A Place Called Home

LORI WICK

HARVEST HOUSE PUBLISHERS
Eugene, Oregon 97402

Scripture quotations are taken from the King James Version of the Bible.

Except for certain well-established place names, all names of persons and places mentioned in this novel are fictional.

A PLACE CALLED HOME

To Bob,
my husband and best friend
who never stopped believing
I could do this.

CAMERON FAMILY TREE

PROLOGUE

"... and to my coachman, Dobbins, I leave 300 dollars, the roan mare from the stables, and my black riding crop..."

The words became distant and far away to the black-garbed young woman, who sat as though she were made of stone. She sat in the large study that had been her grandfather's. This room had been his haven. It had been in this very room, on her grandfather's lap, that he had told her her parents were dead. They had drowned in a boating accident when she was six years old.

She used to love visiting her grandfather in this room. It was big and masculine, as he had been. Of course everything about Joshua Bennett had been big—his laughter, his temper, his love for life. She let her eyes wander around the room, whose walls were lined with books. She had learned to read and write in this room. Large, comfortable chairs were scattered about, and in the middle of it all was her grandfather's massive desk. The desk, the bookshelves, *everything* was walnut. The dark wood would have made it gloomy but for the two huge windows that sat behind the desk and overlooked the street. Her eyes went to the windows. It had begun to rain.

It was fitting that it should rain on the day of her grandfather's funeral and will-reading, since he never liked the rain. But her thoughts were brought abruptly back to the present at the mention of her name.

"... she will receive the house and stables along with the rest of my holdings. In the event of her death, the inheritance will go to my partner, Vince Jeffers."

Again the words of the lawyer faded from her ears. "In the event of her death everything will go to Vince Jeffers." Something is terribly wrong! Grandpa would never have done this! She tried to slow her racing thoughts as she brought her eyes to the man sitting not ten feet from her. Vince was watching her with a look that made her stomach turn. His too-thin face held a self-satisfied smile, making his long nose and dark eyes appear evil. It came to her at that moment that this man might in fact want every dime of her grandfather's money.

She rose and went to her room on legs barely able to support her. Once in her room, she sank into a chair and sat looking out at the pouring rain. Again the lawyer's words returned to her: "In the event of her death." My *death*? Grandpa would never write such a thing, since he was hardly leaving a fortune.

Her mind went back to her grandfather's study and the man who smiled so cynically at her. Fear welled up within her as she thought of her own death. With her grandfather gone, who would care? She didn't care about the money; all she wanted was her grandfather back. The tears she had held in until now streamed unchecked down her face. She had never felt so alone.

1

Mark Cameron paced the spacious entryway of his large, two-story house and looked at his watch for the fifth time. He walked to the foot of the stairs and called up, "Sue, are you almost ready? We're going to be late."

"I'll be right down," came the soft reply.

Mark resumed his pacing until the soft rustle of skirts sounded on the stairs. He turned just as his wife, Susanne, reached the bottom. His eyes lit with appreciation and he moved to take her hands in his. "Is Emily all settled in for the night?"

She answered as he helped her into her sweater, "She's cuddled into Maggie's lap with her favorite book and a blanket."

"And how is this little one down here?" Mark's hand moved down to rest tenderly on his wife's swollen abdomen.

Susanne laughed softly and covered her husband's hand with her own. "If he continues to move like he did today, he's going to make the next two months feel like a year."

Mark's thoughts went back nearly three years in time to the night Susanne had Emily. Mark was 25 and Susanne 23. He was a doctor and she a nurse, and both were experienced and confident. But their medical knowledge was little help that night with Susanne's long and hard labor. After Emily was born Susanne assured Mark it had been worth it all, and, looking at his beautiful baby daughter, he had to agree. Nevertheless, tonight his doubts began to surface and the concern he felt was evident in his voice. "Sue, are you sure you're up to this? If you're too tired, Mac and Julia will understand."

Susanne opened her mouth to reply, but someone pounding on the door stopped the words in her throat. Mark swung the door open quickly to reveal one of the boys from town trying desperately to catch his breath. Mark listened patiently as the boy spoke. Each word came out with a gasp. "Doc Cameron . . . a boy . . . in the alley . . . by the livery . . . stabbed . . . please hurry."

Mark turned to grab the black medical bag that was always kept in the entryway. He bent to give Susanne a quick kiss before moving out the door to follow the already-running boy. He heard his wife call "I'll pray!" as he broke into a run, hoping to cover the two blocks before it was too late.

Susanne closed the door and leaned against it. She took a moment to pray for Mark, the boy, and God's guidance this night. Removing her sweater, she walked up the stairs to tell Maggie the change in plans. Emily was nearly asleep. Once back in the entryway, she walked through a door that sat off to the right. Lighting lamps along her way, she entered her husband's office. She had no guarantee he would be bringing a patient tonight, but either way he would see the welcoming lights. She made sure the office door leading to the street was unlocked. Settling down to wait, she realized she must send word to Julia about supper.

Less than 20 minutes had passed when Mark came through the door with a limp bundle in his arms. He spoke quietly as he laid his burden down. "The cut isn't deep but he's lost quite a lot of blood. We need to get it stitched as quickly as possible."

Susanne picked up a cold, pale hand as her eyes moved over the boy. He was filthy from the top of his floppy hat to the boots on his feet (three sizes too large). His large pants and shirt were covered with a huge jacket, and the left shoulder of the shirt and jacket were stained with blood.

"I'll get his clothes, Mark, while you wash up."

As Mark entered the small equipment room, Maggie came through the entryway door. The two women moved silently and in one accord. First came the jacket. Moving the boy as little as possible, they cut the shirt away. Maggie pressed a cloth to the cut as it began to bleed again. The boy seemed to be wearing some kind of tight undershirt that Susanne cut off. As it fell away the women stared at each other across the body. Susanne moved first and reached for the hat. It was pulled on tight and took a bit of gentle tugging to break free. Again the women exchanged a long glance, before Susanne turned on her heel and walked into the equipment room.

Mark had dried his hands and was reaching for the tray holding all he needed to stitch the cut. Susanne stopped in front of him. "Is the boy ready for me?" He was met with silence.

Alarmed that something had happened, he moved to step around her, but Susanne caught his hand. He raised his eyebrows in surprise as Susanne replied, "Mark, your patient is not a boy—it's a young woman."

2

Mark Cameron's brothers Luke and Silas rode toward town. The warmth of the day, even at 7:00 A.M., told them August was going to be as hot as July. The men were headed to Mark and Susanne's. Luke was then to catch the 8:15 train for Chicago.

Things were still pretty quiet as they rode into town. They tied their horses in front of a large, white, two-story house that had served the town's medical needs for nearly 40 years. Joseph Cameron Sr. had converted the parlor into an office, and with great pride had turned it over to his grandson Mark upon completion of his medical training.

As the men walked to the front door, Luke's eyes went to his brother's work clothes. After Luke caught the train, Silas would be headed back out to the horse ranch they worked together, north of town. Luke was dressed in a suit that usually left the closet only for church. He envied Silas his comfort.

Susanne answered the door and each man hugged her. "We missed you last night at Julia's. Where's Mark?" Silas asked.

"He's upstairs with the patient who came in last night."

The fact that a patient was upstairs spoke of a serious injury. Each man knew better than to question Susanne. She was the soul of discretion, especially concerning Mark's practice.

She turned to the brother-in-law whose face mirrored her husband's. "Luke, will you take some things to Paul? It's not very much if you can fit them in your case."

"Sure, I'll work them in."

"Can you stay for breakfast?" Sue asked.

"I thought you would never ask!" Silas spoke as he moved toward the rear of the house. "Where's my niece?"

Susanne answered as she and Luke followed him. "She's supposed to be in the kitchen setting the table."

Emily was hard at work when the three entered the big, sunny kitchen. Her mother's voice broke through her concentration.

"Emily, your uncles are here." A big smile broke across the little girl's face, and with an excited squeal she moved around the table toward her uncles. Upon spying the way her Uncle Luke was dressed, she stopped in her tracks.

"Is this Sunday?"

"No," Silas answered.

Emily continued to frown in her Uncle Luke's direction until he came over and picked her up.

"How come you're dressed like Daddy today?" She, as well as the rest of the townsfolk, counted on the way the Cameron twins were dressed to tell them apart.

"I'm going on the train today."

"Will you be gone for my birthday?"

"I'm afraid so, but I'll bring you something from my trip."

Emily was more than pleased with his answer and was hugging him when her father joined them in the kitchen. Soon all five of them were seated at the table. Mark prayed, asking God's blessing upon the food, Luke's trip, and the patient upstairs.

After the prayer, Luke asked how serious the patient was.

"We're waiting out a fever right now."

"Is it someone we know?" Silas asked, concern in his voice.

"No, she's not from around here—at least I don't think she is." Mark's eyes went to his daughter and the conversation moved discreetly to Luke's trip. He would be gone about three weeks and planned to see Paul, the youngest of the Camerons, at the seminary he attended in Chicago. He was also to look into buying two mares and a stallion for the ranch.

The time moved quickly. Mark went back to work and his brothers were again on their horses and headed for the train station. Things were bustling at 8:00 and the platform was crowded as Luke bought his ticket.

The brothers talked as they waited for the train.

"You did get over to say goodbye to Grandma Em, didn't you?" Luke laughed at the question. "Let's put it this way, Silas: If I hadn't, I'd better not come back!"

Both men laughed and the train blew it's whistle. They said their goodbyes and Luke moved along with the crowd to board. He settled into a seat and then waved out to Silas as the train pulled away. With the train gathering speed, he reached into his bag for the book he was reading and settled back for his trip to Illinois.

3

Christine Bennett fought against the blackness that threatened to engulf her once again. She was warm now but not burning up, as she had been before. Lying flat on her back on something soft, she knew without opening her eyes that it was daylight. She intended to lie there and try to organize her thoughts, but the sound of someone moving around the room was too much for her.

Peeking out between lids that rebelled at the idea, Christine focused slowly. She was more than a little surprised to find herself in a lovely bedroom that was not her own. Her eyes slowly took in the brightly flowered wallpaper and furniture, all painted white. The bed she was in was big enough for two of her, and sat off to the left side of the room. The far wall had a large window covered with white lace curtains, allowing the sun to stream in. Her eyes also took in a dresser, mirror, and rocking chair before coming to rest upon a woman bent over a plant in the corner.

The woman was dressed in a dark blue skirt and crisp white blouse. Her medium-brown hair was pulled back in a very businesslike bun. She hummed softly to herself as she watered.

Christine knew a moment of panic at not recognizing where she was; the thought made her squirm. The sound of her bedcovers moving brought an abrupt halt to the humming, and the woman advanced upon her with a beaming smile.

"Well, well, my dear. I had begun to wonder if you were ever going to wake up. My name is Margaret Pearson—'Maggie' to my friends. Your fever broke during the night after nearly three days. I can tell you the Doc was glad of that! You've had us quite worried. It would have been a terrible thing to lose you, not even knowing your name. So tell me, my dear, what is your name?"

Christine looked into the face of this kind, smiling woman and realized she had never heard anyone speak quite so fast. Or maybe it was because she wasn't feeling herself.

Christine tried to speak, but the words came out in a croaked whisper. Maggie, immediately seeing the problem, drew Christine up with one arm and brought a glass of water to her lips.

Christine lay back and took a deep breath before attempting to speak again.

"My name is Chris—Christine Bennett. Please tell me whose house I'm in."

"Oh! Christine! What a lovely name. Makes me think of Christmas!" Maggie said with her beaming smile. "As to whose house this is, it's the doctor's house—Doc Cameron, his wife, and his little girl. This room is kept special for patients who need to stay over. I'm Doc Cameron's nurse. Well! Listen to me chatter! The Doc will want to know you're awake and I'm sure you must be starved." Maggie spoke over her shoulder as she headed for the door. "The Doc is a good man, the best doctor around these parts, but let me tell you, my dear, how fortunate you are. A few inches lower with that knife and the doctor would not have been able to help you."

Maggie then moved out the door and did not see the little color left in Christine's face drain away at the thought of her own death.

4

Christine lay looking at the ceiling as she listened to Maggie's footsteps recede down the hall. For a moment she had forgotten the alley, the man with a knife, and all the events leading up to her arrival in the small town of Baxter. She tried to shift around in the bed, but the movement brought a sharp pain to her shoulder. She decided to lie quietly, and as she settled in again she let her mind drift back to Spooner and the morning after her grandfather's funeral.

"Christie, Christie dear, are you awake?"

"Yes, Mrs. Hall, come on in." The bedroom door opened and Mrs. Hall, Joshua Bennett's housekeeper of some 20 years, came over to the bed carrying a small serving tray. Christine pushed herself backward in her bed until she was propped up against the headboard. After setting the tray on the bedside table, Mrs. Hall sat on the edge of the bed and took Christine's hand in her own.

"How did you sleep, Christie?"

The gentle words brought tears that Christine thought she had cried out completely the night before. In an instant the women were both crying and in each other's arms. They clung tightly to each other in an attempt to soothe the hurt they were feeling and to fill the void hanging over them with the knowledge that Joshua Bennett was gone.

They separated after some minutes, each making an attempt to compose herself.

Mrs. Hall's smile was a bit shaky as she gestured to the tray. "I brought you some coffee and muffins."

Christine was not hungry, but as she looked at Mrs. Hall, this precious woman who cared for her and the closest person she had had to a mother since she was six years old, she knew she couldn't hurt her.

"Thank you, Mrs. Hall." Christine tried a smile that was even more wobbly than Mrs. Hall's.

Mrs. Hall squeezed Christine's hand and shut the door as she left the room and Christine to her own thoughts.

Christine reached for the coffee and tried not to let her thoughts wander. She noticed that the rain had ended. It looked like a good day for a ride on Raven, her mare. She would need to sneak down the stairs and go out by way of the kitchen so her grandfather wouldn't catch her in the boy's pants she wore when she rode astride. Christine felt tears sting her eyes as she realized where her thoughts were headed. *Her grandfather was gone.* She decided against riding.

Knowing that if she stayed in bed she would continue to cry, Christine jumped up and began to dress. Her grandfather would not have wanted her depressed. She pushed her sad thoughts aside and was dressed and brushing her hair when another knock sounded at the door.

Opening the door revealed Mrs. Hall again. "Christie, Carl Maxwell was here and he—"

"Oh, Mrs. Hall, please tell him I'll be right down!" Christine interrupted as she turned back to the mirror to finish her hair.

Mrs. Hall followed her into the room. "Christie, he didn't stay." Christine stopped brushing and turned to look at Mrs. Hall. "I'm sorry, dear, but he simply asked me to give you this letter and said he had to be going."

Christine looked down at Mrs. Hall's extended hand. She had not even noticed the letter. Christine took the letter even as she wondered why Carl had not stayed for coffee, as was his usual practice. She dismissed the idea when she realized he was being polite in her time of grief. The truth of the matter was that she would have liked to talk with him.

So caught up was she in her own thoughts that she did not hear Mrs. Hall pick up the tray and leave as quietly as she had before.

Christine settled herself in a large, comfortable chair by the window and stared at the envelope. Christine's thoughts had wandered the night before over her grandfather's will and any involvement that Vince Jeffers might have had. Realizing what she was suspecting Vince of, she pushed all such ideas aside and opened the letter. She was not prepared for what she read.

Christie—

I'm sorry I could not stay to see you, but I had to let you know you are in danger. You must get away. Take the train to Fall Creek and stay there until I send for you. Tell no one where you are going and destroy this letter. When you get to Fall Creek go to the ticket office and find Mr. Franklin. Tell him I sent you. He will take care of you, see you settled, and keep in touch with me. I repeat, Christie, *tell no one*— just get out of the house tonight, and remember: You are in danger. Again, I'm sorry.

Carl

Christine sat frozen to the chair. She was in danger! Was Vince Jeffers involved? She read the letter again. He said to get out of the house tonight. She felt panic. She wasn't even sure where Fall Creek was. And who was this Mr. Franklin? She had to force down feelings of despair as she thought of leaving her home. With her grandfather gone, she didn't even feel she had a home. Thinking of her grandfather reminded her of how ashamed he would be if he saw her sitting there feeling sorry for herself. Her grandfather had trusted Carl Maxwell, and she would too. Her eyes went to the clock as she tried calmly to think of what she had to do and how much time she had to do it. Putting the letter in the pocket of her skirt, she prepared to go out.

At 11:20 P.M. Christine stood before the full-length mirror in her room and with a meticulous eye went over every inch of her appearance. Who would have thought the soberly dressed young woman who had walked sedately to the bank to withdraw money and then to the train station to check schedules could be standing here some hours later looking like the poorest beggar boy in town?

Her eyes started their survey with her boots. They were so big it was hard to walk, but they were all she could find. They must have been an old pair of the stable boys' boots because they looked a hundred years old. Her pants were so large they had to be held up with suspenders. The suspenders were also old, and one side kept coming undone. She had horrible visions of them coming loose as she boarded the train and causing a scene which the town would never forget when her pants dropped down around her ankles.

Her eyes traveled up to her shirt. The too-small camisole she had struggled into helped disguise most of her curves. The old jacket out of her grandfather's closet would finish the job. She blinked rapidly as tears came unbidden with thoughts of her grandfather. She had no time for tears.

Gathering the mass of red-brown curls that fell down her back, she held them atop her head. She jammed the floppy brown hat down hard. The hair made the hat too tight, but at least it would stay in place. Eyes back on the mirror, she reached for the small container of dirt she had dug from the garden. Her white face shone like a beacon under the dark brim of her hat. She powdered the dirt all over her face and down her neck. She also did the backs of her hands. Resisting the impulse to wash it off, Christine knew she would be safer traveling this way. She simply had no choice.

The clock now said 11:45 P.M. It was time to go, or she would miss her train leaving for Eau Claire at 12:45 A.M. She picked up her small bag (one of her grandfather's old cases with very little inside), blew out the light, and headed for the door.

Christine sat in the shadows of the train station waiting for the train to come in. She had her ticket and was trying desperately to stop trembling. She had gotten out of the house without a hitch and the walk to the train station had been no problem; she had been careful to stay away from the saloons. But the enormity of what she was doing was suddenly becoming real to her.

Hearing the train whistle, Christine's thoughts raced with all she was leaving behind. She hadn't even been able to say goodbye to Mrs. Hall. She blinked rapidly as tears threatened, but was under control before leaving her place in the shadows to board the train. No one paid any attention to her as she found her seat and sat staring out into the night. Glad for the cover of darkness as the train pulled out, the tears began to stream down her face. As the dim lights of the train station faded, she wondered if she would ever come home again.

Most everything was quiet in Spooner as the train pulled away at nearly 1:00 in the morning. But on the other side of town a light could be seen shining in the den of one of Spooner's most prominent citizens.

"What took you so long?" The question was barked out in anger.

A scruffy little man stood in front of the big desk twisting his hat in his hands. The man behind the desk scowled impatiently. "I said what took you so long?"

"Well, sir, you said ta wait till all the lights was off."

"There were lights on upstairs at 11:30 at night?" the man behind the desk asked in angry disbelief.

"Well, yes, sir, but it's all dark now and everythin's quiet."

Still scowling, the man behind the desk asked, "Is everything ready for tomorrow night?"

"Yes, sir, me and the boys are all set. We'll be fast and quiet."

"See that you are." He bent over the papers on the desk, a gesture of dismissal for the little man.

"Uh, sir, about the fee . . ."

"You'll get your money when I see the body, and not a moment before. Is that understood?"

"Uh, yes, sir, yes, sir." The small man moved quickly toward the door, but stopped as the man at the desk spoke again. "Start keeping an eye on my new partner. Report back to me on his activities."

The man at the door nodded and moved on, only too happy to escape this big house and the man inside.

5

The rocking of the train was comforting as Christine sat looking out into the darkness. The busy day and late hour were catching up to her, and her eyelids drooped with fatigue. Before the train had covered five miles she was asleep.

When Christine awoke, it was daybreak and the train was pulling into Eau Claire. She was vaguely aware that a voice had called out stops along the way and she had dozed through them. She rubbed her eyes and snuggled her coat around her. She was completely unaware that her tears the night before, combined with the dirt she had powdered on her face, made her appear exactly as she had hoped—a tall, thin boy whose dirty appearance made him of no concern to anyone.

Hoping that none of her hair had slipped out, Christine carefully checked her hat with a small movement, so as not to draw attention to herself. She need not have worried. The hat was pulled on so tightly that it made her head ache!

She picked up her bag and moved into the aisle. The train station was crowded, but she made her way to the ticket window and was told the train to Fall Creek would be delayed. She took a seat further down the platform, being as inconspicuous as possible, and settled down to wait.

By the time her train was called, hours later, she was hot and thirsty and her bottom ached from sitting on the wooden bench. Seated again on the train, she took notice of the other passengers. There was a young woman with a baby, a very thin man with a fat wife, an elderly couple, and a businessman. All seemed to be wrapped up in their own thoughts, and Christine turned her gaze out the window. All of this countryside was new to her. She had been to Eau Claire with her grandfather on several business trips over the years, but never beyond.

She let her mind drift to Fall Creek. *Mr. Franklin.* Carl Maxwell had said to find Mr. Franklin and no one else. Would Mr. Franklin be able to answer some of her questions? Did he know what the danger was or if Vince Jeffers was involved? A chill ran up her spine at the thought of Vince Jeffers. So many unanswered questions. Why couldn't Carl have stayed and explained things to her? She reminded herself that her grandfather had trusted Carl Maxwell. Carl would not send her away unless he knew she would be cared for. Having reasoned this out, she closed her eyes and tried not to think anymore. A rumble in her stomach reminded her that she hadn't eaten today. Well, Fall Creek was the next stop. Hopefully Mr. Franklin would feed her.

"Fall Creek! This is Fall Creek, folks. Next stop is Rosedale. Leaving in 15 minutes. All out for Fall Creek." The conductor's voice sounded bored, as if he had said these words a thousand times before. But the words were far from boring to Christine's ears. At the mention of Fall Creek her heart began to pound and she was afraid her legs were not going to support her. Her hunger and tight hat forgotten, she moved along the near-empty platform toward the ticket window.

"Where to, son?" The man behind the window was looking at her with bored expectancy.

Being called "son" confused Christine into silence for a moment, and when she spoke her voice was stuttering and high-pitched. "Well, I, um, well, I'm looking for Mr. Franklin."

The man's eyes seemed to soften slightly. "Are you a relative or a friend of the family?"

"Uh, well, just a friend."

"Well, son, I'm real sorry, but you missed the funeral. It was this morning at 10:00."

"Funeral?"

The man didn't seem to notice her confusion. "Yes, son, as I said, I'm sorry it was so sudden. But if you go on up to the house, I know the family will welcome you. Nice folks, the Franklins. Why, I remember when my wife was sick, they brought us . . ."

But Christine didn't hear the words. Dead! Mr. Franklin was dead! Buried just today. The day she was coming to him for help. Was it her fault he was dead? Did someone kill him to try to get to her? If that were the case, then she had to get out of Fall Creek.

"All aboard!" the conductor yelled.

The train! She must get back on the train. She moved for the door and fell into a seat just as the train began to move. She stared blankly out the window. In a few minutes the conductor came by for her ticket. She paid him for the trip to Rosedale and again retreated behind her wall of misery.

She tortured herself with thoughts of a man named Mr. Franklin whom she never knew but might have died because of her. The finality of death weighed upon her as she thought of never seeing her grandfather again. Mrs. Hall, her home, and Vince Jef-

fers all crowded into her thoughts. Each time the conductor
came by for her ticket she paid him to ride to the next stop.
Unaware and uncaring of how many miles she had traveled, her
mind was closed to everything around her.

"Reedsburg! This is Reedsburg, folks. Next stop is Baxter. All
out for Reedsburg. Next town is Baxter."

Reedsburg! The fog began to clear as she said the word to
herself. She remembered slowly that her grandfather had business dealings several years back with a man in Reedsburg. The
man had wanted her grandfather to come down, but he was reluctant to travel the 200 miles in winter.

She was over 200 miles from home! She was getting off at the
next stop, not caring where it was or if she knew anyone. She
just had to get off this train before it took her any further from
home. Her bag was in her hand and she was ready to go when
the conductor called Baxter as the next stop. Christine was sure
she had never heard of it before.

She was the only one to get off in Baxter, and her eyes took in
the small, near-empty platform. Her feet were on solid ground
only a few minutes when she heard the conductor call "All
Aboard!" She took a few steps away from the train and turned to
watch it move down the tracks. There was a finality about it that
scared her a little.

Turning back toward the train station, Christine noticed for
the first time that evening was falling. Her eyes went to the sign
posted on the side of the ticket office: Baxter, Population 396.
She took a deep breath and remembered again how hungry and
tired she was. Well, she was in Baxter for at least tonight. She set
off for what appeared to be the downtown section of Baxter,
intent on finding a place to stay and something to eat.

Back in Spooner, Mrs. Hall hurried to answer the knock at the
front door. "Oh, Mr. Jeffers, it's you. I so hoped it would be the
sheriff with some news."

Vince Jeffers spoke as he stepped inside. "What news, Mrs.
Hall? What's happened?"

"Oh, haven't you heard? Christine is missing. She wasn't in her
room this morning and no one has seen her since yesterday."
The old woman wrung her hands and tears filled her eyes.

Mrs. Hall did not see the angry clenching of Vince Jeffers' jaw as he fought to regain control of his emotions. With effort his voice came out calmly. "You did the right thing in calling the sheriff, Mrs. Hall. I'll go around now and see him to offer my help. If he's heard anything I'll come back and tell you."

"Oh, thank you, Mr. Jeffers; I've been so worried."

The polite mask falling from his face, he nodded to the woman and stepped out into the evening. Standing with his fists clenched, he trembled with anger at this change in his plans. He stood for some minutes getting control of himself before stepping off the porch with a determined stride, a new plan already forming in his mind.

6

Christine moved around the back of the train station. There were barrels and crates stacked against the building. A lone wagon was parked nearby. There was little activity with the darkness coming, but as she came around the corner of the building she heard music playing. Looking across at what appeared to be a vacant lot, she decided to ask for help over there.

The backs of the other buildings she passed were as quiet as the train station had been. They had an ominous look, and she walked slowly and squinted into the darkness as she moved closer to the music.

As she arrived at the building it occurred to her for the first time that it was probably a saloon. She hesitated before starting up the alley toward the street and front door. Hating the thought of entering a saloon, she nevertheless had to find a place to stay for the night and a meal. She would have to swallow her fear and ask inside.

Halfway up the alley a voice spoke out of the shadows.

"Where you headed, boy?"

Christine gasped and backed away until she came up against the side of the building. A man then came out of the shadows. He didn't look very tall, but his upper body seemed massive in the dim light of the alley. If there was going to be a fight, there was little doubt in Christine's mind who would win.

"What's in your bag? A little cash, maybe?" His voice was deep and gravelly. "I've got me a thirst, boy, and no money. Maybe your bag there can help."

Christine moved the bag in front of her and grasped the handle with both hands.

"Now, listen boy, I don't want to hurt you. Just hand over the bag so I can see it."

Christine felt like a trapped animal. Her eyes searched for an escape route, but he was too close. Her eyes came back to the man who was slowly approaching her. The injustice of it all began to weigh upon her. The last 24 hours were crowding in. She was tired and hungry and her hat was too tight. Without the money in her bag she couldn't even get home. Home! At this point she could barely remember where that was.

The man was almost within arm's reach when he stopped and held out his hand. "Just give me the bag, boy, and you can be on your way."

"No!" Christine could hardly believe she had said that.

Before she could draw another breath the man moved. In an instant he held a large knife toward her. Christine's breath lodged in her throat.

"Now, boy, I'll say it one more time. Hand over the bag."

Christine acted before she thought. Still clutching the bag with both hands, she brought it up hard under the man's extended arm. His arm went up but he didn't lose the knife. Christine leaped away from him, but he was fast and she just barely missed being stabbed. Her fear turned to anger and new strength. She swung her bag again, but he grabbed it with his free hand. She saw him raise the knife and stood in stunned horror, knowing she was about to die. She heard a long, high-pitched scream, never realizing it was her own. She felt the bag wrenched away as a searing pain shot through her chest. She felt her knees buckle. Blackness engulfed her, and she knew no more.

Christine felt weary at having relived in her mind the events leading up to being in this room. Her weariness led to loneliness as she thought of how alone and far from home she was. What would become of her now?

Carrying a food tray, Maggie reentered the room at that moment. She reminded Christine so much of Mrs. Hall that tears flooded her eyes. Maggie set the food tray down and turned to smile at Christine with such tender understanding that, try as she might, she could not stem the flow of tears beginning to pour down her cheeks. Without a word, Maggie sat down and gently embraced the crying young woman. Wrapped in the loving arms of Maggie, Christine gave way to the healing tears that were to signal a change in her life that she could never have imagined.

7

When Christine awoke again it was to the pressure of a hand on her brow. The room was shadowed, dim, and easier on her eyes. She focused on the owner of the hand. A tall, handsome man with deep blue eyes was smiling at her.

"Welcome back. How do you feel?"

"Thirsty." Christine's voice was a hoarse whisper.

The man helped her drink and then settle back on the pillows before he spoke again.

"You were asleep each time I checked on you today. Maggie tells me your name is Christine Bennett." She nodded and he went on. "I'm Dr. Mark Cameron. I brought you here from the alley. What were you doing in the alley after dark?"

As he spoke, his hands were moving. He held her wrist for a minute and then checked her shoulder. He paused in his movements to meet her eyes, telling her plainly he was waiting for an answer.

"I was looking for something to eat and a place to stay for the night." She had been raised to tell the truth. She would not answer if it meant lying.

"You're not from Baxter?" He knew what her answer would be.

"No."

"Did you come in on the train?"

"Yes."

"You rode the train dressed as a boy?"

He watched her lips compress and an angry sparkle enter her eyes. He knew she was pulling away from him. He placed his hands gently on Christine's upper arms and said in a quiet but firm voice, "Christine, don't close me out. I realize you don't know me, but I want to help you if I can." He paused and watched her face intently for signs of softening. "Whatever it is that made you dress up like a boy and leave your home is not going to go away just because you ran from it."

"You don't know how wrong you are!" she cried in a desperate voice. "I had to get out of Spooner."

Spooner! Mark carefully masked his surprise at how far she was from home. Then a thought came to him.

"Christine, you were stabbed in the alley. Was it someone you knew? Did you have something someone wanted?"

"I didn't know the man in the alley. He said he needed a drink and wanted my bag. He got it too—I mean, I think he did. You didn't find it in the alley, did you?"

"No, I'm afraid not."

She looked so young and vulnerable. Mark's heart went out to her. He decided to try one more time. "Talk to me, Christine. Let me help you."

To her utter horror and embarrassment her eyes filled with tears, and in an effort to keep from crying she began to talk. This man, stranger that he was, was so compassionate. She could not stem the flow of her words as the entire story came spilling out.

Outside of a question here and there, or a word of encouragement, Mark said nothing. His mind raced as he tried to sort through all the facts she was telling him. He agreed that she had no choice but to leave Spooner. He reassured her when she began to fret about the money in the bag, telling her everything was going to work out.

Once through talking, she was exhausted from the strain and terror of remembering. He helped her with another drink, this one mixed with a sedative she never noticed. She whispered a thank you as her eyes closed in sleep.

Not until Christine's breathing had evened out in deep sleep did Mark turn his attention to the third occupant of the room, whom Christine hadn't noticed. Susanne sat quietly near the door, where she had been during the entire exchange. Mark was sure the concern and sympathy he saw in his wife's eyes mirrored his own.

Having left Christine in Maggie's capable hands, Mark and Susanne checked on their own sleeping daughter and retired to the bedroom. As they prepared for bed, Susanne spoke for the first time. "I'm sure you realize she never intended to tell you a thing."

"I'm sure you're right." He paused and then added, "I can't help but think of Emily as a young woman, possibly alone. I would want someone to help her." His voice was heavy with despair.

"Oh, Mark, you know God would take care of her—just as I'm sure God put Christine in our lives because she needs us."

They were in bed now. Susanne lay on her side so Mark could rub the small of her back. She had done the wash today and ached all over. She was relaxed and near sleep when Mark spoke again.

"I'd like to see her up on her feet tomorrow, but I think she'll be embarrassed in front of me after tonight."

"You're probably right. Maggie and I can go in and get her up and dressed if she's ready for it."

"Since she is healing well, that will be fine. Thanks for handling it. Good night, Sue." He pulled her close and kissed her, and they both fell asleep with prayers in their hearts for Christine Bennett.

Back in Spooner, once again in the ornate but dimly lit study, sat a man behind his desk in another late-night interview with the small, scruffy man who did his dirty work.

"Are you all set to get in tonight?"

"Yes, sir."

"Remember, if you get caught you're on your own."

"Me and the boys never get caught."

"Go alone!"

"What?"

"I said *go alone*. The three of you will wake the entire house if you search her room together. You go alone and quietly search through her clothes, drawers, everything. You mustn't leave a thing disturbed or that busybody Mrs. Hall will have the sheriff out again."

"Do you want I should get rid of her?"

"Of course not!" the man behind the desk snapped.

"Will that be all, Mr. Jeffers?"

"Yes, just as long as you continue to keep an eye on my partner and report to me regularly."

"Yes, sir, I'll do that."

"You may go, then."

As always, the little man was more than anxious to get away. He knew he wasn't much, but he didn't smile in a person's face and then pull a knife when his back was turned. Two-faced! There was no other way to describe Vince Jeffers, and he didn't trust him. Drawing deeply of the night air, he stepped out the rear of the house. The house, he thought, smelled evil, if that were possible. As he moved along in the shadows to do his night's work, he decided that when this entire episode with the Bennett girl was over he would take his share of the money and move on. He was getting too old for this type of work. His new resolve made him quicken his pace in an effort to get the job done and be gone.

8

Morning found Maggie, Susanne, and Christine all standing in Christine's room staring at each other. The two older women had entered the room and found Christine up, wrapped in a quilt, and looking out the window. Some minutes went by before Susanne broke the silence. She spoke as she transferred a bundle of clothes from her arms to the bed.

"I'm Susanne, Mark's wife." She paused, uncertain. This was not going at all as she had planned. "I brought you some clothes, but I don't think they're going to fit. I mean, you're welcome to them . . . they're mine, but . . ." She shrugged helplessly.

A smile broke across Christine's face at Susanne's attempt at tactfulness. She topped both of these women by a good six inches. Christine was still smiling when she spoke. "I appreciate your kindness and effort. It's hard to judge a person's height when she is in bed."

Both women returned her smile with great relief, and the tension in the room evaporated.

"Well, now," Maggie spoke in her no-nonsense way. "We'll have to look for something else while you get your bath and have breakfast. Maggie handed the clothes back to Susanne and stripped the bed. "Now, my dear, you sit back on the bed and I'll be back up in a minute with your bath." Both women moved out the door.

Christine was seated on the bed when Susanne stepped back into the room. "You must think me terribly rude, Christine. I didn't even ask how you felt."

Christine responded to the genuine concern she heard in Susanne's voice. "I'm a little stiff, but I guess that is to be expected." The women exchanged smiles and Susanne moved out the door again.

Christine knew a moment's embarrassment as Maggie assisted with washing her hair. The only person who had ever helped her was Mrs. Hall. But Maggie's efficient way soon had Christine at ease.

Christine had just finished breakfast and was seated on the edge of the bed, wrapped in a sheet, when Susanne returned. She handed Christine some undergarments.

"Put these on and I'll help you with your hair."

Christine opened her mouth to protest, but Susanne had already turned away to hang the dress and move the chair in front of the mirror.

Christine sat in silence, feeling a bit strange at having this woman, really a stranger, do her hair. But if the truth were known, her shoulder and arm were not up to it. So she was grateful.

Susanne worked in silence except for an occasional comment on how thick Christine's hair was or what a lovely color. Susanne would have laughed to know Christine was admiring the shining blonde curls on her own head with a bit of envy. As Susanne moved to Christine's side, Christine's eyes fell to her swollen stomach. She had made an effort not to stare, but she had been around so few women with babies that she was fascinated. Her cheeks burned as she raised her eyes and met Susanne's, knowing she had been caught staring.

"Do you like children?" Susanne asked quietly.

"Yes." The reply was just as quiet.

The only sound for a time was that of the brush moving through Christine's hair.

"Maggie may have told you that this is our second child. We have a little girl, Emily, who is with her Grandma Em today. Mark has never said, but I'm sure he hopes for a boy. I guess most men want a son. But either way we'll love and cherish this one too. Children are a special gift from the Lord."

Christine was quiet for awhile, digesting Susanne's last statement. Susanne left her to her thoughts.

"How old is Emily?"

"She'll be four before the baby is born."

"When is the baby due?"

"About seven weeks," Susanne answered as she set the brush down. "But at this point it feels like seven years."

Susanne turned and brought the dress over for Christine. "Here, try this for size."

It was a beautiful dress, plum-colored with small white flowers running through it. Christine looked down at herself and then in the mirror. It wasn't too short in the sleeves or the hem, and she was amazed. Her feelings must have shown because Susanne laughed and said, "Mark has a sister about your height."

The words were sobering for Christine, her pride reminding her that she did not even have money for clothes. The thought saddened her. Susanne didn't seem to notice. "Put your shoes on and I'll show you the house."

Susanne led the way out and next door to Emily's room. All thoughts of sadness disappeared at the sight of this little girl's room. Everything was in pinks, delightfully feminine. Frilly curtains and bed ruffle perfectly matched a flowered quilt and wallpaper. In one corner was a doll's cradle with several doll babies sleeping peacefully. In another corner stood a tiny rocking horse, and a stack of books was resting neatly.

Susanne then led the way to the master bedroom across the landing from Emily's room. It was larger, with windows on two walls, and was dominated by a huge bed. Christine's eyes went briefly to Susanne's petite frame and thought she must feel lost in it. She had decorated the room in warm brown tones with a touch of rust and tan. Beautiful lace doilies donned the tables flanking the bed. Bookshelves near the windows were filled. Christine assumed they were medical journals. The room was warm and bright. Christine praised Susanne's decorating style.

The last bedroom upstairs was the baby's, the smallest of the four bedrooms and perfect for the expected infant. The cradle was filled with quilts and the walls were painted a soft yellow. Susanne opened a chest under the window and brought out a few tiny nightclothes. Christine fingered the soft material, thinking of the two women she had known with babies. They really had been more acquaintances than friends.

Descending the stairs put them in the entry by the front door. To one side of the entryway Susanne showed her a door, explaining that at one time it had been the parlor but was now Mark's office.

Opposite the office door and right off the entryway was the front door, but Susanne led them down a back hall that ran along the stairs and took them to the kitchen.

The kitchen was bright and perky. The cupboards were painted white and appeared spotless. There was an alcove holding a table and four chairs. The curtains, tablecloth, and fabric covering the pantry shelves were all red gingham. Another door, Susanne said, opened to Maggie's bedroom. The massive stove and oven were shiny and clean, making Christine think that Susanne certainly had enough to keep her busy.

Christine followed Susanne from the kitchen to the dining room. All along one wall was a beautiful built-in sideboard and glass-fronted cupboards with lovely glassware and dishes. They walked past the dining table and chairs into the front room.

The front room had a lived-in elegance about it. The couch and chairs were all covered in varying shades of blue, and all sat on a beautiful cream-colored rug. An upright piano sat near the stairs, music opened, looking ready to be played. The piano, bookshelves, and tables were all in a dark wood.

When Susanne stopped, Christine told her how lovely she found the home. Susanne smiled in her quiet way and suggested that Christine sit and rest a bit before lunch.

More tired than she cared to admit, Christine simply thanked her and took a chair by the window. Susanne took her leave to the kitchen and Christine turned her attention to the street.

9

Christine noticed that things were fairly quiet out on the street. She noted that houses across the street were nicely painted and maintained. She watched two little boys walk by, and then a woman with a large basket. Christine sat absorbed with the activity in the street until she heard light footsteps on the carpet. Turning, she found a beautiful little blonde girl regarding her with big blue eyes.

Christine smiled and said, "You must be Emily."

Emily nodded.

"My name is Christine."

"Why are you wearing my Aunt Julia's dress?"

The question took Christine by surprise. "Well, I didn't have a dress to wear and your aunt was kind enough to let me borrow hers."

"Where are your dresses?"

Unaccustomed to speaking with children, Christine was not quite sure how to answer. She opted for honesty. "I left my home in a hurry and my dresses were left behind."

"Will you buy some here?"

"Well, not right now, not until I have some money." (As Christine had been gazing out the window, she had decided to find work as soon as possible.)

"But if you have no money, how will you pay my daddy for making you all better?"

"Emily!" A deep, masculine voice spoke sharply from the edge of the room. Emily spun around to face her father, her small hand going to her mouth as she realized who had heard her.

Mark advanced slowly and spoke quietly to Emily when he stopped before her. "You will apologize immediately and then you will go to the kitchen and help your mother with lunch." Emily turned slowly back to Christine and spoke quietly. "I'm sorry, very much."

Christine reached out a hand and gently touched the top of Emily's shiny blonde head. Unsure of what to say, she simply smiled her kindest smile so Emily would know all was forgiven.

Emily smiled back with a hesitant look at her father to see if she had done all right. His nod was her reward, and she walked quickly from the room.

Mark took a chair near Christine, intending to make his own apologies, but Christine spoke first.

"Emily is right, you know. I haven't a dime to my name. I was, as a matter of fact, just sitting here thinking about a place to live and a job, hoping there would be something right here in town." She smiled a small smile. "I really feel I have traveled enough for the time being."

Mark listened to her speak. As he had half expected, she was calm, self-assured, proud. Gone was the crying girl from last night. She did not take easily to a handout, he was sure of that. She was in a fix and planned to work her way out. Mark could easily pay her way home, but he felt this morning that God was leading him to keep her near for the moment. Christine's own words confirmed this thought. "I thought you might feel that way, Christine. Why don't I tell you of an idea I have during lunch?"

"Oh, thank you, Dr. Cameron, that's very kind of you," Christine replied as she stood and moved toward the kitchen. She turned back to say she was going to lend a hand with lunch, but Mark stood also and Christine found herself staring speechlessly into his chin. Mark watched her eyes drop to his shoes and then her head tilt back as her eyes met his. He had to fight to keep from laughing as he watched her mouth drop open. She stared this way for some moments before Mark spoke.

"My sister Julia is your height. Outside of her husband and her brothers, there are not many men she has to look up to. From the look on your face, it must be the same for you." His voice was full of amusement and Christine's mouth shut with a snap. Her cheeks flamed with embarrassment as she realized how she had been staring, her mouth hanging open like a codfish on a hook.

Not knowing what to say, she mumbled something about helping with lunch and made a hasty exit, thinking as she did so that Baxter had held more embarrassing moments in less than a week's time than Spooner had in 19 years!

Lunch went fine, Mark felt, as he walked toward his grand-mother's house. Christine had been very receptive to his job idea. She was a sweet young woman who seemed to get along well with everyone. Now if he could convince Grandma Em that she and Christine needed each other, everything would be fine.

He found himself wishing Luke were here. Luke had a certain way with Grandma Em. Maybe he would try a bit of Luke's firmness with her if it came to that.

He knocked on the front door and entered. "Hello, anyone home?" His footsteps echoed loudly on the polished wood floor of the parlor before hitting the rug. He passed through the parlor and into the kitchen, spying his grandmother through a window as he walked. She was out by her flower garden in the backyard. Her neighbor, Mr. Turley, was by her side. After kissing his grandmother, he turned to shake Mr. Turley's hand.

"Hello, Mr. Turley, how are you today?"

"Well, I'll tell you, Mark, if I were any better I wouldn't be able to stand myself."

Mark laughed and Mr. Turley spoke again.

"I saw that little Emmy of yours this morning." Emmy was his name for both the old and young Emily Camerons. "You've got yourself a real gem there."

"Thank you, Mr. Turley. We think she's pretty special."

"Well, Emmy, I've got work to do. I'll see you later. You too, Mark." He turned to go home.

"So, what brings my favorite grandson over?" Mark smiled at his grandmother's familiar line.

"I'm here on business today."

"Sounds serious. I best put on a pot of coffee."

Mark walked back to the house at his grandmother's side and then watched her move around the kitchen preparing coffee and setting out cookies. He prayed again about her response to his idea. She could be very stubborn if she chose to be. For an instant he thought about the sparks that might fly if he put these two strong-willed women together. If his guess about Christine was right, she was more than a little independent.

The tinkling sound of china cups broke into his thoughts as Grandma Em brought a tray laden with coffee, cups, and cookies to the table.

They poured their coffee in silence. When Mark felt his grandmother watching him, he looked up and met her eyes squarely.

"I'll start by telling you we have a young woman staying with us."

"Emily said there was a sick lady in the room next to hers and you were going to make her all better."

Mark smiled at his daughter's vote of confidence. "Her name is Christine Bennett, and healthwise she's doing fine. But there has been some trouble involving her, and I'm afraid I can't share it with you. I will tell you that she's not from around here and she has no one to call on for help. Christine told me she wants to find work. I could offer to pay her way home, but I'm sure I would be turned down. I doubt Christine takes kindly to a hand-out."

Mark took a breath and decided to jump in with both feet. "I'd like her to come and work for you."

Emily Cameron stiffened and opened her mouth to tell her grandson exactly what she thought of the idea, but his raised hand stopped the words in her throat.

"You will hear me out." His voice was so stern and command-ing she could do nothing but comply.

Over an hour later Mark was walking back to his office. Grandma Em had balked at the idea of a strange young woman coming not only to work for her but to live with her as well. Mark reminded her of hauling wood in November when her arthritis was giving her fits, of going out in the snow to feed the handful of livestock she stubbornly refused to sell, of a horse that was older than Mark was, of a useless goat who needed his vocal chords removed, of four laying hens now too tough to eat, and of two huge white pigs.

Before the conversation ended she had admitted she was feel-ing a bit tired. Grandma Em even went so far as to confess that when she had dusted the parlor yesterday, she had knocked the portrait of the grandchildren onto the floor and shattered the glass. She had then put the picture away in the closet until she could order more glass.

As Mark entered his office, he felt sure the job would work out between the two. Christine, having lived with her grandfather, would certainly know how to be helpful in a tactful way.

10

Two days later Mark walked beside a silent Christine toward his grandmother's house. He carried a small case belonging to Susanne that held the dresses and such that Julia had sent over for Christine. Mark looked down at Christine's face and saw a mixture of determination and fear. He was on the verge of reassuring her when she spoke.

"Did you talk to the sheriff about my being stabbed?"

"Yes, and I also told him briefly of your situation." Christine looked troubled at this, so Mark spoke again. "He had to know, Christine. If there should be any stranger asking around, the sheriff would need to know why.

"But no one knows I'm in Baxter."

"That's true, but the fact still remains that someone did stab you, and although the sheriff agreed with me that it was probably not related to your home situation, there is no reason we should take chances."

The feelings of safety which Christine had harbored at being so far from Spooner and Vince Jeffers now evaporated. But Mark and Christine were already walking up the wide steps to the large porch and front door of Grandma Em's house. The fact that this house was going to be Christine's new home for an indefinite period of time banished all other thoughts from her mind.

Christine followed Mark into a lovely parlor and sat as he directed. Mark disappeared but returned shortly, preceded by a woman of medium height whose steps belied her 70 years. Her hair was a silvery white and in close curls around her head. Her face was liberally seamed and the expression in her light blue eyes was hesitant. It occurred to Christine at this moment the woman was not very happy about the idea of her working here. This thought put Christine on the defensive, and her eyes went to Mark's face.

After Grandma Em had seated herself across from Christine, Mark made introductions. "Gram, this is Christine Bennett. Christine, this is Emily Cameron—"Grandma Em" to her friends, old and new alike."

The women exchanged hesitant smiles and nods. Each measured the other with different thoughts flying through her head.

Emily knew she was fighting God's will as she sat there hating herself for getting old and hoping to find something about this girl she didn't like to ease her conscience when she told Mark that it would not work out. She feared this girl would come in and take over. Life as she had always known it would be changed forever and she had always struggled with change.

Christine, with her own thoughts, wondered if this woman was kind or unreasonably set in her ways—ways that did not include another woman in the house. Needing this job desperately if she were going to get her life back in control, Christine decided to be sweet and congenial.

Grandma Em broke the silence. "How old are you, Christine?"

"Nineteen, ma'am."

"And you're familiar with work around the home and yard?"

"Yes, ma'am. Mrs. Hall, my grandfather's housekeeper, taught me everything she knew about running a home."

"Well, you understand, of course, that I will be running *this* house and you would be helping me." Emily's voice was sharper than she had intended.

Christine only nodded, afraid to say more lest it be the wrong thing.

"Have you ever stolen anything?" Emily asked abruptly.

All ideas of sweetness and congeniality flew out the window. Christine stood up so quickly that the chair nearly tipped over. Her eyes flashing with anger and pain, she turned accusingly to Mark. "I don't have to sit here and take this. How dare she ask me such a thing!" Too upset to say more, she turned and nearly ran out of the room. Mark caught her at the front door.

Emily sat frozen in the front room, her hand pressed tightly to her mouth, listening to the furious whispers at the front door. She prayed fervently that Mark would bring Christine back so she could ask her forgiveness. Why had she said such a thing? A woman her age should be beyond such foolishness.

Mark escorted a sober-faced Christine back to her chair, eyes wide and suspiciously wet. Mark sat near his grandmother, knowing she would do the right thing.

"Christine," Emily hesitated, but Christine caught the different tone in her voice—gentle, subdued. "Christine, please forgive me. I don't know why I said such a thing." Again she hesitated. "Well, the truth is, I *do* know. I didn't want it to work between us. You see, I'm old and set in my ways and very afraid of change. Mark tells me you're alone, and I think maybe we need each other." Emily's voice became quieter as she spoke, showing Christine that in this area she was as vulnerable as she was. Emily's voice was just above a whisper when she asked, "Will you stay, Christine?" This woman's honesty went straight to Christine's heart. She felt a sting behind her eyes and a tightness in her throat, enabling her to only nod and smile.

Mark's laugh of relief brought all three to their feet. He hugged Grandma Em and then surprised Christine by hugging her also. She had also felt surprised that morning when, after thanking Susanne and Maggie for everything, they had grabbed her and hugged her too. Spontaneous displays of affection were foreign to Christine, but she was beginning to like it.

Mark took his leave after Grandma Em served coffee. The two women spent the remainder of the day working in the garden, sharing companionable conversation, listening and learning with no doubt in either heart that they had found something special.

Christine snuggled down into the covers of the big oak bed. Her bed! The thought felt wonderful. She realized as she lay there that she and Grandma Em had spent so much time outdoors that the only rooms she had really seen were the parlor and kitchen and her own room. Her own bedroom! A feeling of contentment washed over her. Drifting off to sleep with her mind becoming foggy, she would have been hard-pressed to tell you if she had a single care in the world.

— ❖ —

"Are you sure no one saw you?"

"No, Mr. Jeffers, no one saw me."

"You went alone?"

"Yes, sir."

"Where did you say you found this?" Vince Jeffers held out a small piece of paper.

"In the closet, in the pocket of a skirt."

"Did you read it?"

"No, sir, I never learned." The small man stared at the carpet as he mumbled this. He looked up as he heard paper rustling and found Vince Jeffers reading the note. He watched as the man's jaw clenched and then threw the paper to the desk.

"The note is from Carl Maxwell." The small man's eyes widened at this information. "He told her to go to a friend of his in Fall Creek—a Mr. Franklin, it says." Vince Jeffers' voice became very calm as he continued. "Let's call around and visit Carl Maxwell, shall we? We'll ask him about this Mr. Franklin in Fall Creek. It's nearly midnight, but I'm sure we can convince him to talk with us."

The small man followed as Vince led the way out of the room. Once outside Vince spoke again, softly and more to himself than to the man behind him.

"Fall Creek. I wonder why he sent her to Fall Creek. Well, it doesn't matter. Even if she's not there, wherever she is I'll find her, and when I do"—he paused, a cold smile playing over his thin lips—"when I do, everything will be mine."

At 9:30 A.M. Mrs. Hall opened the door to admit the sheriff.

"Thank you for coming so soon. I just had to see you." Mrs. Hall's voice was anxious.

"Of course, Mrs. Hall. The stable boy said you had news."

"Yes. Well, you see, I remembered the day before Christine disappeared"—Mrs. Hall's voice shook and she stopped to take a breath. "The day before Christine disappeared, Carl Maxwell was here. He didn't stay to see Christine, but he left a note for her. I delivered it to her myself."

"Did you read the note?"

"No, of course not." Mrs. Hall's voice was indignant.

"Do you have the note now?"

"Well, no. When I remembered this morning, I went up and looked in her room but found nothing."

"I'll have a look myself." The sheriff moved toward the stairs and Mrs. Hall followed. "Describe this note to me—size, color . . ."

Less than an hour later Mrs. Hall was seeing the sheriff to the door. "I'm going to see Carl Maxwell. Hopefully he'll be able to explain the note."

"Maybe she took it with her." Mrs. Hall suggested.

"That's possible."

"Please, sheriff, please keep me informed. My little Christie is out there, away from home. She's never been away from home, and I fear she needs me." The sheriff watched the old woman's eyes fill with tears. He patted her shoulder awkwardly before moving away with a frown on his face, wishing with all his heart he knew where Christine Bennett was.

— ❖ —

Sunshine crept over the windowsill and into Christine's eyes, waking her into confusion. This was not her bedroom at home, or at Doc Cameron's. Where was she? Grandma Em's! The thought brought her instantly awake. Sitting upright in bed, a smile played across her sleep-flushed face.

She sat and surveyed her room from the bed. A soft blend of greens and peaches greeted her eyes. Everything had looked much darker in the lamplight the night before. The greens ranged from a very dark green rug to a pastel green ruffle around the bed. The wallpaper was in peach and yellow flowers with lots of green leaves and vines. The round table by the bed was covered in the same fabric as the bed ruffle. Lacy curtains in soft peach allowed the sunlight to flood in. In one corner was an oak desk and chair. Opposite the desk was a built-in closet. Below the window sat a low oak chest. Christine sat on it and looked out into the garden that Grandma Em had tended yesterday. Further back was a small barn, the sight of which reminded Christine that she would "meet" the animals today.

Having washed, dressed, and descended the stairs, Christine stood in the parlor, where she had met Grandma Em yesterday. Christine noticed for the first time the very ornate and beautifully carved pieces of furniture. The tables and legs of each chair were all intricately carved and matched.

"The furniture was my mother's." Emily's voice came from the kitchen doorway.

"It's beautiful."

"The chairs and sofa have been recovered." She ran her hand over a chair upholstered in a deep burgundy velvet. Curtains in the same material made things a bit dark for Christine's taste, but lovely nonetheless.

"After my father died, Joseph, my late husband and I, lived with my mother. We moved to Baxter from New York when Joseph Jr.—that was Mark's father—was ten. My mother decided to move in with her sister and gave us most of her furniture. The oak bed in your room was mine as a little girl. Well, we had best get to the barn. If you would let me, I'd reminisce all day."

Once they were in the barn, Christine watched Grandma Em fork hay to a horse who looked too old to be standing. His back swayed to an impossible depth and his nose was as gray as hoarfrost. However, his eyes looked gentle, and he turned like an old friend at the sound of Emily's voice. His name was Caesar.

The quiet bleating that had begun when Grandma Em and Christine entered the barn raised to a sound of desperation by the time Caesar was fed. Chester, Christine was informed, did not like to be kept waiting. Chester turned out to be a goat. He, like Caesar, looked old, but there was certainly nothing wrong with his voice. Christine's eyes widened in surprise at how fast the noise stopped as Grandma Em poured a scoop of grain before him.

Christine was still staring at the silent goat when Grandma Em threw a handful of corn to the hens and moved to sit on a bench near the door. Grandma Em pulled on an old pair of men's work boots, picked up a large pail, and beckoned to Christine to follow her out the door.

Christine caught up with her just as she stopped in front of a pen holding two of the biggest pigs Christine had ever seen. Christine's mouth dropped open in surprise as Grandma Em opened the gate, picked up her skirts, and entered the pen. The pigs ignored the open gate. Pushing and grunting with obvious delight at seeing her, they rushed toward Grandma Em. She laughed and spoke to them in quiet tones as she tipped the pail into their trough.

Emily then made her way back out to Christine and laughed at the look of disbelief on her lovely face.

"My grandchildren feel just as you do about Belle and Betsy. They are forever after me to sell all my animals. They just don't realize how attached I've become." Emily patted Christine's arm. "Don't worry, dear, the animals will get used to you and love it when you feed them."

Emily turned away then and did not see the fresh look of dismay that crossed Christine's face. Christine shook her head in disbelief at what she had gotten herself into.

The women worked well together. They prepared and ate a quiet breakfast. Christine rose afterward, intending to clean up the dishes, but Grandma Em waved her back to her seat. "This is part of my morning routine, Christine." Christine watched her reach for a large black Bible. She opened the book and began to read aloud, giving Christine no time to be embarrassed or to comment.

" 'Give ear to my words, O Lord; consider my meditation. Hearken unto the voice of my cry, my King and my God, for unto thee will I pray. My voice shalt thou hear in the morning, O Lord; in the morning will I direct my prayer unto thee, and will look up.' Psalm 5:1-3."

Grandma Em closed the book and bowed her head. "Dear heavenly Father, I praise and thank You for the beautiful day You have given us and the blessings You daily give us. May we be mindful of You and ever in Your service." Grandma Em continued to pray, but Christine opened her eyes to see if anyone else was in the room. The only people she had ever heard pray were the preachers at her parents' funeral and later at her grandfather's. But neither one had sounded like this. Grandma Em made it so personal, as though God were right in the room with them. With another quick look around, Christine closed her eyes again. "And Father, I thank You for Christine. She is already so precious to me. Having her here has brought added sunshine to my life. Please bless and keep her and give us a special day together. In Christ's name I pray, Amen."

Christine, having never had a person pray for her, did not know what to say. To her surprise, no words were necessary. Speaking as if nothing were out of the ordinary, Grandma Em reached for the coffeepot and told Christine what she wanted to do that day. Quickly doing the dishes so they could walk to town before it got too hot, Christine wondered again about Grandma Em and the other people she had met in Baxter. They were not like any people she had known before.

On the walk to town, Grandma Em and Christine's conversation moved to family.

Christine asked, "Grandma Em, you talk as though Dr. Mark's father was dead. Is his mother alive?"

"No, she died when Paul—that's Mark's youngest brother—was only nine."

"How many brothers does Dr. Mark have?"

"Three—Luke, Silas, and Paul—plus one sister who is married and has two little boys of her own. Paul is at school in Chicago and Luke is there on a buying trip. You'll meet everyone else on Sunday, when we all go to church together and then back to my house for dinner."

Grandma Em stopped walking and turned abruptly to face Christine. "Christine, it hadn't occurred to me to ask you if you wanted to go to church with us. I just assumed you would. You will come with us, won't you?" Grandma Em's face was anxious.

Christine could see this was important to Grandma Em. She wouldn't think of refusing her. It gave her a warm feeling to be included as though she were a member of the family. Her answer was simple: "I'd love to come."

Christine found herself being hugged then, although she never found out why. Afterward Grandma Em hooked her arm through Christine's and they continued toward town, a brilliant smile lighting Grandma Em's face.

They stopped at the post office and then the general store. People greeted them warmly, and when the situation afforded, Christine was introduced. They found out that Lars Larson, who was going to paint Grandma Em's porch and shutters, had broken his arm. Emily brought it up on the walk home.

"Well, I'm sorry Lars broke his arm, but I'm also sorry that my painting probably won't get done before winter."

"Why don't we do the painting ourselves?"

Grandma Em stopped and looked at Christine as though she had never seen her before.

Christine continued, "I could climb the ladder and you could work below. We could do it after we do the canning this next week, or we could start right away."

"Luke would be angry," Emily said in a quiet voice, but Christine could tell she was thinking.

"You said Luke was in Chicago," Christine reminded her with a mischievous light in her sparkling green eyes.

Emily bit her lower lip in an effort to keep from laughing, but she couldn't hold it in. "We'll do it!" she said in a burst of laughter. "We'll start right away on Monday and then do our canning the next week." Grandma Em talked a bit more about the painting and then the women walked in silence for awhile. When the silence was broken, it was Emily asking Christine a question.

"Christine, someone is bound to ask me where you're from or why you're in Baxter. I have no wish to pry or to embarrass you, but, maybe you could give me a little help." Emily stopped talking then, praying she hadn't said too much. If she drove this young woman away, she would never forgive herself.

Christine's answer was long in coming, and her voice was quiet and hesitant. "My grandfather died about two weeks ago. We lived up north. I was on my way south to stay with someone. . . . When that didn't work out, I stayed on the train and found myself in Baxter. Upon arriving, my bag was stolen and I was attacked. That's how I met Dr. Mark. Losing my bag made work necessary." They had continued to walk as Christine spoke and were now home and seated on the front porch.

"But even if I hadn't been hurt, I would have stayed and rested for awhile before starting home."

"Thank you for sharing with me, Christine. I'll be praying for God's special comfort over your loss." Emily stood and put a comforting hand on Christine's shoulder. "Please remember, Christine, I'm here for you. If there is anyone at home you want to contact, feel free to use the paper and stamps in the desk in your room."

Emily left Christine alone on the porch. She was glad she had asked. Christine had been honest with her, of that she was sure, but neither had she told the entire story. Emily's mind went back

to her meeting with the sheriff in the general store that morning.
When Christine had been across the store looking at bolts of
fabric, the sheriff had approached her and asked outright if the
young dark-haired woman was Christine Bennett. Emily had been
a little surprised when he had done nothing more than thank her
and walk away after she had told him yes.

Emily climbed the stairs to her room. A pensive look on her
face, she prayed that God would give her the needed wisdom to
help this girl she was sure He had placed in her life.

Christine was not long in following Grandma Em indoors. Going to her own room, she sat at the desk. As she sat there she
realized she had been trying to block Spooner and its problems
from her mind. And for awhile it had worked. The paper was in
the desk, just as Grandma Em had said. She toyed with it a moment before pulling some out. Determination on her face, she
began to write. Even if it meant confronting Vince Jeffers herself,
she wanted some answers!

Christine could not have known that a small, nondescript man
was boarding the train in Spooner. His destination: Fall Creek.
His purpose: to do Vince Jeffers' bidding.

12

Sunday dawned warm and lovely, but the beauty of the day was lost on Christine. Staring at her reflection in the full-length mirror which hung on the inside of her closet door, her thoughts were more suited to rain.

The dress she wore was mint green, lightweight, and fresh-looking. With short puffed sleeves, a fitted bodice, and a full skirt, the dress was really quite lovely and looked as though it had been made for her. A frown clouded her face as she remembered it hadn't been. Continuing to frown into the mirror, she realized how important it had become that Grandma Em's family and friends like her. Being out of her element and dependent upon other people brought a rush of insecurity to Christine.

As Christine descended the stairs she decided to relax and be herself. Her lack of close friends in Spooner had been because of where she lived, not because people didn't like her. Joseph Bennett's neighbors had been elderly, which probably explained why Christine had grown close to Grandma Em so quickly.

Being busy helped Christine get her mind off her troubles, so with a determined step she headed to the kitchen to start breakfast. Turning from her work, she heard Grandma Em's footsteps approach.

"Good morning, Christine. Oh! You look lovely, and your hair up like that is darling!"

"Thank you." Christine's raised hand to her hair showed Grandma Em how unsure she had been.

"Oh, Christine, there will be three of us for breakfast. Silas and Luke always take care of the stock on Sundays and then take us to church."

Christine noted that Grandma Em talked to her as though she had been a part of the family for years. Emily headed off in the direction of the dining room, counting aloud the number of family expected for lunch.

Christine continued with breakfast preparations when the door leading to the backyard burst open. In strode a man, who without a glance in Christine's direction went to the washstand. Christine stood still, her eyes taking in dark hair and a full, dark beard. His shirt tightened across a broad back and muscular arms as he reached for the soap. His height made him a Cameron.

As he washed, and without looking up, he began to speak in an exasperated voice. "Gram, those pigs are a nuisance. How you stand it is beyond me! And that goat! I was ready to nail his mouth shut this morning. Plus I made the mistake of going out to the pigs before giving corn to the chickens. They followed me and kept up a steady stream of chatter the whole time I was wading in to feed those two monstrosities you call pigs."

Silas Cameron turned from his washing to see he was not addressing his grandmother. He did not know this woman who stared at him as if he had lost his mind, but he was warm to his subject, so he continued. With little more than a flicker of surprise showing in his deep blue eyes (eyes that must be a Cameron trait, Christine thought), he went on.

"Have you seen those pigs?" he asked her directly.

"Belle and Betsy?"

"Right. Well, I'll tell you this family could be eating ham and bacon for years if she'd let us butcher those two. Everyone tried to tell her when she and Grandpa bought this place, but no, she said she felt sorry for the animals and Grandpa never could tell her no. So here we are, how many years later still taking care of—" He stopped when he saw his grandmother standing in the doorway, an amused smile playing across her lips.

Silas was always much quieter than his brothers and sister. He was not one you interrupted—for fear of shutting him up, never to know when he would start again.

Emily now openly smiled at her grandson. Silas returned the smile as he moved over to bend and kiss her cheek. Straightening, he leveled a look at Christine.

"Gram, introduce me to this poor girl who was forced to stand here and listen to me rant and rave."

After the introduction, and while he was still warm to the subject, Silas shot another question at Christine.

"What do *you* think of Belle and Betsy?"

"Well, they do grow on you."

Christine watched him throw back his head and roar with laughter, giving her a glimpse of beautiful white teeth amid his bearded face. His eyes were still sparkling with mirth when he said, "Grow is something Belle and Betsy do very well!"

This brought laughter from both Grandma Em and Christine as they laid out breakfast. While they ate Emily couldn't help but notice how relaxed Silas was with Christine. Since he was normally quiet around people he didn't know well, she couldn't help but wonder if he was drawn to her because of her resemblance to Julia or if he was attracted to her as a woman. She was lovely and sweet. Grandma Em ate her breakfast with a thoughtful heart.

Later, as Silas helped Christine onto the seat of the sturdy, two-seated wagon, she sighed with relief. If the rest of the family was this nice, everything would be just fine.

The drive to church was short—almost too short for Christine to become nervous; almost, but not quite. Her palms felt damp and she hid them in the folds of her skirt, but the sight of the church interrupted her thoughts.

It was white and small and utterly charming. Christine's eyes traveled skyward, taking in the high steeple. The bell caught the morning sunshine, Christine noticed, just as it began to ring. She loved the sound. Grandma Em's hand on her arm brought her out of her daze and they walked up the steps together. Grandma Em, sensing a need in Christine, closely hooked her arm in Christine's and led them to a seat.

With a simple but warm interior, the oak pews boasted a dark stain, as did the pulpit. Off to one side sat a piano that had seen better days.

Unaware of the curious glances in her direction, Christine's eyes moved around the room. A tall, lovely young woman stood out like a Christmas tree on the Fourth of July in a small town like Baxter!

Christine watched as a man stepped into the pulpit. Emily leaned over and told Christine his name was Pastor Nolan.

Christine listened closely as Pastor Nolan made a few announcements before opening his Bible. She watched Grandma Em do the same with a Bible she hadn't even noticed. Christine's cheeks burned; she had no Bible. Without even looking at Christine, Grandma Em reached into the pew rack, took out a Bible, and handed it calmly to Christine.

It took Christine a little time to find Luke 15:11, and once she did, she didn't look at her Bible again. Her eyes riveted on Pastor Nolan, listening intently to every word.

Pastor Nolan was telling a story of a young man who wanted his inheritance early. His father gave it to him. The young man left home and spent every dime, wasting it away on riotous living. When the young man found himself alone and destitute, and knew his father's servants lived better than he did, he picked himself up and started home. The father had been watching for his son and saw him when he was still down the road. The father ran and hugged his son, his heart alive with joy. They celebrated his homecoming and welcomed him with open arms.

At the end of the sermon Pastor Nolan said, "Maybe one of you has been away from home. The Lord Jesus Christ is watching and waiting to welcome you back. Maybe you aren't sure you even have a home. Maybe you haven't taken that step of faith and told Him of your sin and believed He died for you."

Christine stood for the closing song on wobbly legs, not understanding everything he had said but knowing the part about home was making her depressed and teary. She mentally shook herself lest she cry right there in church.

Moving through church, Grandma Em took Christine with her, introducing her and staying close. Christine was unaware of how conscious Grandma Em was of her feelings. Grandma Em had glanced up at one point to find Mark and Susanne's eyes on Christine. She watched them exchange a glance, and Grandma Em's heart felt heavy for Christine. Emily still knew next to nothing about her, but she knew that when Christine was ready to talk she would be ready to listen.

In the wagon ride home, Christine tried to sort out the people she had met. The sermon, along with all the new faces, had been a bit overwhelming. Plus she still had not met Julia and her family.

Upon arriving, Christine went straight to the kitchen, hoping the work would take her mind off her jumbled emotions.

13

"Well, if that isn't the most depressing sight I know—seeing my dress on another woman and having it look better on her!" Christine spun around in surprise upon hearing these words. Her eyes met those of a beautiful, dark-haired woman.

Julia Cameron MacDonald stood with her hands on her hips trying to look disgusted, but the smile in her eyes told Christine the truth. Julia stepped forward then, hand extended and a full smile lighting her face.

"I'm Julia MacDonald. Gram tells me your name is Christine." Julia shook Christine's hand and both women felt a spark of comradeship. Their relaxation was visible as all doubts cleared.

"Yes, I'm Christine Bennett, and thank you for the dress. I hope it hasn't put you out."

"Julia has enough dresses to loan the entire town and not be put out."

It was a man's voice coming from the kitchen doorway that Julia had just vacated. He was the size of a mountain. Christine stared at him, thinking it was the first time she had met someone bigger than her grandfather. But Julia spoke to him as if she were scolding a child.

"Behave yourself, Mac. Come over here and meet Christine." She caught his hand and pulled him over. "Mac, this is Christine Bennett. Christine, this is my husband, John MacDonald, Mac for short." Christine's hand was swallowed in a huge paw that she could not keep from staring at. Mac, seeing the train of Christine's thoughts, said, "My mother always tells me I just didn't know when to stop growing." He smiled before adding, "I can't say as I meet too many women the height of my Julia." Mac dropped an arm across Julia's shoulders and gave her a quick hug.

Christine smiled at Julia. "I was rather surprised when Susanne brought me a dress that actually fit. You can't know how much I appreciate it."

The next hour was spent in dinner preparation and conversation. Christine met Calvin and Charles, Julia's sons. They had their mother's dark hair and their father's expressive brown eyes.

Content with family surrounding her, Grandma Em bustled
around finishing the table with a hug here and a word there.
Christine was again amazed at how accepted she was. When Susanne and Mark arrived, Emily bounced into the kitchen to hug
Christine and inform her of her upcoming fourth birthday. Then
she raced off to find Calvin and Charles.

Dinner was wonderful—with only one embarrassing moment.
Mark prayed, thanking God for the day, the food, and the addition
of Christine to the family. Immediately upon the heels of the
"Amen," Emily wanted to know if Christine was now a member
of the family because she was wearing Aunt Julia's dress.

Seeing Christine's flaming cheeks and Mark about to repri-
mand Emily, Grandma Em broke in kindly and explained that
Christine was family because they loved her and wanted her to
be.

Readying herself for bed, Christine reflected on the long day.
She had read a story to the children and also listened to Julia
and Susanne talk about babies and pregnancies. Mark had
stopped her at one point to ask after her shoulder. She assured
him everything was fine.

Silas had been quiet until Grandma Em announced that she
and Christine were going to paint the porch this week. Everyone
save Julia protested. Conversation was frenzied for nearly 20
minutes, when Silas ended with "Luke wouldn't like this, Gram,
and I think you know it. I also think you know, if he were here,
he'd put a stop to this idea in a hurry." But the determined look
on Grandma Em's face told them they had all wasted their breath.

Reasoning that Luke must be the oldest and the head of the
family, Christine wasn't too sure she would like anyone who was
at all hard on Grandma Em. But then she realized she was being
silly and unfair; Luke probably loved his grandmother very
much. She would reserve judgment until she met the man.

Christine now lay in the darkness waiting for sleep to come.
Pastor Nolan's words came back to her. "Maybe you aren't sure
you even have a home." Home! The thought brought a fresh pain
to Christine's chest. She would finish that letter to Mrs. Hall and
get it off soon. The thought helped ease the ache in the region
of her heart as she drifted off to sleep.

14

The next two weeks were joyful and busy. The painting of the porch and shutters went off without a hitch. Grandma Em was thrilled, though her grandsons were still doubtful.

Emily's birthday party was held at Grandma Em's one Saturday afternoon. Emily's special guest that day was Mr. Turley, Grandma Em's neighbor. Emily usually saw Mr. Turley when she was at her great-grandmother's. The man's kindness and lack of a grandfather in her own life made him a special asset.

Julia came one afternoon. Leaving Calvin and Charles with Grandma Em, she whisked Christine back to the farm to go riding. Christine was more than a little surprised when Julia took her upstairs for riding clothes and handed her a pair of men's jeans. Christine looked down at the jeans and then back to Julia's mirth-filled eyes. Both women broke out in uproarious laughter.

The MacDonald land adjoined the Cameron land, and as the women rode over the wide acres with joyous abandon, it occurred to Christine to ask Julia how Mac felt about her in men's pants, thinking back to her grandfather's reaction. But she thought better of it and kept quiet.

Christine mailed her letter to Mrs. Hall, explaining briefly her situation and that she was well. Christine asked many questions in the letter, making it hard to sit and wait for a reply.

One day brought a confrontation between Christine and Mark, when she insisted upon knowing the balance of her medical bill. Mark assured her there was no hurry, but Christine was adamant. Taking nearly every dime of her first wages from Grandma Em, Christine made her first payment. Mark protested right up to the time she left his office, but to no avail. As he saw her out the door and watched her walk up the street, he realized why Grandma Em and Julia liked her so much: They were three of a kind.

After nearly three weeks in Baxter, Christine was settled and content. Much of the time she was too busy to think of Spooner and its troubles.

Three weeks with the Cameron family was bringing changes to Christine's life. She was very aware that they were something special. At first she attributed it to a big family and many friends, something she had never had. But as time went on it was obvious there was something more. Not having heard from Mrs. Hall, Christine could only hope she would be around long enough to find out what that something was. But for now she was at peace and was more than content to stay where she was.

15

Luke Cameron shifted his weight on the train seat. Why did the last 50 miles to Baxter always feel like the longest? Deliberately taking a night train out of Chicago, it had given him one more day with Paul, and he figured he could sleep on board.

But he had figured wrong. Luke had only dozed, and now he felt achy and irritable. The train was due to arrive in Baxter before breakfast. He realized as he sat there, that it would be hours before he could crawl between the sheets of his own bed. His own bed! The thought brought a smile to his lips. At his height he really missed the length of the specially made bed. It had belonged to his parents, Joseph and Kathrine Cameron, who had both been very tall.

As usual, whenever Luke thought of his parents and the wonderful marriage they had, it brought a painful ache to his chest over his own single state.

He and Mark were both 28 years old. God had seen fit to give Mark a wife. He had also been blessed with Emily, and now another baby was due very soon. Luke felt a bit envious, but had decided long ago that God's will was best. With this acceptance came the desire to live to the fullest, alone or not. This submission, nevertheless, did not deter Luke from praying for the desire of his heart.

At one time he prayed simply for a wife. But the years passed and no feelings of love developed for any of the young women at church. This caused Luke's prayer to change, and he began to pray for preparation. Daily he prayed for growth and wisdom, asking God to help him be ready if ever God chose to give him a wife.

Another thing Luke did over the years was to observe. The two marriages he was closest to were those of his brother and sister. After much time watching Mark with Susanne and Mac with Julia, Luke was sure that God would give him a wife like Susanne. Sue was sweet, gentle, and submissive. Luke loved his sister Julia, but she certainly had a mind of her own. He wondered at times if Mac had any control over her at all.

Luke remembered back to a time when Julia was 12 years old. She had put on a pair of boy's jeans, sneaked out of the house, and gone riding astride. She had gotten in trouble for it, but it had never stopped her. In fact, she was still doing it. Why, just a few days before Luke had left for Chicago, Julia had ridden over, in blue jeans, astride her horse. Luke had stared at her jean-clad legs in tight-lipped disapproval, causing the happy smile on Julia's face to vanish.

That she had come over especially to have a quiet visit with him before he left for his trip only occurred to him after, without dismounting, Julia handed him a basket of his favorite cookies and then with a quiet "I'll miss you, Luke," pulled her horse around and rode away.

Luke, awash with guilt, knew he had to see her and make things right. So after supper he rode over to the MacDonald farm, only to be told by Mac that Julia had gone to bed early with a headache.

Mac stood watching his brother-in-law run long fingers through dark curly hair in mild frustration. Mac was reasonably sure that Luke was the reason Julia had come home from her ride with red, swollen eyes. As strong-willed as Julia was, Luke's approval had always been important to her. Luke was also a bit too stern for his own good.

Luke had not been able to see Julia to apologize until the night of her birthday party. Smiling, she told him it didn't matter, but Luke could see the hurt she was trying so hard to hide.

Luke's hand went to the bag on the seat next to him. He hoped Julia would like the book and small glass dish he had found for her in Chicago. He planned on telling her again how sorry he was, and hopefully they could then have the talk they were cheated out of because of his thoughtlessness.

The dish he had bought for Julia brought his thoughts back to Chicago and Caroline. Caroline Chambers. Luke had been staying with Frank and Lily Chambers. Their massive ranch housed more than 200 head of horses. The same day Luke decided which horses he wanted, Caroline, the Chambers' 17-year-old daughter, returned from a visit to her cousins.

Luke had liked her instantly. She was small and blonde, with a bubbly, talkative personality. The two had gone riding and for walks. When Luke was ready to go and stay with Paul, Caroline had talked him into returning for her eighteenth birthday party that weekend.

Luke had had a wonderful time at the party, feeling more drawn to Caroline as the evening progressed. But the next morning, when Luke attended church with the Chambers family, he felt terribly let down. The church was large, but only about half the pews were filled. Luke listened as the minister read a single Bible verse, shut the Book, and never once referred back to it. His monotone voice droned on and on about the sinful state of the city, but not once did he mention the fact that Jesus Christ died for those sinners.

Frank Chambers slept through the entire service. Each time Luke glanced at Caroline she was looking at him, making him wonder how much of the sermon she had heard.

Later Caroline begged Luke to write. Luke had not committed himself and had only smiled at her, even when she grabbed his hand, pressing her address into his palm. Luke wondered a bit at the mixture of relief and regret he felt as he left.

Luke's visit with Paul had been wonderful. Paul's natural speaking ability was popular on campus, and even though he was still in school, he had already been asked to fill the pulpit at several small churches. His enthusiasm was catching, making it even harder for Luke to leave. The men had embraced for long moments, knowing that it would probably be Christmas before Paul got home again.

It was getting light out now, and Luke could see the countryside. He guessed the train to be within 20 miles of Baxter. "It's beautiful up in our neck of the woods," Luke had told Frank Chambers one evening. Frank decided then and there that he and the Mrs. needed a little time away and that they would deliver the horses together. They would be up in a few weeks; Luke was to wait for a wire.

As the train pulled into Baxter, Luke stood and stretched his cramped muscles. He couldn't keep the smile from his face as his long legs carried him toward Grandma Em's. It felt so good to be home!

16

"Okay, Caesar, you're all set." Christine patted the rump of the big horse and moved toward the high-pitched bleat of Chester, wondering as she did why she never fed the goat first just to keep him quiet. As usual, the din came to an instant halt the moment Chester got his food.

The chickens were happily pecking at their meal as Christine headed around the barn to Belle and Betsy's pen. Both were overjoyed to see her, crowding near Christine's legs as though they were starved. Christine filled the trough and turned to go. Betsy, in her eagerness, rushed to the trough and bumped Christine on the back of the legs. She reacted quickly, dropping the pail and reaching for the fence. Catching it kept her from going facedown into the pig muck, but her knees buckled and she felt them sink deeply.

Having struggled out of the pen, Christine stood and surveyed the damage. The front of her dress was ruined. She watched as the slime dripped onto her boots, and she had to put her hand down to hold the dress away from her legs. She knew she had never smelled worse. Christine shot an angry look at Betsy, but the sow was head and ears into the slop, oblivious to all else.

Muttering under her breath about the tasty dishes made from ham, Christine retrieved her pail and stormed toward the house. Rounding the barn, she ran headlong into a tall, solid body. Christine gasped in surprise and stepped back. Her eyes shot downward and saw boots and pants liberally smeared with muck before looking up to the surprised face staring down at her.

"Oh, Mark, it's you! I'm sorry," Christine wailed. "Look at what I've done to your pants and boots. What a mess!" Christine plucked at the ruined skirt. "It was Betsy. She bumped right into me. I tell you, sometimes those pigs make me furious." Christine's anger made her speak quickly and gesture wildly with her arms, the pail in one hand swinging as she spoke. "Well," she said with an angry shrug, "the damage is done. Come up to the house and I'll try to clean up your boots."

Christine then stalked off with a determined stride, pail still swinging, leaving the confused man to follow in her odorous wake.

Grandma Em stepped out of the house just as they approached the back steps. "Oh, no, Christine, your dress! Which one was it?" Her voice sounded resigned.

"Betsy," Christine answered with disgust.

"Oh, Christine, I'm sorry. Betsy is always so pushy." Grandma Em looked at the man standing behind Christine. His confused face and mud-spattered clothing greatly amused her. Her voice told him as much when she said, "Welcome home, Luke."

Christine, who had been wiping ineffectively at her skirt, looked sharply at Grandma Em's face. Her eyes moved slowly to the man she had just plowed into and covered with pig muck. Her face began to burn as the full realization hit: This was not Mark Cameron. This was not the man who had nursed her back to health, befriended her, found her a job, and then took her lovingly into his own family.

This was *Luke*, the brother who had been on a buying trip in Chicago. Only he was no longer in Chicago—he was here, and Christine had welcomed him home by ruining his pants. Christine stared hard at his face. Why had no one mentioned that Mark and Luke were identical twins? It was unbelievable that two faces could be so much alike. She continued to stare rudely until Grandma Em finally broke into her thoughts.

"Christine?" Still she stared on, and Luke began to feel irritated with her.

"Christine?" Christine turned with a guilty start. "This is Luke, my oldest grandson. Luke, this is Christine Bennett. She lives here and works for me."

Luke's eyes widened at this bit of information, but he recovered quickly and offered his hand. "It's a pleasure to meet you, Christine." His voice was extremely polite.

Christine's own hand came forward to return the shake, but upon seeing how muddy it was, she quickly put it behind her back. Luke's hand was extended expectantly in midair until he finally dropped it to his side. "It's nice to meet you also." Christine's voice was stiff and her face was ablaze once again. Years of training came to the fore as Luke and Christine made an attempt to remember their manners in such an awkward situation. But Christine could take no more and turned quickly to Grandma Em. "I'll go clean up." Without waiting for a reply, she nearly ran up the steps and into the kitchen.

Luke, who was left standing outside with Grandma Em, reached into his pocket for his handkerchief. "Would you care

to explain what this is all about, Gram?" Luke's voice was quiet
as he used his handkerchief to wipe his face, his nose wrinkling
as the smell from his boots traveled upward.

Grandma Em took pity. "Let's get you cleaned up and we'll talk
over breakfast."

Nearly an hour later she concluded, "So you see, Luke, it
doesn't matter that I don't know all about Christine, including
why she is so far from home. Although she has not shared with
me, she has talked with Mark. But if I learned one thing being a
doctor's wife for over 45 years, you don't ask questions about
patients." Grandma Em paused and put her hand over Luke's.
"What I do know is that right now I need her, and I hope her need
for me will lead her to Christ."

Luke was quiet for some time. "I guess the idea takes a little
getting used to. All these years of fighting to remain alone and
independent, and in the three weeks I'm gone you capitulate and
let someone not only work for you but live here as well."

"If it makes you feel any better, Mark sounded just like you
the day he came and told me his idea for Christine working and
living here."

This brought a smile to Luke's face. Luke had, without spoken
word, become head of the family when, over four years ago, Joseph Cameron had died. Emily was always a very capable
woman, and Luke did not move in and take over. He was simply
there when she needed him. Mark and Mac were more than willing to lend a hand, but Luke and Silas, being bachelors, were
more available.

Emily rarely had words with her grandson, but when she did,
Luke usually won. In an infuriatingly logical way he stated his
case. He preferred to deal in facts rather than emotions, and
much to Emily's chagrin, he could talk circles around her.

Luke was usually very sensitive to his grandmother's needs
and wishes. Along the way there had been a few times when he
had simply put his foot right down on the top of some of her
plans.

Luke now sat on the wagon seat beside Silas. He felt strangely
humbled at the thought of how well things went with him not
around. He realized that he and Grandma Em hadn't really finished their conversation when Silas had shown up and offered
Luke a ride home.

Silas hadn't known the time Luke's train was to arrive—just
the day. But Silas was like that. In his quiet way he seemed to

sense when and where he was needed and then just stepped in without pomp or ceremony.

As the wagon neared the ranch, the restless night was quickly catching up to Luke. Suddenly he couldn't quite remember what he had been a bit uneasy about at Grandma Em's. Oh, well, he would think on it later. Right now the ranch was in view, and he was sure Silas wouldn't mind if he got in a quick nap. Whatever today's problems were, they would wait a few more hours.

"You say you received this letter today?"

"Yes, Sheriff," replied Mrs. Hall, relief and concern evident in her voice.

The sheriff turned back to the piece of paper in his hand.

Dear Mrs. Hall:

I'm sorry for the worry and pain you must certainly have experienced these past weeks. I am also sorry I was not able to tell you of my plans before leaving. The letter you delivered from Carl Maxwell told me to leave Spooner immediately. I was to meet someone in Fall Creek. When this didn't work out, I stayed on the train and ended up in a small town called Baxter. I live with and work for an older woman. She and her family are very kind and loving to me. I am physically settled but my heart and mind await answers. Please ask Carl to write me. I need his help. I'll close by telling you once again that I am fine. I hope this finds you well. I miss you. Take care and please write to me so I know you received this letter.

Much love,

Christie

P.S. My address: Christine Bennett
c/o Mrs. Emily Cameron
Baxter, Wisconsin

"Mrs. Hall, has anyone else seen this letter?"

"No, I brought it right to you."

The sheriff nodded and stood still as though in deep thought.

When he spoke, his voice was very quiet. "You heard that Carl Maxwell is missing?"

"I'd heard."

"Without him to question, the only place to go is back to Christine." He paused. "Write her and tell her to stay where she is. Tell her Carl is missing and that until I can dig a bit deeper, she's better off where she is. And of course, warn her about talking to people. The less said, the better. You of course understand it is just as necessary here."

"Of course, Sheriff." Mrs. Hall put out her hand to take the letter, but the sheriff held it away.

"I'd really like to keep this." He saw Mrs. Hall's hesitation and then continued. "I'll copy the address so you can write, but this letter is important."

She nodded reluctantly and replied, "When you're done with it, I'd like it back."

"Of course, Mrs. Hall; I'll keep it safe. Now look on the bright side. Christine has written, and you know she's safe. We'll get to the bottom of this. Don't you worry."

Mrs. Hall thanked the sheriff and he watched her walk away, wishing he felt as optimistic as he sounded.

17

Christine stood in the parlor before the large family portrait that Grandma Em had just asked her to hang. Twins! Why had no one ever mentioned that Mark and Luke were identical twins? Shaking her head, she wondered how many times she had asked herself that question.

Yesterday had been awful. Christine could not stop thinking about how foolish she felt while meeting Luke.

Christine's eyes moved intently over the portrait. The four Cameron brothers stood in the back. Susanne, Mac, and Julia were seated in front, a child in each lap. Silas stood to the far right of the back row, sporting a beard as full then as it was today. The man next to him could be none other than Paul. Dark hair, boyish good looks, and most of all his height marked him as a Cameron. By simple deduction Christine guessed the next man to be Luke. To the far left stood Mark, his hand on Sue's shoulder, a small Emily in her lap. Judging from the changes in Emily, Calvin, and Charles, the picture was probably about two years old.

Her eyes once again centered on the identical men in the back row, glancing quickly back and forth between the two. They were even of the same height and build. Well, possibly not. Maybe Luke's shoulders were a bit wider. Christine turned away from the picture with an angry shrug. What did she care if his shoulders were bigger? If she never saw the man again it would be way too soon. Deciding to put it behind her, Christine walked into the dining room to dust, unaware of Grandma Em standing in the doorway to the kitchen, watching the emotions play across Christine's face.

Grandma Em could feel Christine's frustration. Yesterday must have been terribly embarrassing for her. The look on Christine's face when Grandma Em welcomed Luke home clearly stated that she had taken him for Mark. And who wouldn't? There were only a handful of people who could tell them apart.

Grandma Em's mind went to the conversation yesterday. They hadn't really finished talking, leaving Grandma Em unsure just how Luke felt about Christine.

As Grandma Em continued to ponder, it occurred to her why this was so unsettling. Luke's opinion was of the utmost importance to her. If Luke felt uncomfortable with Christine or disapproved of her in some way, she wanted to know. Grandma Em quickly reined in her wild thoughts. God did not put Christine in their lives simply to pluck her back out again. God would handle it. His timing would be perfect. Emily went back to work quoting Proverbs 3:5,6: "Trust in the Lord with all thine heart, and lean not unto thine own understanding. In all thy ways acknowledge him, and he shall direct thy paths."

18

"You haven't stopped smiling since you got back." Silas' voice broke through Luke's concentration.

Luke did not bother to deny it. His grin just widened and his eyes once again swept over the acres he called home—the same acres in fact that his father, Joseph Cameron Jr., called home, as well as his mother's father, Charles Langley, before him.

Supper over and the dishes done, Luke and Silas were settled on the back porch. The silence they shared was comfortable, each letting the peace and serenity of the evening settle around him.

Sunday mornings brought extra work, with Grandma Em's chores to be done as well as all their own stock to feed, so Saturday evening was usually spent relaxing and then retiring to bed early.

Luke broke the silence with a question that told Silas what had been on his mind. "Si, has Christine been going to church with you and Gram?"

"Yes."

Luke merely nodded and left Silas to ponder on what had brought this up. He would have been surprised if he had been able to read Luke's mind, since his question had been nothing more than a passing thought, not centered on Christine, but on going to church and the day he had attended services with Caroline.

Luke remembered a time in his life when, in his teen years, church had not been one of his favorite places. Caroline, he had to admit, seemed more interested in him than in the sermon. He couldn't help but feel a bit flattered until he remembered how easily the minister had made it to think of anything besides the sermon. He was still praying about writing her, his heart still very unsure of his feelings for her. He also prayed he would not feel desperate—that his wanting a wife so badly wouldn't cloud his mind and make him forget that God's will was more important than his own. Once again, as Luke surrendered his will to God's a peace settled over his troubled heart. He knew without a doubt that if God had a wife for him and he left the choosing in His hands, everything would be perfect.

— ❖ —

In town Grandma Em and Christine were also finished with supper. Settled in the parlor, Christine picked up some mending and Grandma Em chose a book. Grandma Em had held her tongue all evening even though she could tell something was bothering Christine. After pretending to read for a full five minutes, she gave up and plunged in.

"Christine, you seem a bit quiet this evening. I hope you're not coming down with something."

"No, Grandma Em, I'm fine." They both knew this wasn't true.

Grandma Em plunged in again, praying she wasn't being too pushy. "Was the letter you received today from home?"

"Yes." Grandma Em watched an expression she couldn't quite define pass over Christine's face.

"Would you like to talk about it?" Grandma Em was surprised when Christine didn't even hesitate.

"It's rather complicated, Grandma Em. You see, I didn't leave Spooner under the best of circumstances. Being here, working and getting drawn into your family a little more each week, sometimes causes me to forget that there are things at home that need to be settled." Christine paused here, and the emotion on her face became clear to Emily. Fear! Christine searched Grandma Em's face intently before continuing hesitantly. "The woman who wrote me, a woman I trust, advised me to stay here for the time being . . . and, well, we've never discussed how long you need me. If this is a temporary arrangement or . . ." her voice trailed off.

Grandma Em's eyes flooded with tears. When she could speak, her voice was very soft. "Were it in my power, Christine, I would keep you here with me for the rest of my life."

Christine flew into the arms of the older woman.

Christine clung to Emily as great sobs racked her young body and Emily's own tears ran silently down her cheeks. Christine's tears seemed to exhaust her, and so, with a final hug for Grandma Em and a hoarse "thank you," she took the stairs to bed.

Once in bed, exhausted as she was, Christine could not keep her mind off the letter from Mrs. Hall. Even as sleep claimed her, snatches of the letter returned. "Carl Maxwell is missing. Talk to no one. The sheriff is looking into things. Stay where you are. I repeat, talk to no one."

— ❖ —

"You mean to tell me you've been gone all this time, only to return and tell me the job isn't done? How long does it take to kill one woman?" Vince Jeffers' face was mottled with rage. The veins in his neck stood out like cords.

"I'm sorry, Mr. Jeffer's sir, but no one has seen a girl of that description, and the only Mr. Franklin in town somebody said was killed by a runaway horse a few weeks back."

Vince Jeffers was so angry he wanted to strike the man. He stood behind his desk, a heavy glass paperweight clenched in his hand.

Finally he spoke through gritted teeth. "Get out! I need time to think, and don't you dare show your face around me until I send for you!"

The man needed no further prodding. He bolted for the door, nearly frightened out of his wits by his employer's rage. The sound of shattering glass echoed in his ears as he made good his escape.

19

Emily sat on the side of her bed feeling every day of her 70 years. Last night had been awful. She had gone to bed feeling very good about being able to reassure Christine of her job and a place to live, only to be wakened sometime near midnight by her screams.

By the time Emily got to Christine's room, she had stopped screaming. Emily found her sitting up in bed, her eyes glazed over and soaked with perspiration. Grandma Em lit the lamp and took Christine's hand, holding it gently until she noticed her presence.

"He was trying to kill you." Christine's voice was a dry whisper.

"Who was, dear?"

"Vince Jeffers. He had stabbed Mrs. Hall and was going after you. I couldn't stop him." Her voice broke.

"A dream, Christine; it was just a dream. I'm safe and you're safe. It's all right now." Grandma Em rose and brought a damp cloth to bathe Christine's face. She helped her into a fresh nightgown, all the time talking in a calm, reassuring voice. When Christine settled back in bed, Grandma Em blew out the light and once again took her hand. In a quiet, clear, trusting voice she began to pray. "Dear heavenly Father, please cover her with Your loving comfort. Help her to relax and sleep. Help her to forget her fear and trust You to watch over her this night. Thank You, God, for giving Christine to us. Help me to be here for her and to comfort her in any way I can. Thank You, God. Amen."

Christine's eyes had closed. Emily's hand reached to smooth her brow. Her heart filled with anguish over this young woman's pain. Emily sat with her for awhile before making her way back to her own bed. Sleep did not come until nearly dawn.

With all these thoughts going through Grandma Em's mind, she was shocked to find Christine up ahead of her with coffee on and breakfast started.

"Christine, I'm surprised you're up. When I didn't hear you moving around in your room, I assumed you were getting some extra rest."

"I was awake and I just got up." Christine's smile was meant to reassure Grandma Em, but she wasn't fooled.

They worked for a few minutes in silence until Christine spoke. "I feel rather foolish for waking you last night. I've never done anything like that before. I'm sorry."

"Christine, there is no reason to apologize. It's not as if you planned to have a bad dream that scared you senseless." Grandma Em chided her a bit sternly. And then more gently, "Do you want to talk about it?"

The back door opened at that moment, keeping Christine from answering. Grandma Em sent her a look of apology for the interruption and then went to greet her grandsons.

Forgetting that Luke was also a regular guest on Sunday morning, she turned to add more eggs to the pan. Christine no longer felt embarrassed about their first meeting. She realized over the past week that these things just happen.

No, her thoughts this morning were not on Luke, but Mark. She had lain awake most of the night and after much thought had decided to talk with Mark. So far the sheriff had not talked to her, and frankly, she preferred it that way. She much preferred confiding in Mark and letting him decide if and when to talk with the sheriff.

Christine, her thoughts so intense, hadn't realized that Grandma Em had taken Silas into the parlor to show him some new sheet music. Luke sat down silently at the table to await the coffee.

Christine bustled around and finally moved to the table to pour coffee. Not until she was nearly on top of Luke did she realize he was there. Having those startling blue eyes leveled so intently on her face caused Christine's hand to shake, splashing some coffee on Luke's leg. Luke was on his feet in an instant and reaching for a napkin.

Christine stood, the pot now upright, a trembling hand pressed to her mouth in horror. "I'm sorry—are you burned, are you hurt? How clumsy of me! I didn't see you, I'm sorry." The words tumbled out and Christine turned to replace the pot and get a damp cloth.

Luke wondered, as she did, if it was at all safe to be around this woman. He couldn't quite squelch the irritation he felt at having his Sunday pants stained. It was either wear them as they were or go all the way home and change.

Christine returned and handed Luke a wet cloth, seeing as she did that his napkin had been of little help. Not until Luke returned the cloth to her did he see the tears standing in her wide, green eyes. He couldn't have known that lost sleep and worry had brought them on and not just the spilled coffee. Upon seeing them, Luke's irritation drained away.

"I'm sorry, are you burned?"

"No, just a bit damp." He smiled and indicated his pants, hoping she would believe him.

When she just stood there, blushing and looking miserable, he tried again. "Honestly, Christine, I'm not burned; I'm fine, really."

She stared at him a moment more and then with a little nod turned back to the stove, wiping her eyes with the backs of her hands.

Luke thought that for as tall as she was, such a childlike gesture made her look like a lost little girl. He felt sorry for her and hoped she hadn't seen any of his earlier irritation.

When Grandma Em and Silas returned, they all sat down to breakfast. All three of the Camerons noticed Christine pushing her food around her plate. Grandma Em and Luke felt sure they knew why. Silas just felt concern for her.

20

Within the next hour the four of them were sitting in church together. As Silas parked the horses and wagon, Christine had a chance to see Susanne and tell her she needed to speak with Mark. Susanne hugged Christine and promised to pass the word along. Having Mark and Susanne to talk with was a great help.

But these thoughts were far from Christine's mind as she sat in church beside Grandma Em. As usual, she listened intently to Pastor Nolan speak, wondering as before at the strange feeling of expectancy she always felt.

Christine reached for the pew Bible when Pastor Nolan told them today's text was in Luke 19. Her eyebrows rose in surprise, for she hadn't remembered that Luke was a Bible name.

In Luke 19 Pastor Nolan told about Zacchaeus, a tax collector who cheated people. This made him very rich but not very well liked. He was also short. On this particular day in Scripture, Jesus was coming to the town where Zacchaeus lived. Zacchaeus wanted to see Him, but the crowd and Zacchaeus' short height made this impossible.

So the little man ran further down the road where Jesus would be walking. The Bible said that Zacchaeus climbed into a tree and waited for Jesus to pass.

When Jesus was below the tree, He looked up and saw Zacchaeus. "Come down quickly," Jesus bade the man; "today I'm going to eat at your house."

Christine's mind wandered a bit as she wondered how Jesus knew that Zacchaeus was in the tree. She continued to wonder about this even as the pastor spoke on Zacchaeus giving back four times the amount of money he had overcharged people, and giving half his goods to the poor. The final verse was Luke 19:10: "For the Son of man has come to seek and to save that which was lost."

As everyone reached for their hymnbooks and stood for the closing song, Christine kept the pew Bible in her hand. She read the passage once again as everyone sang, thinking as she read that she had missed the part where Zacchaeus called down to Jesus or made himself known in some other way.

The service ended and everyone moved toward the door—

everyone except Christine and Luke. Christine was still reading, and Luke, who had sat on the inside of the pew against the wall, couldn't exit without climbing over her. He stood patiently, waiting for her to finish.

When Christine read the passage through for the second time, she turned abruptly to Luke. "How did Jesus know Zacchaeus was in the tree?"

Luke, who was half expecting something like this, answered quietly, "Because God knows everything."

He could see this made no sense whatever to Christine because her brow was knit with confusion. He continued, "And Jesus is God's Son. Jesus is God." Luke watched her face, unsure of what was so confusing.

Christine opened her Bible again and said, "But where does it say that?"

Luke finally understood. "It doesn't say that in the passage we were in today. Here, let me show you where it does say that." Luke opened his own Bible and began to thumb through it.

As he did so, Christine realized that the church had emptied. How embarrassing! She had stood there reading even though the service was over, and Luke couldn't even get out of the pew until she moved!

"No, Luke, it's all right. I best get to the wagon."

Luke looked up to see Christine's face flushed in a way that was becoming familiar to him. Her movements as she headed toward the aisle were stiff, and she was looking anywhere but at him.

"Christine." His deep voice stopped her just as she reached the aisle. Luke waited until she faced him before speaking. "After lunch today, if you'd like, I'll write some verses down and you can look them up yourself."

She nearly sagged with relief. With a nod and a small smile she headed for the door.

Luke replaced the pew Bible that Christine had dropped in her hurry to escape. He followed, his pace more sedate as he exited, belying the way his mind raced for verses she would understand and, more importantly, would whet her appetite for more.

21

The scene on the front porch was a peaceful one. Story time was over and Emily's small head rested on her mother's round stomach. Susanne's foot kept the porch swing at a steady rock.

Emily's eyes slid shut for the last time and Susanne's hand moved to stroke her shiny curls. She smiled as she realized it wouldn't bother her in the least to have another little blonde girl. Her other hand moved absently over her stomach.

The front door opened and shut quietly. Luke took a seat near the swing and sat in silence, watching his niece sleep. A frown crossed his face as he saw Sue's hand on her abdomen. Luke opened his mouth to speak, but Sue was observant and ready for him.

"I'm fine."

Luke relaxed and smiled. "Can Mark hide anything from you?"

"Nope, not a thing."

"How long now?"

"Mark says two weeks. I say sooner."

"He's the doctor."

"So he keeps reminding me." Sue answered with a smile and a raise of her eyebrows.

Luke laughed softly before asking. "Where is Mark?"

Sue nodded her head toward a huge old willow tree that stood some distance off the corner of the porch. Amid bare switches hanging nearly to the ground, Mark and Christine could be seen and were obviously in deep conversation.

"Your grandmother assured me last night when we talked that I have a job and a place to live for an indefinite period of time. It's good to have that worry off my mind. I plan to write Mrs. Hall so her mind is at ease."

Mark nodded. "Our sheriff spoke to me about contacting the law in Spooner, just so the lines of communication are open. Both towns need to work together on this."

Christine shook her head sadly. "I just don't understand.

Grandpa was not a wealthy man. I mean, we lived comfortably and I had all I needed, but it just doesn't make sense."

"I must admit, it's all rather strange. What we know isn't much. First a note to you from Carl Maxwell, and then the man disappears."

"And don't forget my grandfather's will leaving everything to Vince Jeffers in the event of my death. I'm only 19 years old! He would never have written that. Another thing puzzles me—my grandfather's charity. It was never even mentioned. He gave often and quite generously to a small orphanage in Spooner. It doesn't make sense that he wouldn't even remember them."

The two stood together for a moment in thoughtful silence. Mark studied once again the letter in his hand. "Christine," he began gently, "when a person passes away, it's normal for the surviving family members to go through the loved one's possessions. If you were home, I'm sure you would have already started this, painful though it may be." Mark hesitated, wanting to be tactful. "When you write to Mrs. Hall, why not ask her to look through your grandfather's things? I realize this is highly personal, but maybe she can turn up something that will give us some answers."

As Mark suspected, Christine did not jump at the idea. It still upset her to think about the finality of her grandfather's death. So Mark hastened to add, "What you write is up to you. You don't have to tell me your decision—it was only a suggestion. If it's all right, though, I'd like to show this letter to the sheriff when I see him."

"That's fine, Mark." Christine's voice was preoccupied. "Will you please tell Grandma Em I've gone for a walk and I'll be gone awhile?"

"Sure, I'll tell her."

The words were barely out of his mouth before Christine walked away. The need inside her to escape was so desperate that she nearly ran. Cutting across Mr. Turley's field, her long legs carried her swiftly to a quiet spot along the creek which she had discovered during her first week at Grandma Em's.

An enormous boulder at the edge of the water was Christine's destination. Sinking down to it with a weary plop, Christine let the afternoon sun beat upon her. She welcomed its warmth, though it crossed her mind that she should have worn a hat. She studied the backs of her hands: brown. It was what she got for working in the garden without gloves.

A sudden movement interrupted her reverie. Christine's eyes were drawn to the creek's edge. A fish had swum between the rocks and was trapped in a pool barely large enough to hold him.

Christine contemplated the situation a moment before reaching out to shift one of the large rocks. The hoped-for result was immediate: With a flip of its tail the fish headed downstream. With envy Christine's eyes followed as it moved swiftly out of sight in its newfound freedom.

Freedom. It seemed like forever since Christine had experienced that feeling. Freedom to go home if she wanted. Freedom from worries and fears. A freedom that, up until the time of her grandfather's death, she had taken for granted.

Christine felt a lonely ache within her. Luke said that God knows everything. Did He know why she sometimes felt empty inside? Did He care? So many questions but no answers. Christine ached for her grandfather's presence, yet she knew her pride was keeping her from asking for help. So the afternoon shadows lengthened and Christine sat with only her tears for company.

Back at the house, Luke and Silas had their suit coats on and were headed for the door. After kissing Grandma Em, Luke handed her a piece of paper. He explained about the verses, and Grandma Em assured him that Christine would get them.

For Mrs. Hall, Sunday afternoon was usually spent visiting her sister and family. Mrs. Hall's spirits had been up ever since she had heard from Christine. So, after a good meal and a visit with her sister, Mrs. Hall started walking out to the Bennett residence with a light step.

"Good afternoon, Mrs. Hall."

"Oh! Mr. Jeffers, good afternoon to you! It's lovely, is it not?" Mrs. Hall smiled at him.

"Yes, indeed it is. May I wish you also a splendid week."

"Why, thank you, Mr. Jeffers." Mrs. Hall continued on her way.

Vince sat astride his bay stallion and watched the woman's light step, wondering at her exuberance. She certainly didn't look like the grieving woman he had seen before. Maybe she had had news of Christine.

Vince heeled his horse into a walk. He had finally cooled off from his last meeting with that incompetent fool who worked for him. Maybe it was time to send for him again.

Once again in the Bennett house, Mrs. Hall hung up her bonnet and changed her shoes. It was then that she put her finger on what was different about Vince Jeffers.

She had grown used to his smile, a smile that never quite reached his eyes. He was so different from Mr. Bennett that it was a wonder they had ever formed a partnership. But that wasn't it. What was it, then, that was troubling her about him? *He had stopped her and talked to her but didn't even ask after Christine.* How odd! Rarely had he ever given her the time of day.

Once again Mrs. Hall experienced that strange feeling that she got whenever she saw Vince Jeffers lately, as if there were something she was supposed to tell him or remember that she couldn't quite come up with.

Mrs. Hall did a mental shrug as she reached for *A Study in Scarlet*, the new Sherlock Holmes mystery novel that her sister had just finished. Whatever it was with Vince Jeffers would have to wait until tomorrow.

22

"This week has just flown by, especially since the weather has finally cooled." Grandma Em shifted. "Did you get your letter off?"

"Yes, it's been posted. I also had another confrontation with your grandson. Why does he put up such a fuss when I try to pay on my bill?"

Grandma Em laughed but offered no explanation. The truth of the matter was that Mark's heart was tender to a fault. He and Sue cared deeply for Christine and would do anything to ease her plight. Grandma Em also knew about pride. She knew Christine had plenty of it because she saw herself so clearly in the young woman.

The women were now on Grandma Em's street, her house in sight.

"Is that Luke on your porch?"

"Yes, I believe so." Something in Grandma Em's voice made Christine ask, "Do you think something is wrong?"

Grandma Em slowed down a bit and spoke softly. "Don't ask me how I know, Christine, but I think I'm about to get in trouble for painting my own porch."

Near the porch now, the women exchanged a glance and then quickly looked away lest they should begin to laugh. The days they had spent painting had been wonderful. Getting to know and trust each other through paint spatters and laughter had been a tonic to Christine. Neither woman would have traded the experience for the world.

"Hello, Luke. You're in time for lunch. Will you stay?"

Luke answered as he took his grandmother's packages and held the door for both ladies. "Thanks, Gram."

As lunch preparations were made, Christine was aware of Luke's eyes. They settled on both her and Grandma Em for long, intense moments. The conversation was light, but Luke seemed somewhat distracted.

The three made short work of thick ham slices, freshmade bread, and cheese wedges. The peaches were ripe to perfection, sweet as candy.

A forkful of chocolate cake was halfway to Grandma Em's

mouth when Luke said offhandedly, "I heard today that Lars Larson broke his arm." Luke watched as the women across from him paused ever so slightly in their eating before rushing on, taking care not to look anywhere but at their plates.

Luke felt a sinking sensation in the pit of his stomach. Their pause had confirmed the gossip he had heard downtown to be true.

"Did you know he had broken his arm, Gram?"

"Yes."

"Was he able to get to your porch and shutters before he fell?"

"No, he was not." Her answer was quiet, but firm.

Luke's own eyes dropped to his plate. He was beginning to wish he hadn't even asked. A fight with his grandmother was not what he wanted, but one look at her face told him he had best step carefully or that was exactly what he would have.

Grandma Em's chin was thrust out, her eyes sparkling with defiance. Luke nearly laughed out loud as his eyes swung to Christine. She sported the same mulish look, ready for battle. Two against one. It just wasn't fair. Luke knew that another tactic was needed here.

"Who climbed the ladder?" he asked, as if he didn't really care.

"I did."

"Christine." The women answered in unison.

Luke sat and eyed each woman in turn. Both were on the verge of speaking in their own defense when Luke stood.

"Well, ladies, the porch looks nice. You paint very well." This said, Luke bent and kissed Grandma Em's cheek. "Thanks for lunch. I'll see you both Sunday." And with that he left.

You could have heard a feather drop in the kitchen after the front door shut. Neither woman spoke. Feeling shame at how defiantly they had behaved, Emily and Christine exchanged sheepish glances and moved to do the dishes. As Christine worked, she realized that Luke still didn't know how much she appreciated the verses. Feeling double the guilt, she worked on, determined to let Luke know some way on Sunday.

23

With a final look in the mirror that took in a fresh shirt and clean blue jeans, Silas headed down the hall to Luke's room. Luke, having just slipped into his suit jacket, turned to find Silas standing in his bedroom, eyebrows raised in surprise. Luke would have left the room at that time, but Silas wandered in and dropped down on the bed, eyeing his brother with amusement.

"You've already impressed the Chambers family enough to get the horses at a good price. Why the suit?" Before Luke could answer, Silas went on. "It wouldn't have anything to do with the address of one Miss Caroline Chambers I saw on your dresser, would it?"

"I just thought it would be nice to welcome them to Baxter smelling better than a horse." Luke's voice sounded defensive, even to his own ears, and he wasn't sure why. He really didn't expect to see Caroline, let alone encourage her if he did.

Movement below Silas' beard told Luke he was fighting laughter. Silas looked down at himself before asking with feigned innocence, "Do I smell all right? Maybe I should change into a suit too."

This brought a reluctant smile to Luke's face, and his voice was gruff to hide his amusement. "Get to the wagon, Silas, before I leave you home."

Baxter's train station was uncrowded—unusual for a Saturday afternoon, but a blessing nonetheless. The three horses coming in for the Cameron ranch would be ready for a low-key arrival.

Luke and Silas stood together and watched the train pull in. Luke's hand went to the neckline of his shirt when the second person went by and greeted him as Mark. Silas' laughter didn't help. The train had stopped and people were disembarking, so there was no more time to worry about clothing.

Within minutes Frank Chambers was on the platform, his eyes skimming over the station. Luke stepped over to him, Silas at his heels.

"Luke!" Frank Chambers' hand was extended and his smile was friendly.

"Good to see you, Frank. How was the trip?"

"It was fine, just fine."

"Where is Mrs. Chambers?"

"She didn't come. Our niece had her baby, so Lily stayed home to play mother hen." Frank looked his disappointment.

Luke was about to introduce Silas when Caroline stepped from behind her father. "Hello, Luke," she said softly. The look in her eyes was nothing short of worshipful.

Feeling a bit flustered, Luke made the introductions. Caroline barely took time to nod in Silas' direction before her eyes once again clung to Luke. Frank didn't seem to notice. Silas left immediately after that to check on the horses. Frank went with him, leaving Luke and Caroline alone.

"I've missed you, Luke." Caroline's voice was soft and a bit anxious, nervous eyes shining up at him.

Luke only smiled faintly and asked about the luggage. He then bent to lift the large trunk and missed Caroline's face, her disappointment clearly revealed.

Luke hauled the trunk into the wagon before leaving Caroline to assist the men.

Frank had a mare's lead in each hand. Silas was holding the stallion when Luke approached. "You certainly didn't exaggerate, Luke. He's a beauty." Silas' voice more than words spoke his admiration.

Luke smiled and patted the firm neck, speaking softly to the magnificent animal. Titan was black, completely black, from the tip of his proud nose to the end of his long tail. His eyes showed intelligence and spirit. A sound from the mares caught his attention. He answered with a loud snort, sidestepped, and tossed his finely shaped head.

"Let's get this guy home. We'll drop the Chambers' at the hotel and head out."

Some hours later the three horses were settled in their new home, fed and comfortable. As the men headed back to the house, Silas spoke. "I take it you are not headed back into town tonight?"

"How did you know that?"

"Miss Chambers didn't look too happy with you when we left."

"No, she didn't, did she?" Luke replied with a frown. "It was Frank's idea. He said he was beat and that they would see us in the morning. I forgot to tell Grandma Em that there would be two more for dinner tomorrow."

"It won't matter. I'll tell her in the morning."

"*You* will? Where will *I* be?"

"I figured you would go and have breakfast at the hotel with the Chambers'. I can get Gram's chores.

"Oh. Well, thanks for the offer, Si; I'll think on it."

The men had reached the back porch. It was getting cooler, the days shorter. The sun was sinking low.

"What did you think of her?"

"I didn't really get a chance to talk with her." Silas' answer was accompanied by a small shrug. But the look Luke shot him clearly stated that he believed Silas had sidestepped the question.

With a heavy sigh Silas answered, "She seems young."

Luke's face was pensive. "I think so too."

The men fell silent for a time. As the sun dipped behind the trees and hills it cast an orange glow on the Cameron ranch.

Silas stood and stretched. "I'm headed in, but I want to tell you something—something I believe with all my heart. God won't hide His answers from you. If Caroline is the woman God has for you, you'll know. If you continue to trust, He'll continue to be your guide."

These words said, Silas touched Luke's shoulder and went into the house. Alone now, and in deep thought, Luke sat until darkness completely covered the land.

". . . they arrived on the 4:15 yesterday. Luke would like to bring them to dinner."

"Of course the Chambers' can come to lunch. How did the horses do on the trip?"

"They're fine. You'll have to get out and see them. That stallion is a beauty."

"We'll plan on it. Christine, let's go out this week, maybe Thursday or Friday."

"That sounds fine. I'm a little anxious to see the ranch."

Grandma Em and Silas both stopped eating. They stared at Christine and then at each other before speaking, as though they had forgotten she was there.

"I can't believe this, Gram. All these weeks and she hasn't seen the ranch!"

"I feel just awful. I know she'd love it. She told me she misses her own horse. How could we have overlooked such a thing?"

"Ahem!" Christine felt she needed to remind them of her presence.

Grandma Em turned. "That settles it, Christine. We'll go out this week, rain or shine." With a determined nod, Grandma Em went back to her breakfast.

Christine was left to wonder what was so special about the ranch. Her grandfather's stables housed four horses, one being Raven, Christine's own horse—her pride and joy. The thought of seeing the ranch and its horses left Christine in a buoyant mood for church.

Driving into the church yard and being greeted by name felt good to Christine. Mrs. Nolan was in the entryway as usual. She squeezed Christine's hand and said a few words to Silas about her niece Amy.

A brief flash from last week went through Christine's mind and she moved quickly to be first in the pew and next to the wall.

Pastor Nolan said he was fighting a cold. He would need to keep things short today because his throat was bothering him. Only one song was sung before the sermon began.

"Today I would like you to turn to First John chapter 4, beginning with verse 7." Pastor Nolan read these verses and began to talk about God's love.

"God is love. The Scriptures tell us this over and over. In John 3:16 we see the greatest expression of this love. Listen as I read John 3:16: 'For God so loved the world that he gave his only begotten Son, that whosoever believeth in him should not perish but have everlasting life.' Who is the only begotten Son in this verse? It's Jesus Christ. He alone is qualified to take on the sins of the world, for He is God. In John 10:30 are Jesus' own words: 'I and my father are one.' "

Christine turned the pages and read John 10:30. A smile lit her face. She knew this verse. It was the first one on the list that Luke had given her. Shifting slightly in her seat, Christine looked past Grandma Em in hopes of catching Luke's eye. She need not have worried—Luke was already looking her way. They exchanged a quick grin before turning their attention back to the sermon.

"All have sinned and come short of the glory of God—Romans 3:23. 'All have sinned,' it says. Maybe you think that's just not true. You might say, 'I've never sinned. I've never stolen from someone or killed anyone. Those are sins and I've never done those.' But the verse says, 'All have sinned and come short of the glory of God.' You see, in the light of God's holiness, we have all sinned. Pride, greed, unforgiveness, gossip—the list is a long one. God will not allow these things into His heaven. Heaven is God's home, and He alone decides who will enter.

"But there is hope. Read on. Romans 3:24 says, 'Being justified freely by his grace through the redemption that is in Christ Jesus.' Jesus Christ is the answer to all your needs." Pastor Nolan stopped and cleared his throat. His voice was getting hoarse, but he continued.

"My throat isn't going to let me go on much longer, but I must ask you this: Do you know where you would spend eternity if you were to die today? God loves you and sent His Son for your sins. My friend, have you ever confessed your sin to God and told Him you believe that Jesus died for those sins? Have you ever opened up your heart to Him? He is waiting for you with open arms. Your prayer need not be complicated or elaborate. The Word says, 'Believe on the Lord Jesus Christ and thou shalt be saved!' Do not put it off, my friend. No one knows how long his time on earth will be. Don't wait! Go to Christ and open your heart to Him. He will gladly enter in. He is your only answer to everlasting life as well as an abundant life here on earth. Do it today!"

The closing hymn was led by Silas. His voice was deep and clear. In his closing prayer, he asked for God's healing hand upon Pastor Nolan and for those who had not yet accepted Christ.

Once back in the wagon, Silas managed the reins, with Grandma Em sitting beside him. Christine slid forward from her place in the backseat until her face nearly touched Grandma Em's shoulder.

"Grandma Em?" Emily shifted around in her seat with an expectant smile on her face. "You told me your husband, Joseph, was on the other side. Did you mean heaven?" At Grandma Em's nod she went on. "He believed in Christ and you think he is in heaven?" Again Emily only nodded. "And you also believe in Christ and believe you're going to see Joseph when you die?"

"With all my heart, Christine."

It was Christine's turn to nod. Placing a cool hand on Christine's flushed cheek, Grandma Em spoke through tears. "I know you are searching, Christine. I also know that God is your answer. God loves you so much, and I'm praying, Christine, that you will open your heart to that love."

Even though the horses were at a crawl, they were already pulling up to Grandma Em's house. Unlike on most Sundays, everyone including Luke and his guests had arrived ahead of Grandma Em, so she decided it was best to let things go for now.

"If you want to talk later, Christine . . ." she let the sentence go unfinished. Grandma Em hugged Christine and then Silas was helping her from the wagon. Christine watched as she hurried toward the house.

Christine was preoccupied when Silas helped her down from the wagon. So she was doubly surprised when Silas gave her a big hug. The embrace broken, Christine stood staring at him with wide, surprised eyes. It took a moment for her to realize that in Silas' own quiet way he knew she was hurting. A gentle finger came out to touch the end of her nose, and he smiled kindly at her before moving away to take care of the horses.

Reluctant to go inside, Christine's footsteps were weary as she walked to the house. Knowing there was no way she could be alone, Christine made an effort to put her confusing thoughts aside.

Christine had no more stepped into the entryway when a small blonde person ran through the parlor and hid behind her skirt. Within moments Charles was planted in front of Christine, hands on his small hips. "I know you're back there, Em. It's my marble and I want it back."

"Cal gave it to me." The small voice was muffled, and Christine wondered if she were crying.

"He can't give it to you. It's mine."

Christine, who was needed in the kitchen, was on the verge of stepping in when Mac appeared beside his small son.

"I hope you have a good reason for trapping Christine against the front door." John MacDonald dwarfed the five-year-old, but Charles showed no fear as he pointed toward Christine's skirt. "Emily is back there and she's got my marble."

Mac's eyes followed the direction of Charles' finger and laughter rumbled out of his chest when Christine's skirt moved around her legs as she herself stood perfectly still. "Are you harboring a fugitive, Christine?"

"Not intentionally," Christine laughed with him. She made an attempt to move toward the kitchen, but the little girl behind her had other ideas and held fast.

"Go ahead, Christine, I'll get her," Mac said.

Christine turned then and exposed Emily. In one movement, surprisingly fast for a man Mac's size, she was in his arms. Christine glanced back before walking quickly through the house. Charles was standing below his father, looking up at the little girl in his arms. Emily's hand was clenched into a fist, the coveted marble obviously inside. Mac was smiling and saying something to her, but Emily's lower lip was out a city block and she was looking most unreasonable.

Christine entered the kitchen to find everything under control. "When you came through the house, Christine, were the kids getting along? I thought I heard raised voices." Julia spoke from her place at the stove.

Christine peeked at the gravy that Julia was stirring before moving toward Susanne, who was slicing fruit into a bowl. Christine gently removed the knife from Sue's grasp. Taking the smaller woman by the shoulders, she steered her to a chair at the kitchen table. Christine then took over where Sue had left off, all the time explaining about Emily, Charles, Mac, and the marble.

Julia, Grandma Em, and Sue all laughed at the end of the story. Christine joined them, unaware of how much their laughter was over the way she had maneuvered a very pregnant Susanne.

Julia's eyes lingered on Christine as she worked. She was so much a part of them now—just like family. She felt a sting behind her eyes as she silently prayed that Christine would soon be a member of God's family too.

Earlier Grandma Em had quickly told her and Susanne about the conversation in the wagon. Grandma Em had said a quick prayer as they stood together in the kitchen, asking God to save Christine and to use them as instruments as He needed them.

25

Not until it was time to sit down to dinner did Christine meet Frank and Caroline Chambers. It was to date the most humiliating introduction that Christine had ever experienced.

"Christine, this is Frank Chambers. We bought the new horses from his stables in Chicago." Christine shook his hand. "And this is his daughter, Caroline." Christine's hand went out for the expected handshake, but Caroline's words stilled her movements. "Why, you're as tall as Julia!" Caroline's voice was shocked and slightly outraged.

Joseph Bennett had, from the time Christine was small, instilled in her a pride about who and what she was. She had never been allowed to slouch or to be ashamed of her height. She was told to hold her head up and look people in the eye. But at that moment she felt she would have given a year off her life to be a foot shorter.

Christine's eyes took in the petite woman before her: big, light-blue eyes, very blonde hair, pale skin. Christine felt as big as Mac and as dark as the wooden Indian downtown.

Caroline didn't realize how her words sounded, so she went on. "Of course, I shouldn't be surprised, since most all of the Camerons are so tall." Caroline smiled adoringly up at Luke.

"Oh! I'm not related to the Camerons. My last name is Bennett."

"That's right," Luke said, smiling kindly and putting his hand on Christine's shoulder. "Christine lives here and works for my grandmother."

"She works for your grandmother and she's going to sit down to dinner with us?" Caroline's voice was incredulous.

Christine drew back as if she'd been slapped. Caroline's words had been spoken without thought. Watching Luke and Christine exchange a smile in church, plus watching him put his hand on her shoulder, had been fine—until she found out they were not related to each other.

Slowly Caroline became aware of a tense silence which had permeated the room. Even her father, who thought she could do no wrong, was staring at her as if she had taken leave of her senses.

Surprisingly enough, Christine was the one to save the meal. Quietly and with a calmness she herself could hardly believe, she said, "Let's eat."

For Christine the meal was a strain. She ate mechanically. The food that had smelled so good in the kitchen now tasted like sawdust in her mouth. As the meal progressed, Christine's embarrassment faded to an emotion she could not quite define. Something almost painful stirred within her each time she saw Caroline's hand on Luke's arm and each time she leaned toward him to smile into his face. What Christine failed to notice was that Luke's return smile was forced and that he had glanced in her direction more than once to see how she was faring.

But, no, Christine didn't see any of this. She only saw a pretty blonde who made her feel ungainly, too tan, and unwanted. Plus this intruder had Luke's full attention. So Christine continued to eat, feeling miserable and every bit as green as the color of her eyes. It might have helped to define the word, but Christine, having never before been jealous, was left in the dark. Her thoughts were bleak, even going so far as preferring Spooner with all its danger to being in Baxter today.

"Did anyone see you come?"

"No, sir, no one."

Vince Jeffers grunted and glared at the man before speaking. "Get back to the Bennett house."

"What for?" The small man interrupted.

"Just shut up and I'll tell you." Vince growled at the man. "I think the old lady has heard from the girl. Look for a letter, a paper with an address, anything that would lead to wherever she's hiding." Vince Jeffers' voice lowered to a deadly calm before continuing. "You'd better not mess up this time. I'm nearing the end of my patience. Now get out of here and don't return until you have an address for me."

Long after the hired man left, Vince sat in the shadowy study. Time was running out. Already he had lost out on two deals requiring large sums of money he simply didn't have.

Rising, he went to the window. Winter was nearly upon them. The days as well as his time continued to shorten. He didn't know if he could take another winter in Wisconsin, but without that money he was going nowhere.

Vince's words echoed in the stillness of the room with deadly self-assurance. "I'll find you, Christine Bennett, and when I do, you'll pay for the trouble you've caused me before you die."

26

A loud snort sent a white mist billowing into the crisp morning air as Luke's mount tossed his head and pawed the earth. They had ridden hard, Luke giving the horse his head, willing to follow his lead.

Now the horse stood atop a small rise. Luke was still mounted and surveying the Cameron ranch. The setting was peaceful, and Luke's heart swelled with thanksgiving for the wealth that he and Silas shared—not money (although they never went hungry) but the land, its heritage, loved ones, health, the fine animals they bred. He could have gone on forever.

An hour earlier, when Luke had saddled Titan, his thoughts had not been so peaceful. Not for a moment had his mind been off Caroline and her thoughtless words that had hurt Christine. Luke's emotions had run the gamut: anger, frustration, pity, despair, compassion.

Sunday Luke had waged an inner battle over speaking with Caroline. But it was taken out of his hands on the way back to the hotel. Frank had rebuked Caroline in front of Luke, and, whether out of embarrassment or true belief that she had done no wrong, Caroline had stomped into the hotel without a word of apology. Frank had expressed his own regrets before going into the hotel with a worried frown on his face.

Normally Luke would have put the entire affair in the back of his mind, feeling it was Frank's to handle. But the fact was that the Chambers' were his guests, and he felt responsible.

He would never forget the look on Christine's face; she didn't deserve that kind of treatment. She worked hard and was honest. Luke respected her.

Heeling Titan into a smooth gallop, Luke reflected on his previous time in prayer. He had put all these feelings at Christ's feet and had come away knowing that God's hand was at work. His heart had been settled about Caroline and he had petitioned God from the bottom of his heart about his emotions. Fervently asking God to keep the compassion he felt for Christine from turning into a stronger emotion, he knew that Christine's salvation was the most important goal right now.

With these thoughts settled in his mind, Luke went up to the house for breakfast, still thanking God for whatever His work was to be.

27

Coughing into her apron, Christine squinted against the dust billowing around her. She hated beating rugs. There had been a time as a little girl when she couldn't wait to help Mrs. Hall with her work, but even then beating rugs had been miserable. She couldn't get it done fast enough.

Grandma Em had walked downtown to the post office and to run errands. Christine worked desperately to get finished before she returned.

— ⁘ —

Luke rushed into the livery stable. If he didn't hurry, he would be late arriving at the hotel and lunch with the Chambers'. He tugged at his necktie and prayed for patience. Dressing up for the third day in a row was not his preference. A quick check with Jack about the leather harness to be ordered and he could be on his way.

Jack was bent over a horse's hoof. Luke was standing quietly waiting when he felt a tap on his shoulder. He looked up to see the sheriff beckoning to him and moving a few stalls away. Luke stopped beside the man and nearly spoke when the sheriff said in a quiet voice, "I've heard from the sheriff in Spooner. He's a good man whose reputation precedes him, and I trust him." Luke opened his mouth to ask the sheriff what he was talking about, but the man went on. "He sent a description of Maxwell, the missing man, and has several leads he plans to check out. He'll keep me informed. It's up to you what you share with Miss Bennett, but I thought I'd let you know." With a tip of his hat, the man was gone.

Luke stood frozen, feeling as if someone had just thrown a hard right punch to his stomach. His thoughts were in chaos. The sheriff in Spooner, a missing man, Miss Bennett, Christine?

Stumbling out of the livery, the harness and lunch with the Chambers' forgotten, Luke headed to his brother's house. Somehow he knew Mark had the answers to his questions, and Luke had every intention of getting them.

"You got a letter!" Grandma Em called up the stairs. Christine came rushing down, an excited smile on her face. She remembered her manners just before tearing open the envelope. "How was your walk into town?" she inquired politely.

Emily laughed merrily, shook her head, and walked toward the kitchen. "Open your letter, Christine. We'll talk later."

Christine did as she was bade, her hands shaking.

Dear Christie,

I miss you. The house is empty without your smiles and laughter to warm the day.

The weather is getting cold now. The sheriff said it would be too conspicuous to send a box, so I ordered you a coat. Write me when it arrives.

I realize, Christie, it's hard for you not to be here. I will go through your grandfather's things and treat everything with the utmost care.

The Sheriff also told me to send word to the sheriff in Baxter. I'll send news as I receive it. The search for Carl Maxwell goes on.

Please take care of yourself, Christie. My heart and thoughts are with you.

                                              Love,
                                              Mrs. Hall

Christine folded the letter and put it in her pocket. A tear slid down her cheek. Carl Maxwell was still missing. He might even be dead. A shiver ran down Christine's spine as she thought of death. If Carl was dead, would she be next? The thought rode hard upon her that day and even into the night.

— ❖ —

With a final fist into his pillow, Luke gave up on getting comfortable. Sleep was as far away as the North Pole.

Stabbed! Mark said Christine had been stabbed. Luke's heart wrenched at the thought. His eyes closed and he was once again in Mark's office.

"So you see, I didn't have a chance to tell the sheriff he had the wrong brother. I'll ask you again, Mark. Why is the sheriff in Spooner interested in Christine?"

Mark's battle with his oath was short. His brother's question was from the heart and born out of a fear for his grandmother, Christine, and the entire family. So Mark quietly told him all he knew, beginning with the night he carried Christine into his office and ending with the talk under the willow tree last week.

Luke sat in stunned silence as he listened to all that Christine had suffered in complete innocence. He was in full agreement with Mark: Her arrival in Baxter was no coincidence. God had put her here to find Him.

Luke rose from the bed. The room was chilly, but he didn't notice the cold as he pulled a chair near the window and sat looking at the crescent moon.

Caroline's anger at his being late to the hotel drifted momentarily across his mind before his heart stepped before God. Luke claimed every verse he knew about God's love and salvation for the lost. He placed Christine in God's hands with each verse, unaware of how desperately his prayers were needed at that very moment.

— ❖ —

"No! No!" Christine's screams rent the air. Her door slammed open just as Grandma Em stepped into the hall.

Christine rushed toward the stairs but stopped short at seeing Grandma Em. "He's trying to kill me! I've got to get away. He's got a knife!" Christine's voice was high-pitched and hysterical, her eyes like saucers as she gestured wildly before racing again toward the stairs.

"Christine!" Grandma Em reached for her but Christine eluded her grasp. "Christine!" Grandma Em followed her down the stairs, silently pleading with God for help. "Christine, it was just another dream. Christine—please stop."

Nearly to the parlor, Christine in her haste missed the last step. She fell forward, her head hitting the wall to the side of the staircase before she rolled onto her side and lay in a heap at the bottom.

She sat up and rubbed her head in confusion. Grandma Em knelt beside her, her face lined with worry. Christine's eyes went back up the staircase. It was coming back to her in a rush: She had had another nightmare.

Would she ever get over her fear of death? She was so far from Spooner but still haunted by her fears. She felt helpless. Tears filled her eyes and she began to tremble. "I'm sorry," she choked out.

"Shhh, don't cry. It's all right. I'm right here." Grandma Em's hand smoothed Christine's tumbled hair and gently touched her cheek. "Let's go back upstairs."

Christine was still trembling as she sat on the side of her bed. Grandma Em sat beside her, listening and praying. "He was by my bed at home. He had a knife. I thought it was real and he was right here in the room with me."

"Christine." Something in Grandma Em's voice pulled her out of her miserable shell and made her look up. "Christine, what if you had died tonight, if it hadn't been a dream and you were really killed?" Emily let this sink in for a moment. "Where, Christine? Where would you spend eternity?" Grandma Em's voice ended on an urgent note.

"I don't know," Christine whispered in confusion and misery.

"Were you listening on Sunday, Christine? Did you understand what Pastor Nolan said? Believe on the Lord Jesus Christ and you shall be saved."

"I've never prayed before. I don't know what to do." Christine's voice was slightly breathless. It was coming again, that feeling of expectancy that overtook her whenever she went to church or heard Bible verses.

"Believe, Christine, only believe," Grandma Em said gently. "Pray and tell God that you know of your sins and that you believe Jesus died for them. Trust in Him now, Christine, for your eternal salvation and His loving care for you now here on earth."

Christine sat still for a moment as she felt the wonder of Grandma Em's words bubbling up within her. It was all so clear now—her searching, her fear. God was waiting to take them all—waiting for her, Christine Bennett, to hand them over to Him.

Bowing her head, Christine began to pray. "Dear God, I believe in Your Son, Jesus Christ, and that He died for my sins." Christine's voice broke as she struggled to bring her tears under control. "Thank You, God, for coming into my life. Amen."

Christine turned and looked at Grandma Em, but neither woman could see through the tears that flowed unchecked. Neither woman could speak or find a handkerchief, so the silence

was broken by sniffs and small sobs with an occasional breathless laugh.

Christine drew in a shuddering breath. "I have so many questions."

Grandma Em squeezed her hand. "Will they wait till morning?"

Christine smiled and nodded her head. The women embraced
and Grandma Em made her way back to her room. Her head
barely hit the pillow before she fell into the most peaceful sleep
she had known since Christine had arrived. Down the hall Christine's eyes were also closing. Her plans to lie awake and talk to
God melted as sleep claimed her with a smile on her face.

28

Emily stood at the door of Christine's room. Taking in the made bed, she saw that all else was in place and quiet. She had expected Christine to sleep late. After putting the coffee on, she peeked out and saw Christine coming toward the house.

"Good morning," Grandma Em called as she opened the door. Christine hurried toward her, a smile lighting her face.

"Good morning, Grandma Em."

"How are you, Christine?"

"I feel wonderful. You, on the other hand, are probably ready to boot me out of the house for all the nights' sleep I've cost you."

Grandma Em's answer was quite serious. "Having you find Christ, Christine, has been worth every moment."

Christine's answering smile was serene. "It feels peaceful and wonderful knowing that God loves me so much. I'm sure you understand how lonely I was after losing my grandfather."

"I know, dear. The hurt can feel as though it's going to overwhelm you. But I promise you this, Christine: God is bigger than any hurt you'll ever have." It felt wonderful having Grandma Em to share with, Christine thought as the two women readied breakfast.

That morning during Grandma Em's reading and prayer time Christine prayed too. It was simple and heartfelt and was followed by questions from Christine which took all morning. "If the Bible is God's Word, why was it written by men? How do you know God is everywhere at once?" Christine never seemed to run out of them, and by lunchtime Grandma Em was exhausted.

After they had eaten, Grandma Em went to her room for a nap. Luke and Silas came into the kitchen just as Christine was finishing the dishes.

"Well, hello!"

"Hello, yourself!" Silas answered as he leaned against the dry sink. Luke took a chair at the table.

"Where's Gram?" The question came from Luke. He had prayed so much last night, in ignorance about Christine and Grandma Em, that he felt a bit concerned for them today.

"She's upstairs taking a nap."

"She's not sick, is she?"

"No, no, just tired."

"And you, Christine, are you okay?" Luke asked, but both men had noticed the high color in her cheeks and the almost-fever brightness in her eyes.

"I'm fine. In fact, I'm wonderful. Last night I accepted Christ into my heart." Christine's smile was beaming.

Luke's eyes closed against a sudden rush of tears, his hands tightly clenched in his lap. He felt as if his heart would burst through his chest, so full was his joy.

Silas let out a yell and laughed as he grabbed Christine in a hug that threatened to break her back. Setting her down, he gave her a hearty kiss on her cheek and she joined in his laughter.

Luke had risen from the table and was headed toward Christine. She suddenly felt shy. Luke stopped before her but didn't touch her. The expression on his face was tender and understanding, and when Christine's eyes met his, she blushed furiously.

Silas felt immense happiness that he wasn't attracted to this girl. The only time he had ever seen her blush was in front of Luke. Silas wondered if Luke was aware of it.

Luke, upon seeing the blush, smiled and said quietly, "I prayed for you last night."

"You did?" Christine hoped her voice didn't sound as high-pitched to his ears as it did to her own.

"I'll tell you about it sometime."

"Okay," Christine answered, feeling oddly breathless.

"A woman my age needs peace and quiet for her afternoon naps." A falsely indignant voice spoke from the kitchen doorway. Everyone laughed, and what followed was a chaotic time of excitement and questions, smiles and rejoicing.

Before the day was out, the entire Cameron family knew of Christine's decision. Pastor Nolan also heard. He and Mrs. Nolan came by to talk with Christine and Grandma Em after supper.

Christine fell into bed that night exhausted and overjoyed. As she lay quietly talking with God, she prayed for all the trouble and goings-on in Spooner without being specific. She asked for special protection over Mrs. Hall and a safe end for everyone included in this turmoil. Christine placed her fears and worries in God's hands and fell asleep peaceful and trusting.

— ❖ —

"Baxter?" Vince Jeffers looked once again at the paper in his hand: "c/o Emily Cameron, Baxter, Wisconsin."

"Is this all there was?"

"I think so. The old lady started to stir around and I had to get out of her room."

"You went all the way into her bedroom?" Jeffers' voice was incredulous.

"I had to—that's where her desk is," the small man defended himself.

"Were there other papers—a letter, perhaps?"

"Mighta been a letter, but since I can't read to tell . . ."

Vince Jeffers for once was not angry; he looked thoughtful. "Something tells me we've found her." He spoke as he poured each man a liberal helping of brandy. "Sit down. We've got some planning to do."

29

"Hurry, Daddy, I can't wait to see Luke's ranch," Caroline stated.

"What's your hurry? The ranch isn't going anywhere."

At her father's answer Caroline turned with a huff on the buggy seat. This action brought a grimace of pain to her face.

"Can you believe this buggy? It's ancient and this seat is like a board, and to top it off, it was the best the livery had!" Caroline's voice was heavy with disgust.

Frank slanted a look at his daughter, thinking as he did so how he had courted her mother in a buggy worse off than this one. At the time he didn't have two nickels to rub together. But it hadn't mattered; he and Lily, then and still today, had eyes only for each other.

Before Caroline came along, Frank had taken over his father-in-law's breeding yards. By the time Caroline was four he was well-established, his reputation was spotless, and his stock had more than tripled.

Caroline, too young to remember anything except a fancy house with many servants, had never worked a day in her life. Frank knew it was his own fault that she was more little girl than woman. When his little girl had begged to come north with him in Lily's absence, he couldn't say no.

But he was brought out of his reverie by his daughter's whining. "Are we almost there?"

The road rounded a large clump of trees, and, just as Luke had directed, the house was in view. With an eighth of a mile Frank was turning up the driveway and pulling the buggy to a stop in front of the house.

Silas came out the front door just as Frank helped Caroline down from the buggy. "Hello!" he greeted them with a friendly smile. "Luke is in the barn. Come on, I'll show you."

The three of them made their way around to the side yard and headed for the massive, well-built structure housing the Cameron's 26 horses. They found Luke in the alleyway between the stalls, checking the injured foreleg of a four-week-old colt. The colt's mother beckoned to him from a few stalls away, giving Luke the extra chore of trying to hold the young animal still.

Without a word Silas stepped over to hold the colt's head, freeing both of Luke's hands for the leg.

Frank stood still, admiring the two men as they worked gently and effectively with the horse, unaware that the train of his daughter's thoughts was quite different. Dressed in her yellow riding habit, she expected to catch Luke's eye the moment she walked into the stable. She felt angry at his lack of attention. She determined to make Luke notice her today so he would want to see her every day they were here for the next few weeks.

The Chamberses stayed long at the ranch that day. The cool weather was perfect for riding, and they spent most of the after-noon on horseback.

It was during supper that Frank announced that he and Caroline would be going home Monday. Caroline's reaction told Luke and Silas that she had not known.

"Monday? But we just got here! Why Monday?" Caroline whined and argued, but Frank was adamant. "I'm ready to get home, Caroline. You understand, don't you, Luke?"

"Of course, Frank."

"I'll be back sometime when Lily can come. She would love your rolling hills."

"You'll be welcome anytime," Luke assured him.

Caroline proceeded to pout through the remainder of the evening. Luke, unaccustomed to this in a grown woman, felt he needed to make amends. The way Caroline's face lit up when he asked her to go riding with him Saturday morning told him he had been duped. Realizing it was too late now, and feeling disgust at his own gullibility, he had a date to go riding with a spoiled young woman whether he liked it or not.

— ❖ —

Christine shifted once again before leaving her seat to pace around the room. She turned to find Grandma Em watching her. "I feel so excited about seeing the ranch tomorrow. I can't sit still. What time will we be leaving?"

Grandma Em laughed as she answered. "Right after breakfast so you won't have long to wait." The women talked for awhile before Christine retired early, somehow hoping to make morning come sooner.

Knocking and then pounding at the front door awoke Christine. The pocket watch on her bedside table said 3:45. Christine heard Grandma Em's bedroom door open as she reached the parlor. Upon opening the front door she found Maggie with Emily in her arms, wrapped snugly in a quilt, dead to the world.

Grandma Em appeared as Maggie stepped into the entryway. She transferred her bundle to Christine before speaking. "Sue's pains started around midnight. Her water broke about an hour ago and things are moving pretty fast. The Doc thought it would be best if Emily woke up over here."

"Thanks, Maggie," Grandma Em said; "give them both our love and tell them we're praying." After Maggie left, Grandma Em led the way back up the stairs with a lamp in her hand. When she moved toward the spare bedroom, Christine's voice quietly stopped her. "Grandma Em, can I take her into my bed?"

"Oh, Christine, you don't have to do that. She's slept in here before."

"I know I don't have to, but I want to." Christine snuggled the little girl closer to her. "She's precious, isn't she?"

"Yes, she certainly is. You go ahead and take her to your bed. I'll see you both in the morning."

Wrapped inside the quilt along with Emily was needed clothing for the next day. Christine hung the little dress in her own closet before easing into bed beside a still-sleeping Emily.

As was becoming her habit, Christine prayed before she slept. Tonight she pulled Emily close beside her and asked God for a child of her own.

30

"How many pancakes have you eaten?"

"I think five."

"Five! My goodness, you're going to pop!" This brought gales of laughter from Christine's small charge. Christine couldn't think of when she had had more fun. Emily had thoroughly captured her heart.

They started the dishes together. Emily was on a stool, a drying towel in her hand and teaching Christine a song, when Grandma Em called from the parlor. "Emily, your dad is here."

Squealing, Emily jumped down from the stool and headed through the door, with Christine right behind her. Emily threw herself into Mark's arms. Father and daughter hugged for awhile before Mark took a seat. Emily sat in his lap with an anxious Christine and Grandma Em on the couch across from them.

Mark looked both tired and happy. Grandma Em had asked no more than if everyone was all right, knowing that Mark wanted to share with Emily first. He was careful to talk directly to his daughter, even though he could feel Christine and his grandmother's eyes on him.

"Emily, do you know why you're over here this morning?"

"Yes, 'cause Mama's having our baby."

"That's right. You have a brand-new baby sister."

Mark watched Emily's face as she comprehended his words. Her eyes widened before she asked, "The baby's already here?"

"She's here."

"Can I play with her?" This question brought laughter from the adults. Mark stopped when Emily tugged on his shirt. "What's her name?"

"Her name is Elizabeth. Elizabeth May Cameron." Mark's voice held contentment and pride.

"My name is Emily Susanne Cameron." Emily's voice was stubborn and her lower lip trembled just a bit. Mark immediately recognized the signs of jealousy and lifted Emily until they were nearly nose to nose. "I know that's your name. I remember the day you were born and named you after your Great Grandma Em. And right now Elizabeth is the most blessed little girl in all the world to have a big sister as wonderful as you."

The words were exactly what Emily needed to hear. She gave Mark a hug that threatened to cut off his air before scrambling down from her father's lap and announcing she was off to see Mr. Turley. The back door slammed and she was gone.

"How's Sue?"

"She's good, Gram. Things went much faster this time. Maggie, of course, is incredible. I could have used her when Emily was born."

"Elizabeth is such a beautiful name. What time was she born?"

"Just before 5:00. What time do you think you'll be over?" Mark stood. "I've got to get word to the ranch and Julia."

"Why don't we keep Emily another night and come over mid-morning tomorrow? We were headed to the ranch this week, but that can wait. Maybe when you and Julia go riding on Saturday, Christine, you could stop out there."

"That's fine. Anything to keep Emily another night."

Christine smiled at Mark. "She slept with me last night."

"Did she hog the bed?"

"No, with this cool weather we just cuddled up together in the middle."

"Well, I can't thank you enough, and I'll see you tomorrow."

The next 24 hours went by in a rush. Emily helped Christine with all her work, including the feeding of the stock. It took twice as long to get everything done, but it was also twice the fun. By the time they were walking over to see the baby Elizabeth, she and Christine were fast friends.

Grandma Em and Christine sat in the living room while Mark carried Emily upstairs to see her baby sister for the first time. About ten minutes passed before Mark came partway down the stairs and called to them.

Sue was in bed, sitting up against the headboard. Beside her was Emily, looking proud and holding a tiny bundle in her lap. The women approached the side of the bed. Upon seeing her newest great-granddaughter, Grandma Em began to cry.

Christine didn't cry, but stood in wonder at the tiny person before her. Sue's eyes went to Mark at the foot of the bed. They exchanged a warm look at Christine's reaction.

"Emily, can Christine hold our new baby?" her mother asked softly.

"Oh no!" Christine exclaimed loudly, making Elizabeth start. Quietly now, "I'm sorry. I didn't mean to frighten her."

"She's fine—she'll have to get used to noise if she's going to survive around here," Sue assured her.

Emily spoke from her place on the bed: "This is my baby Eliza, Christine.

It was Christine's turn to cry, and her voice sounded choked through tears. "Oh, Emily, your baby Eliza is beautiful!" Emily began to get squirmy, so Mark rescued his youngest daughter. Holding her, he turned to Christine. "You're welcome to hold her."

Christine shook her head no. Elizabeth was so new and help-less-looking against Mark's chest.

"How about Great-Grandma?" Mark asked with a smile.

Grandma Em, still sniffing, replied, "Let me dry up a bit and I'll sit down and hold her."

Some 20 minutes later Elizabeth began to fuss and Sue looked tired. Mother and daughter were left alone.

Downstairs, Maggie and Christine prepared lunch. Right after they ate, Julia showed up with the boys. She and Mark hugged for long moments, brother and sister sharing in this special event together.

Joseph Cameron Sr. had delivered Calvin, but Mark and Julia were recalling the night Mark had delivered Charles. Susanne, his nurse then and not his wife, had assisted. Mark had commented aloud as he held his minutes-old nephew, his eyes a bit wet, "The only thing better would be to deliver one of my own." As Mark said these words, his eyes locked with Susanne's, the room and its occupants fading from sight as this young doctor and nurse regarded each other, their hearts in their eyes. Julia found out later that Mark had asked Sue to marry him that very night.

Arriving very late back at Mark's office to clean up, Mark had cornered Sue in the equipment room.

"I saw something in your eyes tonight and I want an explanation."

Sue, painfully shy at that time, had tried to step past him, but he would have none of it.

"Move out of my way, Dr. Cameron," she had ordered as firmly as possible, her heart pounding in her chest.

"Not until you tell me," he stated quietly. She could see he was not going to budge.

"All right," she cried, "I'll tell you. I did exactly what you told me not to do after you hired me: I've fallen in love with you. But you need not worry that I'll be a problem, Dr. Cameron, because I'm leaving first thing in the morning." This painful admission out, Sue buried her face in her hands and burst into tears.

Mark's arms had come out and gently pulled her against his chest. Remembering the day a few weeks after she had arrived when he had uttered these words, Mark was disgusted. What conceit! He saw now that he had said them as a defense against the attraction he felt for her immediately upon seeing her, an attraction he fought as it grew daily.

Mark had pulled out his handkerchief as Sue's crying subsided. He gently dried her tears before bending his head and tenderly brushing her lips with his own. A declaration of love fell easily from his lips and came straight from his heart. Sitting in his office, they had talked until sunup.

The next day a beaming Mark and radiant Sue had announced to the family that they would be married.

Now, five years later, the family did a little reminiscing. Christine was all ears when Julia began to question Mark about the birth, the water breaking, the time spent pushing, etc.

Remembering the night when Raven was born, Christine spoke without thinking. "It's a little like when a horse foals." This statement brought complete silence—and then uproarious laughter. Christine's embarrassment was saved by Charles, who was quite interested in the idea of a horse having a baby—something he had never witnessed but wanted to. He began to question her. The adults in the room were more than a little surprised at her knowledge. Grandma Em questioned Christine on her experience.

"We didn't live right in town," Christine explained, "so there were no children or young people nearby. When I first came to live with my grandfather, his stables were full—about 15 horses. When I was ten he first allowed me to watch the births. By the time I was 12 I was assisting, but then Grandfather had begun to sell out. Without friends near, seeing them only at school, horses became my world.

"I never told him, but it was torture every time he sold another horse. It had always been just a hobby with him, and he said that when a hobby gets to be more headache than fun, it's time to call it a day. By the time I was 16 we were down to three mares, one of which was pregnant. I helped when Gypsy gave birth to a perfect little mare. Had it been a stallion he would have sold it, but it was a mare so Grandfather gave her to me." Christine fell silent then, a bit appalled at the way she had shared so much of her past.

Christine would have been horrified if she could have seen the wheels turning inside the heads of the three adults seated across from her. It was as if the lights had come on: Christine was a new Christian and she had just shared with them her knowledge of horses. There were two unmarried men in the family who ran a breeding ranch!

Julia went upstairs to see Sue and the baby. Mark had a call to make, and Grandma Em took the children to the front room for a story. Christine rose to help Maggie with the dishes, unaware of the new development in everyone's mind. Christine didn't stand a chance!

31

"Aren't they a bit tight?" Christine stood in front of the full-length mirror in Mac and Julia's bedroom, scrutinizing her jeans-encased legs.

As she pulled on a boot Julia answered, "Maybe a little. But with no one around to see us, I wouldn't worry about it."

Christine shook her head, her voice rueful. "Even if someone does see us, it's better than riding in a skirt!"

"Oh, I heartily agree. My brother thinks I'm rebellious, but he's never worn a riding habit."

"How does Mac feel about pants?"

"If I go right over to the ranch and back, I can go alone. If not, I have to ride with someone and stay on MacDonald or Cameron land."

Once mounted and ready to go, Julia knew a moment's pricking in her conscience. She knew she had stretched the truth, but she shoved her guilt aside, not wanting to spoil the day.

Christine and Julia moved past the MacDonald cornfields, ready for the harvest. They rode in silence, taking in the beauty around them. The horses' sturdy legs ate up the acres as the crisp October air surrounded them.

The fall days brought cool mornings and brisk nights, but by ten in the morning the sun was warming things up to a comfortable temperature that didn't call for sweaters or coats.

Julia pulled her horse atop a small mound and Christine followed suit. Below them sat the Cameron ranch. The house was a single-story rectangle about a hundred feet from the stable, a low-ceilinged structure set at the edge of a well-built corral area.

Christine's eyes took in the horse barn. It seemed enormous to her. "How many horses do they have?"

"I think the three that just arrived made it 26, but the stables will hold well over 30."

Julia sat still for a spell, letting Christine take in the beauty of the ranch setting. After they turned their horses away, Julia led them down along the creek. They let the animals rest and graze, each woman taking a rock and getting comfortable in the morning sun.

"How did you meet Mac?" Christine asked. For the first time

in her life the relationships between men and women weighed
heavily on her mind.

"He came to the ranch to see my father. Well, actually, it was
the first time I had seen him in many years. He had left home
when I was still quite young. But when Mac's dad got sick, he
came home to work the farm. I was only 13 but already showing
signs of being tall, and Mac was so big and acted so grown-up.

"He was 18 at the time, and very kind. He never told me to get
lost like Luke and Silas did." Julia laughed softly. "I used to lie
awake at night and think about him. Because of his size, I would
dream he would come and take me away and then beat up my
brothers when they were mean."

Christine laughed at this before asking, "When did he first notice you, I mean . . ." she grew flustered and silent.

"You mean as a woman."

At Christine's nod, Julia continued. "The summer I turned 15
I had gone into town one day to shop. Mac was in the store and
we talked. Later he walked my things out to the wagon for me,
and I swear I was head over heels in love. That night after supper
he came to call. We sat on the porch and laughed and talked for
over an hour. By the time he left I was sure I was in love."

"After Mac left, my father told me I couldn't see him socially
again. I remember crying and crying.

"But why, Julia?" Christine's voice was aghast.

"Oh, Christine—I'm sorry. I forget sometimes that you weren't
raised around here. Mac and his family were not Christians,"
Julia explained gently. "And the Bible is very clear on its guide-
lines for a Christian courting or marrying a non-Christian."

A week ago Christine would have been angry at such a
statement. But now she realized it was another of God's truths
she needed to learn.

"I best finish the story. I obeyed my father and told Mac I
couldn't see him and why. It nearly broke my heart when he
accused me of thinking I was too good for him. I didn't see him
for quite a few months after that, but I prayed every day that he
would trust Christ and understand why I had to obey my father.

"I didn't know until much later that while he had been away,
working in the South on a plantation, the plantation owner's
daughter used him. She flirted with him and made promises she
had no intention of keeping before she up and married another
plantation owner's son. She told Mac after the wedding that he

would never have been good enough for her. He was very bitter, to say the least." Julia's voice was sad with remembered pain.

"But he did eventually get saved." Christine broke through her friend's melancholy.

Julia beamed at her. "Yes, he was saved. About six months later he came to church. He sat in the back and didn't talk to anyone. It went on like that for some time. Then my father did something that surprised us all—he asked Mac to Sunday dinner. After that the pattern changed. Mac would sit with us, come to dinner after church, and stay until near dusk.

"It was one of those Sunday afternoons when Mac was over that he and Paul, who was only 13 at the time, were talking on the back porch. Paul went over the plan of salvation with him, prayed with him, and helped lead him to the Lord.

"It wasn't long after that my father died. I don't know what I would have done without Mac at that time. He was there for all of us. Less than a year later his own father died. It was a rough time, but we grew closer to God and to each other because of it.

"Mac asked my grandfather for my hand when I was 17. Grandpa said yes but that he wanted us to wait until I turned 18. So we were married in the fall of 1879, eight years ago this month."

Julia's eyes were filled with tears, her wonder at God's goodness not at all dimmed after all these years.

Christine, caught up in the miracle of Mac and Julia's courtship, asked, "Do you think, Julia, that God has someone for me?" Her voice was wistful, her eyes also filling with tears.

"Oh, Christine, I don't know exactly what God has for you, but I promise it will be wonderful!" They embraced, cried, and talked nonstop for the next hour. The sun was high and Christine's stomach growled, or else they might have been there all day.

— ❖ —

"Do you plan to expand anytime soon, Luke?"

"Expand?" Luke's questioning gaze swung to Caroline.

"Well, yes, I simply assumed with all this land you would be building more stables and adding to your stock."

"Silas and I have no plans at this time to add on," he told her patiently. "We're about to our limit as to what we can handle ourselves."

"Oh, but you just need to hire some help . . ." she was off again.

It was as if she hadn't heard a word he had said. Luke was beginning to wonder if the morning would ever end.

For being a horseman's daughter, Caroline didn't ride very well. She was too busy trying to keep her riding habit in perfect order. Straighten here, brush off there. And that hat! It was a useless little number that caused her to keep her head at an odd angle in order to ensure that the hat was in the exact place she wanted.

They had been out for nearly two hours, and as yet Caroline had not stopped talking or giving advice. Luke was getting hungry and his patience was wearing thin.

Caroline was so busy explaining about the way her father had built up with additional stables and help (evidently forgetting Luke had been there) that she failed to notice the two other riders moving in the direction of the MacDonald farm.

Without conscious thought Luke adjusted his direction and speed. Caroline innocently followed his lead, talking all the while. "Why, a man from Europe came to see Father's horses. His reputation is flawless, you know." The sound of approaching hooves finally put a halt to Caroline's chatter.

"Hello!" Julia called a greeting as the four riders came together in a small circle.

"You ride in blue jeans?" Caroline's voice was outraged.

Undaunted, Julia just smiled and said, "Oh, Caroline, it's unbelievably comfortable, and we didn't expect to see anyone." Julia's eyes took in Caroline's slightly rumpled appearance, her hat a bit askew and rather dusty.

Christine only saw the flawlessly-made blue riding habit and how it accentuated Caroline's blonde hair and blue eyes.

Luke, on the other hand, had completely forgotten there was a Caroline Chambers. Julia and Christine had raced away from the creek. Julia's pins had held, but Christine's hair, thicker and falling past her waist, had pulled free. It moved with the breeze gently around her face and shoulders. Luke could only stare.

Christine at that moment became aware of Luke's perusal. She made an attempt to bring a little control to her hair, but without pins it did little good. She gave up and let it go. Christine felt her cheeks grow warm under his steady regard, even as a tiny feeling of pleasure began to stir within her.

Luke sat there feeling hypocritical. All these years he had objected to Julia in pants on horseback, and here he was thinking that Christine looked beautiful.

In all fairness to Julia, he knew she was careful of where she rode, and often Mac was with her. She and Christine would not have seen anyone today if Luke hadn't maneuvered it.

It occurred to Luke just then why Mac never protested to Julia about her riding astride: He liked the way his wife looked in pants. *His wife.* The words seemed to echo loudly in his ears until Julia spoke.

"Have you seen our new niece, Luke?"

He smiled, "Last night."

"Isn't she precious?"

"She is that," Luke agreed with her. "What do you think of her, Christine?"

"I think she's beautiful." Luke's breath caught at the smile on Christine's face when she thought of the baby.

"You were in town last night and didn't stop at the hotel?" Caroline's stringent voice cut through the air like a knife. A brief moment of uncomfortable silence ensued before Julia spoke.

"Well, we're starved and headed for home. We'll see you tomorrow." Luke and Caroline watched them ride away.

In a rare moment of maturity, Caroline watched Luke as his eyes followed Christine's departure. It became crystal clear just then: Luke Cameron was not the man for her. Never once had he hung on her every word the way the boys back home did. And the look in his eyes when he had seen Christine today! Caroline had to admit to herself that she wouldn't know what to do if Luke ever looked at her with that same intensity.

The couple returned to the ranch in silence, Luke feeling regretful. It was never his intent to hurt Caroline. He wished he had known how to handle things better.

Caroline, knowing she had made a fool of herself one too many times, also kept silent.

32

"Mama's back! Mama's back!" Charles' cry was excited and it brought Mac out of the barn.

Both of Julia's sons hung onto her legs after she dismounted and bent to kiss them.

Christine, in watching the little boys at Julia's legs, missed the tenseness that passed between husband and wife.

Once in the barn, Christine moved to unsaddle her horse for a rubdown, but Mac stepped in. "Here, Christine, I'll get that. Boys, take Christine out and show her the puppies."

Christine had no time to protest as each little boy grabbed a hand and dragged her outside.

Julia could feel Mac's eyes resting upon her. She stopped her work and met his eyes over the dividing wall between the stalls. "I'm sorry, Mac."

"Why, Julia? We have an agreement. Why did you break it?"

"I wanted to be alone with Christine so she would feel free to open up with me."

"The boys and I were gone all morning. You could have talked here at the house."

"But she loves to go riding. I thought it would be relaxing for her and she would want to talk."

"Those are all excuses, Julia, and well you know it!" Mac's voice was stern but not angry. "Does Christine know you broke our agreement?"

"I lied to her." Julia began to cry. "I told her I had to ride with someone if I went further than the ranch, and not specifically with you or one of my brothers. I'm sorry, Mac, so sorry. I don't know what I was thinking. I'm sorry!" Julia was engulfed in Mac's embrace, his arms holding her tightly against him.

"I've got to talk with her," Julia hiccuped. "I've got to tell her I was wrong and ask her forgiveness. You forgive me, don't you, Mac?"

"You know I do." The words came out just as he covered Julia's lips with his own.

This was the scene that Christine, Charles, and Calvin came upon when they returned to the barn. Christine held back, but the boys, evidently accustomed to such sights, ran directly to their parents. Mac and Julia each bent to scoop up a child, the four of them sharing a family hug.

Julia broke away and came toward Christine. Upon seeing the wetness on her cheeks, Christine became concerned.

"Julia?"

"We'll talk later," she assured her with a smile. "Come on, we'll change clothes and get lunch on the table."

The MacDonald kitchen was small but cheery. Christine listened with a bit of awe as first Charles and then Calvin thanked God for the meal. To know Christ at such a young age was wonderful.

The conversation around the table turned to the topic of the weather.

"We'll have snow next month, won't we?" Calvin asked.

"I don't know, Cal. It's getting colder every day, but there's no sign of snow." Mac answered.

"Well, it's got to snow in November," Charles stated.

"Why is that?" his mother wanted to know.

"Mama! You can't have Thanksgiving without snow! How would you go sledding?" His young voice was incredulous, as if he couldn't believe his mother didn't understand such important details. The adults all hid amused smiles at this declaration.

After the meal the boys begged Christine to swing with them. Christine hesitated, but Mac spoke his encouragement. "Go ahead. I'll help Julia with the dishes."

Later, as they washed, Mac looked out at the three at play. "Christine looks enough like you to be a sister."

"Considering her face and figure, I'll take that as a compliment, but today I don't believe Luke was thinking of her as a sister."

Mac became instantly alert, his hands going still on the cup he was drying. "Julia, are you matchmaking?"

"No." His wife turned to him with wide, innocent eyes. But Mac looked skeptical. "Honest, I haven't said a word." Mac only shook his head in resignation and went on drying.

Julia watched out the window a moment. "I must admit, I did think of what a good-looking couple they would make, but I wasn't going to say anything."

"Just remember, the Holy Spirit doesn't need your help." Mac felt the need to remind his well-meaning wife.

Julia watched again as Christine pushed first Charles and then Calvin. All three were laughing. The boys shouted at the air as they swung up higher and higher.

Julia sighed. "They would have made such a cute couple. It seems so romantic."

Quietly, so quietly that Julia almost missed it, Mac said, "I think so too."

Julia looked over to see her husband taking special pains with the dish he was drying. Julia moved until she was standing directly in front of him, her height allowing her to look directly up into his face. Mac finished with the dish and reached for another, but Julia's hand stayed him. "Did you picture Luke and Christine together as a couple?"

"It did cross my mind," he reluctantly admitted.

Julia stood there until their eyes met and they both began to laugh. Throwing her arms around his neck, Julia said, "I love you, John MacDonald."

"And I love you, Julia MacDonald."

Once again Christine came upon the embracing couple. This time without the boys, she withdrew quietly to give them privacy.

Moving through the house, Christine went into the parlor and took a comfortable chair. Seeing this happy Christian family caused Christine to feel discontented. Unbidden, Luke on horseback, handsome and masculine, flashed through her mind. She shoved the picture aside as she also saw Caroline, lovely and dainty in her blue riding habit, on the horse beside him.

Christine was still praying for she knew not what when Julia joined her. "I really should be getting back to Grandma Em's."

It was tempting for Julia to simply agree to this and take Christine back, but she knew it was best to get it out right now.

"I wanted to talk to you before you go." Christine, remembering Julia's tears in the barn, waited quietly. "I did something wrong this morning, Christine, and I need to tell you and ask your forgiveness."

Christine's eyes widened but she kept her peace. "Earlier I told you when I rode further than the ranch I needed to go with someone. I was not completely honest. My agreement with Mac is that I ride with either him or one of my brothers." Julia stopped, her eyes on the clenched hands in her lap, too ashamed to even look at Christine.

"You're my new sister in Christ. And instead of being an example and a help to you, I lied to make myself look important and to impress you. I would ask you, Christine, from the bottom of my heart, for your forgiveness."

"It's all right, Julia . . ."

"No." Julia cut her off. "Christine, it's not all right and I don't want you to say that it is. Saying it's okay would be condoning what I did. Saying you forgive me would tell me you understood I've done wrong, but you accept my apology and we can forget it and go on. Can you forgive me, Christine?"

Christine saw the truth and importance in Julia's words and was thankful for them. She took Julia's hands in her own. "I forgive you, Julia. I love you and thank you for coming to me. You *have* been a wonderful example to me today. More than you'll ever know."

"Thank you, Christine. I couldn't have asked God for a more special friend."

All four MacDonalds took Christine home that afternoon and stayed to share a light supper with her and Grandma Em. Mac, Julia, Charles, and Calvin hugged Christine as they left, thinking that their lives were a bit sweeter with the presence of Christine Bennett.

33

Since it was too soon for Sue and the baby to be out, Sunday dinner was at their home. Sue stayed up in bed, allowing one visitor at a time, but Elizabeth was brought downstairs and she made the rounds.

The table space at Mark and Sue's did not allow all the adults to eat in the dining room. Christine cheerfully agreed to eat in the kitchen with the children. Luke scowled in Christine's direction as she headed for the kitchen. He was unaware that her reason for going to the kitchen was because she genuinely loved spending time with the children and not because of Caroline's remark the week before. He thought about going after her, but decided against it.

Christine saw the frown and wondered at it. It stayed with her even as she enjoyed a wonderful time with the kids. The three children tried to outdo one another on memory verses. Christine was amazed at all they knew.

Finally she asked, "Why do you memorize Bible verses?"

Calvin answered, "It helps you not to sin. There's even a verse about it." The children all thought for awhile, but could not remember it.

Luke, standing unobserved at the doorway, came in and whispered in Emily's ear. She beamed at them and said, "I will hide God's Word in my heart." She hesitated, and Luke again bent to her ear. Emily nodded and started over. "I will hide God's Word in my heart that I might not sin against thee." Luke kissed her cheek before pulling up a chair at the table.

Suddenly Christine lost her appetite, so conscious was she of Luke's presence right across the table. She listened to him and the children but only sipped her milk and pushed her food around for something to do with her hands.

"Aren't you going to eat? You can't have dessert unless your plate is clean. Don't you like chicken?" Emily's innocent questions set Christine's cheeks ablaze. She looked over at the little girl next to her and then back at her plate, knowing that the table was quiet, awaiting her answer.

Christine wished with all her heart at this second that the floor would open up so she could fall through.

"Have you always embarrassed so easily?"

Christine's head snapped up at this casual question to find Luke regarding her thoughtfully, his elbow on the table and his chin propped up in his hand. Christine's blush only deepened as he studied her face.

"Uncle Luke, you shouldn't tease Christine." Calvin, who knew his uncle well enough to have caught the teasing tone in his voice, admonished him in a grown-up way.

"You're right, Cal," Luke answered, all teasing gone and without taking his eyes from Christine's face, "but Christine is beautiful when she blushes. It's nearly impossible to resist." Luke smiled at her then. Perfect white teeth stood out against his tan features.

He continued to smile and regard her with such warm amusement that Christine couldn't stay at the table. Luke, who half expected her to give as good as she got, felt badly when, too flustered to speak, Christine fled the table and began to prepare water for the dishes.

Luke sat a bit longer with the children. He noted how Christine was careful to keep her back to the room. Her every movement spoke of tenseness, and he knew that saying anything, even in kindness, would only make matters worse. So, taking pity on her, he left the kitchen.

— ❖ —

"How long have you been a nurse, Maggie?"

"Ah! Now that would be telling. You might even be able to guess my age." As usual, Maggie was businesslike.

Christine laughed and said, "It must have been wonderful to see Elizabeth come into the world."

"You're right about that. In all my years of nursing it's a sight I never grow tired of."

"Are you the only person in your family in medicine?"

"No, no, my father was a doctor and my oldest brother has a practice. His daughter, my niece, is in nurse's training right now. So you can see that my decision to become a nurse was an easy one."

"Well, for purely selfish reasons I'm glad you are," Christine told her.

Maggie laughed, "Let's get this coffee to the front room."

Christine carried a tray full of cups and saucers. Maggie's tray held the coffee, cream, and sugar. Christine's idea to help Maggie serve went out the window when, after she set her tray down, she noticed the occupants of the couch.

Luke sat comfortably holding his baby niece, her downy blonde head moving, her eyes open and searching as Luke talked to her. Next to him, leaning over his arm to see the baby, was Caroline. The entire pose was so tender and familylike that Christine felt tears beginning to form.

Mumbling an excuse to no one in particular about checking on the children, Christine turned for the back door. Once outside, Christine drew in great gulps of cold air, somehow hoping to freeze the ache in her chest. She could hear the children at the side of the house and took a quick peek to see if they had their sweaters on. Christine thought absently of the coat that Mrs. Hall had ordered. She would be needing it soon.

Christine strolled around the backyard, noticing that the remnants of Sue's vegetable garden looked lonely and cold. Lonely and cold—the way Christine had begun to think of Spooner. The thought of leaving Baxter made her want to cry. "Not Baxter," Christine told herself, "but the people." How could she leave these people? The thought hurt. But if she were honest, it would be easier to go than stay and see Luke and Caroline get married. Christine was shocked at the anguish it caused her to think of this prospect.

"You've done it now, Christine Bennett." Christine's voice broke quietly through the cold air to her ears alone. "You've fallen in love with a man who is interested in another woman. You're going to be hurt and it's no one's fault but your own."

Wanting nothing more than to sit down, feel sorry for herself, and have a good cry, Christine knew she had to get her mind off Luke and Caroline.

Grandma Em had once said that God is bigger than any hurt we might have. Christine prayed as she went around the house to play with the kids, "Please, Lord, be bigger than this hurt that threatens to overwhelm me. Help me to trust You for my future and accept Your will for my life."

34

Luke stood on the platform until the train was completely out of sight. The sound no longer echoed in his ears, and the vibration beneath his feet was now still.

The send-off had been easier than he had hoped. Caroline had been reserved but not sullen. Frank had praised him for his stables and the fine work he and Silas did. He had promised to try and get up next spring if the Mrs. could come.

Luke knew he had some things to get done at the ranch, but if he hurried to the post office he would be able to squeeze in a trip to see his grandmother, not once admitting, even to himself, who he really hoped to meet.

His horse tied out front, Luke opened the door for a woman carrying a box so big it nearly obscured her. A muffled thank you came from somewhere beneath the box as the woman moved out the door and a few steps past. Luke suddenly realized who it was.

Large hands on Christine's shoulders brought her to a surprised halt. Before she could turn, those same hands reached around and lifted her box up and over the top of her head.

Even as Christine turned, some sense told her it was going to be Luke.

"Good morning, Christine."

"Good morning," Christine answered and reached for her box. Luke let it go.

"How are you today?" Luke again took the box from her grasp.

"I'm fine. What brings you to town?" The box was once more in Christine's hold.

"I was seeing the Chamberses off." The way he had casually stated seeing his girlfriend off, as if he didn't care, made Christine angry, and when Luke reached to take the box again she stated firmly, "I can carry it myself. It's not heavy." Had Luke known her better, he would have realized that her temper was coming to the fore. She had realized he had been flirting with her at the table yesterday, only to go in and sit cozily with Caroline on the couch. That night in bed Christine had made a decision to stay away from Luke Cameron as much as possible until it was time for her to go home. Now, running into him the next morning was almost more than she could take.

Luke, thinking to keep things light, said exactly the wrong thing. "I don't know about where you come from, but around here a gentleman helps a lady with her packages."

Christine, believing he was playing false with Caroline in the pretense of being a gentleman, let her temper boil over. "I do not need *you*, of all people, to remind me of the social amenities, Mr. Cameron," Christine gritted out icily between clenched teeth.

Luke was stunned. What in the world had he done to anger her?

Christine, taking advantage of his silence, said, "Good day, Mr. Cameron," and turned on her heel.

Christine seethed all the way home. Her long stride eating up the blocks, she walked and saw nothing. People waved at her but she missed them. The box grew heavy but she gave it little notice. "What nerve!" she fumed. "Put his girl on the train one minute and forget she exists the next. What a flirt!"

Christine stomped up the porch steps. Letting the box slide down until it landed at her feet, she reached for the handle, but the door opened before her hand could make contact.

To her utter surprise, Luke reached out and took her box under one arm. With his free hand he pulled her inside.

The door shut firmly and he spoke. "I will know, Christine, before I leave here, why you are angry."

The two faced each other in Grandma Em's parlor. Christine's surprise at seeing him did not diminish her anger. Her voice was heavy with sarcasm. "Did you have a nice visit with Caroline, Luke? It must have been hard to put her on the train and say goodbye. I imagine you'll miss her very much." Christine's eyes spoke her disappointment and hurt.

Luke finally understood. Her anger was a cover for the hurt she felt.

"Christine, there is no commitment between Caroline and me."

Christine looked confused before she asked, "Does Caroline know that?" thinking back to the adoration she saw in her eyes.

"She didn't when she first arrived, but she does now."

Christine couldn't look at Luke. How many times was she going to make a fool of herself in front of this man? Her eyes took in the carpet with great interest as she spoke. "I'm sorry I was angry at you. I have a nasty temper."

"You have a temper? I didn't know that!" There it was again. That supremely innocent voice and expression that told Christine he was having one on her. To her amazement, she didn't blush.

"I really am sorry," she repeated, now able to look him in the eyes.

He was sensitive to her serious tone. "I'm sorry too, Christine. There was no way you could have known there is nothing between Caroline and me." Or that my interest is right here in this room, he added silently to himself.

"Thank you for explaining to me. Considering it's really none of my business, that was kind of you."

"Aren't you a little curious about what's in the box?" Luke was ready to change the subject.

"Oh, it's a coat." At Luke's questioning look, she explained, "Mrs. Hall, a friend of mine at home, wrote that she ordered it for me."

"Aren't you going to at least look at it?" Luke asked, wondering, and then thinking better of it, if he should tell her he knew she was from Spooner and who Mrs. Hall was.

When the box gave her trouble, Luke slipped a small knife free from his front pocket and with a few cuts had the box open.

Christine's hands moved the wrapping aside until she spotted a bit of white. Without thinking, she pulled, and out came a lace-trimmed cotton camisole that she held at arm's length.

"I wonder if there's been a mistake." Christine looked over at Luke, who was standing beside her. His eyes took a short glide over the very feminine garment before saying to Christine, "If that's the heaviest thing you're going to wear this winter, you're going to be cold."

With a gasp Christine realized what she had been standing there holding for his inspection. Quickly she shoved it back into the box. She should have known Mrs. Hall would order more than just a coat, especially since it was such a big box.

Christine couldn't keep the stammer from her voice as she attempted to right the box to carry it upstairs. "It would really make a mess—I mean the box. I should open the rest later—well, that is, in my room." When she realized how she sounded, she stopped and said, "I have to go now." With that she grabbed the box and ran quickly up the stairs.

Grandma Em came in some minutes later to find Luke in the

exact spot that Christine had left him, simply staring at the place where Christine had been standing.

"Luke, is everything all right?"

He turned absently to his grandmother. "Did you say something, Gram?"

"I said, is everything all right?"

A beaming smile broke across Luke's face. "Everything is just wonderful, Gram." Grandma Em watched him walk to the door, whistling a little tune. He gave her a small wave before exiting.

Emily shook her head as she went to find Christine. "I wonder if there has ever been a case history of spring fever this close to November."

35

November began much like October, but by halfway through the month the temperatures had dropped. Luke rose one morning to find that the fire had gone out in the kitchen stove. Blowing into his hands, Luke stomped around for warmth before attempting to light the fire.

When the fire was stoked and the coffee on, Silas came out, barefoot and shivering. He and Luke huddled near the stove, waiting for the coffee to become drinkable.

"Why don't you get married so we've got someone here to take care of us?"

To this long-standing joke between the brothers Luke answered as expected: "If I did get married, the first morning she got a look at that furry face of yours she'd go screaming from the house and we'd be alone again."

Silas was a sight first thing in the morning. His dark, thick hair stuck out in all directions. His beard, usually brushed down in some semblance of order, was in riotous disarray. Luke said he looked like a grizzly bear.

Two cups of coffee later, both men were warmly dressed and headed for the stables. They worked together feeding the 26 horses.

"Gram and Christine will be coming out to the ranch Friday morning," Silas commented offhandedly.

"They will?" Christine's name snared Luke's complete attention.

"They were supposed to come a few weeks ago, but with Elizabeth's birth and Emily staying with them, it just didn't work out. I'll be going to get them midmorning."

"Don't you have a buyer coming Friday morning?"

"Yeah, but I'll have time."

"I'll go for you."

"It's cold, Luke—I couldn't ask you to do that," Silas answered with his face averted, and it took Luke some minutes to realize he was being teased.

"Am I that obvious?"

"Not to anyone else. You forget I live with you." The men finished up in silence and went to the house for breakfast. Silas was a great cook, but this morning Luke's attention was elsewhere.

He finally spoke. "Si, are you and Christine more than friends? I mean, are you interested in her?" Luke wasn't sure why he had asked, but the thought came to him in the stable and he couldn't quite shake it.

"If you're trying to ask me if I'm in love with Christine, the answer is no." Silas leveled a look on his brother. "Are you in love with her?"

"I don't know. I'm attracted to her—I have to admit that. I was attracted to her before she got saved. I did a lot of praying in an effort to keep my feelings in obedience. I think it was almost a relief to have her be saved so I could relax when I was around her. Now being able to relax around her has just increased the attraction."

"How do you think she feels about you?"

"I think she's scared to death of me. I was barely able to exchange two words with her Sunday."

"Calvin told me she cried because you teased her."

"She cried?" Luke's voice was alarmed.

"It was the Sunday we ate dinner at Mark and Sue's. Calvin said when she came out to play with them, her eyes were wet and that earlier you had teased her at the table."

Luke was looking miserable. Were the tears because he had teased her or because she thought he was committed to Caroline?

"Luke, why don't you go see her this afternoon? Go and stay for supper. Tell her you're looking forward to her coming Friday. Next week is Thanksgiving. We'll all be together the entire day. If there's a strain between you two, you'll both be miserable. Go see her. Talk to her."

Christine pulled the pie from the oven. It smelled wonderful. "I wonder if Luke likes apple pie. Stop it, Christine!" she told herself in frustration, wishing she had a nickel for every time she had thought of him today. As close as it was to afternoon chore time, she would be a rich woman.

Keeping busy had always kept Christine's mind off her troubles, but not so where Luke Cameron was concerned. When she was sweeping she remembered the warm way he smiled at her.

When she ironed she remembered the warmth of his hand, lightly and briefly on her back so she could precede him out of the door of the church.

Time between Sundays was long, and when at last the next Sunday came, Christine determined to make the best of it. But when Luke had complimented her dress, and innocently asked if it had come with the new coat, Christine was so painfully reminded of the scene with the camisole that she didn't even answer him.

She hadn't said ten intelligent words to the man. He probably thought her addlepated!

Christine scolded herself. "You, Christine Bennett, are not getting paid to daydream!" A quick peek at her roast and she had to get to the barn.

"Grandma Em, I'm headed out to feed!"

"Okay," Grandma Em's voice answered from somewhere upstairs.

Christine tugged on the ancient overcoat she used for her barn chores and slipped out the back door.

Luke took his brother's words to heart. He finished his work and was back in the house by 3:30 for a shave and a bath. Silas kindly saddled a mount and Luke was on his way to town by 4:00.

He rode at an easy pace, allowing his mind to work on the feelings he had for Christine. He would never have been so presumptuous as to assume that God had placed Christine in Baxter and saved her just to give him a wife. But maybe God did have something special for the two of them.

Luke praised God daily for Christine's salvation and her interest in Christian growth. Grandma Em had told him that she and Christine studied together nearly every morning, and that Christine was an avid student.

Luke asked himself if he loved Christine. He just wasn't sure. Loving was risky business. His parents and grandfather had been most dear to him. It had not been the same relationship as husband and wife, but it was a painful loss nonetheless.

He was not worried that Christine was going to die, but she did live in Spooner. There was nothing stopping him from going to see her there, but the idea of not having her in Baxter really bothered him. He wanted a chance to get to know her and was not quite sure how to go about it.

If he found he loved her and she didn't return that love, the rejection would be bitter. On the other hand, if she fell in love with him and his feelings were not that strong, she would be hurt. Luke rebelled strongly against this idea. She had been hurt by too many people, and he was determined not to be one of them.

Luke had just arrived in town when he really began to listen to himself. He wasn't trusting God at all. He was worrying and fretting about something over which God had complete control.

Luke began to pray silently, his heart humbled before his heavenly Father. He confessed the pride he had felt when thinking he could deal with this issue without God's help.

A special peace stole over Luke as he communed with God. He asked God's help in obeying His will, come what may, and in listening to his own heart about Christine. Luke remembered what Silas had said: God won't hide His answers. If God wanted Luke and Christine together, Luke would eventually know it.

36

The first hit of cold air took her breath away as Christine stepped from the warmth of the kitchen. She shivered a little as she walked to the barn. The door was kept closed in this weather, and when Christine got inside she lit a lamp to see.

"How's my sweet old Caesar tonight?" Christine said affectionately to this faithful old friend as she fed him. "Are you keeping warm out here? I'm afraid it's going to get much colder before we see spring." Christine stopped talking abruptly and stood still a moment. She thought she smelled smoke. Figuring it was from someone's stove, she went back to work with a shrug.

"You're going to get fat and lazy . . ." her words died off.

She *did* smell smoke. But where? Not until Christine stepped completely out of Caesar's stall did she see the cause.

The barn was on fire, over by the door. Christine did not panic but ran toward the blaze, stripping off her coat as she hurried.

With the coat she began to beat at the flames, but they were spreading quickly out of control. Feeling the heat on her face, Christine knew she had to get out.

The animals! Quickly Christine ran to Chester's stall. He had been strangely quiet tonight, Christine thought absently as she grabbed the scruff of his neck and began to pull. She knew opening the door would fan the flames, but she had no choice.

Throwing the door open, Christine ran out into the cold. Taking deep breaths of fresh air, she left Chester some ten feet away before running back to the barn.

Hesitating at the door, Christine could see that the flames had multiplied in those few seconds. Taking the hem of her skirt, she covered her face and charged back in.

"Please, God," she prayed, "please let Caesar come willingly," knowing how fearful horses were of fire.

Once in the stall, Christine grabbed his halter and tried to move him. He tossed his head, his nostrils dilating as he inhaled the smoke. Trying to resist her, his eyes rolled fearfully in their sockets.

Thinking that an eternity of breathing smoke and praying had passed, Christine miraculously felt the horse back out of the stall.

"Thank You, God," she sobbed as she looked toward the barn

door. The leaping flames made their passageway to safety small, but Christine determined to get Caesar out of the barn or die trying.

Caesar fought Christine as she pulled him along the alley between the stalls. Quickly losing visibility, Christine tried to coax him along with words, but her voice was choked off by the smoke.

The smoke nearly blinding them now, Christine began to feel dizzy and lightheaded. She felt her way along the stalls, silently pleading with God for strength.

Amazingly, the door was in sight! Fresh air! They were going to make it! Caesar picked that time to lunge for the door, knocking Christine against the wall. She felt the flames burn her ankle and calf. A quick turn and she was through the door, only to trip on the threshold. She put her hands out as the ground came rushing up to meet her, but suddenly strong arms were surrounding her, lifting her high against a solid chest.

Christine squinted up through painfully dry and burning eyes to see the clean cut of Luke's jawline above her. He looked down then, his features sharp with concern and then softening with tenderness as his eyes met hers.

It was the *tenderness* she saw there amid all the places she hurt. Turning her soot-blackened face into his coat and clinging with all her might, Christine began to sob.

She was still clinging to Luke and crying when she felt the softness of a mattress beneath her back. Luke laid her gently on her own bed and stayed bent over her. He realized, prior to this night, that he had never known the meaning of the word "fear."

Upon arriving and seeing the smoke, Luke had run to the backyard. His grandmother had just come out of the house and called to him that Christine was in the barn. Luke had thought his heart was going to stop.

"Luke?" Christine croaked in a dry cough.

"Shhh, don't try to talk. Gram sent a neighbor for Mark."

"The animals?"

"The animals are fine. Now, not another word."

"Please don't leave me." Again another cough seized her.

"Shhh," he said as he gently placed a finger on her dry lips. "I'm right here, I won't leave you." Luke attempted then to straighten away from the bed, but Christine grabbed frantically for him. He bent over her once again. "I'm just getting out of this coat. I'll be right here." Her eyes slid closed at his comforting words and she wondered if she had imagined the kiss she felt on her brow.

It could have been a minute or an hour later—Christine could not gauge—when she felt someone pulling her shoes off.

"Luke?"

"Luke is in the hall. He hasn't left you. Maggie and I are here to take care of you. When we're done, Luke can come back in." Mark's reassuring voice came from somewhere above her.

Christine lay still after that, only protesting when her ankle was touched. Gentle hands washed her and helped her into a soft, fresh-smelling nightgown. When a glass was held to her lips, she drank without question. The door opened and she heard Mark's voice. "You haven't much time before the powder does its job." Before Christine could work through these cryptic words, Luke was back beside the bed.

Easing down on the bed beside her, Luke watched as Christine focused in on his face and smiled. Luke smiled back as he placed a hand on either side of her, knowing the medicine was taking effect.

Christine reached to the face above her and touched Luke's cheek. Her smile broadened when she realized he was really there.

"I'm here," he said softly. Christine's hand dropped to the front of his shirt, where she grabbed a fistful of material and hung on. "I have to go to sleep now." Her voice was slurred and she made no move to release him.

"All right, I'll see you in the morning."

Her eyes slid shut and Luke sat quietly a moment before Christine's eyes flew open again.

"Luke?"

"I'm still here."

"Do you like apple pie?"

"It's my favorite," he answered in bemusement, wondering what had brought this on.

Her eyes closing again, Christine let out a huge sigh. Luke sat with her long after her breathing evened out and the hand holding his shirt fell slack against her side. Luke found it hard to breathe when he thought of how close he had come to losing her. You didn't withhold your love from a person just because it might be risky. This was clear to him now.

"She'll be fine, Luke." Mark's voice spoke from the foot of the bed.

"What if she wakes in the night and calls for me?"

Luke loved the fact that she wanted him there. And soon he would tell her just how much he wanted to be there.

"Maggie is staying in the guest room just in case she wakes up, but it's not likely. She'll sleep through the night and you can come back in the morning. Your losing a night's sleep is not going to help anyone."

Luke nodded reluctantly and Mark moved toward the door.

Luke turned down the lamp until the room was bathed in a soft glow. Christine's head on the pillow was turned toward Luke. His eyes moved a final time over her lovely face. He bent and kissed her cheek. "Good night, Christie." Luke's words came softly as he sat, almost in wonder over the realization of the love he felt in his heart for this woman.

37

For the second time in not many months, Christine awoke to find Maggie nearby. Gone was the fear of the unknown, replaced this time with just a calm security at seeing her familiar face.

Maggie helped Christine drink a glass of water and then left to tell Mark his patient was awake.

Within minutes both Mark and Maggie were at her side. Christine, still drowsy, lay quiet as Mark checked her leg. It was tender and, he told her, not badly burned. As Christine began to come fully awake, many questions were coming to mind. Mark pulled the desk chair up to the head of the bed and sat down.

"Your leg looks good. The only thing I'm concerned with is your nose, throat, and lungs. You took in a lot of smoke, and I want you to stay in bed until I give you leave to get up. And no talking!"

"No talking?" Christine croaked, thinking of all the questions she had.

"Does your throat hurt?"

Christine knew what he was getting at and stubbornly refused to answer.

"Christine!" Mark's voice was very stern, and he sounded amazingly like Luke. "Does your throat hurt?"

Her jaw set, Christine gave him a short nod.

"Until it stops hurting, you are not to talk."

"How am I to communicate?" Tears sprang to Christine's eyes, born of a sore throat and frustration.

Mark answered with his best bedside manner. "There will be someone here to check on you at all times." She watched Mark produce a small pad of paper and a pencil from his pocket. "If you can't answer with a nod or shake of your head . . ." Mark tapped the pad and put it on the bedside table.

Christine was on the verge of telling Mark to take his orders and get out of her room, but she began to grow weary and she ached all over. Suddenly the fight went out of her and her eyes closed, not wanting to fight sleep or anything else.

Mark took Christine's sleep as a peaceful acceptance of her situation. Unaware of how far this was from the truth, he headed out to see what Mac and his brothers were finding.

Mark found Mac, Luke, and Silas, along with a few other neighbors, looking around the charred remains of the barn. There was
talk of possible causes for the fire. The family was thanking the
men who had carried water and soaked the ground surrounding
the barn, seeing that the structure itself was going too quickly
to be saved. It had been a small barn, and thankfully the closest
building was well over a hundred feet away. But the water surrounding the barn had been an extra safety precaution.

When Luke found a moment with Mark, he asked about Christine.

"Her leg is in good shape but I think she's feeling pretty weak.
She was asleep when I left her."

"She sounded so hoarse last night. Will her throat be okay?"

"I've told her to be quiet until her sore throat is gone, but I
think she'll be fine. She wasn't too happy with the idea of not
talking."

"Telling a woman not to talk is like saying 'sic 'em' to a hound
dog." Both men laughed at this and started toward the house.

Close to an hour later, with everyone just finishing breakfast,
Maggie came down to prepare a tray for Christine.

Christine, wrapped warmly in her robe, was sitting up in bed
brushing her hair. She could hear voices downstairs and wondered what was happening.

Christine reached for her Bible but didn't open it. She leaned
her head back against the oak headboard and began to pray.
Christine told God what an awful patient she was. She was rarely
sick, and when she was, she made herself miserable by fretting
about things not getting done until she could be up and around
again. She and Grandma Em worked so well together. Christine
asked God to soon put her back on her feet so she could be of
help again. Christine's prayer was interrupted when the questions she had had earlier that morning began to roll once again
through her mind. They destroyed her peace and made her feel
weary. Did the barn burn down completely? Where were the animals? Who was taking care of them? Did anything else burn?
Was anyone hurt? Tears again filled Christine's eyes as in frustration she asked God to help her obtain some answers.

She was feeling sleepy again, and try as she might she couldn't
stop herself from drifting off.

Less than five minutes passed before Luke came through Christine's door bearing a breakfast tray and a smile, only to find her sound asleep. She had scooted down a bit and was curled against her propped-up pillow. Luke adjusted the pillow and covered her with the bedclothes, as Christine continued to sleep. He wondered if he would get to see her at all today.

As it turned out, he did not. When Maggie reported that she slept through lunch and on into the afternoon, Luke knew he had to get home. So with a final check on her he made his way home, hoping that tomorrow she would feel up to company.

38

Grandma Em's hands joined Christine's as she briskly rubbed her wet hair with a towel.

"We're both going to be in trouble when Mark finds out about this. If Joseph were alive, he'd take me to task."

Christine opened her mouth to speak, but Grandma Em dropped the towel over her face. "I know, I know, your hair smelled like smoke and you couldn't stand it. There. Now, can you sit up for a bit longer?" Christine nodded. "Good, we'll brush your hair out while you sit in this patch of sunlight in front of the window."

As Grandma Em brushed, she talked. Knowing that Christine was concerned about the animals, she started with them. "Caesar and Chester are fine. They're both out at Mac and Julia's. Belle and Betsy are at Mr. Turley's. And the hens I'm afraid didn't make it." Christine turned to look at Grandma Em, but she only patted Christine's shoulder and went on. "The barn burned completely down, but nothing else was damaged and you were the only one hurt."

The look Christine threw at Grandma Em told her she felt she was fine, but Grandma Em only ignored her. A few more strokes and she was done.

"Okay, back into bed. How about some lunch?"

"Gram!" A man's voice sounded at the bottom of the stairs.

"It's Luke. We're in trouble now," Grandma Em said before she left the room.

"How's Christine? Can I go up and see her?" Luke spoke before his grandmother even hit the landing.

"She is much better. In fact, she was up this morning."

"You mean she was out of bed? Why was she out of bed?"

"I'll let her tell you—I'm going to fix lunch." Grandma Em went to the kitchen feeling like a coward.

Once upstairs, Luke knocked on the open door jamb and walked into Christine's room. She was sitting up in bed, looking content with a book in her hand. Christine watched as Luke took in the wet towels, hairbrush, and chair near the window. Next his eyes went to Christine's hair, still unbound and a little damp, falling in soft waves around her shoulders.

Luke's voice was calm and measured. "You got out of bed today against Mark's orders in order to wash your hair?" Christine nodded calmly.

"Why?"

Christine wrote and handed Luke the pad.

"It smelled like smoke?" Again, the calm nod. "You washed your hair because you didn't like the smell of smoke?" When Christine didn't answer but only looked at him, Luke opened up to a rare show of temper.

"That's ridiculous. Absolute foolishness. It's freezing outside and it's cold in these upstairs rooms. You had no business getting out of this bed." Luke ranted on, but Christine had tuned him out and reached for the pad. She handed Luke one sheet of paper and smiled when he sputtered to a halt.

"Hush up, Luke," he finally read out loud, his voice incredulous.

The two eyed each other for endless seconds before Luke spoke more to himself but still aloud. "How did your grandfather control you?"

"He didn't try." Even though her voice was hoarse, Luke caught the underlying steel in her tone. He turned then and walked from the room, leaving Christine to wonder if he would ever be back.

Luke sat down at the kitchen table with a heavy sigh. "You shouldn't have shouted at her," Grandma Em began.

"She deserves more than to be shouted at."

"No, Luke, she doesn't."

"You sound as if you agree with her getting out of bed."

"I helped her wash her hair."

"Why, Gram?" Luke asked in total bemusement.

Emily sat at the table with him. "Luke, try to see things from her standpoint. She slept yesterday away. She had had no news about the barn or the animals you know she cares for. The smell of her hair and sheets was making her sick to her stomach. She also feels much better, and I for one could not see standing on ceremony and waiting to ask Mark. So I grumbled at her and got her washed and back into bed as quickly as I could."

"How do you know all of this?"

"She had written me quite a long letter full of questions and frustration. She was standing next to my bed when I woke this morning so she could deliver it personally. I told her Mark would not like it, but she was determined and I could not say no.

"I hope, Luke, that you won't let your pride punish both of you. Christine and I talked for some time this morning about why God would let this happen. I know it was hard for her not to have an answer land in her lap. She's also feeling good enough to be bored. If you are not going to stay, please go by Julia's and tell her Christine needs company."

Again, Grandma Em went back to the tray she was preparing to bring upstairs. She delivered it and then returned to the kitchen to get lunch for Luke and herself. Luke made the mistake of not returning to Christine's room until after lunch. He would find out the hard way that when Christine was left upset and alone with her thoughts, they moved like wildfire and usually in the wrong direction.

"He had no right shouting at me," Christine told herself. "I am not answerable to him. If I want to wash my hair when I feel good enough to do so, it's none of his business. How would he like to smell like smoke?" This was the train of Christine's thoughts as she picked at her lunch. It had been easier than she expected to not talk; her throat *did* hurt. Her leg throbbed some, like a sunburn, but other than that she felt pretty good.

So with all these thoughts in mind Christine made a decision. As soon as she was on her feet, she would take the train home. She didn't see any problem in being home by Thanksgiving.

"Hello," Luke said as he came through the doorway. Christine politely set her lunch aside and watched as he pulled her desk chair around and straddled it. Even in her irritation that he had come back when once again she had decided she had made a mistake about him, she couldn't help but notice how he spilled over the chair. It was so rare to find someone who could make her feel small and protected. It was getting harder to hold onto her anger as she remembered those arms holding her, his presence when she needed him most.

Luke could see she was angry with him. He felt he should apologize for shouting at her and should tell her his anger stemmed from the fear she would get sick, that he cared too much about her to want that to happen. Not knowing how to start, he said, "Silas told me you were to come to the ranch tomorrow."

Christine nodded.

"I was thinking we could change your visit to next week, the day after Thanksgiving. Would you still like to come?"

Christine reached for her paper. When Luke saw her answer was longer than a simple yes or no, he felt a sinking sense of dread. He read the paper she handed to him. "I'm sorry I won't get to see your ranch, but I'm going home next week. Thank you anyway."

"Home?" Christine nodded. "To Spooner?" When her eyes turned wide with surprise, Luke said, "Yes, Christine, I know you're from Spooner. The sheriff mistook me one day for Mark and told me some things. I went to Mark immediately and demanded that he tell me the entire story."

"You're very good at demanding things, aren't you?" Christine's voice was icy.

"Yes, I can be very demanding, just as you can be extremely stubborn," Luke answered her.

Christine turned her head away from him in anger and looked out the window. She heard his chair move and, assuming he was leaving, was surprised when he moved it up to the head of her bed and leaned close to her.

Christine wouldn't look at him. Luke waited patiently, and when she still didn't turn he reached and took one of her hands in both of his.

This brought her head around as she looked first at the way his hands swallowed her own, then up into those deep blue eyes glued to her own.

She looked confused, but she didn't pull her hand away, and Luke was encouraged. When he spoke, his voice was deep and quiet, his eyes probing hers. "When I got to the backyard Tuesday night and Gram said you were in the barn, I thought my heart was going to stop. And then today, when I shouted at you, it was out of fear you would get sick when I desperately want you back on your feet again."

A tear slid down Christine's cheek. "You confuse me."

"I don't mean to," he answered gently.

"It's not you, it's me. Everything confuses me." She began to cry. When she tried to speak, no sound came out and she cried harder.

Luke, unsure of what to say, sat holding her hand and rubbing it gently until she had composed herself. After she had dried her face and looked at Luke, she watched him bow his head. Christine followed suit.

"Dear heavenly Father, thank You for Christine's safety. Thank You for bringing her out of the fire. She was not hurt in the fire, Lord, but she is hurting. Please comfort and heal her. Dry her tears and hold her close. Calm her confusion as only You can do. Help her to trust You, Lord, for her every need, and help me to be here to encourage and care for her. I praise and thank You, God, that You saved Christine and put her in my life. Help us to trust You for our needs and feelings toward each other. In Your Son's holy name I pray. Amen."

Luke was still holding Christine's hand, and after the prayer he reached out and gently touched her cheek. Again their eyes met. "Please don't leave Baxter, Christine. I can't take care of you in Spooner. I can't get to know you if you're so far away. Please don't leave me, Christine, now that I've just found you." The desire to kiss her was almost overpowering, but Luke saw the confusion and fatigue in her eyes.

"I'll go so you can rest. I'll see you tomorrow." Reluctantly he withdrew, knowing that they both needed to be alone with their thoughts and to pray.

39

"Well, Mr. Buelow, please come on in." Maggie answered the front door to find the hotel proprietor on the step.

"I know it's the dinner hour, but I need to see the Doc."

"Of course. I'll get him."

Mark appeared within seconds. "Hello, Al. Good to see you."

"Sorry to get you away from your lunch, but I need to see you."

"Certainly—come on into my office." Mark held open the office door that led off the entryway, and Albert Buelow preceded him inside. When both men were seated Mark said, "Now, what can I do for you?"

"It's not me that needs ya."

"One of your guests?" This was not an unusual occurrence.

"Yeah, we've had a man in number three since the weekend. When we didn't see him around for a few days, Ina thought she should check on him."

"Is he sick?"

"Not exactly. His arm is burned." Mark sat completely still as the weight of this news hit home. Al Buelow watched him, his look one of compassion.

"Is he from around here?"

"I've never seen him before."

"Who else knows about this?"

"Just Ina and myself."

Mark continued to sit very still, his heart hammering in his chest as he asked God for wisdom.

"Al, will you do me a favor?"

"Anything, Doc."

"Go to the sheriff and tell him all you've told me. Also tell him I'm headed over right now to check the man's arm. One more thing, Al—*keep this to yourself.*"

The man nodded solemnly before asking, "How is Miss Bennett?"

"She's doing fine, Al. It was kind of you to ask."

Mark had just seen Al Buelow out when Susanne came into his office. Her smile quickly faded at the look on her husband's face.

"Can you tell me, Mark?"

"There's a man at the hotel with a burned arm." Mark watched the color drain from his wife's face. Sue sat down heavily in the chair that Mark led her to.

"I'm afraid."

"I am too, but we're both being a bit premature. I haven't even examined the man. I'm headed there right now."

"Oh, Mark, please be careful!"

Mark pulled his trembling wife into his arms. "Shhh. You know I'll be careful." He kissed her gently. "Cover me with your prayers." Mark reached for his bag and was gone."

" 'Bye Silas, thanks for coming."

"Any time. I imagine Luke will be along about supper-time. The buyers today were a little more than we expected. It might not be fair to tell you this, but I could tell his mind was here and not at the ranch."

Christine smiled at him, and he and Grandma Em left the room. If Luke didn't come tonight, she would be tempted to get on a horse and go to him. It was hard to believe how much she wanted to see him.

After much prayer and thought, Christine realized she had been ready to run from the man she loved because anger was clouding her judgment.

In the last 24 hours Christine had done a lot of praying, confessing, and giving over her fears to God. It was time to get to know Luke. They really had shared a very small amount of time together. When he arrived, she planned on telling him that yesterday she had overreacted. She wanted to stay in Baxter in hopes of getting to know him better.

Yet doubts assailed her. Worrying that her approach was too forward, she prayed, "Please help me to know what to say."

Christine reached for her notepaper and scratched out a quick note. Then she moved down in bed to a more comfortable position for a short nap.

"I told ya I didn't want to see no one."

"Well, the doctor's here and he's going to look at that arm."
Ina Buelow's hands were planted on her ample hips as she tow-

ered over the small, dirty man lying in agony upon one of her beds.

His eyes were clouded with pain, but he tried again. "I tell ya it ain't nothin' but a scratch. Now leave me be."

Mark decided to step in. "I'm Doctor Cameron, and whether or not I look at your arm is entirely up to you. But you *will* answer questions when the sheriff arrives. I can try to alleviate your pain before he comes or you can suffer through the questions."

The small man on the bed sagged with defeat. Or was it relief?

Mark moved forward. The man had a second-degree burn that ran from his left forearm to the back of his hand. He lay quietly, gritting his teeth as Mark examined, cleaned, and wrapped the swollen, oozing skin. By the time Mark finished, the man was bathed in perspiration but hadn't made a sound.

The sheriff had arrived and stood waiting to talk with him. The Buelows left and Mark stood near the door to listen.

Nearly two hours later Mark walked away from the hotel. The man had spent the first half-hour denying there even was a fire. After the sheriff looked around and in the closet found a raggedy overcoat with a badly burned sleeve and a wine bottle with a few tablespoons of kerosene sloshing around in the bottom, the man changed his story.

He insisted that he had been near the barn, but didn't start the fire. He could give no reason for the coat or the wine bottle and nearly came unglued when the sheriff told him the charge for attempted murder was the same in Baxter as it was in Spooner.

The sheriff told Mark when he left that he would be posting a man at the hotel until he could move the burned man to the jail. He never did give his name, but the sheriff planned on holding him until he could wire Spooner.

Mark arrived home to find his brother's horse in front of his house. He was thankful for the saved trip to the ranch.

Silas was on the front-room floor with Emily. They were reading a book together. Much to the delight of his niece, Silas' voice changed with each character.

Mark's cares momentarily evaporated as he listened to the antics of his brother.

The story ended when Emily spotted her dad. She danced around his legs until he swung her up into his arms. Silas folded his long frame into a chair and Mark took the couch.

"Is Luke coming into town tonight?"

"That's a silly question," Silas said with a raised brow.

Mark nodded. "Yes, I suppose it is."

"I just came from Gram's. Christine looks much better," Silas remarked.

"I saw her this morning and she seemed to be coming along. A bit down perhaps, but not physically."

"Luke's arrival will take care of that."

"Do me a favor and ask Luke to stop here when he gets into town."

"Sure, I'll tell him."

"Thanks."

Silas knew better than to ask, but his brother really looked upset about something.

Not long afterward Silas rode toward the ranch, realizing that he could pray even without knowing any details, but his mind kept returning to Luke and Christine. Silas wondered if they had figured out that they were in love. Well, God would take care of it. As Mac liked to say, the Holy Spirit didn't need anyone's help.

The wind had picked up, as did Silas' mount, with both man and beast ready to be home.

40

Luke tied his horse in front of Mark's place and knocked on the door. Mark answered and led Luke wordlessly into his office.

"Al Buelow came over today to tell me a hotel guest was hurt. The man's arm was burned. The sheriff questioned him and he found a burned overcoat and some kerosene hidden in the man's closet. The sheriff plans to hold him until he can get word to and a reply from Spooner."

Luke reeled under the weight of the news. He leaned against the wall, feeling as if the pins had been knocked out from under him.

Mark let Luke catch his breath before saying, "I don't know how to tell Christine without upsetting her."

"We won't tell her," Luke replied after some moments.

"What?"

"I said we won't tell her," Luke repeated calmly.

"Luke, that's not fair. She has a right to know."

"It will only frighten her. Anyway, the man is in custody. It's over now."

"Luke, it's not over. Christine is not dead and I'm sure whoever wants her that way will not give up so easily." Mark knew the words were harsh, but he could see the need to be blunt.

"I'll be here to take care of her."

"Luke, be reasonable. Even if you two were married, you wouldn't be with her all the time. She needs to know about this so she can be on her guard and less vulnerable. She's not a little girl, Luke. We can't protect and treat her like one."

Mark continued on in his argument, but Luke was adamant. Mark even considered going to Christine himself, but put the idea away when he saw how single-minded Luke was to keep the information from her. He watched his brother leave, a heavy feeling in Mark's heart.

— ⋮ —

The ride to his grandmother's house was short, but in that span Luke was even more determined to keep the recent developments from Christine and to proceed as he hoped. By the time

Luke arrived and found his grandmother in the kitchen, he had nearly succeeded in pushing the barn fire from his mind.

"I found this on Christine's bedside table when I checked on her." Grandma Em handed him the note.

> Grandma Em, please wake me if Luke comes.
> Don't let him leave.

"Is she awake yet?" Luke asked, still holding the note.

"I don't think so. It's pretty quiet up there."

Luke began to pace. "Was she upset? Did she tell you why she had to see me?"

Grandma Em opened her mouth to answer when they both heard a sneeze. Luke gave his grandmother a small smile and walked with a determined stride up to Christine's room.

The room was chilly and Christine was settled back against the pillow, the quilts tucked in tight around her. She heard someone on the stairs and watched as Luke came in. He was without a doubt a man with a purpose.

Not a word was spoken as Luke moved the desk chair to the head of the bed and leaned close to Christine, much like yesterday.

"I've done a lot of thinking since yesterday, Christine. I was insensitive to your needs and I'm sorry." Luke leaned a bit closer, his voice almost urgent. "I realized after I left yesterday that we've had almost no time together." Luke hesitated, knowing it was too soon to tell her he loved her.

"I care deeply for you, Christine. And I want you to stay in Baxter. Stay and give us time to get to know each other. I can't believe how little I know about you. We've both lost our parents and I think we have a lot to share. Please stay, Christine; give us a chance."

A tiny bubble of laughter, in contrast with the tears sparkling in her eyes, sounded from Christine's throat. "I had the same speech planned for you."

"You mean about staying in Baxter and getting to know each other?"

Christine gave him a happy nod. Luke's laughter sounded through the upstairs and Christine joined him. Their relief was more precious because they had both asked for God's guidance.

Christine touched Luke's arm. "I need to say something else.

I'm sorry about the way I acted yesterday. I've never been a good patient."

"Oh, really! I hadn't noticed." Christine bit her lip in an effort to keep from smiling, knowing that if she did he would only be encouraged to tease her more.

When Christine asked Luke to give her a few minutes alone he left the room, shutting the door behind him, and waited in the hall. Supper aromas were drifting up the stairs, and he decided that he and Grandma Em should bring their plates up and eat with Christine.

"All set!" Luke turned in surprise at Christine's voice as she came out into the hall, dressed and wrapped in a quilt. She smiled at him as she moved toward the stairs. "I'm starved." Christine spoke again and was partway down the stairs before she realized that Luke had not followed.

Christine stopped and spoke without turning, "I'm fine, Luke. My throat doesn't hurt, and if I have to stay in that bed another minute I'll go out of my mind." Christine was relieved when she heard Luke move onto the steps behind her.

His presence was so comforting. She had to stop herself from leaning into him as he reached her on the stairs and put his hand on her back to guide her to the parlor.

"I rather thought I'd see you down here tonight, Christine." Grandma Em's eyes twinkled with mischief as she kissed Christine's cheek. "Your room is lovely, but 24 hours a day gets to be a bit much."

Grandma Em went back to the stove. Christine put her quilt on a chair, intending to follow. She had only stepped twice before she felt the quilt drop back onto her shoulders and Luke's hands guide her to a seat.

"I need to help," she protested after he had sat her down.

"I'll help her."

"Luke, I can't just sit here."

"Yes, you can." Christine heard the words correctly but knew that his look and tone were really saying, "You had better."

Luke, who was bent over Christine to talk quietly into her up-turned face, saw the exact moment she gave in. His knuckles brushed feather-lightly down her cheek before he moved to aid his grandmother.

Christine's earlier statement of being starved had not been far from the truth. She filled her plate twice and had two pieces of pie.

"That was delicious." Christine sat back with a sigh.

"Did you think I had forgotten how to cook?" Grandma Em asked with feigned indignation.

"No!" Christine laughed.

"Well, the truth is, you do have me pretty spoiled."

"What I'd really like to do is spoil you some more by doing the dishes. But," Christine continued quickly as Luke began to protest, "your grandson has other ideas. So I'm headed to the parlor so I won't have to watch you work."

After Christine left, Luke began to gather the plates, but Grandma Em waved him away. "I can get them, Luke. Go sit with Christine."

Luke, much to his grandmother's amusement, didn't even hesitate. He found Christine curled up on the couch and he joined her.

"Are you warm enough?"

Christine nodded in contentment, willing to just sit with Luke in comfortable silence. She was feeling tired and Luke also was content to just be near her.

As the silence between them continued, Luke grew pensive. His thoughts were turning bleak before he realized that Christine had leaned forward and was looking into his face.

"Did I cause that scowl?"

"No." Luke reined his thoughts in and smiled into Christine's eyes. Christine realized she was leaning rather close. Hastily she sat back and began to nervously pleat the quilt in her lap. "Tell me about your ranch." Christine spoke, wishing she couldn't feel his eyes on her.

"No."

"What!" Christine felt a bit taken aback at his abrupt answer.

"I said no, because I want you to come and see the ranch. Next Friday."

"I'll have to check with Grandma Em." Christine smiled with relief. "But I'd love to."

The next few hours flew by. Grandma Em finished the dishes and the three sat in the parlor. Talk moved rapidly from one subject to the next.

When Luke was ready to leave, Christine walked him to the door. With his coat and hat on, he leaned against the door and took Christine's hand.

"I won't see you tomorrow. But," he said with mock sternness, "I expect to hear that you rested and took it easy when I get here

Sunday." He pointed a finger at her. "Do I make myself clear, Christine Bennett?"

"Yes, sir!" Christine spoke with exaggerated sweetness.

Luke only groaned and rolled his eyes, knowing she would do exactly as she pleased. This groan brought a smile to Christine's face.

Suddenly Christine knew she was about to be kissed. She couldn't stop the tensing in her body, the clenching of her hands at her side.

Luke didn't miss her stance. She looked like a frightened animal about to bolt. Slow down, Luke, he told himself—don't rush her.

Careful not to move toward her in any way, Luke let go of her hand and reached for the door handle. "Good night, Christine. I'll see you Sunday."

"Good night." Christine stood for a long time after the door shut, the cold air no longer swirling around her legs. "If I didn't want Luke to kiss me, why am I so disappointed that he didn't?"

Long after Christine bid Grandma Em good night and took herself off to bed, the question plagued her.

41

"Come in," Christine called to the knock on her bedroom door, assuming it was Grandma Em this early on a Sunday morning. "Oh, Mark! It's you!" Christine sent up a quick prayer of thanks that she was dressed.

Mark came into the room and saw that his brother's suspicions had been right: Christine was ready for church. He also wondered absently how Christine was able to tell him and Luke apart, no matter what they were wearing.

"I'm on a mission for my brother," Mark said.

Christine laughed, feeling quite certain she knew what that mission was. "Why don't you tell me about it over a cup of coffee."

"Lead the way," Mark said as he gestured gallantly toward the door.

"So," Christine said after she had put the coffee on, "what's up? I assume when you say 'brother,' you are referring to Luke?"

"Correct. Luke wants me to make sure you are well enough to be out today, and if not, to make you go back to bed."

Again Christine laughed. "What would you like to know? My throat feels fine. My eyes and nose no longer burn. My leg is still tender and I think the skin is going to peel. I must admit I tire easily, but I just rest when I feel the need. Other than the fact that the animals are not here to feed, it's almost as if the fire never happened." Christine shrugged and moved to get the coffee.

Mark watched as she poured two cups. "Yes," he thought, "she's ready to be out again." Unbidden, another thought followed: "It's easier to keep her safe if she stays in."

"Mark, if that look on your face means you're about to tell me to go back to bed, then I best warn you, you'll have a fight on your hands."

Mark looked up to see that Christine had put the coffeepot back on the stove. Her hands were planted on her hips, her chin was thrust out, and she was ready for a battle.

Mark could not keep the smile from his face. "Luke, my dear brother," he thought to himself, "you have met your match."

Christine's battle stance turned to confusion upon seeing that smile. She watched as Mark drained his coffeecup, amazed that he could drink it so hot. Standing, he said, "I'll see you in church, Christine," and then he was out the door.

"And men think women are hard to explain," Christine said to a supposedly empty room some minutes later.

"There's no hope for you, Christine, if you're talking to yourself at 19. What are you going to be doing at my age?"

The women shared a good laugh and Christine explained Mark's visit, none of which was news to Grandma Em. She didn't miss much of the goings-on in her family.

The women took some time to pray and share a verse before starting breakfast. Christine had begun to memorize Scripture. Reading Psalm 121 for the first time the night before, she had determined to put all eight verses to memory.

Luke and Silas came in to find Grandma Em setting the table for breakfast and Christine stirring the cooked cereal with one hand and holding a Bible in the other, completely engrossed. Luke asked his grandmother what Christine was doing, and he was not surprised at the answer, for he was learning that Christine did most things with a fierce sense of purpose.

Silas had stepped to the stove to pour a cup of coffee.

"Memorizing is hard work."

"I think so, and it gets harder as you get older," Silas replied. "I can't believe how fast the kids can learn those verses. Of course Julia is an exception—she can memorize today as well as she could when we were kids. She used to beat the pants off us boys. Maybe it was the Lord's way of making her extra-special. Being raised with three older brothers who were always a little faster and stronger has a way of discouraging a girl. Even when she stopped competing with us and began to grow up, we teased her for putting her hair up or wearing ribbons. Not until she turned 15 and fell so hard for Mac did we have any compassion."

Luke came out to the kitchen, and he and Christine exchanged a smile before Christine turned back to Silas.

"Were you really compassionate toward her?"

"I don't think we ever said anything to her, but I sure remember the day after she told Mac she couldn't see him again. All the sparkle went out of her."

Luke joined the conversation at this point. "She did her work and never complained, but when we teased her, there was no reaction. It went on like that for nearly a month before our father blew his stack."

"That was a bad night," Silas went on. "It was at the supper table. He really raked her over the coals. Told her to stop moping around and get back into the family or he'd find so much work for her to do that she'd have no time to pout."

"Julia was already doing the work of a grown woman and had been since her mother died." Grandma Em had come in and talked as she cracked eggs into a pan. "We all make mistakes, and I'm afraid that was one of Joseph Jr.'s worst."

Breakfast preparation was finished in silence and the four sat around the table. Prayer was said and they began to eat before Luke continued the story.

"Julia came around after that. She would laugh and talk with us when we were around. But she also lost weight and spent more time alone than she ever had in her life. It was as if she decided on her own to take Dad's word and to work to forget Mac."

Silas shook his head and took off where Luke had finished. "She never stopped working. Dad began to see that he'd been too harsh with her. Then she got sick. She was down to skin and bones and collapsed one day in the kitchen. Paul found her and came for us in the stable. She burned up with fever for three days. It was during this time that we found out just how painful it had been to tell Mac she couldn't see him.

"She kept saying, 'I'm sorry, Mac, I had to obey my father. I don't think I'm too good for you. I love you, but I have to obey my father. Please, God, please save Mac and help him understand.' It never came out at one time, but she would cry and talk. Paul never left her side, and he heard most of it.

"Paul became Julia's champion. He told all of us, including our father, that we'd been unfair and that we owed her an apology and some help with the work around the house.

"He cried, didn't he, Luke? And he told the family that if things didn't change, he and Julia were going to move into town to Grandpa's. He was so upset after his speech that he wouldn't even speak with us."

It was time to do the dishes or they would be late for church. As they worked, Luke finished the story.

"It took Julia some time to get back on her feet. While she convalesced, Silas did most of the housework and we helped. He became a very good cook, by the way. Anyhow, after Julia was up and about, we all apologized to her and promised to help her with her work. We also began to pray daily as a family for Mac's salvation. Having us behind her turned Julia around. She became her old self, and it wasn't long afterward that Mac came to church. He began to eat Sunday dinner with us, and one day Paul led him to the Lord. Now, eight years of marriage later and two little boys down the road, it's just like Silas said—she can still memorize with the best of them."

Christine was amazed at Julia's story. Julia had said that things had been hard, but she had never once hinted at the real pain she had experienced. These thoughts stayed with Christine until the four of them bundled into the wagon and headed for church.

The proximity of Luke on the rear seat with her drove away all thought of Julia as Christine reached between them to steady herself on the seat. Luke took her hand, holding it all the way to church.

He released her hand only after the wagon had stopped in the churchyard.

They had arrived in time for the service, and in the few minutes before it started Luke asked Christine about her memorizing.

"Gram tells me you're working on Psalm 121. How is it going?"

"Well, I just started last night. I read it and read it, then close my Bible and can't remember a thing."

Luke laughed softly and Christine studied his face. He looked so tan against the crisp whiteness of his dress shirt. His hair was a little mussed from the wagon ride and a few stray locks fell on his forehead. His teeth and smile were beautiful. And those eyes! Sapphire! Christine looked away—how would she ever concentrate on the sermon?

Mrs. Nolan had started the piano prelude, and Luke quickly leaned over to Christine. "I worked in Psalm 121 when I was a kid. I could use a refresher course. Why don't we work on it together?"

Christine's look was uncertain and Luke misinterpreted it. "If you'd rather not . . ."

"No, it's not that . . ." Christine was not allowed to explain because Pastor Nolan had stepped to the front.

The sermon was on fear—specifically, the giving over of fear to God. Christine and Grandma Em had talked on this subject several times, and Pastor Nolan confirmed much of what she had said. "When we start to feel that some fear will overwhelm us, we should immediately pray and keep praying until we've given that fear to God and can rest in Him," Grandma Em had said.

Luke seemed restless, Christine thought, but then maybe she had imagined it.

Pastor Nolan ended his sermon by suggesting some good verses to refer to when fears assailed. Joshua 1:9: "Have not I commanded thee? Be strong and of good courage; be not afraid, neither be thou dismayed, for the Lord thy God is with thee wherever thou goest." Psalm 27:1: "The Lord is my light and my salvation; whom shall I fear? The Lord is the strength of my life; of whom shall I be afraid?" Hebrews 13:6: "We may boldly say, 'The Lord is my helper, and I will not fear what man shall do unto me.' " Isaiah 41:10: "Fear thou not, for I am with thee; be not dismayed, for I am thy God. I will strengthen thee; yea, I will help thee; yea, I will uphold thee with the right hand of my righteousness."

The service closed with the congregation standing and reading the 23rd Psalm. Christine noticed that Luke recited it from memory. Christine was discouraged as she left church. There was so much to learn. With this on her mind, Christine failed to notice Luke's rather quiet demeanor on the way home.

42

Luke thought much about the sermon on the wagon ride home. He felt very convicted about not giving his fears to God. It was fear, plain and simple, that kept Luke from telling Christine about the burned man at the hotel—fear that she would panic and go back to Spooner, and he would lose her forever.

These thoughts rode him hard, even as they arrived back at Grandma Em's and went in for Sunday dinner.

"There's my girl." Susanne spoke tenderly to her infant daughter as she transferred her to Christine's arms. "Fed and dry, Christine, you're getting Eliza at her best."

Christine laughed softly. "I never would have believed how much fun it could be to be chased out of the kitchen. I put up a fight, but Julia was adamant. I'll have to thank her."

The two women were in Grandma Em's room. Sue buttoned her blouse as Christine gently rocked the baby. The usually quiet Sue surprised Christine when she broke the silence with a question.

"Should we be asking God to give you a baby, Christine?"

Christine's look was so startled that Sue laughed.

"Don't you think I should start with a husband?" Christine finally asked.

"Do you have anyone in mind?" When Christine didn't answer the question, Sue went on. "If you don't, I do."

"I rather thought you might. Does he happen to be the spitting image of your husband?"

Susanne smiled, not at all sheepish about being so transparent. "It is a nice face to wake up to every day." When Christine blushed, Sue went on softly. "If Luke lets you get away, Christine, I may never speak to him again."

A few minutes later there was a soft knock on the door and Mark entered. He joined his wife on the edge of the bed and smiled at the sight of Elizabeth on Christine's shoulder.

"I was just asking Christine if we needed to ask God for a baby for her."

"Don't you think she should start with a husband?"

"Who should start with a husband?" Christine could hardly believe her ears. How could a man of his size move so quietly?

Luke stood patiently awaiting an answer. When none came, he approached the rocking chair and knelt down next to Christine and Elizabeth. Christine watched him look at the baby before turning his attention to her. "She's to fair to be . . . yours." Luke stopped just short of saying ours, and Christine didn't miss the pause.

"I would take her anyhow." Christine spoke quickly, hoping to direct Luke's attention back to his niece, but to no avail—his eyes were still searching her face.

Christine was glad of Sue's interruption just then. She took the baby and put her in the basket by the bed. All four adults quietly left the room. Mark and Sue led the way down the stairs. When it was Christine's turn to follow, she held back, causing Luke to stop behind her.

Turning, she asked, "Luke, is anything bothering you?"

"Tell her, Luke," an inner voice prompted. "Tell her about the man at the hotel." But when he spoke, it was only "No."

Christine smiled at him, thinking again that she had imagined his restlessness at church.

The day sped by with good food and fellowship. Christine was moved away from the kitchen every time she headed that way, even for the most innocent of reasons.

By the time Luke said goodbye, with the time drawing near for the horses to be fed, Christine had completely forgotten that she had thought something was wrong. Luke had been happy and charming all afternoon. They had worked together on Christine's memory verses. Laughing away her earlier hesitation that stemmed from a fear of not being able to memorize all eight verses, Luke said they would take as much time to memorize together as they needed.

Twice he had held her hand, once at the dinner table and again after she had read Emily a story. Christine climbed into bed that night with a glow about her as she remembered the way Emily had fallen asleep in her lap and the way Luke had reached for her hand and held it between them. She marveled again at the way he made her feel little and protected with the mere act of placing her hand in his.

With these happy thoughts Christine fell asleep, praising God for love, happiness, and Luke Cameron.

43

"It snowed! It snowed!"

Mac squinted up at the little boy sitting in the middle of his chest. Beside him he heard Julia's breath leave her in a rush as Charles landed on her stomach, enroute to joining his brother.

"It snowed, Papa," Charles added, in case his father had missed Calvin's words.

"And you two are going to see that I can't enjoy it by crushing my chest!" The boys grinned indulgently at their father. Both were quite sure that *nothing* could crush John MacDonald's chest.

"We prayed and God sent the snow, didn't we, Cal? We prayed every night in our beds."

"Charlie's right. We prayed and asked God to send it for Thanksgiving. We asked for Christine."

Mac had pulled Julia close, and with her head pillowed on Mac's shoulder she asked, "Why for Christine?"

"Because that day she came out to swing with us, she told me and Cal that she'd never been in a snowball fight."

Mac cleared his throat. "That was very kind of you boys to think of Christine. I'm proud of you."

"Don't cry, Mama! The snow is here. It's okay now." Charles' concerned look and caring words just caused Julia to cry harder. Mac reached past her for the handkerchief she usually kept under her pillow.

After handing it to Julia, Mac again spoke to the boys. "Your mother's tears are because she is just as proud of you as I am, that you prayed and thought of Christine's happiness."

"Is Christine going to marry Uncle Luke?"

"Why do you ask, Charles?" Julia asked as she dried her face.

"They were holding hands on Sunday and Uncle Luke smiles a lot."

"Yeah," Charles joined in. "He still plays and talks with us, but his eyes are always watching Christine."

"Well, I think that Luke and Christine care for each other, but marriage is a big step, and until they decide what they want and share it with us—" Mac paused here to make sure he had both boys' attention—"we are not going to ask them or bring the subject up. Understood?" Both boys nodded solemnly. "Okay, go get bundled up. We've got some shoveling to do."

The boy's shouts and laughter echoed back to Mac and Julia's ears as they ran for their room.

"What's the frown for?"

"Well, you just told the boys we're not going to ask Luke and Christine what's going on, and I was hoping you would talk to Luke and find out how he feels."

"Julia, my sweet, that is none of our business." His voice was patient.

"I know! That is precisely why I was trying to figure a way to find out." She stated this so matter-of-factly that Mac burst into gales of laughter. Julia hit him with a pillow, but to no avail. He was still chuckling when he was dressed and ready to leave the room.

He bent over Julia, who was buried beneath the covers in bed, his face close to hers.

"Do you know what I'm thankful for?"

Julia smiled, sure she would hear a loving endearment.

"I'm thankful that being married to Julia means never being bored." Mac kissed the tip of her nose and scooted toward the door. He slipped out an instant before another pillow sailed through the air.

"Go ahead, Luke, I don't mind staying."

"Don't be ridiculous. I'm not leaving you here."

"You haven't seen Christine since Sunday. Go, Luke! It doesn't take both of us to check on this colt."

"Forget it, Silas! We're in this together and I won't hear another word about it."

Silas turned away. When Luke made up his mind, there was no swaying him.

The men had come out that morning to find a mare had foaled unexpectedly. The colt seemed to be all right, but it was small, and for the sake of both horses it was best to be sure there was no problem.

So Luke stubbornly stood at the stall of the first-time mother and newborn colt, thankful for its safe arrival but wishing he could be with Christine.

— ❖ —

"I hate having Paul gone on the holidays. You wouldn't think with the mob we'll have here that I could miss anyone, but I do." Grandma Em's voice was wistful.

"Who is Paul the most like?"

"Oh, he's such a combination, yet he's his own person. He's a wonderful listener like Si and a gentle presence like Mark. But he can also be very commanding and behave like Luke. And like Julia, there's also that side of him that flaunts convention."

"He sounds too good to be true."

"No, no. He's far from perfect! He struggles with doubts and fears, and they sometimes get the best of him."

"You never did say what you were the most thankful for in Paul's life."

Grandma Em stopped her peeling and looked thoughtful. "I guess I'm most thankful he went to seminary school. It was no easy decision, I can tell you. He was so unhappy at the ranch. He'd been raised with those horses but he wasn't satisfied to stay on, as Luke and Silas were. He considered going into medicine. He even went out with Mark a few times, but it just wasn't for him. His letters home are filled with the joy of the Lord. So I guess I'm thankful he's where he's supposed to be and happy about it."

The women went on with their dinner preparation. The turkey was cooking and the potatoes were peeled. Christine was working on pumpkin and mincemeat pies. Both Julia and Susanne were bringing dishes so that everything would not be left to Grandma Em and Christine.

"You never asked me what I'm thankful for today."

Grandma Em looked surprised. "You're right, I didn't. Will you tell me now?" she asked kindly.

"I'm thankful for you," Christine answered with her head down, her voice quiet and thick with tears as she rolled out the pie dough. She stopped when she felt Grandma Em at her side. The women hugged and cried silently for a time.

"Do you remember how awful our first meeting was?"

"Yes, I was scared to death of you."

"I said that awful thing about you stealing."

Both women found this all highly amusing. So when the Mac-

Donald family entered a few minutes later, it was to find Christine
and Grandma Em with the giggles, their eyes still wet with tears.

Mac hugged both women and then stood regarding them in
turn "There must be something in the air. Julia has been crying
today too."

"Ours were tears of joy," Christine told him.

"Hers were too," he smiled back at her.

"Well, look at you two!" Grandma Em spoke to the little boys
standing around Mac's legs. "You look like you're ready to brave
the snow."

"We're here for Christine," Calvin announced.

"That's right, we're going to show her how to have a snowball
fight."

Christine laughed with delight and knelt down to pull both
heavily garbed boys into her arms. They both became suddenly
shy, and Christine said, "I'll go get ready."

"Not very good, am I?"

Trying to be tactful, Calvin hesitated, but Charles spoke right
out.

"You're a terrible thrower, Christine! You haven't hit a thing
you've aimed at!"

"Well, she throws it pretty far, though—just not in the right
direction." Calvin spoke now in an effort to soften Charles'
words.

Christine bit her lip to keep from laughing out loud. The boys
were so serious. Charles had generously taken her onto his team
against Calvin, but Calvin was killing them. He never missed.
Charles was a fair shot, but Christine was awful. She tried to be
optimistic.

"Well, it's my first time. Let's try it again." The boys were
agreeable and they spent some time building up their arsenal.

"Okay, I think we're ready." With that the war was on in ear-
nest. What Christine lost in throwing she made up for in ducking
Calvin's barrage. At one point he took her by surprise and hit
her right on the side of the head. She let out a false bellow of
rage that had both boys in stitches before winding up like a pro
and letting a snowball fly. As usual, her aim was quite poor at
best, but she did hit someone, causing all three snowball throw-
ers to become deathly quiet and watch as Luke wiped the snow

from his face. Knowing beyond a shadow of doubt that Christine's throw was a mistake, Luke couldn't pass up the opportunity to tackle her into the snow.

Her cheeks were cherry red with the cold and her eyes were bright with suppressed laughter. Her hat was tilted a bit and had snow on one side. Luke couldn't think when she had ever looked more beautiful.

He spoke slowly as he approached. "So this is the way I'm treated when I don't see you for three days!"

"It was an accident, I'm sorry," Christine said on a bubble of laughter.

"Oh, you sound very sorry!" Luke fought his own mirth.

This made Christine laugh harder, and she began to back away. "What are you going to do to me?"

Luke smiled at this question and Christine, a little afraid of that smile, turned and ran. She had rounded the far end of the house and thought freedom was in sight when her legs went out from under her.

Christine rolled onto her back and put both hands up to wipe the snow from her face. When she felt Luke's hands join her own, she looked up to see him kneeling beside her.

It was on the tip of her tongue to tell him what a rascal he was for knocking her in the snow, but he was leaning over her now, his eyes locked with hers, his lips descending.

"Christine," he breathed, his lips nearly touching hers.

"We'll save you, Christine!" The spell was broken. Calvin's gallant cry reached them.

Before the boys could round the corner of the house, Luke helped Christine to her feet. He pulled her into his arms and held her close under the guise of dusting the snow off her back. The boys bounced on to the scene just as he released her.

Even as the boys danced around their legs, Luke and Christine's eyes locked once again. "I'm sorry," Christine said, the words for his ears alone. Luke took her hand and squeezed it gently. "Later," she heard him say. The look in his eyes told Christine it was a promise he would keep.

The dishes were done and Susanne had just fed Elizabeth and put her down for a nap. Grandma Em called everyone into the front room. Christine was surprised as Silas sat down at the piano and played a few hymns. Everyone sang and then Grandma Em asked the children to share what they were thankful for.

Emily was thankful for a new sister and that she only cried some of the time. Charles was thankful for the snow and for turkey dinner. Calvin made Christine cry when he expressed thanks for snow and that Christine had played with them.

Luke and Christine had no time alone together, but Christine was thrilled at the way he stayed by her side throughout the day.

The day was a long and happy one. It was late before Luke and Silas left. If Christine hadn't known she would see him the next morning, she would have begged him to stay.

After Christine climbed into bed, she kept the lamp turned up and reached for her Bible. Holding it unopened, she began to pray.

Christine thanked God for the wonderful family to whom He had brought her. She knew in her heart that God had led her right to them. Tears slid down her cheeks as she thought of her grandfather, wishing with all her heart he could have met Luke and his family. She knew they would have liked one another.

Christine fell asleep hoping that at some time her grandfather had made that step of faith. She asked God to help her keep from dwelling on the subject and to go on from where she was, in obedience to His will and not to fret about things she couldn't change.

Visions of Luke and the ranch floated through her mind. Tomorrow! Tomorrow she would see him again.

"Ready to go?" Luke asked the women who stood before him.

"We've been ready to go since—"

"Yes, we're ready!" Christine interrupted Grandma Em loudly and sent her a pleading look. But it was too late.

"Up early, Christine?" Luke asked innocently.

"What makes you think that?" Christine threw over her shoulder as she moved through the snow toward the cutter.

The three of them on the seat was a tight fit, but it was nice for warmth. Christine was thankful that Luke had dropped the subject of when she awoke. She was not at all willing for him to know she had awakened very early and had paced until it was time to go.

Luke had his own reasons for not rekindling the subject. He too had risen some two hours earlier than usual and had made coffee and tried to read but ended up pacing just like Christine.

Baxter was a world of white, much to Christine's enjoyment. The trees and housetops were powdered and glistening in the morning sun.

Grandma Em was snuggled for warmth between Luke and Christine, and Christine was able to lean over the side and watch the sleigh runners race along the snow-covered ground. Her attention was brought back to the road when the horse snorted loudly and picked up his pace; home was in sight.

Christine's first close-up look of the Cameron ranch house was a sight she would never forget.

The rectangular snow-covered roof sported two chimneys, both billowing smoke. The front door, off-center and to the left, was preceded by a wide, multipillared porch.

Luke pulled up in front of the porch and surprised Christine when he took her by the waist and swung her all the way onto it. Grandma Em was shortly beside her and Silas was out to bustle them into the house.

Grandma Em went directly to the fire burning in the stove. Christine stood admiring the immense room. It was a combination front room, kitchen, and dining room. She took in the beautiful oak furnishings, from the piano to the kitchen table.

Everything was orderly, though not without its bachelor

touches: a stack of papers spread across a table by the sofa, a pair of boots standing in the corner with socks dangling from the top. The atmosphere was welcoming and this made Christine smile.

"I hope that smile means you approve." Luke was standing beside her, intently watching her face.

"I think your home is wonderful!" Christine replied in all seriousness.

"Why don't I show you the stables before you take off your coat?"

Christine readily agreed. She and Luke walked down to the stables, Luke leading the horse and cutter.

Christine stepped in when Luke threw the door open wide to admit the sleigh. She breathed deeply of the familiar aromas of hay, horses, and leather. Rows of windows allowed the November sun to stream in and take some of the chill from the air.

Christine walked along the stalls, admiring the beautiful coats and healthy looks of the Cameron's quarter horses.

Luke went to park the cutter and rub down his horse. Christine had continued her tour until she came to a stall that housed the most magnificent black stallion she had ever seen.

She stepped close to speak softly with him. "Hello there, fella. What's your name? Oh, you are a beauty! You remind me of Raven."

"Who's Raven?" Luke spoke from his place at Christine's side. She was growing accustomed to the way he could move so silently.

"Raven is my horse in Spooner."

"Is she as black as her name?"

"Yes. I helped our coachman with her birth, and when he saw her he said, 'She's as black as a raven's wing.' The next day my grandfather reminded me she had been born after midnight and on my sixteenth birthday. He gave her to me and I named her Raven." Christine stopped abruptly, feeling as though she were babbling, but Luke was fascinated.

"When is your birthday?"

"Next month."

"What day?"

"The 24th."

"The 24th! You're a Christmas Eve baby! Christine for Christmas Eve." Luke sounded delighted, but Christine was a bit embarrassed. She wished sometimes that he wouldn't watch her so intently. It was most unsettling.

"Does anyone call you Christie?" In his mind she had been Christie for some time.

"My grandfather used to. And his housekeeper, Mrs. Hall, still does."

Christine moved down the stalls then to escape those blue eyes that were able to frustrate and confuse her so.

Luke followed along, giving a short history of any horse that Christine showed an interest in. She was delighted with several foals, and Luke returned to the subject of Raven's birth. They discussed it further and he was impressed with how knowledgeable she was.

They were about halfway through when Luke asked, "Are you warm enough?"

"Oh, yes, this coat is very warm."

"I don't think I've ever told you, but it looks wonderful on you."

Christine hated herself for it, but she was embarrassed by the compliment, so she changed the subject.

"Luke, I've been meaning to ask you. How did you get to Grandma Em's ahead of me on the day my coat arrived?"

"It's no great trick, Christine, I assure you," Luke answered with a smile. "You were so angry that you didn't even see me ride directly past you."

"Oh," was all Christine could think to say before moving along and looking into the next stall. She stood for a few minutes watching the very pregnant mare within before turning to ask Luke about the animal.

To Christine's surprise Luke had stepped directly behind her, so that when she turned she found herself face-to-face with him as he bent slightly over her.

Christine couldn't move, so trapped was she by the love she saw written in his eyes.

"Christie," Luke spoke as his hands came up to frame her face, his lips brushing her forehead and then her cheek.

"I'm in love with you, Christie." The words came out in a breathless whisper just before his lips met hers.

Christine's hands came up to cling to Luke's arms in an attempt to steady herself as Luke tenderly kissed her. It was brief and sweet, and when Luke raised his head, Christine felt her hat being tugged off. Luke touched the thick tresses that fell from beneath the hat and marveled at the softness.

"I've wanted to touch your hair for so long, to see if it's as soft as it looks."

"I've been tempted to cut it many times." Christine's voice was little more than a whisper.

"If you ever cut it, I'll paddle you." Luke spoke before once again lowering his head. It was the most natural thing in the world when Luke broke the kiss for Christine to share what was in her heart.

"I love you, Luke."

"Oh, Christie, Christie, I had begun to think I would never hear you say those words. I could see it in your eyes, but I was afraid you would be too shy to say them. When, Christie, when did you first know?"

"The Sunday morning I spilled coffee on your pants and you tried so hard not to show your irritation. When was it for you?"

"Well, I must admit I was attracted to you immediately, but with you not knowing Christ, I took special care to keep the attraction in check. For me it was the night of the fire. I knew when I carried you away from the barn that I wouldn't be feeling the way I did about almost losing you if I didn't love you."

Christine beamed as she heard the words again.

"Do you know how close you come to getting kissed every time I see that smile?"

"I think so. It makes me a little bit afraid of you."

"Really, I hadn't noticed!"

Christine shook her head at him. "Calvin is right. You *are* a terrible tease!" They had begun to walk toward the door, but Luke stopped abruptly.

"Christie, did I make you cry the Sunday I teased you at Mark and Sue's?"

"No, it wasn't your teasing." She tried to keep walking, but Luke pulled her to him.

"Please tell me, Christie."

Christine hesitated and then sighed. "I had finally begun to admit to myself that I was in love with you, and when I saw you and Caroline on the couch together with Elizabeth, I thought it was hopeless." Christine's words came out with heavy reluctance, and she didn't look at Luke. "Caroline is so dainty and fair. I felt as big as Mac and as dark as a thundercloud."

"Christie!" Two fingers beneath Christine's chin tipped her head back until she was looking Luke in the eye. The tenderness she saw there, combined with the loving way he said her nick-name, had a way of breaking down all her defenses.

"Caroline Chambers is a sweet, rather spoiled girl, and I do mean girl. I am in love with a woman—a tall, beautiful woman whose green eyes and chestnut-colored hair drive me to distrac-tion."

He pulled her into his arms then and once again kissed her thoroughly.

Christine couldn't remember the walk back to the house. She was once again on the front porch with Luke, and he was telling her he loved her. He didn't kiss her this time, but held her close before opening the door to the warmth within.

46

"I think it's snowing too hard for Grandma Em and Christine to go home."

Silas looked at the miniscule flakes barely falling out of the sky. The men were walking to the stables, and Silas' laughter echoed in the cold air.

"Are you afraid Christine is going to get away from you if you let her out of your sight?"

Luke was disgusted at Silas' lack of sympathy. "You just wait, little brother"—a ridiculous statement, since Silas was only an inch shorter than the twins and a year younger. "When you fall in love, it will be *my* turn to give *you* a hard time."

Silas was undaunted. "Oh, so you've finally figured out you're in love?"

"What's that supposed to mean?"

"Well, I've known for some time."

"Is that a fact?"

"Sure, a blind man could see it. Christine blushed to the roots of her hair every time you got within ten feet of her, and you spent most of your time trying *not* to look at her."

Luke stopped dead in his tracks, so accurate was the description of his and Christine's relationship a few weeks back. Silas just thumped him on the chest and walked into the barn, still laughing. He was most pleased with himself.

— ❖ —

"Do you think it will snow too hard for us to get home?" Christine asked Grandma Em, trying not to sound too excited.

"I take it you'd rather like spending time with Luke?" Grandma Em asked kindly, wanting very much to laugh.

"Does it bother you that I'm . . . interested in Luke? Would you rather we didn't care for each other?" Grandma Em *did* laugh then. Christine was such a delightful combination of confidence and insecurity. Luke would certainly never be bored with this woman.

"Christine, I would love nothing more than to see you and Luke in love, married and filling these bedrooms with babies."

Christine was surprised speechless. Marriage? She had not thought that far. It caused an incredible flood of apprehension and worries to flow through her head. Was Luke thinking of marriage? What about all the unsolved trouble in Spooner? Maybe Luke didn't really know everything, and if he did, would he still want to marry her?

"Christine, your face tells me I just opened a Pandora's box," Grandma Em said as she poured two cups of coffee.

Not until after Christine was seated and sipping her coffee did Grandma Em speak again.

"It was not my intention to interfere, Christine. What you and Luke do is between the two of you. I'm sorry if I upset you."

"You haven't upset me—it's just that I hadn't thought as far ahead as marriage. It's not that the idea is unappealing; it's just new to me and takes a bit of getting used to."

Grandma Em reached for and patted Christine's hand. "Believe it or not, Christine, I know what you're feeling. Joseph asked me to marry him four weeks after we met. He scared me to death."

"What did you do?"

"I ran."

"You ran away?" Christine was incredulous. Emily Cameron was not a woman who ran from anything.

Grandma Em nodded slowly. "I told my mother I wanted to go visit my aunt, who lived about 30 miles away. I was there for nearly two weeks before Joseph showed up. He was furious.

"The three of us—Joseph, my aunt, and I—sat in the parlor and talked for a bit. Aunt Eleanor was thrilled that a young man had come to see me. She was sure that at 20 years of age I was destined to be an old maid. So when Joseph asked if we could go for a stroll she was delighted, and I had no time to protest as he nearly dragged me out of the house. I remember we walked and walked. He was so angry that he didn't even speak. When we finally did stop, he turned to me with such pain-filled eyes that it nearly broke my heart.

"We talked for hours. I told him of my fears and he listened patiently. I was afraid of leaving home and going to live with a man I barely knew. Joseph's practice was still unsettled. I was used to having anything my heart desired. What a materialistic young woman I was!"

Christine refilled the coffee cups and Grandma Em went on. "After I told Joseph of my fears, he just stood and looked at me for some minutes. When he spoke, Christine, his voice was quiet and deep, his heart in his eyes. 'I don't know what tomorrow holds, Emily, or if I'll be able to give you all the things your parents have. But I promise you, there won't be a day that goes by that you won't know, beyond a shadow of a doubt, that I love you with all my heart.' "

With this Grandma Em had both her and Christine in tears. "Don't, Christine, don't be afraid to talk with Luke. He is very understanding, and if you ever want to share your doubts, I promise he will listen."

Christine thanked Grandma Em for her words and the women continued to talk. By the time Silas and Luke returned, Christine was at ease again.

Within the hour Luke drove the women back to Grandma Em's. He stayed for a spell to get warmed up before heading back home.

Christine and Luke had a few minutes alone before he left.

"Thank you, Luke. It was a wonderful day."

"It was, wasn't it? The only thing missing was a good snowstorm that would have stranded you at the ranch a bit longer."

"Will I see you tomorrow?"

"I doubt it. Knowing that makes Sunday feel a week away." They stood in silence for a few minutes.

"I love you, Luke," Christine said, her eyes shimmering with unshed tears.

"Christie, why are you crying?"

Christine didn't know and could only give a small shrug. Luke was understanding and didn't push for an explanation. He simply drew her against him and held her, his cheek resting atop her head.

Much too soon he stepped back. "I have to go."

Christine tried to smile. "I'll see you Sunday."

"You'd think the way we're acting, it was going to be a year."

This did bring a smile to Christine's face, and in an instant Luke's lips were on her own. With his lips still touching hers he said, "Good night, Christie," and was gone.

47

"Good morning, Mrs. Hall. I hope I'm not calling too early."

"No, Sheriff, please come in."

"Is there someplace where we can talk?"

Mrs. Hall led the way into Joshua Bennett's study. She offered the sheriff some refreshment, but he declined.

"We found Carl Maxwell's body. He drowned."

Mrs. Hall's hand flew to her mouth and she gasped in horror.

"From the condition of the body, my guess is it was some time ago. There's no way for us to tell if it was an accident or deliberate."

"You mean suicide?" Mrs. Hall asked unbelievingly.

"No. I mean murder." Mrs. Hall sat heavily into a chair. The sheriff stood over her. He hated to upset her, but she was his link to the Bennett family and he needed her.

"Are you all right?"

Mrs. Hall fanned herself with her handkerchief. "Yes, Sheriff, I'm okay. I just wasn't expecting any news of this sort."

"I can assure you, Mrs. Hall, if there were any other way to handle this, I would."

"Of course, Sheriff." Mrs. Hall breathed deeply to compose herself. "What can I do to help?"

"Have you found anything in your search here in the study?"

"No, I've been through hundreds of papers but nothing that appears to be of utmost importance. I wish Christine were here." Mrs. Hall shot up out of the chair. "Christine! If Carl Maxwell was possibly murdered, they might be after Christine!"

"That's the next thing I needed to discuss with you." The sheriff summarized what the sheriff from Baxter had written. By the time he got to the burned man at the hotel, he was sure Mrs. Hall was going to faint.

But to his surprise she was made of tougher stuff than that. She composed herself after some minutes.

"I must admit to you, Sheriff, I have been most ignorant of how serious all this has become."

"And I'm sorry to upset you, but you can see why I need your help. I've been to see Vince Jeffers twice, and he nearly slams the door in my face over a few simple questions."

"Mr. Jeffers is not an easy man. There is something about him I can't quite place." Mrs. Hall shrugged.

"Will you write Miss Bennett about Carl Maxwell?"

"I hate to, but I really must. She needs to be on her guard. Her letters are very cheerful and I hate to put a damper on her happiness, but she must know."

"Please tell her to be careful and that I'm continuing my investigation here."

Mrs. Hall went then to prepare a light tea and handed the sheriff a few papers she had put aside. There was nothing pertinent, and as he left he encouraged her to keep searching.

48

"Oh no!"

"Bad news?"

"Yes, it's from Paul. He's not coming home for Christmas."

"Does he say why?"

"Oh, let me see." Grandma Em looked back at the letter in her hand. "It says here he'll be helping in a small church whose pastor was suddenly taken ill. He says 'As much as I want to be with you right now, these people need a pastor at Christmastime.' " Grandma Em stopped and blew her nose. "It just won't be the same without him."

Christine didn't know what to say. She knew the entire family would be sorely disappointed, since it was already December 12 and Christmas was less than two weeks away. It was too late to send Paul's gifts along to him.

"On Christmas morning we'll set aside all of Paul's gifts to box up and send to the school. They'll be waiting for him when he returns."

"That's a good idea! Thank you, Christine." Grandma Em was beginning to look happier.

Christine sensed that Grandma Em wanted to be alone, so she bundled up for a trip back downtown.

"But you just went," Grandma Em said in surprise.

"Yes, but there are a few things I forgot." Christine smiled and went out the door.

Baxter's general store was small but packed to the hilt with barrels of molasses, kerosene lamps, sacks of flour, a shiny new plow, and bolts of fabric. Christine could have looked all day.

She picked out the buttons she needed to finish Luke's Christmas present and then found two beautiful ribbons for Emily. She picked up extra yarn to finish the mittens for Calvin and Charles.

Christine took a few minutes after paying for her purchases to count out her money, and decided to pay some more on her medical bill.

The walk to Mark's place was cold, and Christine kept her head down against the wind. Had she been looking up, she would have seen a familiar horse out front.

"Well, Christine! What are you doing out on such a cold day?" Mark spoke and stepped to take her coat.

"Oh, I'm not staying. I just came to pay on my bill. Please, Mark, please let me pay without a lecture this time."

Mark agreed, but Christine could see he was not happy about it. He was still standing by the front door after Christine left when he heard Luke's footsteps on the hardwood steps.

Luke looked at the money in Mark's hand before turning questioning eyes to his brother.

"Don't say it, Luke. I've tried to talk with her, but you've got one independent woman on your hands."

Luke certainly couldn't argue with that. His hand went to his back pocket. He handed some bills to Mark. "If this doesn't cover it, let me know. If it's too much, put the balance in Christine's bank account." Luke reached for his coat and hat.

"Are you going to tell her?"

"Right now. If the next time you see me I have a few battle scars, you'll know why."

Christine had just taken off her things when Luke came in the front door.

"Hello!" he called out, and Christine came from the kitchen.

"Luke, I didn't know you were in town!"

"Actually, I was just at Mark's, but you left in such a hurry that you didn't see me."

"Oh, well, I just needed to pay on my bill and get home. It's too cold to be out."

Luke took Christine's hand and led her over to the couch. "I talked to Mark after you left. I paid off your bill." Luke watched as a frown covered Christine's face.

"Why?" she asked flatly.

"Why what?"

"Don't mince words with me, Luke. I don't like to be a burden to anyone. You did not need to pay my bill."

"I realize I didn't need to pay your bill, but I wanted to. It was no burden. I had the money and it was my pleasure."

Christine couldn't come up with an argument after the simple, practical way he stated his case.

Luke watched as she stood and paced a bit before coming to stand before him.

"It just doesn't seem right."

"I love you, Christine, and I want to take care of you. What could be wrong with that?" Again she had no argument.

Christine stood for a moment in thought before bending and kissing Luke's cheek. "Thank you," she stated humbly, and Luke knew it had cost her. He was sure that in her own mind she was accepting a handout.

Before Luke could yield to the temptation of pulling her down into his lap he said, "Where's Gram?"

Christine sat beside him before she spoke. "I think she's upstairs. Your brother Paul wrote and he's not coming home for Christmas. I'm sorry, Luke."

Luke's face fell. "Our first Christmas without Paul! It won't be easy. I'll go up and see her."

Christine went into the kitchen to work on lunch. She prayed for Grandma Em and the family, asking God to give them a special peace about Paul's absence. She ended her prayer with a thankful heart that God had led her to a man as kind and sensitive as Luke Cameron.

49

"Hey, you're all bundled up! Don't tell me you're going some-where. I just arrived."

"Luke, I got a letter from Spooner today. I need to go see Mark. Will you take me and then stay while we talk?"

Luke looked at Christine's face. She was pale and he could tell she had been crying. Wordlessly he led her to the cutter. Some of the snow had melted off and Christine wondered absently whether Christmas, only a few days away, would be a white one.

When Luke and Christine arrived, with Christine obviously up-set, Maggie discreetly took the children and withdrew upstairs with them.

After the four adults were alone, Mark astutely guessed the problem. "You've heard from Spooner."

Christine nodded. "Mrs. Hall's letter came today. Carl Maxwell is dead. Mark, how could God let this happen? Carl was the only one who could answer my questions." Christine began to cry and Luke's arms went around her from his place next to her on the divan.

Sue's eyes also filled with tears and Mark reached for her hand.

"Christine," Mark said after she had composed herself, "what else did the letter say?"

Christine sniffed and pulled the letter from her skirt pocket. She handed it to Mark, who read it and then gave it to Luke.

"Listen, Christine, Mrs. Hall has not finished going through your grandfather's things yet. The sheriff is still on the job. And I think you've known deep in your heart for some time now that Carl Maxwell was probably dead. Am I right?"

Christine nodded.

Luke spoke up, correctly reading her mind. "Christine, none of this is your fault. I'm sure you feel helpless, but right now all that any of us can do is trust God to straighten this out."

Mark and Sue added their words of encouragement and Chris-tine began to feel somewhat better. When Christine seemed in control again, Sue went to the kitchen to fix coffee. Mark went with her.

Once Luke and Christine were alone, Christine stood up and moved away from him. She didn't look at him when she spoke.

"Everyone I get close to dies. If you don't want to see me anymore, Luke, I'll understand."

Luke was across the room in an instant and taking Christine's arms in his hands. Turning her around to face him, his words of rebuke at her foolish talk died in his throat at the misery he saw in her eyes. How could he explain to her that he was in over his head? If he told her about the burned man now, it would scare her witless. And the idea of no longer seeing her was like asking Luke Cameron to stop breathing.

"Christine, you haven't been listening to me. I love you. When a person loves someone, he doesn't run when he's needed the most. I'm going to be here beside you, taking care of you, loving you, and praying for you until you're sick of me."

"I will *never* be sick of you."

Susanne had started through the door back into the living room when she stopped so abruptly that Mark nearly ran into the back of her with the tray he was carrying.

Shifting to one side, Mark saw what had stopped his wife. In the front room stood Luke, holding in his arms the woman he loved. Knowing the way Christine was hurting, Mark and Sue wouldn't have interrupted them for anything, save another fire.

Mark put the tray back in the kitchen and leaned against the counter. "I think my brother had the right idea," Mark said as he pulled Sue against him. Sue looked up as she leaned against Mark's chest, her head not even up to her husband's chin.

"It's almost like watching *you* out there holding Christine."

Mark's eyebrows rose in surprise. "I can see, Mrs. Cameron, that if you've had time for such wild ideas, I've been neglecting you. I will remedy that instantly."

Susanne giggled and raised her mouth for his kiss.

The Cameron twins' thoughts at that moment were running on identical tracks: Home is anywhere as long as this woman is in my arms.

50

Christmas Eve Day. Christine lay in bed and stared up at the ceiling. If she were in Spooner right now and her grandfather were alive, they would be getting ready to go uptown for their traditional birthday breakfast. They had missed only one year since Christine was seven. The year she had turned 12 there was a blizzard, and Grandfather didn't want to risk getting caught in it.

Twenty years old! "Thank You, Lord," Christine prayed, "for finding me now when I still have most of my life to live with You in my heart." At the thought that her life might be cut short by a selfish man's greed, Christine pushed out of bed and refused to dwell on the idea.

Christine found Grandma Em up and breakfast ready. Grandma Em hugged Christine in the doorway. "Happy birthday, Christine!" Christine was surprised, since the only person she had told was Luke.

Grandma Em led her to the table. Christine was speechless as she sat down at her place to find a small, brightly wrapped package.

"I don't know what to say."

"Don't say anything. Just open it."

Under the wrapping Christine found a small black-bound diary.

"I know you came from Spooner without your things. The new year is upon us, and with all the changes you've been through, I thought you might find this helpful. Recording answers to prayer and then looking back on them can really lift your spirits."

Christine was too moved to speak. She turned the pages to see that Grandma Em had written in the front, "Happy 20th Birthday, Christine. May God bless you today and always. Love, Grandma Em. Proverbs 3:5,6."

Moving around the table, Christine kissed Grandma Em's cheek and hugged her. "Thank you," she said softly.

"You're welcome." Grandma Em smiled at her. "We've got a full day ahead of us. Let's eat."

Grandma Em was not kidding about the schedule. Silas would be bringing a tree in this afternoon and the parlor needed to be readied. At 6:00 there was to be a Christmas Eve service at church, and then the Cameron family would be headed back to trim Grandma Em's tree and have cookies with hot apple cider.

The day rushed by in a flurry of activity. Christine took a bath and dressed for the evening with special care. The dress she had made for the season was a deep green, near the color of her eyes. It had a high neck with long sleeves and a stark white collar and cuffs. Christine's hair, freshly washed, was brushed out and left long down her back.

The women were ready to go when Luke and Silas arrived to collect them. Christine was surprised but not disappointed when she saw Silas lead Grandma Em to a larger sleigh, one she had never seen before, while Luke guided her to the cutter and bundled her inside. The night air was crisp and Christine snuggled close to Luke.

The service that evening was one that Christine would never forget. The lamps were low, Pastor Nolan explained, because he didn't want the people to follow along in their Bibles but to just listen as he read.

"Luke 2. And it came to pass in those days that there went out a decree from Caesar Augustus that all the world should be taxed. (And this taxing was first made when Cyrenius was governor of Syria.) And all went to be taxed, everyone into his own city. And Joseph also went up from Galilee, out of the city of Nazareth, into Judaea, unto the city of David, which is called Bethlehem (because he was of the house and lineage of David), to be taxed with Mary, his espoused wife, being great with child. And so it was that, while they were there, the days were accomplished that she should be delivered. And she brought forth her firstborn son, and wrapped him in swaddling clothes, and laid him in a manger, because there was no room for them in the inn. And there were in the same country shepherds abiding in the field, keeping watch over their flock by night. And, lo, the angel of the Lord came upon them, and the glory of the Lord shone round about them, and they were sore afraid. And the angel said unto them, 'Fear not, for behold, I bring you good tidings of great joy, which shall be to all people. For unto you is born this day in the city of David a Saviour, who is Christ the Lord. And this shall be a sign unto you: Ye shall find the babe wrapped in swaddling clothes, lying in a manger.' And suddenly there was with the angel a multitude of the heavenly host, praising God and saying, 'Glory to God in the highest, and on earth peace, good will toward men.' And it came to pass, as the angels were gone away from them into heaven, that the shepherds said to one another, 'Let us now go even unto Bethlehem, and see this thing which is come to pass, which the Lord hath made known unto us.' And they came with haste, and found Mary and Joseph and the babe lying in a manger. And when they had seen it, they made known abroad the saying which was told them concerning this child. And all they that heard it wondered at those things which were told them by the shepherds. But Mary kept all these things and pondered them in her heart. And the shepherds returned, glorifying and praising God for all the things that they had heard and seen, as it was told unto them."

Christmas took on a new meaning for Christine that night. She sat in awe as she thought of God coming to earth in the form of a tiny infant to one day become the Savior of her soul.

No hymnbook was opened and no music was played, but the congregation raised their voices in one accord. They sang with reverence and thanksgiving in their hearts.

Christine cried through most of the service and had to ask Luke for his handkerchief. When Pastor Nolan ended the service, Luke bent to tell Christine he had offered to douse the lamps and close up.

There were many hugs and much laughter. And when the last person left, Christine went to the stove for warmth as she waited for Luke to finish.

When the only light was a lamp burning up front and the fire, Luke joined Christine by the stove.

"Oh, Luke, it was such a beautiful service!"

He smiled tenderly.

"It makes such a difference hearing the story of Christ's birth when that same Christ lives within you."

They stood quietly together, unsure if the warmth they felt came from the fire without or within.

Luke reached into his pocket and brought out a thin gold chain. He held it for Christine's inspection. Hanging from the chain was a delicate gold locket, in the middle of which was a tiny diamond.

Luke waited until her eyes raised to his. "Happy birthday, Christine."

Christine struggled desperately to keep from crying and ruining this precious moment. Luke moved behind her and, raising his arms, clasped the necklace on her.

When Christine felt the locket drop below her throat, her fin-

ger reached for it and she gently opened it up to reveal an empty
space within. Her eyes went questioningly to Luke.

"I was hoping you would put our picture inside, Christine—
our wedding picture."

Christine's breath caught in her throat. She could only stare
at the man before her.

"I wanted to ask you here, Christine, in church so you would
know I've prayed and trusted God in this. Christine, will you
marry me?"

"Oh, yes, Luke!" Christine spoke without hesitation and went
into his arms. Luke held her as if he would never let her go, and
Christine clung to him.

"When, Christine, when will you marry me?"

"Anytime you want." Christine was in a daze.

"January."

"But that's next month!" she answered, some sanity returning.

"January 21st. That's four weeks from today."

It was on the tip of her tongue to tell him it was too soon, but
she looked into his eyes and knew she wanted it as well.

Without a word Christine nodded her head and Luke kissed
her with all the love and longing he felt. In that kiss Christine
knew it would be the same for her as it had been for Grandma
Em. Every day she would awake and know that Luke Cameron
loved her with all his heart.

51

January 5, 1888

My Dear Christie,

My heart is filled with joy over your wedding plans. I wish I could be there, and you know I would be if it were at all possible.

I continue on here, as I hope is your want. The house is in fine order and the horses are well taken care of. The sheriff spoke to the bank as you requested, and extra money was made available for salaries and household needs.

I hope this finds you safe. Please write and tell me about the wedding.

Love,

Mrs. Hall

"Her letter is a little shorter than usual and she didn't say anything about my accepting Christ," Christine commented to Luke as they sat at Grandma Em's kitchen table.

"Maybe she's afraid it will change things and she'll be out of a job."

"I've been thinking about that. I will have to go back home at some point. Things aren't really settled with grandfather's estate."

"When are you going to start thinking of Baxter as home?"

Christine could only stare at Luke, unsure of what he meant. Luke tugged on a strand of her hair. "I was just teasing, Christine. I didn't mean to upset you."

"There are times I don't know where home is, Luke. Can you understand that?"

"Considering what the last year of your life has been like, it's completely natural." He stood up. "I've got to go. As usual, I told Si I wouldn't be long, and then I stop over here and you won't let me leave."

"Oh no you don't, Luke Andrew Cameron! You're not going to blame your tardiness on me!" Christine shook her finger at him.

"You, Madam," Luke said with mock sternness, "are entirely too big for your britches and much too sassy. That is all going to change after we're married. Is that understood?"

"Yes, Luke," Christine answered with all the meekness she could muster.

"All right. Now act like a good wife and get my coat and hat." Christine moved like a humble servant and barely kept a straight face. While Luke was putting his coat and hat on, Christine moved around the kitchen table away from him.

"All right, I'm ready to go. You may come and kiss me good-bye."

"No."

Luke regarded his playfully defiant fiancée from across the table.

"Come here, Christie." His voice was no longer commanding but deep and persuasive.

Christine shook her head and stepped away from him as he moved toward her. His use of her nickname told her she would be kissed or he wouldn't be leaving.

"Come here, Christie, come and kiss me."

"You'd better kiss him, Christine, or Silas is going to end up feeding all those horses by himself." Grandma Em spoke matter-of-factly as she brought up jars of fruit from the basement.

Luke looked barely patient at the interruption but Christine was highly amused. She sauntered out from the kitchen to the parlor. "I'll walk you to the door." Her eyes told Luke she felt victorious.

"Bye, Gram."

"Bye, Luke."

"You think you're pretty clever, don't you?" They were at the front door and Luke was buttoning his coat.

"Pretty and clever, both," was Christine's sassy reply.

Luke threw back his head and roared with laughter. Christine never failed to delight him. Long after he kissed her goodbye and headed home, he was still laughing.

52

"Do you have the ring?"

"Yes, Luke. For the third time, I have the ring." Silas was calm as always, a steady rock in the storm.

"Did Julia get all of Christine's things moved in?"

"Last night. Christine will bring the last of her things after the ceremony."

"Does the house look okay?"

"It looks fine."

"Listen, Si. I've been thinking, and I just don't feel good about you staying with Grandma Em. This is your home. I don't want to do anything that will make you feel unwelcome. I know Christine feels the same . . ."

"Luke!" Silas' raised voice stopped Luke's tirade. He never shouted and Luke stood speechless.

"I do not feel that you and Christine are kicking me out of the house. It was my idea and it will only be for two nights. I'll be back Monday. Luke, you are bringing your bride home tonight and it's her I'm thinking of. The two of you need time alone together, if only for a few days, to start off your marriage on the right foot." Silas' voice was more firm than Luke had ever heard it.

Luke was grateful for Silas' words and nodded his agreement.

"Besides," Silas spoke as they headed out of the house, "you're only going to have her until Monday. Come Tuesday morning, she'll get one look at my hairy face and go screaming from the house." The men laughed at the long-standing joke and the tension evaporated.

The 2:00 o'clock sun was shining brightly overhead as Silas mounted his horse and Luke climbed into the cutter. They had a wedding to attend.

"How does it look?"

"You look beautiful," Julia said earnestly.

"I look ten feet tall in all white," Christine replied with dismay. Julia and Susanne dissolved into giggles; both women agreed they had never seen a more radiant bride.

The women were in Grandma Em's room, and with less than

an hour to the 3:00 o'clock ceremony Christine looked about to come unglued.

"She needs to see Luke," Julia said softly.

"I need my grandfather." Tears filled Christine's eyes as she spoke. "He should be here, to give me away. And Paul—Paul wasn't able to come, and that's not right." She was becoming frantic.

Christine did not notice Sue leave the room. But she was back momentarily, and with Grandma Em. She and Julia left them alone.

Upon seeing Grandma Em, Christine burst into tears. Grandma Em, drawing wisdom from every one of her 70 years, said nothing—not a word about teardrops on her wedding dress or how close it was to 3:00.

She knew Christine had slept poorly last night and had eaten nothing today. She also remembered how her own father had been too ill to walk her down the aisle and how devastated she had felt over this.

"I don't know what's wrong with me," Christine finally choked out. "I love Luke and I want to marry him. I just don't know what's wrong."

Grandma Em gently pulled Christine to the desk chair. She then moved the rocker close and began to pray. "Dear Father, help Christine. Please draw her near to Your throne, where she can find comfort and rest for emotions she herself may not even understand. You know of the love she and Luke have for each other. Calm her nerves and give her a peaceful heart to go down and marry the man she loves. If, Lord, there has been blindness, and Luke and Christine are not to be wed, please put Your hand down and prevent this marriage. Speak to Christine's heart so she will know Your will. We give this day and its glory to You. Amen."

Grandma Em sat quietly as Christine dried her face. "Would you like me to go get Luke? You know he'll come in an instant if you ask him."

Christine looked at the clock. 3:10. "Do you think he's upset with me?"

"No. Probably worried, but not upset."

Christine took a deep breath. "Will you please send Silas up in about five minutes?"

"I most certainly will. Do you want help with anything? Maybe Julia should come back up."

"No, I'll be fine. Thanks, Gram." Grandma Em didn't miss the use of the nickname that her grandchildren used. She hugged Christine and nearly glowed with happiness as she left the room.

Christine stepped before the full-length mirror. Her hair was still in place, swept up in curls atop her head.

Her dress was snow-white satin. The skirt was full and gathered at the waist. Puffed sleeves at the shoulder fit snugly along Christine's arms and buttoned tightly at the wrist. The satin on the bodice was overlayed with handmade lace that ran in a V from the nipped-in waist to a high, stand-up collar. The same pearl buttons that buttoned at the wrist ran full length down Christine's back.

Luke loved Christine's hair and had asked her not to cover it. Christine was taking a close-up check for signs of tears when Silas knocked.

Silas kissed her cheek before offering his left arm. They paused at the top of the stairs. "Are you okay?"

Christine nodded. "Thanks, Si."

Luke stood in the parlor awaiting his bride. The urge to go to her had been nearly overpowering, but Grandma Em had told him that all was fine and that Christine would be down in about five minutes. He didn't care that the ceremony hadn't started on time or that the kids were getting squirmy; he just wanted to see Christine and know she was all right.

The relief he felt upon hearing the rustle of her dress on the stairs just before she came into view was poignantly sweet.

Nothing could have prepared Luke for the vision of Christine in her wedding dress. He could only stare. Christine's eyes searched his out and the rest of the room faded from view.

Christine remembered little of the ceremony. She would always cherish Luke's eyes as he said "I do," the pressure of his hand holding hers, watching his hand slip the ring onto her finger, and their first kiss as man and wife, tender and warm.

Mark and Julia had stood up with them. Pastor Nolan performed the ceremony while Mrs. Nolan played the piano. The parlor was filled with family and friends from church.

The reception was well under way. Gram, Julia, and Sue had prepared a feast. When Luke and Christine were finally seated, their plates full, Luke asked, "Are you okay?"

"Just an attack of nerves. Are you angry?"

"Furious," Luke stated with a smile.

The time flew by, and before long everyone was at the front

door waving and shouting blessings and good wishes to the newlyweds as the cutter bore them away.

The horse's fast pace and the gusty wind made conversation nearly impossible. Christine was starting to feel chilled as they reached the house.

Christine was picked up and carried into the front room of the ranch house, then set down and a lamp lit before either person uttered a word.

"Welcome home, Mrs. Cameron."

Christine's face glowed with happiness. "I like the sound of that."

Luke handed Christine the lamp. "Go get warmed up while I take care of the horse."

Christine stood still a few moments after the door closed behind Luke, smiling at her surroundings.

With the lamp in one hand and a small suitcase in the other, Christine headed toward the hallway that led off the dining area.

Luke's room, and now hers, was halfway down the hall and at the back of the house. It was a huge room with a massive four-poster bed, a matched set of wardrobes, and the largest bureau that Christine had ever seen. In one corner, having been stoked that afternoon, burned a wood stove, making the room comfortably warm.

Julia had shown Christine through the bedrooms the week before. She ran her hand over the beautiful quilt on the bed. Luke's mother had made it—a mother-in-law that Christine would not know personally, but only through Luke's words and her handiwork here and there in the house.

Christine opened the wardrobe door. Seeing her things hanging beside Luke's gave her a feeling of contentment. She heard a door close and knew that Luke was back.

Luke followed the light from Christine's lamp and found her in his bedroom, *their* bedroom. Upon entering, Luke closed the door and leaned against it.

Christine was still in her wedding dress, her hair coming loose around her face. Luke was in his dark suit and crisp white shirt, so tall and handsome. Husband and wife stood in silence regarding each other. Luke spoke from his place at the door.

"Christine, it's been a long day. I know you're tired, and if you'd rather . . ." Luke halted as Christine moved toward him, her heart swelling with love at how thoughtful he was of her well-being.

When she stood directly in front of him, all she could think to say was, "I love you, Luke."

Luke understood and drew Christine to him, hardly able to believe that a man could be so happy and blessed.

Theirs was a love sprung deep from within, willing and able to stand the test of time, come what may, with Christ at the head of their home.

53

Never would Luke or Silas have believed they could be so spoiled so quickly: baked goods in abundance, hot meals served, coffee always waiting on the stove, the house spotless, and clothes always clean—all brought on by Christine's presence.

Christine was a morning person, and Luke's only complaint was that the warm person beside him all night was not there most mornings when he awoke. But the warm kitchen and hot coffee could not be faulted.

For nearly two weeks Christine laughed at the sight of her new brother-in-law first thing in the morning. Silas would try to act as grumpy as he looked, but Christine only laughed harder and he gave up.

Every Thursday Christine spent the day at Grandma Em's. Christine insisted upon coming back once a week to help out. There had been a battle, but Christine won.

"You'd think I was 100 years old the way you're acting."

"I do not think you are 100 years old. I know very well you'll be 71 next month, but that's beside the point."

"But, Christine, you have your own house to take care of now!" Grandma Em said as she tried a new approach.

"My house is not going to suffer the one day I come to see you. Now, what day shall we make it?" Grandma Em was stubbornly silent.

"All right! I'll pick a day myself. Thursday. I'll be here Thursday morning at 8:00."

"Less than a month you've been married, and she sounds just like you," Grandma Em said accusingly to Luke, who was sitting quietly on the couch, watching his wife in battle.

Luke opened his mouth to defend himself, but Christine broke in. "Luke has nothing to do with this. It was my idea, and I will not change my mind."

Grandma Em could see she was not going to win this battle, but she was not about to give in gracefully. "Is your salary to be the same as before?" Grandma Em asked innocently.

Christine was out of her chair in a flash and standing, arms akimbo before her husband. "Talk to her! Tell your grandmother I *will* be here on Thursdays to give her a hand and if she gives me one cent, I'll burn it!" This said, Christine stomped into the kitchen. Luke and Grandma Em listened a minute as she banged and slammed around preparing some coffee.

"How do you really feel about Christine coming?"

"I'm delighted to have her."

"That's what I thought," Luke said, his eyes twinkling. "You really shouldn't have teased her. You got me in trouble."

"That was the best part!" Grandma Em replied as she headed to the kitchen to make her peace with Christine.

54

Using the back of her hand, Mrs. Hall brushed a fallen strand of hair from her face. Her eyes fell on a small slip of paper sticking out of a stack she was reading through. 284539. She contemplated the odd set of numbers for a time before setting the paper aside.

Sunday was no time to be going through the study at the Bennett residence, but she was drawing close to the end and was anxious to be done. Her fingers went to her temples and she rubbed gently. 284539. What an odd combination of numbers. Combination! The safe! Mrs. Hall reached quickly for the paper. She had nearly forgotten the safe.

Mrs. Hall went to a small wood cabinet that sat inconspicuously behind the desk below the two windows. The door opened easily to reveal the black safe within.

Mrs. Hall looked again at the numbers in her hand and then knelt on the floor. The first two tries with the dial were unsuccessful, but on the third attempt she heard a click. Reaching carefully for the handle, she turned it and pulled.

Her heart was pounding as she swung the door open. She rose quickly and moved the desk lamp close. A musty smell hit her nose when she resumed her place on the floor.

For a moment she touched nothing, but she held the lamp high and peered within the small cavern of the safe. A large, yellowish bundle of papers caught her eye and she reached for it.

Mrs. Hall recognized Joshua Bennett's own handwriting on the first page. It took the weary housekeeper some minutes to realize she was reading a will—Joshua Bennett's last will and testament written in his own hand.

With sudden clarity Mrs. Hall was transported back through time: ". . . she will receive the house and stables along with the rest of my holdings. In the event of her death, the inheritance will go to my partner, Vince Jeffers." Carl Maxwell had read those words in a quiet, almost apologetic voice.

What a blind fool she had been! To be sure of her theory, she quickly scanned the pages in her hand. There was not a word about Vince Jeffers. Nearly everything was left unconditionally to Christine.

Mrs. Hall struggled up from her cramped position on the floor. Donning her coat and hat, she quickly grabbed up the incriminating papers and rushed for the front door.

— ❖ —

"I think we should eat at 7:00. How is that for your families?"

"Sounds fine," Julia answered.

"No problem that I can think of," Susanne said, then added, "Pending as always Mark's work. We'll just bring Grandma Em with us."

"Julia, are you going to do the pies?" Christine asked.

"I'd planned on it. I put up jars and jars of peaches, and that's her favorite."

"Okay, Sue's doing a chocolate cake and I'm covering supper, so I think we're all set." Christine would have said more, but the moment Grandma entered the kitchen, the three women stopped talking.

When the silence lengthened through Grandma Em washing a spot on her dress, she became suspicious. "Why do I get the distinct feeling I was being discussed?" Grandma Em asked while approaching the table.

The women knew she had to be told, but they hated to spoil her Sunday. In their hesitation, she figured it out for herself.

"Oh, you girls! You're planning something for Friday, aren't you? I told you last year there would be no more parties, but you didn't listen. You need to be spanked and I'm going to go get your husbands."

Christine looked a bit thunderstruck, but Julia and Susanne had heard all this before.

Within minutes Mac, Luke, and Mark entered the kitchen. Julia stood and gave Mac her chair. As she expected, she was pulled down into his lap as soon as he was settled. Mark stood behind Susanne, his hands resting on her shoulders. Luke took the chair next to Christine after moving it close beside hers.

"Where are the children?" Sue asked. "Emily is out for the count on the sofa and the boys went out to play with Silas," her husband answered.

"And Gram?"

"She headed upstairs after telling us you three were in plot against her."

"You must have been discussing Friday," Luke guessed, since he and Christine had already talked it over.

"Is it true she says no more parties every year?" Christine wanted to know.

"Just about, but she loves them and always has more fun than anyone else."

"By March, when the cold weather feels like it's never going to end, everyone is in need of a party."

The six adults talked around the table for awhile. When Christine heard one of the boys run by outside and Silas call to him, she commented absently and to no one in particular, "I wish Silas were in here with his wife."

It was a subject that had crossed everyone's mind at one time or another.

"Has Si said anything to you, Christine? About wanting a wife, I mean?"

"No, not directly, or even indirectly, for that matter. It's just that at times he looks a bit lost and lonely. I didn't mean to make you cry, Julia." Christine felt bad.

Julia shook her head in mute apology over the display of tears and Mac said, "It's not your fault, Christine. Some people are born with an overabundance of tears. Julia has enough for six people." Everyone laughed at this, and the spell was broken.

They continued to talk and make plans until Elizabeth began to complain about an empty stomach from the cradle in the parlor.

Soon everyone broke up to return to their own homes, the prospect of a party on Friday buoying everyone's mood.

— ❖ —

"I need to see Mr. Jeffers." The sheriff in Spooner spoke as soon as the housekeeper allowed him into the entryway.

"I'm terribly sorry, but he's not home. Perhaps you'd like to leave a message."

"When will he be back? It's urgent."

The housekeeper hesitated.

"I repeat, it is urgent that I speak with him."

"He's not here and I don't know where he is. When I arrived this morning, there was only a note saying he would be away and to keep the house in order." The servant looked frightened.

"Let me see the note." The sheriff's voice was abrupt in his agitated state over Vince Jeffers getting away. The housekeeper scurried to comply with the order.

Upon reading it and taking a quick look around, the sheriff's hopes plummeted. From all appearances, Vince Jeffers had disappeared without a trace.

Luke rolled and stretched, his body protesting the idea of getting out of bed. When something tickled his nose, Luke reached up and pulled away a stray hair. He smiled as it just kept coming. He wound the strand from Christine's head around his finger.

It was time, he knew—time to come clean and confess to Christine what he had been holding back. He had been feeling the pain of disobedience in his heart long enough. It was time to talk with his wife and to trust God.

"Oh, Luke, I thought you would be up! I really need to make that bed. I have so much to get done before the party." Christine spoke as she bustled around the room.

The party for Grandma Em. Luke had forgotten all about it. "Tomorrow, Lord," Luke promised; "tomorrow I'll tell her."

"Luke Cameron, are you going to get out of that bed today?" Christine stood at the foot, her brows raised in question.

"You could come over and help me up." Luke's voice was gravelly with sleep.

"Do I have your word that you will come out and I won't get pulled in?" At Luke's silence, Christine laughed. "I thought not." With a flick of her wrist Christine threw back the covers, causing Luke to shiver and leap for the stove.

"You're a cruel woman," he grumbled as he dressed quickly. But Christine had the bed half made and just ignored him.

When the men came back in from the horses, Christine asked about the road. "I really need to get to town. The storm this week has put me behind schedule. I didn't even get to Grandma Em's this week."

Silas answered her. "I've got to go in this afternoon. You can go with me."

"That's fine, Si, thanks. I can have supper almost ready before we go."

It crossed Luke's mind to tell Christine he would rather she stay inside today. Knowing she would ask why and that he had no reason, he held his tongue.

"You're sure?"

"Yes, I'm sure. I'll go straight over as soon as I'm done here and ride with them. You go back and I'll see you tonight."

"Okay, but you be careful."

"I'll be fine. Thanks for the ride, Silas."

Christine turned away, but Silas still hesitated at the door of the general store. His business in town had been brief, and he had heard from some buyers and wanted to get home to tell Luke. Christine was to go to Mark and Sue's for a ride home. Silas went ahead out to the sleigh. Christine was a big girl and she would make the two blocks safely.

"Is it almost time?" Emily danced around her mother's legs.

"Almost. I've got to wrap up this cake and bundle up your sister. Don't forget, we have to pick up Grandma Em too."

"Won't Aunt Christine be surprised that we're coming early to help?"

"I'm sure she will. Now don't forget to say Happy Birthday to Grandma Em when we see her, and don't tell her what's in the box we wrapped."

"I won't. Is it time to tell Daddy we're ready?"

"Yes, you go ahead and tell him about 15 minutes."

Emily, always happy to be of help, skipped off toward her father's office.

"Red or blue," Christine said under her breath. She needed calico for the border of her new quilt and could go with either color.

"Ma'am." A voice broke through her thoughts.

Christine looked down at the small child standing beside her. She did not remember seeing this child before. Wordlessly, Christine was handed a note and the child ran from the store. She stared after him in some surprise before reading the paper in her hand.

"Christine," it read, "come immediately to the house. Grandma Em has been hurt."

The note was unsigned, but Christine was sure it was from

Mark. The snow was deep and it hindered Christine's progress as she rushed with a fearful heart. Of all things! Grandma Em injured on her 71st birthday!

Christine quickly climbed the front porch steps and rushed in the front door.

"Gram!" Christine called as she quickly unbuttoned her coat and moved into the parlor.

"By all means, Christine, take off your coat. You're going to be here awhile."

Christine's movements stilled and she felt her blood run cold. Until that moment she believed she would never hear the voice of Vince Jeffers again.

He was seated on the sofa. Resting beside him on the seat and close on his right was a long, wicked-looking knife.

"Take off your coat, Christine." This time it was an order, and Christine obeyed. She laid the coat over the nearest chair and looked up to see Vince's eyes moving over her. A leering smile played across his lips and Christine felt dirty beneath his perusal.

"Please, God," Christine thought, asking for she knew not what, just needing to cry out to her Savior.

"What are you doing here, Vince?" Christine was amazed at how calm her voice sounded.

"I'm surprised you have to ask that, Christine. You didn't actually think I was going to let you get away with all that money, did you?"

"What money?" Christine asked in genuine confusion.

Vince's scornful laugh grated on Christine's nerves. "You're as big a fool as your grandfather was," he snarled at her as he stood up.

Christine was still completely baffled, and Vince could see this. She watched, horrified, as the snarl on his face became almost a pleasant smile. This man was mad.

"The railroad stocks," he informed her, as if he were announcing the time of day.

"The railroad stocks? The ones you advised Grandfather to sell because they were worthless?"

"Yes, one and the same. He was a fool. He never even checked on my story—just handed me the papers so I could take care of it."

"But the stocks are worth something after all?" Christine asked, trying desperately to get some understanding of the situation while praying constantly for help, helpless as it was. No one knew that Vince Jeffers was here or that she was at Grandma Em's.

"Worth something?" Again that scornful laugh. "They're worth a small fortune, but I can't touch it. By the time I realized I needed your grandfather's signature, he was already dead.

"No, I didn't kill him," Vince assured her upon seeing the look on her face. "But it was very nice of him to die when he did. I really am in deep financial trouble, you know." He stated this so calmly that Christine felt her stomach lurch.

"Do I nauseate you, Christine?" Vince had not missed the look of revulsion on her face, and he approached slowly as he spoke. "That's really a shame, you know." He was almost next to her. "Because we're going to get to know one another very well." Christine had backed up flush against the wall and Vince stopped within inches of her. His hand came up to her face and Christine tried to turn into the wall. Vince fed on her fear, and his laugh was a low hiss as sour breath fell on her face. She felt his fingers at the side of her neck. "Yes, Christine, very well indeed."

"It's Mark," Silas said from his place at the window.

Luke felt relief wash over him. He had been anxious all day about Christine and couldn't wait to see her.

Grandma Em was the first one in the house. Silas and Luke both hugged her before she could get her coat off, wishing her birthday greetings. Not until Susanne and Emily were inside, and Mark, with the baby in his arms, began to shut the door did Luke ask.

"Where's Christine?" The room became completely still at his question.

"Isn't she here, Luke?" Mark asked.

Silas broke in. "She was supposed to come to your house after she was done in town and ride back here with you."

"We left a little early. Maybe she missed us," Grandma Em suggested.

"It wasn't that early," Mark said, his eyes locked with Luke's.

Luke felt as if the walls were closing in. The feeling of dread and worry that Christine was in trouble had been with him all day, and already it could be too late. He took control just as the MacDonalds walked in the door.

"Silas, take Mac's sleigh and ride for the sheriff. I'll go with

Mark. Bring him as fast as you can to Grandma Em's. Mac, stay here. Sue can explain everything." In a flurry of grabbed coats and hats the three men were out the door.

Luke never would have believed the ride to town could take so long. Mark was whipping the horse into a near frenzy in order to gain speed but the snow was deep and it seemed as though an eternity had passed.

As his stomach churned in fear, Luke allowed himself to imagine that Christine was all right. He pictured her shopping in the general store, ignorant of anyone intending to harm her.

But the image did not last. The sense of foreboding which had rode him hard throughout the day assured him—Christine was in danger. How could he possibly live with himself knowing his own sin had cost him the most precious person in his life.

"Please God," Luke prayed under his breath as both sleighs nearly flew into town, "please let us be on time."

"Take your shoes off!" Vince suddenly snapped into Christine's face. When Christine hesitated, again feeling a sickening horror at his change of moods, he picked up the knife. "I've always hated it that you were taller than me." Christine moved quickly to do as he bade. The low heeled boots made little difference, but he seemed pleased.

His eyes were undressing her again and Christine thought frantically on how to divert his attention.

"Vince, do you know anything about Carl Maxwell's death?"

"Don't mention that spineless fool to me." He waved the knife around as he spoke. "I needed a new partner to help me with a few things in your grandfather's estate but he turned out to be a gutless idiot. Oh, he had no trouble drawing up that fake will but he became quite squirmish when I said you had to die. He thought he was so clever, sending you to Fall Creek."

"Did you kill that man in Fall Creek?" Christine whispered.

"No, no, that was just a freak thing. It caused me a lot of trouble too—you running all the way down here. It took us forever to find you and then when we did, my man couldn't even burn a barn properly. Never send a boy to do a man's work." Vince sneered, his face an ugly scowling mask.

What little color was left in Christine's face drained away. The barn burning was attempted murder! "Oh, God," she prayed silently, "please help me!"

"How many people have you killed in your greed, Vince? What was in grandfather's will that you had to change? He was good and generous." Christine was crying now, not even sure of what she was saying, and it angered Vince.

"Stop your blubbering. Your grandfather was soft. Why, he left over a thousand dollars to that orphanage. What a waste! Carl Maxwell was soft too, and he got in my way." The sneer in Vince's voice softened as he approached Christine again. "And you're going to find out, Christine, when people get in my way, I must remove them."

He was in front of her again, the knife held straight at her. When she felt the tip of the knife move against a button on her blouse and heard it hit the floor, she prayed again. "Please God, please help me." Luke flashed through her mind.

"I'm through with the games now, Christine," Vince said in yet another tone of voice. "Take off the blouse."

"No, please, Vince," she whispered.

"Take it off!" he screamed at her, and Christine felt the knife prick her throat. Visions of another knife in an alley made Christine's hands shake so much she couldn't loosen the buttons.

With an angry curse, Vince reached to the neckline of the blouse and yanked. Christine's head was snapped forward and buttons flew everywhere.

Her hands came up to hold the gaping blouse together and she heard her name.

"Christine!"

Vince turned to the intruding voice and Christine saw Luke and the sheriff coming into the parlor from the kitchen.

Vince spun back quickly and raised the knife over Christine, but a shot rang out and Christine watched the knife fly from Vince's hand. At that same instant, he clutched his bleeding elbow and began to scream in agony.

Christine watched as the sheriff, with little regard for the screaming man's elbow, dragged him from the room. Christine could hear his hysterical tirade, shouting against her grandfather and her until the kitchen door slammed, and the room was covered with an almost eerie silence.

Unaware of any other presence in the room, Christine started when she felt gentle hands on her upper arms. Even upon seeing it was Luke, Christine could not stop herself from bolting away from his touch.

Luke felt a myriad of emotions flood through him as his wife recoiled from him and backed toward the stairs. Her eyes were wide with panic. Her blouse was ripped open and there was a cut bleeding on her neck. Luke felt sick with the knowledge that this was his fault.

He had thought if they could just be in time, everything would be fine, never once considering the shock his wife would be in. He knew in that instant if it took the rest of his life, he would put this behind them. He would be there for her so she would have nothing more to fear.

"Christine." Luke's voice was quiet, his eyes moist. At that soft familiar voice calling her name, Christine seemed to gain a bit of control.

"He ripped my blouse," she said, her voice like a lost little girl's, and Luke's heart broke.

Luke continued on in the same quiet voice, tenderness in every syllable as his heart overflowed with love for this woman.

"It's over now, Christie. He's gone. The sheriff has him and he can't hurt you anymore. It's my fault. I should have told you about the barn fire. I wanted so much to take care of you, and all I did was hurt you. I'm sorry." Luke's voice broke on these last words.

"I was so scared," Christine began to sob.

"It's over now," Luke still did not approach her for fear of frightening her more. With his arms outstretched he said, "Come to me, Christie. Come and let me hold you."

Luke waited until Christine took one step and then covered the distance between them and swept her into his arms. They clung together and cried. Tears of frustration, anger, fear, and relief. Tears of joy and thanksgiving. Holding tightly to each other, they cried tears that marked the end of a pain-filled season and the beginning of a time for healing.

EPILOGUE

May in Baxter meant sunshine, warm weather, flowers bloom-
ing and spring planting. Christine had begun to think it would
never warm up, but May brought a warmth that let the grass
grow tall and green.

Christine sat among the grass atop a small knoll thinking back
over the past year and all its changes. Her mind went back to
the night when a frightened 19-year-old woman had, in a boy's
disguise, run from her home. Arriving in Baxter, meeting the Camerons, seeing her need for Christ and accepting Him. Her marriage to Luke and the awful confrontation with Vince Jeffers. A
frown covered Christine's face. Vince and the man who had
started the barn fire had been sent back to Spooner. They would
both stand trial for their deeds.

Soon Luke and Christine would head to Spooner to clear up
Joshua Bennett's estate. Christine would also have to testify
against Vince Jeffers, a task she did not relish. She watched Luke
come out of the house, and when he looked her way, she waved.
She smiled when he started toward her.

Was it possible to be so in love? Every day was more precious
than the last. Christine's hand went to her still flat stomach. She
would have to tell him her suspicions soon. She hesitated only
because she wanted to be sure.

Upon spotting his wife sitting off by herself, Luke became alert.
She had had another nightmare last night. They had decreased
some, but as always, Luke was concerned for her. They both
knew when it was time to return to Spooner, there would be
memories to upset her. Luke was reluctant to do anything that
would stir up the hurt, but they had little choice. Christine stood
and they shared a sweet kiss before Luke asked, "Are you okay?"

"I'm fine," Christine assured him. "I was just thinking over the
last year."

"It hasn't been an easy one. Are you thinking about going
home?"

Christine smiled and shook her head at him. Luke, misinter-
preting, was about to tell her they could possibly delay the trip
if she was uneasy about it, but Christine spoke.

"Luke," Christine's voice was whisper soft, her eyes shining with love. "Home is here in Baxter with you. Our time in Spooner will be temporary. You are my home, and wherever God leads you, I'll be by your side, knowing we're within His will."

Luke smiled at her and spoke gently. "My precious Christine, I have prayed so long for that peace in your heart. I've known for some time that where you are is a place called home."

A Song
for Silas

LORI WICK

HARVEST HOUSE PUBLISHERS
Eugene, Oregon 97402

All Scripture quotations in this book are taken from the King James Version of the Bible.

Except for certain well-established place names, all names of persons and places mentioned in this novel are fictional.

Music and lyrics for "My Rock, Refuge and Savior" by Timothy Barsness and Lori Wick. Used by permission.

A SONG FOR SILAS

Copyright © 1990 by Harvest House Publishers
Eugene, Oregon, 97402

2 in 1 ISBN 1-56865-551-7

Printed in the United States of America.

To Mary Vesperman,
secretary and dear friend.
I couldn't have done it
without you.

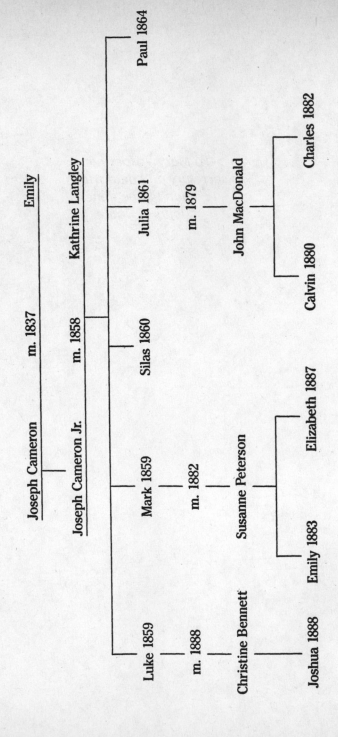

CAMERON FAMILY TREE
1889

Joseph Cameron — m. 1837 — Emily

Joseph Cameron Jr. — m. 1858 — Kathrine Langley

Paul 1864

Julia 1861 — m. 1879 — John MacDonald

Calvin 1880

Charles 1882

Silas 1860

Mark 1859 — m. 1882 — Susanne Peterson

Emily 1883

Elizabeth 1887

Luke 1859 — m. 1888 — Christine Bennett

Joshua 1888

FOREWORD

Neillsville, Wisconsin
February 1889

"Amy!" Grant Nolan called from inside the house and waited for an answer from the front porch.

He raised his voice and tried again. *"Amy!"* When there was still no answer, he walked to the porch from the living room. Grant stood and stared at his daughter a moment before speaking. "Amy, are you alright?" His brows drew together in a sharp V as she again failed to respond.

He tried again. "Amy, where is Thomas?" Grant watched as his daughter turned to look at him as though seeing him for the first time. Seeing he finally had her attention, Grant repeated, "Where is Thomas?"

"He left." Her voice was oddly flat and she turned her head once again to stare out into the yard at nothing in particular.

"Did you two have a disagreement?"

"No, he just came by to tell me he can't marry me because he's in love with Debra Wheeler."

Grant stared at his daughter's sober profile. The wind tossed her hair and she lifted her left hand to remove a few strands from her cheek. Grant's eyes were drawn to that hand. Empty. He felt his throat tighten at Amy's loss of the small ruby ring which had belonged to Thomas Blane's mother.

The empty ring finger confirmed the words his daughter had spoken. The sparkle the ring had brought was completely snuffed out.

Two months ago Amy had nearly floated into the house after she and Thomas had been on a Sunday afternoon ride together, her eyes sparkling, her face shining with happiness.

"Dad." Amy's voice had been hushed as though afraid that uttering the words aloud would somehow break the spell. "Thomas asked me to marry him."

She then had held out her left hand to show the lovely ruby set in a thin gold band. "It was his mother's, and he wants me to wear it so the world will know I am his."

Staring at his daughter with a mixture of emotions, Grant had risen to take her in his arms. Pain had mingled with overwhelming joy as he realized that his daughter had grown up and found a Christian man to spend her life with—his sorrow was over the fact that her mother wasn't there to see and share this special moment.

As though able to read her father's thoughts, Amy had raised her eyes to meet the loving ones above her. "I feel like Mother can see us and we have her blessing." Grant could only nod, his heart overflowing with joy for his daughter.

But now that peace had been shattered in a moment's time. Grant struggled to control his feelings of anger at the thought that anyone would reject his daughter. She had suffered more than enough pain and loss in her young life.

He knew some adults who would not have stood as strong as she had. But Amy was special, gifted and loving, taking each blow in stride, as she placed her small hand in the all-encompassing grasp of Jesus Christ as He had led the way through the dark tunnels of pain. Emerging from each trial more refined, Amy grew stronger and lovelier with every passing year.

Realizing he was still just standing and staring at Amy, Grant noticed absently the way the sun turned her golden hair to a fiery glow. As he walked to join his daughter on the porch swing, he prayed, wanting to comfort but not to intrude. He asked God to help Amy turn to her Lord for comfort as she had always done in the past.

As Grant shifted and settled his weight on the swing, Amy reached for his hand. Father and daughter sat side by side and were comforted with one another's presence.

Grant Nolan knew without a trace of prejudice that his daughter was the most wonderful one in the world. "Please God," he prayed silently, "please let Your will for Amy be as special as she is."

1

Baxter, Wisconsin
April 1889

Luke Cameron rolled onto his side to better see the little person in bed with him: his son . . . six months old . . . Joshua Luke Cameron. Luke's eyes moved over the cap of dark curls and down to the fan of equally dark lashes that lay still in sleep.

Joshua slept with his chest against the mattress and his little round bottom in the air, one tiny fist pushed into his flushed cheek.

It had been last year, Luke reflected, when Christine was still pregnant, that he and Mac had been talking on Grandma Em's front porch. Mac's words came back to him as he looked at the miracle of his son. "God is still faithful even amid our foolishness."

September 1888

John MacDonald stretched and flexed his massive back and shoulders, causing the chair on Grandma Em's porch to creak in protest. Luke Cameron was settled on the porch railing, letting the afternoon sun warm his back. It was warm for September—Indian summer—but no one was complaining. The snow would be upon them soon enough.

Mac, short for MacDonald, watched as his two sons, Calvin and Charles, charged out of the house. He followed their progress as they raced down the front porch steps and off to the willow tree to swing on some of the bare switches. His face reflected the pride he felt.

"It's hard to believe Cal is nine years old." Luke nodded as he also followed the progress of the boys—his nephews—as they raced around in the autumn sun.

"What's even more amazing," Mac replied, "is all your sister went through to get him here."

"I don't remember Julia having a hard time with labor and delivery," Luke answered, with a puzzled look on his face.

"She didn't have a hard time having Cal, just carrying him, and I'm afraid it was all my fault."

Luke stared at his brother-in-law, wondering what in the world he was talking about. Mac met Luke's stare and confessed, "I was scared to death for Julia to have Calvin."

Luke squirmed a bit at hearing these words. They so closely echoed his own thoughts now that Christine, his wife, was nearly seven months along with their first child.

Mac, seeming not to notice Luke's discomfort, went on. "Julia was over six months along before I realized she knew I was scared." Mac shook his head at the remembrance.

"Everything was fine with Julia and the baby and she knew it, but to give me peace of mind she worked twice as hard as she needed, carefully not showing me her exhaustion and never complaining about the way her body ached. But I didn't see any of it. The worst part was, I stopped touching her. I was afraid that if I even hugged her, I'd hurt the baby. Julia was over two-thirds of the way into her pregnancy, and I had never even felt the baby move. I can't believe how much I missed. She was working like a horse, and I was treating her as though she were made of glass. She told me later she had never been so hurt, thinking I was repulsed by her pregnant shape."

Mac again shook his head at his own stupidity. "Sometimes God allows us to go through some painful times. But we learned from it, and the rest of Julia's pregnancy was wonderful. God is still faithful even amid our foolishness."

Later that night, Luke knew he had to confront his wife. The lamp was blown out, and Luke lay in the darkness gathering courage to speak, knowing if he waited too long Christine would fall asleep. Wordlessly he moved and took her into his arms. Christine was so surprised by this action that for a few minutes she uttered not a sound, but lay in tense silence. When was the last time Luke had held her like this? How many times had she begged God, "Please, Lord, let Luke's affection for me return after the baby is born"?

But his touching her so suddenly like this was not a comfort. Her back began to ache with the tense way she held herself, waiting for whatever bad news he must have to tell her. When she could no longer stand it, she asked in a shaky voice, "Luke, is something wrong?"

Luke knew this was his chance. She was waiting and ready. All he had to do was explain to her about his fear and how much he loved and wanted to take care of her. But Luke decided foolishly not to burden her with all his fears. "No, Christine, everything is fine."

The next week was torture for both husband and wife. Luke, having decided to show Christine how he felt, only managed to confuse her by the change in his behavior. By Sunday of the next week, Christine's confusion had turned to anger and, after serving breakfast, she had quietly informed her husband she would not be going to church that day.

Christine was in the bedroom when she heard the horses move away pulling the wagon, so she was very surprised to hear someone walking down the hall.

Luke stopped just inside the doorway and found his wife in the rocker by the stove. Her eyes met his for just an instant before returning to the mending in her lap. "I thought you went to church with Si."

"You're angry." It was a statement and not a question.

"What makes you think that?" Christine asked as she viciously jabbed the needle into the shirt in her hands.

"Christine, we've got to talk."

Something in her husband's tone made Christine look up. Their eyes met and she knew he was as miserable as she. What followed were hours of soul-baring. Fear, pride, anger, hurt— they all were confessed to each other and then to God. The fear Luke had felt about losing Christine in childbirth, and the rejection Christine felt because of that fear, turned to love and new commitment.

Later, as Luke's hands lay on Christine's stomach feeling their child move within, Mac's words came back: "God is still faithful even amid our foolishness."

The sound of booted feet coming down the hall brought Luke back to the present. He rolled to his back and watched his wife enter the room.

Christine Cameron, even in denim jeans and a man's shirt, was poised and lovely. Luke smiled at the sight of her.

She sat down on the edge of the bed and leaned to kiss her husband.

"Did I wake you?"

"No."

Husband and wife spoke in hushed tones even though they knew it was unnecessary. The high activity level of their son caused him to sleep deeply whenever he slowed down long

enough to let slumber claim him. Saturday had developed into a routine of Luke and Josh taking a nap together giving Christine a bit of free time. Most days she went riding with Julia.

Christine reached across her husband to tenderly pat her son's bottom. She smiled as he moved and shoved his balled-up fist into his mouth.

"You weren't out for very long. Would you care to join us?"

Luke's inviting smile was tempting. The bed was plenty big enough to hold them but she felt dusty from her ride. Luke saw her hesitation and began to pull gently on her arm. Christine had just settled comfortably in Luke's embrace when they heard the front door open and close.

"Anybody home?"

Luke and Christine were out of bed in a flash upon hearing that deep voice from the living room. Silas was home.

2

Chicago, Illinois

Silas Cameron stared in stunned silence at the man across from him. The beautiful book-lined study with its elegant chairs and tables faded from view. He couldn't believe Frank Chambers had just asked him to come and work for him.

"I can see you're surprised, Silas, but I can assure you the offer is genuine." The older man's voice was slightly amused.

"Surprised is putting it mildly, Frank, and I'm very flattered but . . ."

"No, no, Silas. I don't want an answer right now," Frank cut him off. "You owe it to Luke as your partner, as well as your brother, to discuss it with him. I also realize the thought of leaving Baxter has probably never occurred to you, so I want you to give it some time. Think on it. I'll tell you exactly what I have in mind, and after you go home, I'll wait a few weeks to deliver your horses. I'll get your answer after I get to Baxter."

Frank then went on to explain the position in detail. Captivated, Silas listened closely.

"I delivered your horses last year because I liked Luke immediately upon meeting him, as well as all he had to say about his home. But, it is not normally my job. You can understand our operation here is too big for me to handle all the traveling."

"You deliver all the horses you sell?"

"Yes, we do. It has always been our policy. There have been a few times over the years when I have returned with the horses. No amount of money will make me leave my animals in a place where I feel they will be mistreated. I realize this is an unusual concept, but I've never been sorry and my reputation has been all the healthier for it." There was no boasting in his tone as he stated these facts, just a certainty he was doing the right thing. Considering the success of the Chambers' stables, Silas couldn't help but agree.

"What I have in mind for you is to deliver to our special customers. You have a calm way about you and can deliver our most valuable animals with the utmost care. Of this I'm sure. You would be traveling all over the United States and abroad probably at least once a year."

"Abroad? As in Europe?"

"Right! As I say, it's not very often, about once a year, but the job needs someone with your skill."

Frank talked on as Silas listened. He explained the other duties he had in mind and, when he named a salary, Silas had to work at keeping his mouth closed.

Silas went to bed with visions of travel and money floating through his head. He did not sleep well.

As Silas expected, Frank brought the matter up again on the way to the train station the following morning.

"There is one more thing I want you to understand, Silas. The salary I named is completely above and beyond any travel expenses you may have. We, of course, pay train fares for both you and the horses, and any time you must stay the night we'll cover that bill.

"Also, Silas, I am not insensitive to the close bond in your family. Anytime you are in the Baxter area with nothing urgent pressing here, you are more than welcome to stop and see them for a few days."

Silas was aware that Frank was talking as if he'd already accepted the job. It made him uncomfortable, and he was glad when the train station came into sight.

Frank's parting words as Silas stepped on the train were, "Think on it, Silas. I'll be up in a few weeks." Again, Silas had the impression Frank was already sure of the answer.

As the train moved along at a steady pace, the restless night began to catch up to Silas. He settled in and was nearly asleep when a child's crying woke him.

Across the aisle sat a woman with an infant and a toddler. The woman and the baby in her arms were fast asleep. The woman appeared to be literally limp with exhaustion. On the seat beside her was a little girl in a panic because she couldn't rouse her mother or fit into her already-full lap. Silas moved to the edge of his seat and held out his arms. There was a moment's hesitation, and then the little girl was in his arms.

With some coaxing, he discovered her name was Laura and that she was thirsty. When the tears were all dried and the thirst was quenched, Silas found her mother still sleeping, so he settled Laura in his lap.

Playing first with his tie and then his beard, Laura entertained him for the next hour, all the time talking to him in not-quite-recognizable English. When he asked her age, three little fingers went proudly into the air. Laura's head had just dropped onto

Silas' chest when her mother awoke. Silas would have liked to prevent the frantic look he saw in her eyes before spotting her daughter, but he didn't want to move and wake Laura. He assured her in a quiet voice that Laura was fine where she was and, after giving Silas a grateful smile, the young mother settled back in her seat to feed the baby.

With all of the thoughts Frank Chambers had put into his head, Silas, strangely enough, found his thoughts turning to the child in his lap—not specifically Laura, but children in general. Silas had two nieces and three nephews whom he adored. But lately it was not enough. He had begun to ache for a home of his own, with a wife and children to fill his heart and life.

He even knew the exact place he would build his house. It was not far from Luke and Christine's, and the group of big oaks that stood on that spot would give a feeling of privacy to both homes. He and Luke had talked about it just last month. Luke had been all for it as long as Silas didn't feel as though he and Christine no longer wanted him with them. Silas had assured him this was not the case.

Now Silas' thoughts turned to Chicago and the job with Frank Chambers. It would save him the cost of building a home. Frank had a two-bedroom cottage not far from the main house and had said the rent would be a part of Silas' salary.

Silas shook his head as though trying to clear it, and Laura stirred. She sat up and spoke a few words to him before noticing her mother was awake. Silas' lap was deserted quickly and he once again settled in for a nap.

The remainder of the trip was uneventful, and Silas was relieved to step onto the platform at Baxter. Greetings from townsfolk enveloped him as he made his way to the livery. As planned, Luke had left a horse for him. Within a half hour of leaving the train station, Silas was headed to the ranch.

As he rode through the familiar surroundings, Silas couldn't help asking himself, "Could I actually leave all this?" Baxter was the only home Silas had ever known.

The ranch hadn't changed in two weeks, although Silas halfway expected it would because it seemed to him he'd been gone forever.

No one came out as he rode up, and it was so quiet he wondered if anyone was home. He wished for an instant that he'd stopped at Grandma Em's. Maybe everyone was there.

The smells were familiar as he stepped into the front room.

He smiled. The aroma of whatever pie Christine had served for
lunch still lingered in the air. Home. Silas couldn't believe it felt
so good. As he quietly closed the door behind him, he called out,
"Anybody home?"

3

Barely finishing a piece of pie and cup of coffee, Silas began answering questions. Luke and Christine wanted to know everything. Their first questions were about Paul, the youngest brother in the Cameron family, who was at seminary in Chicago.

Silas, understanding their concern for the brother they missed so much and saw so little of, started right in.

"Paul is great. He misses everyone but loves school. He fills a different pulpit in the area nearly every week. He also told me that as much as he loves his studies, there is no feeling in the world like that of preaching a sermon. I couldn't believe how excited he was."

"Do you think he'll take a church in the Chicago area when he graduates?" Christine wanted to know.

"Somehow I don't think he will. He's still too much in love with small-town life. But then again, he said this weekend that God has been teaching him a lot about surrendering his will to God's. His most fervent prayer is that he, Paul Cameron, will be God's man for the job."

"When does he think he'll be home again?" Luke couldn't keep the wistfulness out of his voice. It seemed like forever since he had sat down and talked with his youngest brother.

Silas looked apologetic as he answered. "I wouldn't watch for him until sometime this summer."

Further conversation was interrupted by a small cry from the direction of the bedroom. When Christine rose, Silas stopped her. "Sit down, Christine. I've been waiting patiently for that sound since I walked in the door. I need to see my little Josh." Silas threw a beaming smile at Luke and Christine before moving to get his nephew.

Joshua Cameron always had a smile for his Uncle Silas. Always, that is, except for today. Silas scooped him off his parents' bed to hug and kiss him hello, but Joshua just stared at the bearded face above him. Silas was not too surprised when Joshua's little arms reached for Christine as soon as he saw her.

Completely unoffended, Silas headed for the piano. He played a few quick notes and then held his arms out to his nephew.

Joshua's smile was his reward and soon both were seated in their usual positions on the piano bench.

Completely hemmed in, Joshua was snuggled onto the piano bench with Silas' stomach at his back, the keyboard at his front, and Silas' arms stretched out on either side to reach the keys.

Silas never played from sheet music while Joshua was in his lap. He watched the little hands pound the keys in front of him or reach to the hands so much bigger than his own as they moved over the keys. If Joshua was especially tired, he would simply lay back against Silas and listen. Not so today. Fully revived from his nap, Joshua was ready to go.

The remainder of the afternoon flew by as Silas settled back into his home. When Joshua had been put to bed, Silas brought up to Luke and Christine the offer from Frank Chambers. They were as stunned as he had been. Christine had to bite her tongue to keep from coming right out and telling Silas he simply couldn't go. They talked for some time and Silas told them honestly he wasn't sure what he was supposed to do.

Knowing it would be best to sleep on it and do some more thinking and praying, Silas retired early. As he lay waiting for sleep to come, he knew he wanted God's will. But if he were completely honest, he also knew he hated to leave home, even for a short time. Coming home just felt so right. He asked God before he slept, If submitting to His will meant changing homes, would it ever feel as right as this one did?

The next day was Sunday and Silas awoke looking forward to church and then lunch with the family. He wanted very much to share the news of the job offer with the rest of the family and to ask for their advice and prayers. But as it was, the subject never came up.

Pastor Nolan had finished the closing prayer, but before dismissing the congregation, he spoke again. "Before I dismiss you this morning I would ask a few minutes of your time. Our niece Amy has written us to say that my brother has broken his leg." He paused as a ripple of murmurs moved across the room. "As most of you know, my brother has a farm in Neillsville where I grew up. I would ask for your prayers for Grant and Amy. A farmer's schedule does not allow for being laid up like this. I'm writing them tomorrow, and I'd like to tell them you are praying."

When the service was dismissed, Silas had to wait his turn to talk with the pastor. The men shook hands for a long moment before speaking, giving Silas time to see the lines of strain around the older man's eyes and mouth.

"I'm sure you know why I stayed to talk with you. Would I be out of line to ask if you can share more with me than you did from the pulpit?"

"It would be a relief to talk with you, Silas. Just let me see the rest of these folks out and I'll be right with you."

Silas was seated back in a pew but a few minutes when Mrs. Nolan joined him. "Thank you for staying, Silas."

"You know I'll do all I can." She met his assurance with a nod and they waited for the pastor in silence. When Pastor Nolan was finally seated, a conversation seasoned with the warmth of time began.

"The letter from Amy came yesterday. She wrote that Grant fell from a ladder and broke his leg. She also writes that the doctor has given him medicine for the pain and that he is completely bedridden. They haven't even started the planting. The letter went on to say that Amy is doing all the milking and she will be pulling money from their savings to pay for some help with the fields." Silas could hear the worry in Pastor Nolan's voice.

"Where is Evan?" Silas' voice was a bit angered.

"Nothing has changed with Evan. He never goes to the farm or anywhere near Grant. It's been four years. I have my doubts as to whether he'll ever get over Maureen's death. He's never said, but it's obvious he blames my brother for his sister's death."

They sat in silence for some minutes before Silas spoke. "When you write, tell them I'm coming."

"Are you sure, Silas? You've only just returned." The pastor's voice held genuine concern, but his eyes were hopeful.

"I'm sure." Silas spoke in a firm voice and in short order explained his plans and was on his way to see his family for the first time in two weeks, his heart a bit heavy at having to tell them he was leaving again.

4

Walking to Grandma Em's house from the church stirred up a bittersweet feeling in Silas. He knew that before the next Sunday dawned in Baxter, he would be on a small farm in Neillsville, Wisconsin, some 85 miles from his home.

As Silas walked up Grandma Em's street, he savored the approaching spring. It was his favorite time of year. He liked to pray for new growth in his own life as he watched the flowers come alive and the trees sprout new leaves. The weather was a bit chilly and the new growth really hadn't started yet, but there was a feeling of anticipation in the air, as though the plants and trees themselves knew something was about to happen.

Silas reflected a bit on the family with whom he was going to stay. Grant and Amy Nolan. Four years ago, upon the request of Pastor Nolan, Silas had gone to help Grant with his fall harvesting. Grant's wife, Maureen, had died suddenly and both Grant and his 14-year-old daughter, Amy, were in shock.

Amy. Silas smiled. The sweetest little girl Silas had ever met. Not demonstrative and very quiet, she had grieved silently, keeping to herself in a way that was heartbreaking. She had not spoken over five words to Silas the first week he was there. But in time the ice had melted and they became close, despite the 10 years difference in their ages.

They had not corresponded through the years, but Silas had kept abreast of the family through Mrs. Nolan. Grant had not remarried and Amy had been engaged but that was off now. She would be 18 now—a grown woman. Silas found himself hoping, as he climbed the steps to Grandma Em's front porch, that Amy would be as sweet as he remembered.

Sunday dinner was on the table and Mac had just prayed when Silas opened the front door. There was a round of hugs and kisses before everyone settled back down to the meal.

Silas had been all set to tell his family about his plans, but he was sitting next to his niece Emily, and she didn't let him get in a syllable. She questioned him thoroughly about Paul and then moved on to the horses.

"Did you get horses?"

"I sure did."

"What color are they? Can I ride one?"

Silas wasn't going to touch that one. He shot a look to Emily's mother, Susanne, but all she did was smile at him. No help there. A glance back at Emily told him she was awaiting his answer. Her eyes turned to him with hopeful anticipation. He knew he had to tell her the truth.

"I can't promise you a ride right now, sweetheart, because I have to go away again." As Silas expected, this statement captured everyone's attention. He might have been surprised to find out they had suspected this when, after church, he'd told Luke to take the buggy and that he'd walk to Grandma Em's.

"When do you leave?" The question was directed to him by his grandmother. He met her understanding eyes before looking at Luke to answer. "I was hoping Friday, but Luke and I have yet to talk."

Luke nodded and the meal progressed. The subject of Silas' departure was dropped, everyone realizing that Silas and Luke would have to talk this out on their own.

The front porch ended up hosting the conversation between the brothers. Luke's twin brother, Mark, and Mac were also present. Silas told them the added information Pastor Nolan had relayed, and concern was evident on every man's face for the trials of this family.

"How long do you expect to be gone?" Luke's question was matter-of-fact, knowing Silas' decision to go was already firmly planted in his mind.

"I could tell you a couple of weeks, but that's what I said last time and was gone for six." Silas was on the verge of saying more, but Luke cut in. "Actually, Si, I don't know why I ask you. I think your decision to go is just exactly that—your decision. I also know you have not made this decision lightly. I know we'll miss you, but we'll manage."

"I was thinking the same thing," Mark spoke now. "Why wait until Friday? The Nolans need you right now and we can help at the ranch whenever Luke gets into a bind, unlikely as that is."

Silas felt great relief at how supportive his family had been, until his sister-in-law Christine appeared. One look at the men on the porch told Christine the matter was all settled.

"Just like that. It's all settled isn't it?" No one said a word. "You've only just returned and you're leaving again." Her voice was not angry—resigned and sad, but not angry. "Well," Christine's voice had changed to determination just that fast, "if you don't write to us at least once a week, don't bother to come home."

The tension was broken at this and Silas moved to give Christine a hug, thinking as he did, what a relief it was to be leaving with his family's blessing.

5

"Did you write to Frank?" The question came from Luke as he and Silas headed toward the train station.

"Yes, I wrote. But if I know Frank, he'll not accept my answer."

Luke asked no more, fairly certain what Silas' answer had been. The train was a bit late, giving the men some time to talk. Silas seemed a bit edgy, and Luke couldn't keep from commenting on it. "Is anything bothering you, Si?"

Silas' answer did not come immediately. He was feeling very unsure of what he would find once he got to Neillsville, and he didn't want to burden Luke. In an instant he decided against it. "I'm just thinking ahead about my trip to the farm. I've got a long day ahead of me." All of which was true.

Luke noticed the evasive answer but only said, "I hear the train. Be sure you write or I'll be hearing from Christine. She really is in a stew over this. When she found out Grant Nolan had an 18-year-old daughter, I got the third degree."

Silas laughed in delight at this. "She can certainly be the mother hen at times, can't she?"

"Oh, Si, if she ever heard you say that . . . well, I hate to even think of the tongue-lashing we would both get."

Silas agreed with him. While the men shared a laugh, the train pulled in and they stood. Luke opened his mouth to say goodbye, but Silas interrupted. "About your question, Luke, I'm not sure what I'll find in Neillsville, and it's troubling me. Will you please just pray?"

"Every day," Luke answered with assurance and, as he stood on the platform watching the train become a dot in the distance, he began right then to keep his word.

Silas, on the other hand, was not at all prayerful. Indeed, he was very tense. He attempted to empty his mind of all thought, but he failed miserably. His mind kept returning to the young woman at the end of his journey: Amy.

Silas settled back in his seat and gave in to the desire he had felt ever since Pastor Nolan spoke on Sunday, trying to picture in his mind what Amy was like now.

She had been rather coltish at 14. A bit on the awkward side, as if she were not sure what to do with all her limbs. Awkward, that is, until she sat at the piano. Silas had been mystified the first time he'd heard her play. Silas played piano and his family thought he was the best, but they'd never heard Amy Nolan. The keys somehow came alive under her small hands. And her face—it positively glowed while she played.

She was gifted, there was no doubt about that. At 28 years of age, Silas had listened to his share of pianists and he knew Amy was in a class all her own.

Silas had learned to play piano at his mother's knee—the only one of five Cameron children to show a genuine interest. Being able to play the piano that his mother had taught him on somehow helped ease the pain of losing her. Kathrine Cameron's deep love for music was transmitted to Silas through those times of practice and play.

For a short time right after her death, Silas had not played at all, out of consideration for his father. He could tell that hearing the piano pained his father greatly.

When the house was empty one afternoon, Silas sat down and played some of his favorite hymns. He had played along in a bittersweet state for nearly 30 minutes when he looked up to see his father watching him. Silas could only guess how long he'd been there.

Silas bolted from the piano bench, stumbling through an apology as he straightened the music sheets with shaky hands. His panicky movements and words came to a halt as his father started toward him.

Silently, Joseph reached for the sheets of music. He looked through them slowly before placing a single sheet back on the music rest. A quick glance told Silas it was one of his mother's favorites. "Play this one, Si. Play it the way your mother taught you." He gave Silas' shoulder a pat and moved to take a nearby chair. Before he finished the song, the entire family had gathered. One by one they entered the room, no one bothering to disguise the sound of sniffling noses. Silas barely made it through the piece.

Silas played regularly after that. The keys beneath his fingers felt like a balm applied directly to his soul.

Amy also had learned piano from her mother, but there had not been the same comfort for her. Silas had been in the Nolan home for over two weeks when, after supper one night, Grant asked Amy if she felt like playing. Silas hated the shy way she looked at him before telling her father no. He did not want to make her feel uncomfortable.

He had wished he could tell her he understood the hurt. He had been only 13 when his mother died. It had been only three weeks since Maureen Nolan's funeral, but Silas knew from experience that to Amy it felt like a year.

Standing quickly, Silas made a snap decision. He faced Grant and spoke. "I know I'm a poor substitute for Amy, but if you've no objections, I'd like to play."

Grant answered with a small smile, "Please, Silas, feel free." But Silas didn't move with Grant's consent alone. He turned to the sober young girl in the room, who was regarding him with big, surprised eyes.

"Do you have any objections, Amy?"

"No." She didn't hesitate in answering, but her voice was so low that Silas saw more than heard her answer.

At the piano, Silas played wholly from memory. Within minutes, the other occupants of the room were forgotten as he moved from one song to the next. The piano's tone was beautiful, and Silas pulled deep within himself as he played piece after piece.

He would never know exactly what brought him back to the present, but just then he looked over at Amy and she smiled at him. For an instant, Silas was so surprised he didn't respond. It was the first time this quiet girl had shown anything past an indifferent, neutral acceptance of him in her home.

When Silas finally returned the smile, Amy's grew wider. They sat there grinning at one another while Silas finished the song.

Not long afterward the three retired for the night. As Silas readied himself for bed in his small attic bedroom, he was sure the ice had broken through for Amy and him. He really did want to be her friend.

Every day for nearly three weeks Silas had worked alongside her father, working steadily even when Grant slowed down or came to a complete halt. After a week, Grant began to talk and Silas listened without comment to the man's heartache, his concern for Amy foremost in his mind.

The days the men worked and talked seemed to be a gentle push for Grant onto the road of acceptance and recovery.

Not so with Amy. She grieved silently without complaint or comment. It was at this time Silas realized how much he'd taken his siblings for granted. Amy needed a big brother to help shoulder the grief.

As Silas settled into bed, he knew he wanted to be that big brother. "Please, God," Silas prayed as he dropped off to sleep, "help Amy open up to me. Let her know that I care and understand." Remembering the smile she had given him, he fell asleep, sure that tomorrow would be different. But it would be a few more days and a ruined breakfast before the ice broke completely.

Silas was jolted out of his reverie when the conductor passed through the train and announced there would be a delay at the next stop. There were grumbles throughout the car, but Silas was just glad he'd left Baxter early.

The conductor said to feel free to get out and stretch a bit, so Silas moved out of his seat toward the door.

They were stopped in Elroy, a small town not too many miles out of Baxter. Silas quickly decided not to wander about and took a bench in the shade to watch the busy activity of the depot.

It wasn't long before the sights of the depot grew mundane and Silas' thoughts wandered back to the time he and Amy finally became friends.

Grant and Silas walked from the barn to the house. The milking was done and both men were ready for a big breakfast. They were greeted at the door not by the smell of fresh coffee and biscuits, but by the pungent odor of burned bacon and eggs.

Amy stood with the frying skillet in one hand while waving a dishcloth over the smoky mess with the other. When she saw her father, she simply said, "I'm sorry, Dad. Breakfast will be a little late this morning."

"Don't worry about it, Amy. I'll wash up and give you a hand." And that was the end of that. Amy didn't cry or offer a long excuse, just a simple apology and it was over. Silas was impressed.

The moment of friendship arrived when Silas also washed up and, stepping behind Amy, took the burned skillet from her hands. "I'll get this for you." The look of surprise on her face could only be matched by the expression on her face when he'd asked to play the piano a few days earlier.

Silas didn't wait for a comment from Amy but simply proceeded to scrape the pan clean. Amy's surprise turned to genuine puzzlement when he did not return the skillet but put in strips of bacon and began to crack eggs into a bowl.

The three worked together in silence, Grant and Amy both sending a look in Silas' direction now and then. The meat was eaten as silently as it had been prepared. Grant and Silas were still at the table with their coffee when Amy was ready to leave for school. She kissed her father goodbye and then moved over to Silas. He smiled at her and said, "Have a good day, Amy."

"Thank you, Silas." Amy spoke these words just before bending and planting a quick kiss on his cheek. Silas turned to stare at her as she bolted for the door. Neither man spoke of it the rest of the day, but Silas noticed for the first time that Grant whistled while they went about their daily work.

A precious friendship began that day and Silas boarded the train with a feeling of contentment in his heart brought on by his reflection of that time. The friendship he and Amy shared had been special, one that no amount of time could obliterate. Each held a special place in the heart for the other.

The remainder of the trip, if uneventful, was less worrisome for Silas. By the time he arrived in Neillsville, it was raining. Silas had planned to hire a horse from the livery and ride the two-and-a-half miles out to the Nolan farm, but the rain caused him to reconsider.

Reasoning to himself there was no guarantee the rain would let up tomorrow, Silas went ahead toward the livery. He might as well get wet today as tomorrow.

It was dark and gloomy as he rode out of Neillsville, and he could feel the reluctance of the animal beneath him. Not that he blamed the poor beast. This was not fit weather for anyone. Silas only hoped, as he picked up the pace a bit, that Pastor Nolan's letter had arrived and his appearance would be expected.

6

Amy muffled a small groan as she stood up from her cramped position on the milking stool. How excited she and her father had been at the freshening of two more heifers just last month. Now, with only two more cows to go and her back screaming, Amy couldn't help wondering what they'd been so excited about. The morning milking never hurt her back like the afternoon milking did, and Amy, in her tired state, never stopped to think that the full schedule she kept between the morning and afternoon milking may have something to do with that fact.

The milking and cleanup finally completed, Amy threw her cape over her shoulders and, with head bent to watch every step, she moved carefully across the puddle-strewn yard to the house. Doctor Schaefer was scheduled to see her father sometime that night, and Amy wanted to be present.

Not until Amy was on the porch did she look up to see if Doc's carriage was in the yard. Although on this rainy night he would probably have come right into the barn, Amy peered through the rain-darkened evening for signs of him and saw none. Satisfied she had finished before he arrived, she went in to check on her father.

Grant sat back against the pillows of his bed and heard the front door open and close. He waited quietly, without calling, knowing Amy would come to check on him as soon as she was dry. The pain was only a dull ache, but the frustration was ever-present. Having to lay in bed while his daughter did his work was almost more than he could bear.

"Doc should be here anytime, Dad. How about some supper?" Amy spoke as she entered the room and sat down gently on the bed, moving carefully so as not to jar his leg.

"Let's eat after he comes. First, tell me if there is any trouble with the cows."

Amy was accustomed to this question. Even when her father had been in great pain, he asked after the cows. He went on before she could answer. "I hate to see you go out in this rain. You didn't get a chill, I hope." Amy almost laughed over the fact that he asked about the cows before checking on his daughter. He was like an overanxious mother where those cows were concerned. But considering they were the source of family income, she couldn't say as she blamed him.

"The cows are fine, including the latest milkers, who are doing great. Everything is closed up for the night, and I did not catch a chill," Amy recited quickly, hoping she had omitted nothing and that his worries would be eased, but a funny look came over his face.

"Amy, am I driving you nuts?"

Amy was so surprised by this question, she laughed outright. "Dad," she gasped, "what in the world are you talking about?"

But he did not join in her merriment, and she tried hard to pull a straight face. "When have I ever had trouble milking? If there was a problem, you would be the first to know. And the second you start to drive me crazy, you'll also be the first to know."

This brought a small smile to Grant's face and he asked, "You're sure everything is fine?"

"Positive." Amy said with a smile. "How's the leg?"

"Better, much better. It usually throbs in the night, so I'm afraid you'll have to get used to sleeping the days away for a bit longer."

"Well, as much as I'd like to see you out of that bed, I'll tell on you in a hurry if you rush things."

"I'm sure you will. You're as bossy as your mother was." They both laughed at this. Maureen Nolan had been the most *un*bossy woman on the face of the earth.

Old Doc Schaefer arrived as Amy was fixing supper. He readily agreed to stay for the meal, and the amount of stomach stretching his binders gave proof that he rarely turned down such offers.

Doc checked Grant over and was pleased to see him progressing so well. Between Amy and the doctor, Grant was able to eat at the kitchen table for the first time in nearly two weeks. Conversation was lighthearted for most of the meal and, having escaped the bed, Grant was in high spirits.

Over coffee and dessert, Doc Schaefer asked a surprising question. "Had you heard? Carltons were robbed last night."

"Robbed?" Amy was incredulous. "What in the world was there to steal?" Amy's question was valid. The Carltons had a very small farm and usually had a hard time making it from month to month.

"Well, Harold must have told one too many people he was

planning on taking some of that inheritance money from Ruth's aunt for farm repairs."

"But Ruth said that money was in the bank."

"It was until yesterday and then was stolen last night."

The table was silent as Grant and Amy digested this bit of news. More coffee was served and the three talked on until it was evident Grant had overestimated his strength. The rain had not let up and so as soon as they had Grant settled back in bed, Doc took his leave.

He and Amy talked for a bit but, with the rain continuing, Amy wanted to get out and check the stock one last time before settling in for the evening.

"Amy," Grant said as she was leaving, "take the shotgun out with you." Amy's eyebrows rose in surprise at this, and for a moment she hesitated. "Please, honey, it would make me feel better."

Amy nodded silently and headed for the door. She realized that until just then she hadn't even thought of the thieves still being in the area.

The gun felt cold against Amy's side as she made her way across the yard for a final check on the animals. She tried to squelch the fear she felt as she stepped carefully around the puddles, but the desire to do double checks on the shadows was a temptation. Psalm 56:3 came to mind as she moved toward the barn: "What time I am afraid, I will trust in thee." After thinking of these words, Amy knew instant comfort.

The rain was not a hard downpour, but a steady shower. The warmth and familiar smells of the barn were an added comfort as Amy stepped within. She leaned the gun against a post while lighting the lantern.

The wind seemed to pick up as did the rain as she walked along the stalls. Amy was angry with herself for the fear she felt. She knew God was watching over her and once again claimed the verse in Psalms. Everything was in order and Amy had just blown out the lamp and picked up the gun, when the door was opened wide.

Having just ridden in the dark, Silas was a few steps into the barn before his eyes made out a lone figure pointing a gun at him. He froze and felt his heartbeat accelerate. He had wondered how he would be greeted at the Nolan farm, but this was ridiculous.

"State your business, mister, and do it quickly." The voice

speaking from behind the gun was high-pitched with fear, but Silas recognized it.

"I'll state my business, Amy Nolan! You've got exactly two seconds to get that gun pointed in another direction, or I'll do it for you!" His voice was gruff with relief, and he was just a bit angry.

The gun lowered slowly. "Silas?" The voice went up still another octave.

"Silas?" Silas mimicked in a high imitation of her voice.

With that the words came pouring out as she tried to light the lamp. "Oh, Silas! Oh no, I'm so sorry! I can't believe I held a gun on you. You scared me and you see there was this robbery and well, I wasn't expecting anyone to come in." The words stopped as abruptly as they had started when the lamp was finally lit and turned high. Amy could only stare at the drenched man before her. Silas stared back. Amy watched the flash of white in his beard as a slow smile started.

"Hi." Silas' voice was soft now, and deep.

"You mean you're speaking to me?" Amy asked, her tone dry. Silas' laughter echoed in the barn, and he reached to give her a quick hug.

"I take it from your reaction, I've arrived ahead of your uncle's letter?"

"There's been no word on your coming, but I'm so glad you're here." Amy's voice was sincere and childlike all at once.

"How is your dad?"

"He's doing better, and he'll be thrilled to see you."

They stared at each other for a few more minutes, Amy feeling like she could hug him again but remembering she was not 14 anymore. Silas thought how grown up she was.

They worked together to stable Silas' horse and, as they made their way across to the house, Silas had the odd sensation he was coming home.

— ❖ —

"You would think the boss could have put this off for one night. I'm freezing."

The man to whom he spoke only grunted in reply and continued to stare out into the rain. Within ten minutes, coming from the direction of town rode a black-cloaked figure on an equally black mount. The men stood silently as the horse and rider entered the broken-down barn that had stood abandoned for years.

Without dismounting, the rider spoke. "You have the money?" The voice was husky and low, and the two men within the barn tried to make out the face of their mysterious employer. The turned-up collar of the cloak, along with the low brimmed hat, kept the rider's identity as dark as the night.

Wordlessly, bags were exchanged. A large sack was handed up to the rider and quickly concealed beneath the cloak.

Anticipating the next move, the two men caught small bags as they sailed from atop the horse.

The chink of coins as the bags landed in the outstretched hands was the only sound made as the two men watched the rider turn the mount and disappear into the wet gloom.

"Who do you suppose he is?"

"I don't have a clue, but if we start asking questions the money will stop," the other man spoke as he tucked the moneybag into his belt. "And *that* is a risk I'm not willing to take."

7

Silas lay on his back in bed. The vaulted ceiling was familiar, as were the smells and sights of his attic bedroom. The room was simply furnished with a bed, washstand, and dresser. Moonlight streamed through a small, yellow-curtained window and shone on Silas' clothes where they hung from a hook on the wall. Next to the hanging clothes was a small wooden chair. For Silas there was a strange sense of comfort in seeing everything as he remembered.

Silas had the same feeling with Grant and Amy, even though there had been changes. The three of them had taken about an hour to get reacquainted, and Silas was amazed at how welcome they had made him feel. It was as if they had never been separated.

As he lay musing, Silas remembered that Amy had said something about a robbery. He would have to ask her tomorrow. Right now he was too tired to think. He knew the morning would bring hard work—not that he had ever been afraid of work, but getting a good night's sleep was beginning to blot out all other thought.

He knew this was where God wanted him, and it gave him a feeling of contentment as he drifted off to sleep that could only be matched by that of the two people readying for sleep downstairs.

Amy had never prepared for bed so slowly. Her mind kept going over and over the events of the last two hours when Silas had appeared in the barn, and then seeing her look of surprise mirrored on Grant's when Silas' large frame had filled her father's bedroom doorway.

Silas carried with him an air of confidence that brought with it a sense that all was going to be well.

Four years ago God had given Amy a big brother, for six weeks, in the form of Silas Cameron. Silas had come to them like an armored knight in days of old, at a time when their pain and confusion over losing their wife and mother was so great, they didn't believe their world would ever be normal and happy again.

Quiet and sensitive, Silas had offered comfort and stability in his warm, gentle way. Amy had never known a better listener. She smiled to herself as she began to brush her hair. Silas was back, and everything was going to be just fine.

For the first time in over two weeks Grant's mind was not on the throbbing in his leg as he tried to fall asleep.

Silas Cameron! Who would have thought God's answer to his prayers would be Silas Cameron? Grant had never even thought of him as he had prayed and asked God to help them through this time of hurt.

But he was here, and Grant knew all was going to be well. Amy had been an angel, but Grant could see the extra work was weighing on her. She was used to the long hours and even the milking, but not the handling of the milk cans and all of her regular work besides.

Grant had also been more than a little worried about borrowing from savings to hire field help. But the crops had to be planted, and as frustrating as Grant's helplessness was it didn't change that fact.

If the crops did not go in, money from savings would be needed to buy feed for his stock. He would be forced to buy through the winter and until next years' harvest—a very unsettling thought.

"Silas can do the planting and take over the milking and hauling. I'll get back on my feet, and by the fall I'll be off my back and ready for harvest. . . ." These were the thoughts with which Grant fell asleep.

8

Amy was halfway across the yard before she realized the barn door was partially open. Quickening her steps while avoiding mud puddles, Amy approached the barn in unbelief. Silas had actually beaten her to the milking.

Amy stood a few minutes just inside, recovering from her surprise, when a deep voice spoke from amid a row of various-colored cows. "There is no reason for you to be out here, Amy. I can take care of everything."

Amy followed the voice until she stood at Silas' side. When he raised his head, she spoke with a teasing voice, "Am I being dismissed?" Before he could answer, Amy began to laugh at his appearance. "Oh, Silas," she said between giggles, "I forgot how much you look like a bear in the mornings."

Her words so mimicked Luke's opinion of Silas' morning appearance, he had to smile. Amy returned the smile with a warm one of her own and said, "I'll have breakfast ready when you get in."

Within the hour Silas was in the kitchen bending over the washstand. After brushing his hair and beard into some semblance of order, he headed to the table that was the focal point of the Nolan kitchen.

The room was not overly large, and the table and stove took up most of the floor space. Over six feet in length and easily four feet wide, the table was space-consuming by any standard, but seemed especially so with just Silas sitting and watching Amy dish up food from the stove.

She had outdone herself this morning. Silas' eyes took in eggs, sausage, bacon, fried potatoes, biscuits, three choices of jam, oatmeal, milk, and coffee. As Amy continued to work, Silas' eyes skimmed over the room he had briefly passed through the night before. It was as he remembered. Two small windows looked out over the front yard. The curtains were very plain white cotton, but somehow fitting in this simple room. Hooks on the wall, a washstand, stove, and small, low worktable along one wall—yes, everything was as he recalled.

When Amy joined Silas at the table, she asked him to pray. She was impressed again with the feeling that all was going to be well as Silas petitioned God on behalf of Grant Nolan. Silas asked God outright to ease Grant's pain and put him back on his feet. He prayed with such assurance that Amy felt that was exactly what God would do.

When the prayer ended, they ate in companionable silence until Silas questioned Amy about the robbery. Amy told him what they had learned from Doc and then ended with, "I plan to drive into town tomorrow. I always take time to see Aunt Bev, so I'm sure she'll give me any news we've missed out here."

"Does she ever come out here to see you?" Silas asked, although quite sure what the answer would be.

"No. Uncle Evan forbids it." Her voice was so sad that Silas wished he'd kept his question to himself.

Grant woke not long after breakfast and Silas went in to see him. The two men spent the next two hours in deep conversation. Amy moved between the bedroom and the kitchen getting her father's breakfast and then bringing coffee as the morning slipped by.

When Silas finally left the bedroom so Grant could get some more rest, he knew exactly what Grant wanted done in the next several weeks. The milking and hauling, the fields, and care for the animals—they had covered it all. Silas would also be finishing the painting of the barn and house—the very cause for Grant's bedridden condition, and not a comfortable subject.

When Silas had first brought up the matter of doing the painting, Grant had said absolutely not, the painting could wait. But Silas was undeterred and, after some coaxing and reasoning, Grant had agreed to tell what his plans had been prior to falling from the ladder.

When Silas sat down to the table for noon dinner, he was holding a list of supplies he would need from town. He and Amy discussed the list and agreed that it would be easiest if he accompanied her. They planned to leave the following morning after breakfast. They would stop on the way so Amy could ask a neighbor to check on Grant at midday and get his meal.

The remainder of the day went by with chores and small talk. Silas helped Grant to the kitchen table for supper, and the three of them talked and laughed long after the dishes were cleared and the coffeepot empty. It was a warm and special beginning to Silas' stay with the Nolans.

9

Two-and-a-half miles northwest of town nestled into the base of a rocky bluff sat the Nolan farm. It was not a farm handed down from earlier generations of Nolans, but it had been home to Amy for as long as she could remember.

Grant's father, as a very young man, had come to Neillsville to work in the logging industry there. Grant was born into this rough existence and even worked for a time in the logging trade.

But the work was dangerous and Grant, with a wife and young daughter, had wanted out. He borrowed money from the bank which was subsequently owned and operated by his wife's uncle and brother, and bought a small, ill-kept dairy farm not far from town. Grant moved his wife, Maureen, and small daughter, Amy, to the farm when Amy was 3 years old.

The barn was large, with more than enough room to house the 19 healthy cows Grant milked. His milk went daily to the Daisy Cheese Factory at the edge of town, a steady income he'd banked on for years.

The farmhouse was small and white with a high-pitched roof. A small porch led up to the front door that opened into the kitchen. Two bedrooms and a living room completed the downstairs. Simple-cut stairs in the living room went up to the bedroom in the attic.

Silas and Amy emerged from the house as a clear morning sun warmed the ground. Silas in clean, blue denim pants and a red plaid shirt walked beside Amy whose dress was a soft yellow print. She tied on a matching bonnet as the couple moved across the yard to the barn where Silas had the wagon and team waiting.

Silas watched Amy glance back at the house and broke into her thoughts. "If you're worried about your dad being alone, I could take your list for town."

Amy shook her head in rather sad resignation as she answered, "No, Silas. Dad would be upset if he thought I stayed on his account. But thanks for the offer." Amy stopped by the wagon and looked up to meet Silas' eyes. "I suppose you think I'm being rather silly, but he's so helpless in that bed. I would just feel sick if anything more happened."

Silas answered as he helped her into the wagon. "On the contrary, I would think something was wrong with you if you could leave without a backward glance. Do you trust Mrs. Brewer to check on your dad?" At Amy's nod he continued, "Then I think you should leave with a peaceful heart, knowing you've taken care of everything."

Amy was thankful for his logic, and when a quarter mile up the road they stopped at the Brewer's farm, all doubts vanished.

"Of course I'll check on your father," Mrs. Brewer assured Amy. "I'll take Sammy with me, and we'll see to his every need. You know I'm always happy to give you a hand. It's important for a woman to get out to town when she can. Lifts the spirits, I always say."

Amy smiled at this woman who, along with her husband and sons, had been such a help and encouragement since her father's accident. It was to them she had run when her father had called from the yard in agony. The bone in his leg had actually come through the skin, and his entire body had seemed to lie at an impossible angle. Amy had been unable to move Grant from his crumpled position at the bottom of the ladder. So, upon arriving at the Brewer farm, Mr. Brewer and their oldest son, Dave, raced with Amy back to the house while Sammy was sent for the doctor.

Among the three of them, they had moved Grant to his bed and were keeping him warm when the doctor arrived.

"Yes, Silas was right," Amy thought as she introduced him to Mrs. Brewer. "I completely trust my father to this woman's capable hands."

The prospect of time in town had Amy's mood high as the land leveled out and the houses of the main street came into view.

Their first stop was at the bank where Amy hoped to catch sight of her Uncle Evan. Much to her disappointment, he was out. Amy made a withdrawal while Silas returned his rented horse and saddle to the livery.

When Silas picked her up, Amy asked him to drive the team to the general store. She had her list of household supplies and Silas had Grant's list for the farm. Amy saw familiar faces everywhere as they made their way past the hat shop, a boardinghouse, saloons, and numerous lumber dealers. The sight of Amy aboard her own wagon with a strange bearded man at the reins brought many stares and a few hesitant waves.

Hesitant that is, until Silas pulled up in front of one of the general stores. Mrs. Anderson, the owner's wife, who was always on the lookout for new faces and news, nearly ran into them on the boardwalk out front.

"Well, Amy dear, you've been such a stranger lately. How is your father? We've missed you on Sundays the last few weeks. We really do hope you'll be out soon. No one can play like you do. I'm afraid you've got us all spoiled."

Amy noted with amusement that while all the comments and questions were directed to her, Mrs. Anderson's eyes rarely left Silas Cameron's handsome face.

"Well, Amy dear," Mrs. Anderson said with some reproof in her tone and a raised brow, "aren't you going to introduce me to your friend?"

A quick glance at Silas told Amy he was as amused as she was by the woman's long-winded speech, but his manners were impeccable as Amy did the honors.

"Mrs. Anderson, this is Silas Cameron, a friend of my family's from the Reedsburg area. Silas, this is Mrs. Anderson. She and her husband run the general store and post office."

Even as Silas shook the woman's hand and attempted to greet her politely, she began to speak. "Well, how nice to meet a friend of Amy's." No one missed the emphasis she put on friend.

"Tell me, Silas—I hope it's alright to call you Silas?"

"Certainly."

"Tell me, Silas, are you looking to settle in this area? Possibly planning to make your home here?"

"Well no, ma'am. Actually I'm here to help at the Nolans' while Grant gets back on his feet."

"Oh well," her voice was filled with disappointment. "I hope you have a nice stay." She looked at Amy with genuine regret in her eyes. Then with a sudden "oh goodness," Mrs. Anderson's regret was replaced by curious interest. "There's Milly Baker with her new baby. You two go on inside. Ed will see to you."

Silas stared after the once-again-talking woman until he felt Amy's hand on his arm. "Is she always like that?"

Amy laughed. "Oh yes, she's never the same twice. The only thing that stays the same is her ever-present desire to see her daughters marry. I'm afraid you crushed her by telling her you were not going to be living here for the rest of your life."

Silas kept his thoughts to himself as he entered the store, but the idea of Mrs. Anderson as a mother-in-law was a bit disconcerting. Once inside, the couple wasted no time selecting the items on their list. In short order everything was loaded and paid for and they were on their way to see Bev Randall.

10

One of Neillsville's most prominent citizens in 1888 was Evan Randall. He owned and ran the largest bank in town—a business and position he had inherited from his uncle, Dell Randall. The Randall name was one of importance and commanded respect in the town of Neillsville. The Randall men were not known for their warmth or social skills, but over the years no one could fault them for their shrewd business sense and the way they turned a profit at every hand.

Amy knew all about her uncle's business acumen, and she was not blind to the fact that he completely blamed Grant Nolan for his sister's death. He believed life on the farm was too hard and that the work had shortened her life. He was sure she would have stood stronger against the illness that claimed her if her life hadn't been so rough.

In fact, he had never approved of the marriage between his sister Maureen and Grant, even before Grant began to farm. Older than Maureen by five years and already working under his Uncle Dell at the bank, Evan's aspirations for his sister went much higher than a man who worked for one of the small logging firms in town.

The fact that 18-year-old Maureen was head over heels in love with Grant Nolan or that his Uncle Dell had given his complete approval made little difference. The whole idea was repulsive to him and he was thoroughly against his beloved sister marrying someone he felt was beneath her.

He rarely spoke to Maureen during the first 18 months of her marriage to "that logger" as Evan disdainfully put it, until Maureen presented him with a tiny blonde niece named Amy.

Evan's heart melted at the sight of the little girl, and this was the Evan Randall Amy knew. He was never too rushed to talk with her. Opinions that he was cold were completely groundless in the presence of his niece.

The plain truth was, Evan Randall was willing to do anything for her. The love Amy had for her uncle was straight from her heart, and she recognized that not even his sweet wife, Bev, received the special smiles she did and this bothered her.

Bev never seemed upset with her or jealous, but to Amy it was obvious, as she was sure it was obvious to everyone else, that Evan Randall thought his niece most special—as special as his sister had been. As Amy grew older, she began to see that Evan was pouring into her all the love he hadn't been able to give to his sister in the last four years.

This special relationship between Amy and her uncle had always been a source of security and joy to her. But recently something had come up, and Amy was unsure how to deal with it. Worry invaded her peace. Amy was thinking of it even as Silas pulled the team to a stop in front of a huge white mansion.

A deep, wide porch ran along the entire front of the majestic-looking home. Thick white pillars supported the flat porch roof that gracefully fronted the second-story windows.

The tenuous thread that held the Nolan and Randall families together had been abruptly severed with Maureen's death, so Silas had never been here. He let out a low, appreciative whistle as his eyes moved over the exterior.

Amy smiled with some pride. "It's beautiful, isn't it? My mother grew up in this house. I had forgotten until this moment that you haven't seen it or met my aunt and uncle."

Silas usually took hospitality for granted, but with the little information he had on these two families, and the quiet way Amy had ridden in the seat beside him, he had to ask, "Amy, maybe it would be best if I didn't stay. I could get lunch downtown and come back for you later. It would give you a chance to have a private visit with your aunt."

The shock on Amy's face was genuine. "Silas, why would you think such a thing? Aunt Bev knows all about you, and I know she'll want to meet you. You couldn't be more welcome in this home."

Silas immediately assumed he had mistaken her pensive look in the wagon. "Honestly, Amy, I meant no offense. It'll be a pleasure to meet your family."

Amy stood and looked at Silas even after he lifted her from the wagon. Silas smiled into the light-blue eyes regarding him so intently. She seemed very vulnerable to him at that moment. It became clear that his meeting and liking her aunt and uncle must be important to her.

Silas gently placed his hands on Amy's small shoulders and his smile became very tender. "Amy, I know the relationship between your father and uncle is painful for you. I would be a liar if I said I never thought of it, because it bothers me too. But I want to meet the Randalls. I know how special they are to you, and I'm sorry my question sounded so insensitive."

After a moment Amy smiled back. "You're always so logical, Silas. I think we get along very well together."

"I think we do too. Besides," he spoke as he took her arm and led her toward the door, "*that* is what big brothers are for."

Amy continued in his light-hearted mood. "It's a nice arrangement I've got, having a part-time big brother. If we'd grown up together, you would be bossy and tease me all the time. This way if you step out of line, I won't feed you."

"Ah, but you're forgetting, I can cook!"

"That does pose a problem. If I can't get to you through your stomach, I'll have to come up with something else to keep you in shape."

They shared a final teasing smile before Silas reached up to knock at the front door. It was by mutual, unspoken consent that they waited in silence for the door to open.

11

"Hello, Perkins. Is my aunt home?" After some moments the front door had opened and Amy was addressing her question to an elderly gentleman with a full head of gray hair and a stately manner about him that he wore like a cloak.

"Of couse, Miss Amy." The man nodded, his face expressionless. The couple moved into the foyer as Perkins stepped aside and opened the door wide. "I'll tell Mrs. Randall you're here." His manner was so formal that it was almost comical.

After he moved away, Amy looked at Silas. She had to stifle a giggle with her hand as she watched his brows raise and eyes twinkle. Knowing her laughter would only start his own, Silas turned away from her to survey his surroundings.

Dual staircases rose from the foyer to the second floor in a straight, formal fashion. To the right of the foyer was a small parlor with large windows overlooking the porch. In one corner stood a small fireplace.

Another room—appearing to be a library—branched off the parlor, but Silas did not move to investigate. His eyes swung to the left of the foyer and took in a large living room running almost the full length of the house.

This room, as well as the foyer sported huge windows, some accented with colored or ornately etched glass. The living room overlooked the porch and was full of beautiful furniture. Several doors exited off this room, and Silas felt an urge to explore. He glanced at Amy to find her watching him.

"Were you hoping I'd be impressed?" Silas' expression was knowing.

"Are you?" Amy's grin was downright cheeky.

"What if I said no?" Silas asked with an elaborate shrug.

"I'd say you were a poor liar, Si Cameron."

"You'd be right," Silas said with a laugh.

"Amy," a deep, almost-masculine voice called from the living room. Amy turned and rushed into the arms of a tall, reed-slim woman.

Silas watched as the two shared a long hug. When at last they separated, Bev Randall held Amy at arm's length. The unfeigned concern Silas saw written on her face endeared her to him immediately. "How is Grant?"

"A little better every day, but he's been in so much pain," Amy answered in a trembling whisper, and Silas knew without seeing her face that she was fighting tears. Her aunt knew also and pulled her once again into a firm embrace.

"I wanted to come, but . . . well . . ." The words died in the older woman's throat as Amy nodded her head in silence. Once again the two hugged, this time in unspoken understanding.

Silas suddenly found himself the center of attention. Both women had turned to him and Silas stood quietly, studying Amy's aunt as intently as she was studying him.

The face before him was thin, cheeks nearly sunken. Something about her mouth led Silas to believe she didn't smile often. Her eyes were shrewd but not unkind, nor did they waver from his own as she began to speak in an almost-stern tone of voice.

"From Amy's description, you can't be anyone other than Silas Cameron." She paused, and the young people in the room were almost tense as they waited for her to continue. But when she did, there was kindness in her rather gravelly voice. "I must admit that when Amy told me about you four years ago, I believed it could only be a 14-year-old's imagination that could create such size. But I was wrong," she said as she stepped forward with her hand outstretched. "You *are* big."

"It's a pleasure to meet you, Mrs. Randall."

"Please call me Bev and allow me to thank you for coming to help Grant and Amy."

"Aunt Bev," Amy broke in, "how did you know Silas was here to help us?"

"Oh, that's easy. Two nights ago a large, bearded man arrived by train when the skies were dumping rain on Neillsville. He rented a horse and headed in the direction of the Nolan farm." Bev smiled at Amy, who was beginning to catch on, and continued her story to a still-confused Silas. "You see, Silas, there isn't much in this town that goes on without my knowledge. Remembering Amy's description of you and the direction you headed that night along with finding you in my front room . . . well, you see it didn't take a detective."

The three laughed at this logical explanation for Bev's nosiness, but Amy sobered quickly upon remembering something.

"Aunt Bev, had you heard about the robbery at the Carlton farm?"

Bev nodded silently, and Silas and Amy watched a pained, troubled expression cross over her features. She opened her mouth to speak, but just then the front door burst open and in strode Evan Randall.

12

Silas spooned soup into his mouth from the most beautiful china bowl he had ever seen. The spoon in his hand was heavy with a large, ornate "R" engraved on the handle. It was obvious even to the most casual observer that everything in the Randall dining room, and probably the entire house, was of high quality and cost.

As he continued to eat, Silas watched Evan Randall converse with his niece. Silas tried to look at Amy, but she was partially hidden by a vase of fresh flowers sitting on the table between them.

Silas found it odd that Evan made no attempt to include him or his wife in the conversation. Still, Silas continued to study the man.

He was slim like his wife and a few inches taller. His hair was a medium shade of brown but his thin mustache and short, pointed beard were nearly black. Silas studied the man's eyes. They were unsmiling eyes—even when the corners of Evan's mouth had turned up, his eyes had stayed flat, almost expressionless. Silas remembered the way they had skimmed over him earlier when they were introduced. Silas had the distinct impression he'd been assessed and found wanting.

Silas' thoughts were interrupted when the soup bowls were removed. He met Amy's blue eyes just over the top of a red rose when the butler announced the serving of roast duck. Those eyes twinkled at him before Amy turned to answer a question posed by her uncle.

The meal progressed, and by the time dessert arrived Silas was a bit antsy. He was not used to taking so much time over a midday meal, and especially when he had not been allowed more than two sentences' worth of conversation.

Amy also must have been aware of the time. Not more than ten minutes passed after the end of the meal when she said they had to be leaving. She hugged her aunt good-bye and promised to return soon. Silas stayed in the house a moment longer to add his thanks to Bev Randall as Evan walked Amy to the wagon. Once outside, he caught part of their conversation as he approached.

"Please, Amy, don't reject the idea out of hand. You'll always be welcome in this home. If you don't feel good about leaving your father in someone else's care, then plan to come when he's back on his feet."

Amy opened her mouth to speak, but Evan held up his hand to forestall her. "Don't give me an answer now. Just think on it and know the offer I made before your father's accident still stands."

"Alright, Uncle Evan, I'll talk to you later." Amy's voice sounded almost sad.

Silas had boarded the wagon and was surprised when Evan reached across Amy to shake his hand. His smile was almost warm. His words were even more surprising. "I'm glad you're here, Silas. I hope with your help Amy's father will be up and about soon." He didn't wait for a reply but turned and walked back to the house.

Silas sat for a moment and stared at the woman beside him. When she did not look at him, but sat staring somewhere beyond the horse's ears, he spoke. "I don't suppose you'd care to tell me what that was all about?" He watched Amy frown and bite her lower lip, telling him she'd heard his question, but she made no move to answer.

Just as silently, Silas urged the team forward. Amy still had not spoken at the edge of town and Silas left her to her thoughts even though his were racing. He had not liked the bit of conversation he'd heard or the unexpected words directed to him from the town banker. Something told him Evan Randall never acted unselfishly. Silas shook his head slightly over his judgmental attitude. The last thing Evan Randall needed was Silas' condemnation. What he really needed was prayer, and Silas was suddenly thankful for Amy's silence as he began to pray silently.

Amy, sitting so quietly on her side of the wagon, was praying also. Not just praying, but begging God for wisdom in this impossible situation that was bound to bring pain to someone she loved.

A few weeks before her father's accident, Evan had approached her about coming to live in town with him and Bev. Amy had been so surprised that she had not known what to say. She had rarely seen her uncle so excited. "You have no social life when you live so far out of town. Bev and I have more space in this house than we know what to do with. I know you would never make this move without talking to your father. But I'll say this much, Amy," and here his voice grew very stern, "if your father really loves you he won't stand in the way of your happiness."

Amy had been dumfounded by his words. She had never expected to receive such an invitation from her uncle, and she wondered where in the world he got the idea she was unhappy on the farm. Amy was still reeling from shock when her uncle spoke his first insensitive words to her. "I don't have to remind you, Amy, that Debra Wheeler is a town girl. Now I think Thomas Blane is a fool to give you up and obviously not good enough for you, but the truth is that the most eligible men are from town and they would naturally want wives from town."

Had Amy not been so stunned by his words, she would have burst into tears. She was well on her way to getting over Thomas. In fact, she was doing so well she wondered if indeed it had been love she felt for him. But these words coming so cruelly from her adored uncle, that somehow her being from the farm had made her not good enough, were almost more than she could bear. Even now they caused a sharp pain in the region of her heart. It didn't help that Amy thought Debra Wheeler very beautiful and her pride had suffered a severe blow at being tossed over for one of the most attractive girls in Neillsville.

Suddenly she wanted to talk it over with Silas. But after the way she had treated him in front of her uncle's house, she wasn't sure he was speaking to her.

"Silas, are you angry with me?"

"No, should I be?"

"Yes."

"How do you figure?"

"Well, you asked me a question in town and I wouldn't even look at you."

"That's true. But did you stop to think that I asked you a question that was none of my business?"

Amy shifted on the seat to look at Silas and he pulled the team to a halt. They were still about a half mile from the house.

"Oh Silas, I wasn't offended by your question—never think that, but I'm in a terrible mess and I really need someone to talk to and it can't be my dad. If he ever found out, he'd be just crushed."

"Found out about what?" Silas asked, his eyes leveled on her face. Had she not said a word he would have known something or someone was playing havoc with her heart. For an instant he thought it might be the man she had been engaged to and wondered why this idea bothered him so much.

Amy was unaware that her face was a mask of confusion and grief as she answered. "Before Dad's accident, Uncle Evan asked me to come and live with him and Aunt Bev. Today he assured me the offer still stands."

Amy spoke the words quietly, and Silas understood almost instantly the dilemma she was in. She had long been an envoy of peace amid these two families, and now she found herself between the kettle and the coals. No matter what her choice, someone she loved was going to be hurt.

13

Grant was starved for news from town and fired many questions at Silas and Amy during supper, much to the relief of both. Time had not allowed them to sit long on the road, and they were still both in deep thought over their unfinished conversation.

"Amy," Silas had said, "I don't have answers for you right now. I need to think and pray before I can advise you, and I'm not even sure I should do that. You may need to work this out for yourself. But I'm glad you told me and when you want to talk, you know I'm here." Amy had thanked him. The regret and concern she had seen in his eyes had somehow given her a small measure of peace. She didn't feel quite so alone in her pain.

Amy had just finished the dishes when Grant called her to his room. Silas had helped him into bed after supper, then he went out for a final check on the cows. Grant asked Amy to play for a while, and Silas found her seated at the piano and playing softly when he returned.

Moving quietly, Silas settled onto the couch and let the music flow over him. Amy was in profile to him as she played, and Silas watched with the eye of a fellow musician. As always, her style and grace were beyond compare. Her hands moved with confidence as she played from memory. Silas recognized the music, noticing she went from hymns to a more difficult piece that had a soothing, almost haunting melody. His head fell back to rest on the couch and, as his eyes slid closed, he began to reflect on the day.

The Randalls wanted Amy to come and live with them—what a mess! The conversation Silas had overheard at the wagon now made complete sense. Judging from the words Evan had directed at Silas, he seemed very confident Amy would come as soon as Grant was on his feet. Silas had to admit to himself, his first reaction to the idea was negative, but who was he to judge? Maybe God wanted Amy living in town.

Amy, as far as he could see, had been working hard all her life to balance her affection between her father and uncle—a position she had not asked for but one which had been thrust upon her at birth. Judging from the relationships Amy had with both men, it was obvious she was doing an excellent job. Silas felt a bit of anger that she should now be forced into making this kind of a decision. Possibly some of the anger could better be termed frustration at having no advice to give this young woman. She held a special place in his heart, as a younger sister would. His feelings must have shown on his face because he opened his eyes when the music stopped to find Amy watching him. "The music is supposed to relax you, Si, not make you frown." She smiled at him as she spoke, but her eyes were questioning.

"It wasn't the music, Amy, I can assure you. Nothing has changed in four years; you still play like an angel."

"Just exactly how many angels have you heard play?" Amy's voice was a bit mocking.

Silas gave her a stern look. "I can see there are other things that haven't changed in four years; we've talked about this before. When someone compliments your playing, you thank them—not belittle your work with some light remark."

"But Silas, that's just it, it's not work. My playing has always come so easily that I feel guilty accepting compliments."

"It's still a gift from God, and to make light of it is wrong." The two sat regarding each other in stubborn silence for some moments. Amy spoke first.

"Were you frowning over what I told you in the wagon?" Amy was sure her dad was asleep, so she did not drop her voice.

Silas' voice was serious as he answered. "It hasn't been far from my thoughts since you told me. Would you like to talk about it?"

Gone was the big brother who scolded her for a flip response to his compliment. In fact, Silas' voice was so tender that Amy nearly cried. She spoke slowly and Silas listened without interruption.

"A few weeks before my dad's fall, Uncle Evan approached me about coming into town to live with them. Somehow he has the impression I'm unhappy out here on the farm. Nothing could be further from the truth." She paused, but Silas kept quiet.

"Silas, had you heard I'd been engaged?" At his nod she continued. "The boy I was engaged to is from town and well, Uncle Evan felt I would meet someone else if I lived there. I've so wanted to talk with my dad, but I'm afraid he'll think I'm staying here out of some sort of obligation and it wouldn't be the truth. I don't want to move into town, but I have no idea how to tell my uncle without hurting him or making him think Dad is forcing me to stay.

"I know my uncle never meant to be mean, but he said the most eligible boys were from town and they would naturally want a wife from town. Debra Wheeler lives in town. She's Thomas Blane's new fiancée, and Uncle Evan thinks if I had been from town Thomas would not have broken up with me. I didn't tell my uncle that I plan to never marry, but I couldn't help but feel a little hurt when he implied I wasn't good enough. I also know my uncle has never accepted Christ, and I'm afraid that if the bond between us is broken, he'll never come to know the Lord."

Even in the light of this man's need for salvation, Silas was working hard at keeping a normal expression on his face as rage boiled within him. How dare her uncle make Amy feel as though she were not good enough! Thomas Blane was a fool and obviously didn't deserve her. Silas would have laughed if he'd known how closely his thoughts echoed those of Evan Randall, a man he was having more and more trouble liking all the time.

"I know you can't tell me what to do, but thank you for listening, Silas."

Silas' heart nearly broke at the forlorn look on her face. "You're right, sweetheart, I can't tell you what to do. But I will say this: I think you're doing your father a great injustice. Part of the hurt you're feeling is because you want to talk to him. I know he'll listen and help you, and you know it too. Even with a broken leg he's still the father who loves you with all his heart. He'll not let you down."

Amy sat and stared at Silas as the truth of his words came through to her. How many times had she asked God for help while possibly missing how close it had been all the time? "Thank you, Silas." Amy spoke the words softly and moved to her bedroom. Silas blew out the lanterns and headed for his own room.

Grant lay quietly in his bed listening as Silas climbed the stairs to the attic. He stared at the ceiling, feeling old beyond his years and helpless. He wanted to pray but didn't even know where to begin. After all he'd overheard tonight from the living room, the pain in his heart overpowered the pain in his leg. He felt a single tear slide down his temple, his heart crying out to God as it had so many times past, "Please God, let Your will for Amy be as special as she is."

"You got the note?"

"I got it." The voice answering was sharp with anxiety.

"What's it say? We got another job to do?"

"Patience man, this barn's been standing alone for years. A light burning in here and we're as good as found out."

The testy man's companion peered out into the ebony night. There didn't appear to be anyone about, but one couldn't be too careful. Suddenly the attention of both men was drawn upward by the sound of fluttering wings—bats, no doubt. Each man reacted in his own way—one suppressed a shiver, the other pulled his hat a bit closer about his ears, and whispered, "Well, if we can't read it here, let's get back to town." The man was not about to admit his fear, but he nearly sagged with relief when his partner moved toward the horses.

As always the two were plagued by the identity of their employer, or rather the lack thereof. When at first their services had been employed, the jobs were nondescript and, even though the margin was narrow, within the confines of the law. But all this had changed a number of weeks back when they were asked to rob a farmhouse. The amount taken was very small, but it became obvious that they were being tested when the next farm robbery had yielded a substantially larger amount.

Even as the men climbed stairs at the back of the largest saloon in town and entered their room, each harbored a small hope within his breast that this note would give some clue as to the identity of the mysterious, darkly-cloaked figure with whom they were doing business.

14

The letter began "Dear Silas" and it was from his grandmother. She wrote of herself and the family, along with asking many questions as to the welfare of the Nolan household. Silas had had precious few moments with his Grandma Em in the last month, what with his trip to Chicago and then leaving almost immediately for Neillsville. He missed her more than he thought possible. The letter was the next best thing to talking with her, but it made him feel the void of her missing presence all the more.

Unbidden, the fact came to Silas' mind that his grandmother was not getting any younger. He couldn't imagine life without her, and he immediately pushed the thought aside. She was with them now and he could see no reason to torture himself with images of a future without her.

An unfamiliar man's voice drifted up through Silas' open bedroom door to interrupt his musing. He listened for a moment from his place on the bed and caught sounds of Amy's voice before setting his letter aside and descending the stairs to appease his curiosity.

"Oh Silas, I'm glad you came down," Amy spoke the minute she spotted him. "This is Doc Schaefer. He's here to check on Dad."

The men shook hands and exchanged pleasantries. Both Silas and Amy watched as the doctor moved into Grant's bedroom with easy familiarity, shutting the door behind him. Amy headed back into the kitchen and Silas went outside.

The weather was warm, surprisingly so for this early in the year, but the ground was still too wet to even start thinking about the crops. Silas' mind turned to the painting of the house.

Grant must have worked quickly because the front and sides of the house were done, leaving just the back and the trim. Standing at the back of the house, Silas could see where Grant had started to paint at the apex of the gabled roof. His eye measured the distance from the spot near the roof to the ground. No wonder Grant was in pain. Silas winced at the thought of Grant's fall.

"When do you plan to start?" Amy spoke as she came around the corner of the house.

"Monday morning, pending the weather."

Amy nodded and looked to the small section her father had already painted, far above the ground. She didn't say anything to Silas but she was determined: Come Monday she would be out here holding the ladder when he climbed it.

The couple began moving toward the front of the house. "I've asked Doc to stay for supper, it's nearly ready."

"I thought I smelled pie," Silas said with a pleased grin.

"That you did—last year's peaches." Silas held the door for Amy and, as they entered the house, the aromas that assailed Silas told him Amy had been hard at work.

Doc Schaefer was an easy man to talk with or rather to listen to. He knew everyone within miles and loved to give the latest news to any willing ear. Silas learned that Carrie Nelson had just given birth to a large, healthy girl and that he suspected Maria Southern was carrying twins.

The doctor's diagnosis on Grant had been a little less than encouraging. The healing process was slow and Grant would be off his feet for an indefinite period of time. Grant had not joined them at the supper table this night, and Silas strongly suspected his spirits were low. Both he and Amy had been in to check on him before retiring for the night and, even though Grant was talkative, Silas knew he was discouraged over his bedridden state.

Amy went to bed with much the same thought as Silas. She reached for the Bible she kept on the table by her bed and turned to the Book of Isaiah. In the fifty-fifth chapter, verses eight and nine she read, "For my thoughts are not your thoughts, neither are your ways my ways, saith the Lord. For as the heavens are higher than the earth, so are my ways higher than your ways, and my thoughts than your thoughts." Reading these words helped restore some of Amy's peace and calm her questions about why so many painful things had entered their lives.

Suddenly Amy remembered something. She jumped out of bed to look for a poem she had written after her mother died. It was in the bottom of the chest which sat at the foot of her bed. After reading it over again, Amy thought of how good it would sound put to music.

Amy got back into bed with a purpose in her heart. She would try not to dwell on her dad's accident or on the answer she must give to her uncle and she would give special attention to putting some notes to the words of her poem.

When Amy finally did drift off to sleep, it was with a more peaceful heart and with joy that tomorrow was Sunday, a day set aside for fellowship and learning about her Lord.

15

Silas stood fingering his beard before the mirror that hung over his washstand. The words ending his grandmother's letter came back to him: "You are such a peaceful, consistent part of our lives, Silas. You never seem to change as the years go on, and sometimes I think this is what makes you so special."

He knew very well that his grandmother had meant this in only the kindest terms, but somehow the words bothered him. Silas did not believe for a moment that a man's physical appearance altered his personality—to which he was sure his Grandma Em was referring, but somehow he had this tremendous urge to change something about his looks.

He glanced down at the razor near his hand, still a little bemused at what might have compelled him to bring it along. It had been years since he'd used it. Once more he looked up into the mirror. "I'll do it," he thought. And having made up his mind, it was as good as done.

— ❖ —

Amy closed the door to her father's room. He had told her the night before that he planned to sleep late and not to worry about breakfast. He'd assured her he could wait until they got home from church to eat. But when breakfast was on the stove, Amy decided to check on him anyhow. Just as he'd predicted, he was sound asleep.

Amy was just turning away from the stove when Silas entered the kitchen. At least she thought it was Silas. The bowl of oatmeal dropped from her hands and landed hard on the table.

Silas stood completely still and watched Amy move toward him as though she were in a trance. Her beautiful blue eyes were wide as she surveyed his new face. His beard was gone. His upper lip still sported a full, dark mustache, but his beard was completely gone. Amy had always thought Silas nice-looking, but suddenly those words were a gross understatement. His jaw was strong and his chin had a tiny cleft in it. His cheeks were leaner than you would have expected to find under all that hair. Somehow the absence of his beard made his eyes stand out, and Amy noticed for the first time how blue they were. The skin of his lower face was several shades lighter than his upper cheeks and forehead, but it didn't detract from his looks. One word came quickly to mind: beautiful.

Amy was unaware that she had spoken the word aloud until Silas smiled so wide the cleft in his chin disappeared. Amy blushed to her hairline. Silas, on the other hand, was pleased beyond words.

Amy turned away in confusion, realizing that until that moment she had never looked at Silas as being anything more than a big brother. Seeing him like this, as a woman sees an attractive man, was a bit disconcerting. Suddenly she felt rather childish and wondered if maybe this was the way Thomas had perceived her, as a little girl.

"Do I really look okay, Amy?"

Amy immediately picked up the hesitancy in his voice and turned to find she was right. This big, self-assured man was in need of a little encouragement. Amy doubted that Silas knew his insecurity was written all over his face. Suddenly he was her big brother again, and Amy answered with sincerity. "You look great, Silas. I've just never noticed what pretty eyes you have." She grinned mischievously before she went on. "The girls at church will be begging for introductions. And Mrs. Anderson, before she recognizes you, will be sure I've got another suitor for her girls."

Silas touched his bare face. "I wonder if I could stick the hair back on."

Amy laughed at his chagrined tone and gave him no mercy. "Come now, Silas, you might find one of the Anderson girls very nice."

"It isn't the girls I object to. It's the idea of Mrs. Anderson as a mother-in-law that has me doubting."

Amy laughed again, but it sounded hollow to her own ears. She couldn't understand the funny feeling coming over her at the thought of Silas interested in one of the girls at church. It was still on her mind when they pulled out of the yard in the buggy.

Amy would have been surprised to know that Silas' thoughts were along the same vein. What was it that caused a man to become more attracted to one woman than another? His brother Luke had known the women at church for years, and yet by his own admission he had had to fight his attraction for Christine almost from the moment he laid eyes on her. Had she been a Christian when they'd first met, Luke would no doubt have carried her off and married her within the first week. Silas missed them terribly, especially little Josh, but it was almost a relief to be away for a spell. Luke and Christine's marriage was a warm and loving one, and even though they never made Silas uncomfortable with their shows of affection, they did make him long for a wife and child of his own.

Suddenly Silas' thoughts turned to Amy. How was it for her after planning to be married, expecting a home of her own, with a husband at her side, only to have those plans dashed in an instant?

April Nolan, Amy's aunt who lived in Baxter, knew Silas cared deeply for Grant and Amy. After Amy had written to her about the change in her wedding plans, April had talked with Silas. He was sure Amy was unaware that her aunt had shared with him.

Maybe it was because Silas had met Amy as a vulnerable 14-year-old girl who had just lost her mother, but he knew he was more than a little protective of her. The idea of seeing her hurt caused him deep pain. He worried a bit over what his reaction would be if he were to meet Thomas Blane.

Silas was so deep in his own thoughts and prayer he did not notice Amy's own silence. In fact, he was still praying as they pulled into the churchyard.

16

Silas and Amy spent the first few minutes at the church reacquainting Silas with members of the church family. Many of the faces were familiar, giving Silas a warm sense of belonging.

Amy's prediction had been correct. Mrs. Anderson bore down upon them with surprising speed, dragging two very shy-looking daughters in her wake. Even though Silas must have been a lost cause in Mrs. Anderson's eyes, he was introduced to Brenda and Clare. They were indeed shy, and Silas felt a little sorry for the awkward situation in which their mother had put them.

With the introduction over, Silas turned to see if Amy was ready to go only to find her studying him intently.

"Did you change your mind about my looks without a beard?" Amy didn't answer his teasing question, but continued to stare at him for a few moments, completely unaware of her scrutiny. "Amy, is something wrong?"

"Silas, why aren't you married?"

"What?" Silas bent low over Amy to lessen the difference in their heights; he was sure he had misunderstood her. "What did you say?"

"I asked why you have never married, but I'm sorry I did. It's none of my business." Amy could feel the warmth in her cheeks as Silas looked at her in confusion. What was the matter with her? She was never uncomfortable with Silas and not at all used to making a fool of herself. Amy watched as Silas opened his mouth to speak, but the church bell began to ring and Amy was sure the relief she saw on Silas' face was just as evident on her own.

Silas sat in the second bench as Amy moved a few feet up to the piano. Her movements were sure and graceful, but to Silas she looked preoccupied. Whatever had prompted her question to him regarding his marital status? Silas wanted to mull the thought over, but the service was starting and he tried to shift his mind to the present.

Silas watched as Pastor Johnson stepped behind the small pulpit at the front of the church. The man was small, petite in height and frame. But he had an air of authority about him, and his sermons were doctrinally sound. As much as Silas enjoyed his preaching, he had a feeling that today his mind would be elsewhere. With effort he pulled his mind away from Amy as the pastor led the small congregation in a few songs. The pastor then directed everyone to turn to Psalm 121 and to follow along as he read.

I will lift up mine eyes unto the hills, from whence cometh my help. My help cometh from the Lord, who made heaven and earth. He will not suffer thy foot to be moved; he that keepeth thee will not slumber. Behold, he that keepeth Israel shall neither slumber nor sleep. The Lord is thy keeper; the Lord is thy shade upon thy right hand. The sun shall not smite thee by day, nor the moon by night. The Lord shall preserve thee from all evil; he shall preserve thy soul. The Lord shall preserve thy going out and thy coming in from this time forth, and even for evermore.

They sang two more songs and then were launched into the sermon. Snatches of the message from 1 John came through to Silas, but for the most part he was miles away. He glanced at Amy often and noticed she didn't even have her Bible open. When Amy rose from his side to play the closing hymn, Silas was appalled. What was the matter with him that he could not even take time from his own thoughts to hear God's Word preached?

For the most part, Silas and Amy were quiet on the ride back to the farm. Amy's mind kept returning to the few words she had with Silas before going into the church. Her embarrassment kept her quiet not only for the ride home but for most of the day.

Sunday was usually spent relaxing, so when Grant was settled back in his bed after the noon meal Amy went off to her room for the rest of the afternoon.

Silas spent the day in his room also. He prayed and read his Bible for over two hours. For some reason his prayers were very concentrated on Amy, and by the time supper rolled around he couldn't even think of her without feeling tears at the back of his eyes.

The day passed so quietly that Silas couldn't help wondering what Monday and the new week would bring.

17

"Amy, you don't have to do this." Silas spoke the words for the third time, but the girl on the ground stood mute, holding the ladder in firm determination. Silas tried one more time, but she wouldn't even look up at him.

He sighed in exasperation. They had argued over breakfast, they had argued while milking, and then again as Silas climbed the ladder. Or rather, Silas had argued—Amy had just listened in stubborn silence after announcing that morning that she planned to hold the ladder while he painted.

Silas started back down the ladder. Amy moved aside as he neared the bottom. He stood frowning at her, and Amy returned his look without apology. Silas was tempted to order her into the house, but he knew she wouldn't go. It would also hurt her feelings, and that was something he would not do. With this thought in mind, his words to her were kind.

"Amy, I'm not going to fall."

"That's right, you're not." The firmness of her statement would have been more believable if her lower lip had not trembled.

Something inside of Silas melted as he witnessed her fear and vulnerability. He grabbed her into his arms and gave her a fierce hug. When he set her from him, the hands holding her upper arms were tight. "Amy, I understand your fear, but I don't believe God is going to let me fall from the ladder. Your dad and I have talked. Even if you had been out here that day, you could not have stopped his fall. In fact, from what Grant described, he would have fallen on top of you had you been standing here."

Amy followed his finger as he pointed to the foot of the ladder. "Amy, you're going to have to trust God in this even though it frightens you. If it makes you feel better to hold the ladder, that's fine. But God alone has control over this."

Silas' arms dropped to his side, and Amy turned to look out over the surrounding landscape. With the way she was chewing on her lower lip, Silas was sure she wasn't seeing the land at all.

Silas figured Amy must have come to some peace because she turned to Silas after a few minutes and said, "I'll be out to check on how you're coming a little later."

Once in the kitchen, Amy stood and tried to calm the pounding of her heart. Silas was right—she could do nothing outside. It did feel better to hold the ladder, but Amy knew if she did that she would be trusting in herself and not God to keep Silas safe.

Almost of their own volition, Amy's feet moved toward her father's bedroom.

Grant was awake and looking almost as though he had been waiting for her. The curtain moved slightly against the window, and Amy instantly knew he had been. With the window open slightly, he had heard her entire conversation with Silas.

Grant patted the edge of the bed and Amy settled herself next to him. "Silas is right," he said without preamble. "God sent him to us in our time of need and I trust that God will take care of him. When he first asked me about finishing the painting I was against it, but I realized this was pride. I've had to face the fact that right now I can't climb that ladder and may never be able to again. Well, I wasn't about to let you finish the painting, so you can see I didn't have many options. Amy, your fear is understandable, but everything is going to be fine. God will take care of Silas."

Grant stared at Amy as she studied the carpet in silence. She was a young replica of Maureen. In fact, they were so much alike he even knew what she was thinking. Her silence meant she was still pondering over the situation and praying it out—so like Maureen.

Maureen. Even now a pain went through his chest. His precious Maureen—oh, how he missed her. How proud she would have been of Amy, grown into a beautiful, godly young woman.

Suddenly, almost desperately, Grant wanted Amy to know the kind of love he and Maureen had shared.

What was the matter with Thomas Blane? For him to have Amy's love and reject it was beyond comprehension. Would Amy ever give her love again?

Movement at the back of the house drew his attention, but Amy didn't change positions. Silas Cameron. A smile broke across Grant's features. For the first time Grant was very glad Thomas had broken off with Amy. He tried to slow his mind down, but it didn't work. Silas was the perfect man for . . .

"Dad, are you alright?"

Grant started and moved to see Amy looking at him with concern. "I'm fine, honey. I was just listening to Silas bump around out there and thinking." He reached over to pat his daughter's hand, and Amy looked relieved.

Amy stood. "I think I'll head out and see how he's doing."

Grant's voice stopped her at the door. "Amy, if you want to talk about anything, you know I'm here."

Amy saw the look of tender concern on her father's face and wondered exactly what had brought that on, but she simply thanked him and went out.

18

Silas stood over the basin in the kitchen and scrubbed at the paint on his right hand with a small brush. It felt as though he were removing more skin than paint. He figured he could take more time tomorrow and use some turpentine, so he put the brush down and finished washing up for supper.

Silas had already helped Grant to the table, and he and Amy were waiting patiently for Silas to sit down. Grant's spirits, which were already high, soared when Silas told him he had finished the back of the house and would concentrate on the trim the rest of the week.

They talked about the planting which could be started next week if the good weather held. Grant could see that Silas was starving, so he took pity on him and held his conversation for dessert.

Silas was on his second piece of cake when Grant said, "I'd like you to head into town this week, no later than Thursday. There are a few things you'll need for next week. Even if we get rained out of our plans, I'll feel better when we have what's on that list."

"That's fine. Amy, do you need anything from town?"

"Yes, about six items if you think you'll have time."

"I'm sure I will." He smiled and Amy smiled back. As the day progressed, the two of them seemed to be back on old terms—warm, friendly, and a bit teasing.

After Silas thanked Amy for the meal and complimented her cooking, he turned to Grant. "Grant, where would you like to be?" Silas asked the older man, able to tell he was not at all taxed from his time at the supper table as he usually was.

"I thought you'd never ask," Grant said with a twinkle in his eye. "I'd like to go into the living room and listen to my daughter play the piano."

"Well, do I have anything to say about this?" Amy said with a teasing tone. She, too, could see that her father was in fine form this evening.

"No, you don't. You just do as you're told or I'll see you out to the woodshed."

"But Dad," Amy said with a laugh, "we don't have a wood-shed."

"I know, but we did when I was a kid and that threat always worked on me."

— ❖ —

Silas wondered as he settled back on the couch if he could ever grow tired of hearing Amy play. Not likely, he was sure.

The window near the piano was open, and Silas watched as the breeze lifted a strand of her golden blonde hair. With the lanterns turned high, her hair shone with health and cleanliness.

As he continued to watch her, he remembered how good she had smelled as he'd passed her in the kitchen—like spring flowers and fresh air.

Amy looked up then and smiled at her dad and then Silas. Silas' breath caught in his throat at her beauty. Even as special as she had been as a child, Silas would never have dreamed she would grow into such a beautiful young woman. Talented, loving, giving, godly—really all the things a man would want in the woman he lov . . .

Between one heartbeat and the next, Silas Cameron fell head over heels in love with Amy Nolan. Silas sat frozen as his heart thundered painfully in his chest. "I'm in love with her!" he thought in wonder. Silas, having thought of himself as just a big brother, a friend, and a confidant, sat looking at Amy in stunned disbelief.

He realized it had been coming for a while. He had labeled it protectiveness and the special way a brother felt for his little sister, but it was love.

Now he knew why he could listen to her playing forever—because he wanted to be *with* her forever. He wanted her for his wife.

This joyful realization lasted only seconds. Amy thought of him as a big brother. At one time, this was special beyond words, but a big brother was the very last thing he wanted to be to Amy right now.

Despair quickly set in as Silas remembered Amy had said she planned to never marry. Silas looked quickly away from Amy. He was afraid she would glance over and see in his eyes all he was feeling.

Silas' heart nearly stopped as he averted his eyes from Amy

only to have them lock with Grant's. Grant's look was one of compassion and understanding. *He knows*, Silas realized. *He knew even before I did.*

Amy ended the number just then and Grant quickly spoke up. "I think I'm ready to turn in now, Amy. Thank you, honey, you played beautifully."

The two men went alone to Grant's room and Silas saw Grant settled in for the night. Silas turned to leave, but Grant caught his arm. Silas had been avoiding the older man's eyes. He wanted desperately to be alone with his newfound feelings. But with Grant's hand holding him, he had little choice.

Grant said not a word as Silas' eyes met his. He held the young man with his eyes as well as his hand for a long moment. Whatever he had been searching for in Silas' face he must have found, for he slowly nodded his head in silent approval and bid Silas good-night.

Silas' good-night to Amy was hasty. He had to escape to his room. He wasn't the least bit tired, but the need to be alone was overpowering. It was long into the night before he slept.

19

"Silas, do you miss your mom?"

"Very much."

Amy's mind was four years back in time. Silas had been scheduled to leave for home in two days. They were talking up on the bluff behind her house, seated beneath the big oaks. The spot was Amy's favorite thinking place.

"Do you think about her all the time?"

"Not so much now, but right after she died I thought about her constantly."

Amy was silent for a long time. When she turned to Silas, there were tears in her eyes—the first he'd seen. "It's not fair," she whispered. "It's not fair that she's gone and now you're leaving, too."

"Oh, sweetheart," was all he could say as he folded her within his arms. Amy sobbed then. The arms holding her close and the loving endearment were too much. The tears came in a torrent.

Silas continued to hold her and speak quietly to her, stroking her hair and calling her sweetheart. He told her God understood her pain and that He was there for her.

Amy could not remember anything after that. The next day Silas had told her she had cried herself to sleep in his arms. Silas had carried her all the way back to the house and delivered her into the arms of her anxious father who had been watching them from the house.

What Amy did not know, since her father put her to bed and she slept through the night, was that Silas had retired to his room to let his own tears fall. Tears for the 13-year-old boy he had been while watching his mother's body being lowered into the ground. Tears for the 14-year-old girl who had had no siblings with which to share her grief. This young girl who was lonely and scared, who was having to say good-bye to him now that their friendship had become so special.

— ❖ —

Amy came out of her reverie when she heard the team and wagon in the yard. For a moment she stood at the kitchen window and wondered what had brought on her memory. She loved it when Silas called her sweetheart. He was the only person who did, and it gave her a special feeling inside. Maybe that was what she wanted—that special feeling. Silas had been so distant for the last few days. Amy told herself he must be homesick. But even as she thought it, she knew it wasn't true. As Amy watched out the window, she thought she saw some white paper in Silas' shirt pocket. She hoped he had gotten a letter from home. That was sure to cheer him up.

Silas spotted Amy at the window, but he kept his face turned away. He had received letters from home, but he hadn't even looked at them. He had also seen Bev Randall in town, and she had given Silas a verbal message for Amy. It was not a happy message and, along with trying to keep his feelings for her hidden, he had the starting of a headache. It looked to be a long evening.

Silas was sure he should wait until tomorrow to deliver his message to Amy, but when Amy said her dad wanted a tray in his room, Silas knew the time was now.

He knew he was acting oddly from the looks Amy kept sending him. She had been eyeing him curiously for the last few days. He was not succeeding in his act, wanting her to believe nothing between them had changed.

The signs of love—watchfulness, the need to be close, wanting to touch—were new to Silas and, because he had to hide them, painful.

Silas had worked at not reaching for her hand or touching her hair more than once in the last few days. The times when Amy had casually touched his arm as she spoke had been torture. Silas wanted to take her small hand in his own and hold it for hours.

Last night Amy had teased him and flicked water in his direction while they were doing the dishes. When she had turned to him, her face wreathed in smiles and laughter, Silas had gripped the dishcloth tightly to keep from grabbing and kissing her.

"Silas, did you hear from home?" The silence between them continued to lengthen as they ate, and Amy could no longer stand it.

"Now, Silas," he said to himself as he faced Amy across the table. "I did get letters from home, but I haven't read them yet." Amy's brow rose in questioning surprise, but she stayed silent.

"I saw your aunt while in town. She sent you a message." Silas' somber tone frightened Amy. "There will be no summer wedding for Thomas Blane and Debra Wheeler because they were married quietly on Monday. She said to tell you that it's not town gossip. She spoke directly to Thomas." Silas paused and his voice dropped low. "Thomas told your aunt that Debra is pregnant; the baby is due in the fall. Mr. Wheeler insisted they move the wedding up and Mrs. Wheeler insisted they live with them until the baby is born.

"Your aunt said she wanted to tell you herself, but felt a message from me was better than waiting and having you possibly hear the news through the gossip lines."

Silas watched as dismay and sadness showed in Amy's eyes. Silas knew that any emotional pain he had previously felt was minimal compared to the pain he felt in knowing the woman he loved was in love with another man.

"I'm sorry, Amy." Silas' voice was husky with raw emotion.

Amy looked at the big, gentle man across from her and knew she had to clarify things for him. He was hurting for her, and she knew that in a few words she could lessen the pain.

"Si, I'm not in love with Thomas. In fact, I've begun to wonder if I ever was. I'm sorry for both Thomas and Debra. In fact, a part of me can understand how easily it could happen. But as painful as Thomas' rejection was, I'm glad we're not married. It obviously would have been a mistake."

Silas felt as though the weight of the earth had been lifted from his shoulders. But his feeling of euphoria didn't last.

"You see, Si, I feel that my dad needs me here. This is my home. My decision not to marry has nothing to do with Thomas breaking off with me. I feel this is God's way of showing me this is where I belong—here, taking care of my father. And even if I had doubts about my feelings, Dad's accident confirmed them. He needs me here."

"Amy does your dad know you feel this way? Somehow I think he would want you to have a home of your own." Silas made no attempt to hide the distress her words caused him.

But Amy didn't take his words personally. "Oh Silas, I know you mean well, but this *is* my home. You're going to think it's silly, but whenever I'm away even for a trip into town, as soon as I spot our farm my heart begins to sing. I know this is where I belong."

"Well Amy, your aunt will be glad you were not overly upset."

The statement sounded inane even to his own ears, but he couldn't possibly tell her what he was really thinking.

Amy noticed Silas' surprise upon hearing her beliefs, but she knew she was right. In fact, so sure was she that her mind had already moved back to Thomas and Debra. She didn't even notice when Silas refused dessert and quickly excused himself to check on the cows.

20

Dear Silas,

Baxter is not the same without you. I feel as though you have been gone for months. Josh continually crawls down the hallway to your room and bangs on the closed door.

Luke said the extra work from your absence is not nearly as hard as your missed companionship. Enclosed is a letter from Frank Chambers. He wrote while here to deliver the horses and asked me to send it with mine. Frank took the entire first evening of his visit to try and talk Luke into convincing you to go to work for him in Chicago. Luke heard him out, but told Frank in no uncertain terms that the decision was yours and he would not interfere.

We, of course, want God's will in this, but the thought of you living elsewhere makes me unhappy. We're praying you will know what to do, for this is the only way you'll be at peace.

Please write us. God bless you.

Love,
Luke, Christine, and Joshua

— ❖ —

Dear Si,

I saddled my horse today and rode down by the creek. I ended up in the spot where we had that huge mud fight as kids. As I recall, Dad warmed our backsides for that one. Sitting in that spot, I missed you so much I cried.

The boys are ready to be out of school for the summer. It shows in their restlessness. Last week Cal locked Charlie in an old trunk in the barn. Their father found them, and I noticed they both sat down carefully at the supper table that night. I guess things never change; each generation gets their share of spankings.

Mac said to tell you Sunday dinner at Gram's is not going to be the same until you come home.

If you don't hear from Sue, it's because she isn't feeling very well these days. She hasn't said, but I suspect she's pregnant.

Please tell the Nolans that we're praying for all of you and that they can't keep you forever.

Love,
Julia and family

— ⋰ —

It was the afternoon of the following day before Silas sat down to read his letters. Silas prayed immediately for Sue and the new life possibly growing within her. She and Mark were so happy together that Silas was sure this would only add to their joy.

"Oh God," Silas prayed in his heart, "another niece or nephew. When God? When will I have children of my own? Surely this desire to be a husband and father is from You." Silas sat in painful confusion and tried very hard to thank God for the things he had and not the things missing in his life.

"Be still and know that I am God." The words came gently to Silas. He wasn't even sure of the reference. Maybe somewhere in the Psalms. For the first time, the words became real for him. God was in control. Be still, for He would have His perfect way.

Silas stopped praying. He lay back on his bed and looked toward heaven. Even as he saw the beamed ceiling above him, his heart grew calm and peaceful.

God was in control of Grant, Amy, and him. If Amy was meant to live with her father for the rest of her years, then she and Silas would be miserable as husband and wife. If Amy was to be his wife, then God would change her heart and Silas would have to learn patience.

"Be still and know that I am God."

"Please God," Silas prayed, "keep those words before my eyes."

Silas lay still for long minutes before he reached for the letter from Frank. He had just started it when Amy called to him. She sounded anxious, and Silas rushed down the stairs.

"Oh Silas, will you help me? Dad has caught a spring cold. He said he would feel better if we put some pillows behind his back." Grant did indeed sound congested, and Silas was glad to do anything to make him more comfortable.

Silas was still in the room when Amy left and returned with a large bottle and spoon. Grant ignored the spoon and took two healthy swigs. Returning the bottle to Amy's hand, Grant said, "This will put me right. Thanks, honey."

Amy followed Silas from the room, taking the bottle with her. Once in the kitchen, Silas noticed she looked a bit pale. He wondered if maybe she was coming down with a cold, too.

"Are you okay?"

"I think so. I'm just a little tired." As Amy spoke, she reached for and began to peel potatoes. Silas was instantly by her side. "Amy, let me get supper so you can rest."

"No Si, you still have the milking to do and it's not fair that you get your own supper." Silas didn't argue with her but decided to get the chores and milking done quickly. He could tell Amy needed help whether she would admit it or not. He checked Grant as he went out and found him soundly sleeping.

Two hours later Silas was just finishing outside. On this of all the nights, when he was in a hurry, everything seemed to go wrong. He'd been kicked twice by an uncooperative cow, and he was not paying attention as he lit a lantern and nearly set the barn ablaze. Those were just a few of the things that delayed his finishing. He moved toward the kitchen, worry for Amy hurrying his steps.

Amy was at the stove when he came in. Strangely, she did not have a greeting for him. Silas washed up in record time and went to her side near the stove. She was looking at a large pot and did not acknowledge his presence.

"Amy, how are you doing?" She did not reply or look at him. "Amy?"

"I can't find my spoon."

Silas picked up a large spoon that was sitting very near her hand. Amy's head came up and, after she focused in on the spoon, her face broke into a huge smile.

Silas saw that her face was flushed and her eyes too bright. "Amy, I think you're sick. Let me do this." The smile turned instantly into a fierce scowl and Amy waved the spoon about as she spoke. "I can do it, Silas. It's my kitchen."

Silas watched as she thrust the spoon into the pot, nearly submerging her hand, and began to stir vigorously.

Silas stood in confusion. Amy was not acting at all like herself, and her speech was slightly slurred. His gaze swung away from her and his eyes caught something on the kitchen table. The large bottle of medicine was sitting open with a wet spoon beside it.

Silas walked toward the bottle with a sinking heart. His head jerked back in repulsion after waving the bottle beneath his nose. Silas was no judge of liquor, but if smell was any indication, the stuff was 90 proof.

Amy was drunk.

Silas quickly set the bottle down and returned to the woman at the stove. Her stirring had slowed down to a methodical movement that seemed to be hypnotizing her. He wondered how much she had taken.

Silas headed for Grant's room. That girl needed to be in bed, and Silas needed some help if nothing more than advice. But Grant was sound asleep, out cold. Silas headed back to the kitchen in consternation.

He arrived to see Amy lift the pot and nearly scald herself. She righted the pot just in time, but Silas' mind was made up. He gave her no time to protest as he took the spoon and pot from her and began to guide her out of the kitchen. But his touch was too light on her arm and she easily pulled away from him, saying as she did that she must finish supper. At least, that's what it sounded like.

Silas tried to reason with her: "Amy, you're sick and should be in bed." But Amy chose to ignore him and tried to get back to the stove.

Silas' next move was to get behind Amy. With his chest to her back and walking slowly, he got her as far as the living room before she turned around and Silas found himself hugging her. At any other time hugging Amy would have delighted him, but his skill with inebriated women was nonexistent and he just wanted to see her safely to her room.

Amy let out a little squeal when Silas gave in and swung her up into his arms. Her head swam and she threw her arms around his neck and closed her eyes.

She did not open them until Silas sat her down on the chest at the end of her bed. Silas hunkered down in front of her and

Amy tried hard to concentrate on what he was saying. Everything felt so warm and fuzzy.

"Amy, you need to get ready for bed. I'll get your gown if you tell me where it is." Silas hated even this small intimacy, but he had no choice.

Amy continued to look at him with a small smile on her face, so Silas tried again. "Amy, sweetheart, please try. . . ."

"I love it when you call me sweetheart." Amy's smile grew to just short of a leer.

"Oh boy," Silas thought, "I've got to get out of here or I'm going to kiss her, drunk or not."

Silas' hands flew to Amy's shoes, removing them quickly. A fast search of the room produced Amy's robe and nightgown from the hook on the back of the door. When he set the garments beside her, she informed him that some beast was wrapped around her waist. Silas unknotted the apron strings she had been demolishing and pulled her quickly to her feet.

He thrust the clothing into her arms and commanded, "Put these on, Amy. Now!" With that he exited the room, nearly slamming the door in his haste.

Silas leaned back against the closed door and prayed. He heard bumping sounds from in the room, and then Amy broke into song.

Silas rolled his eyes toward the ceiling and headed for Grant's room. He was still very deep in sleep.

All was quiet in Amy's room as Silas returned to stand outside the door. He waited a moment in indecision and then quietly opened the door.

Amy lay across the bed in her nightgown and robe humming to herself. She raised her head, and Silas could see she was very sleepy.

With utmost care, Silas pulled the covers back and lifted her into his arms. He tucked her within the blankets, robe and all. She was asleep before Silas could straighten. He stood looking at her a moment, wishing he could tell her what was in his heart, before quietly leaving the room.

21

The small copse of trees had seemed like a good hiding place the night before when running from an outraged farmer with a shotgun. But as dawn began to light the sky, the joints and muscles of both men were doubting the wisdom of their decision.

"You think it's safe?"

"Yea, I just hope nobody found the horses."

"If we're gonna get shot at, I'm gonna ask for more money."

"You just let me do the talkin', little brother. You go shooting your mouth off, and we'll be out of work fast."

"Okay, okay, I just don't like sleeping out of my bed. Makes me sore for days."

"Stop whining. We got the money and that means we get paid. Come on, let's get back to town."

— ⊹ —

Silas moved slowly in an attempt to relieve the ache in his back, brought on by a night on the living room sofa. The piece of furniture was neither long enough nor wide enough to support his frame, and he had found little rest upon it.

The night before Silas had made sure that both bedroom doors were open. Amy had slept through the night, but Grant had stirred twice. Silas had seen to his comfort both times and once had given him more medicine.

Grant had shown no pity on Silas when he described Amy's bout with the medicine. He laughed and told Silas that a man who had been allowed to stay the night in the barn a few years ago had given it to him. The man swore it would knock a cold or flu right out of your system.

Grant had not had any suspicions about the contents until his next cold. But it had worked so fast that he didn't care what was in it.

Amy, to his knowledge, had never used it. But then, she rarely got sick. He had asked Silas to check on her then for his peace of mind. Silas had found her warm, but not alarmingly so. Knowing Amy was fine, Grant had gone back to sleep with the help of more medicine. Silas had returned to his temporary bed in the living room and asked God to heal both father and daughter quickly.

Now it was time to do the milking and, with a quick check on both his sleeping patients, Silas headed outside.

— ❖ —

Amy stretched and squirmed under the heaviness of the bed covers. Something felt strange to her, but she was too sleepy to figure it out. Well, at least her head was clear. Last night as she was fixing supper she knew she had caught a cold along with her dad. She could not believe how fast her head had stuffed up.

On impulse, she had taken some of his medicine and, being unsure of the proper dosage, had drunk several tablespoons. Amy's mind stopped in confusion then. The rest of the evening seemed rather vague.

No worry, really, she thought. It had obviously done the trick with as good as she felt. With a sweep of her arm, she threw back the quilts and swung her feet to the floor.

She stared down at her feet in surprise when she noticed she still had one stocking on. Catching sight of herself in the big oval mirror over her dresser, Amy saw that the extra weight in her bed had been her robe and that her hair was still pinned up.

A sudden vision of Silas carrying her through the door and then of him untying her apron at the foot of the bed made Amy's eyes go wide. She began to notice small things. The curtains were not pulled closed and her clothes were thrown all over the room. And her Bible—it was closed. She always opened her Bible to the place where she was reading so she could reach right for it, first thing in the morning.

She reached for it now, and it somehow gave her comfort. "Oh God," she prayed, "You know what I'm thinking, but it just can't be true. Silas would never do that."

Amy was by nature a levelheaded girl. She now used some of her logic to calm herself. She would go about her normal routine and simply ask Silas when she saw him.

Amy dressed, made her bed, and read her Bible. After she closed her father's door to give him quiet, breakfast was the next step in her routine.

But all Amy's coolheaded thinking flew out the window when Silas came in from milking. Before even washing up, he came toward her with a wide smile and asked how she felt.

To Amy's embarrassment, she blushed a fiery red and blurted out, "Silas, how did I get to bed last night?"

Horror overcame her as Silas' own cheeks turned pink and he stared down at the toes of his boots. "Oh no," Amy's mind protested.

When Silas looked up, he knew immediately what she was thinking. "No, Amy, no." Silas was equally horrified. "I just helped you with your shoes and apron. You got yourself ready for bed. You were falling asleep on top of the quilts and I tucked you in. I swear that was all."

Amy looked relieved but still embarrassed. "I guess Dad's medicine is a bit strong."

For the first time Silas saw humor in the situation, and his grin clearly showed his amusement. "You, Miss Nolan, were quite drunk last night."

Amy eyed him warily and asked, "What did I say?"

"Ah, now that would be telling."

"Silas Cameron," Amy scolded, "how dare you tease me about something so embarrassing."

Silas laughed then and assured her she had been a perfect lady. Amy did not look completely convinced, but she couldn't have been too upset for she served him an enormous breakfast and they talked like old friends during the meal.

22

The next weeks were spent in long hours of planting. As long as there was light in the sky, Silas was in the fields. Amy was back to doing most of the milking.

Silas worked out a deal with the man from the cheese factory who always picked up the Nolan's milk. The man would haul the cans—not Amy. Amy protested, but Silas was adamant.

Silas had been furious to discover the man had let her do all the hauling for the two weeks prior to Silas' arrival. They argued about it one day after the man left.

"I can't believe he let you haul those cans. Can he really be that lazy?"

"Yes, I'm afraid he can."

"Did your dad know about this?"

"Honestly, Silas, Dad had enough on his mind. I am a big girl, you know, and I can take care of myself."

This was the real rub, and Silas knew it. He wanted it to be his place to take care of her. The subject was dropped, but it continued to bother Silas.

— ⁘ —

Silas had finally read his letter from Frank Chambers. As expected, he had not accepted the refusal Silas sent before he came to Neillsville.

With the farm work and emotional changes going on in Silas' life he had given very little thought to Frank's offer, even though Christine had warned him of the man's persistency. He needed to continue in prayer regarding that offer. Frank had said to take his time and think it over. With all the unsettled things in Silas' life right now, he needed to do just that.

Silas' relationship with Amy was good, if not as comfortable as it once was. Silas smiled wryly to himself at the different way a man thinks of his little sister and the way he thinks of the woman he wants for his wife.

Little things he had never noticed about Amy before were becoming very dear to him: the way she chewed her lower lip whenever she was anxious about something; the way her voice took on a childlike quality as she prayed, so trusting and sweet; her concentration and sparkling eyes whenever she played the piano. These and so much more made up the whole of Amy.

Amy. Amy Cameron. Silas had tried the name out loud one day in the barn when there was no one to hear but the cows. He loved the way it sounded, but not knowing if it would ever come to pass was disheartening. He tried not to dwell on it.

He petitioned God constantly to give him strength and wisdom in this situation where he felt so helpless. Silas was unable to see it right now, but this time in his life was bringing him closer and closer to God.

There were even moments when he felt God had forgotten him, but they were brief. For even amid the pain of wishing for a life with Amy and not knowing if he would ever have it, was a sweet, peaceful knowledge that God had not deserted him and that His will for Silas was perfect and complete.

23

Grant was getting stronger every day. Each evening he and Silas talked about the planting and Grant was able to give much advice and encouragement from his many years in the fields. He fretted some, too, at not being able to man the plow himself.

The difference in the men's ages came home hard to Grant when Silas reported each night how much he was able to do in a day. Even with Grant's best team, those days were behind him.

But truthfully, he was not really very envious. He just asked God to let him walk again. This he prayed for with his whole heart.

Doctor Schaefer had been pleased with how well Grant had come out of his cold, but was worried nevertheless. He told Grant he wanted to see him up in a chair, increasing the time each day as he felt stronger. Doc informed them that he had lost more patients from a bedridden state because of their chest filling up, than by deaths resulting directly from accidents such as Grant's.

It was during one of these times with Silas in the field and Grant sitting in the living room that father and daughter were able to talk.

Amy had just walked some food and water out to Silas—the last he would get until he came in for supper. When she returned, Grant asked how things were going. Knowing how close it was to milking, he was surprised when Amy settled into a seat.

"It's going well, I think. Silas can sure cover a lot of ground in a day."

"Yes, he's a lot faster than your old dad."

"I never think of you as old, Dad," Amy said softly and then fell quiet. Grant waited and hoped. Amy would never know how long he had prayed for this time.

"There is something I have wanted to talk to you about Dad, but I'm afraid you'll be upset."

"A parent has to be careful not to make any promises with a statement like that, but I will hear you out."

Amy studied the man across from her. His sandy-brown hair was liberally streaked with gray. There were laugh lines at the corners of his eyes, and his skin was a permanent shade of red from years in the sun.

He was a wonderful father, and Amy knew he loved her dearly. Yes, he would hear her out; he'd always been fair.

Without introduction Amy began. "Uncle Evan asked me to come into town and live with them." Amy paused, but Grant said nothing. Other than a slight lift of his eyebrows, his expression didn't alter.

"I knew when he asked me that I didn't want to, but I was so surprised I didn't say a word. And then the last time I was with him, he said something that really bothered me. He said if my father really loved me he'd let me go. I've known for a long time that there was no friendship between you two, but I can't stand the thought of having Uncle Evan believe the reason I'm saying no is because you won't let me go."

"Should you say no?" The question was spoken so calmly that Amy could only stare at her father.

"You mean you want me to go?"

"I want you to be wherever God leads you. As much as I'd miss you, I know Evan and Bev would take good care of you."

"But Dad, what about you? Who would take care of you?"

"Amy, honey, you must not build your life around me. What did you think would happen to me when you and Thomas moved into your own home—that I would wither up and die?"

"Well no, but Dad I just figured that the breakup with Thomas was God's way of saying, 'Stay here and take care of your father.'"

"Amy, do you really think me that selfish? I've been where you are—young and ready for love, and I found that love. Your mother and I loved one another deeply and when God gave us you, there wasn't anything more in the world we would have asked for.

"I want you to experience the things that I have—marriage and family. I can't imagine a man wanting a more wonderful wife than you would be. And when it comes to babies, well I've seen your face light up when you hold them at church.

"You know I'll respect your decision about living in town or not, and there are no words to describe how much I would miss you if you go. But Amy, do not, *do not* base your decisions on a need to stay here and take care of me."

"But it's not just that. This is a good life here. I love it on this farm."

"You're right—it is a good life, we've been blessed many times over. But God may have a completely different plan for you, Amy, and I'll not hold you back."

There was silence in the room for a long time. Grant's compassion for his only child was great and, even though his words had shocked her, they needed to be said.

Amy stood. "I best get to the barn." Grant nodded. Amy hesitated and then walked to his chair. They hugged long and hard. "This is the only home I've ever known."

"I know, honey, and I'm not pushing you out, but please don't close your eyes to what God might have for you beyond these acres."

Amy stepped back and held her father's hand. She squeezed gently and said, "Thanks, Dad." On these words she moved for the door.

24

The following day was Saturday, and Silas came in from the fields a bit early. Amy surprised both men at the supper table when she asked if Silas would take her to town after the meal. Silas assured her he would be glad to oblige. Amy then looked to Grant.

"You're sure, Amy?"

"I'm sure. I should have told Uncle Evan the first day he asked me."

Amy did a quick cleanup on the kitchen and they were able to leave while there was still light in the sky.

Neillsville on Saturday night was a busy place. In front of each saloon was a crowd, and the noise spoke of boisterous activity within. Amy was glad for Silas' presence. A man would have to be crazy to challenge someone of Silas' proportions—crazy or drunk.

Amy wondered a little at her decision to come into town at night, but she knew it was time to resolve this with Uncle Evan. She had prayed about little else since her talk with her dad and knew without a doubt the answer to her uncle must be no. If Amy was honest with herself, she did not really believe she would ever move away from the farm. The only reason she could think of would be to marry, and there were simply no men in the area in whom she was the least bit interested. She knew her father meant well, but for now just knowing she would be able to settle things was peace enough.

The entire downstairs of the Randall mansion was lit. For a moment Amy thought her relations might be entertaining, but the carriage house was closed and there did not seem to be any extra vehicles about.

For the second time in Silas' visit, he and Amy stood in silence at the Randalls' front door. Silas did not need to ask how Amy was feeling. Her attempt at gnawing her lower lip off was answer enough.

Bev Randall was surprised but also very pleased to see Amy. She greeted Silas warmly and, after seating them in her elegant living room, rang for refreshments.

After the servant left them, Amy wasted no time in stating her purpose. "Aunt Bev, is Uncle Evan here?"

"No dear, he went out for awhile. He didn't say where he was going, so I really have no idea when he planned to return."

Amy looked as distressed as she felt. "Is there something I can do, Amy?"

"Well, I'm not sure. I think I should tell Uncle Evan first but I . . ." Amy's voice trailed away in uncertainty.

"Is it about your coming to live here?"

Amy nodded.

"Evan told me that he'd asked you."

"You mean he didn't discuss it with you before he talked with me?"

"Amy dear, your uncle rarely sees fit to discuss anything with me." Bev smiled, but Amy thought she caught a trace of bitterness in her aunt's words.

"I'm sorry he didn't discuss it with you first. He should have," Amy stated firmly and went on before Bev could interrupt. "I've come tonight to tell him no. I know the offer was made in love, but I want to stay on the farm. I've never had a strong desire to live in town. I know Uncle Evan will think my dad is holding me back, but that's not true. The farm is where I want to be and would be even if Dad had not been hurt."

A servant entered the room then and served small sandwiches and cookies for three. Amy's plate of food sat untouched, and she was quiet a moment as she sipped her coffee.

"Aunt Bev, I really wanted to give my answer to Uncle Evan. Please don't be hurt, but I need to be able to express how I feel to him in person."

"I'll not even tell him you were here," she stated in kind assurance. "You can tell him the next time you see him."

"You're not hurt?"

"No, I'm glad for the special relationship you have with Evan. You make your uncle very happy." Amy knew the words were sincere, and she felt some relief from her heavy task.

They stayed awhile longer with Silas joining into the conversation. Evan did not arrive before they left, and Amy resigned herself to the fact that she would have to deliver her answer to Evan Randall another time.

25

Amy played the piano and sang a solo the following morning in church. Feeling his chest expand in pride, Silas watched her. Her gifts of singing and playing were beautiful as she used them to give glory to God.

Silas immersed himself into the sermon in 2 John that morning. Pastor Johnson dwelt especially on the point of walking in the truth to show our love to God. Near the end of the message he spoke to the unbeliever.

"Allow me to repeat some of what I've said and speak to those of you who may not truly know of the love I've been speaking on.

"The way we show our love to God is to walk in the truth. This means obedience to the Bible and the commandments written within. The Scripture says, 'We love him because he first loved us.' What is this first love? Salvation. The greatest example of love was God sending His Son, Jesus Christ, to die for us. He took our sins; He is our salvation. Until you understand this act of love, your sin divides you from God. Christ's death on the cross covers that divide, bridges that space.

"I quote this verse to you often, but if you haven't ever reached out to God, you need to hear it again. John 3:16: 'For God so loved the world, that he gave his only begotten Son, that whosoever believeth in him should not perish, but have everlasting life.' "

Amy played the piano for the altar call at the end of the service, and a little girl came forward with her mother. They both looked a little frightened, and Silas' heart went out to them even as he hoped they would come to a saving knowledge of Christ that morning.

When the service ended, it seemed most of the congregation was of a mind to stand and visit. One of the women from town said there had been another robbery the night before.

Unable to stop the shudder running through her, Amy thought of her and Silas out after dark. As frightened as she was by the talk, she couldn't stop herself from listening.

"They all seem to be related to the bank. When someone makes a withdrawal, his money is taken."

"How many robberies have there been?"

"I think about 20."

"Twenty? I heard it was more like 30."

"Well, I think someone at the bank is involved. I want to withdraw my money, but I'm afraid we'll get robbed, too."

"We should all go in together. They can't rob all of us."

"Yes, that's it. We've all got to band togeth . . ."

A large hand gently took Amy's arm and led her from the circle. No one within the group seemed to notice her presence, nor did they see her leaving.

"Silas did you hear—"

"Shhh, sweetheart. Let's get to the wagon." Amy allowed herself to be led to the wagon and be lifted to the seat as though she were a child.

She couldn't believe they were talking about the bank with such anger. Uncle Evan did not have many friends, but he would never . . . but where had he been last night? Aunt Bev had not even known.

Shame engulfed Amy over what she was thinking. How dare she or any of the women at the church judge Evan Randall.

Amy started when the wagon stopped. They were not home yet, and Amy looked to Silas questioningly.

"Talk to me, Amy. I only heard part of what the women were saying."

When she had finished, Silas exclaimed "Thirty robberies? Amy don't you see that in their panic the facts are being blown completely out of proportion? Your uncle is not the most social of men, but you're right—no one has grounds to call him a thief."

"What if everyone does want their money?"

"I don't know. If there was another robbery last night, I have a feeling this whole affair is going to come to a boil in the next few days."

Silas' prediction was partially right. Things did come to a head, but it didn't take a few days.

Evan Randall's small, gleaming black buggy, pulled by an equally black horse, drove into the Nolan farmyard the very next night.

Evan had not been to the farm since Maureen had died, over four years ago. Knowing this, Amy did not move to the front door in joy but with an awful feeling of dread growing in the pit of her stomach.

"Good evening, Amy. I'm sorry to burst in on you like this, but

I need to speak with your father." There was none of the softness that he usually had for Amy. His voice was brisk, and his words to the point.

"Of course, Uncle Evan. Please come in."

Grant was sitting in the living room, and it was obvious to the younger people that their presence was not needed.

Amy and Silas headed outside to the porch to wait and be out of the way. They were both surprised at how quickly Evan reappeared and was on his way to the buggy.

Amy stood in silent confusion. Evan was seated before he looked up and seemed to realize she was standing there. He maneuvered his rig close to the porch and, ignoring Silas, spoke directly to his niece.

"You must understand, Amy, that nothing between us has changed. I care for you deeply, as I always have." His tone was very businesslike. "I'm sure you'll see that I had little choice." He paused here, and Amy could see genuine regret in his eyes. "It grieves me to withdraw my offer of you living with us, but things have become very complicated in the last few hours and I feel right now it would be best if we postpone the offer indefinitely. Good night, Amy. Please don't hesitate to visit. You know you'll always be welcome in my home."

Without giving her a chance to reply, he turned the buggy sharply and rode away. Silas and Amy stared after him and then at each other.

They found Grant in the chair they'd left him in, but he was slumped low and seemed to have aged years in the few minutes they were outside.

He looked at Amy as he spoke. "There's been a run on the bank and Evan has called in our loan. I've got a week to come up with the money."

26

Forty-eight hours after Grant had uttered those devastating words, Amy was on the verge of panic. Trying not to pace, she waited for Silas to come from her father's bedroom, but she couldn't sit still.

The night Evan visited, Grant had briefly told them what he'd come to say. Evidently, in a panic, about half of the bank patrons had come in on Monday morning demanding their money. A few were large depositors. If not for those, the bank would have stood its own. As it was, Grant felt Evan had panicked a little himself by calling Grant's loan and two others.

After some discussion Monday night, the subject had been dropped. Now Amy waited for Silas who had gone into Grant's room after supper to see if something could be worked out.

When he appeared in the kitchen, Amy was seated. She frantically wrung her hands and asked, "Is Dad okay?"

Silas was surprised at her state of agitation. He had not realized how upset she was. "Oh Silas, what are we to do? What was Uncle Evan thinking? We don't have money put aside to pay off that loan. Does he think we're hiding it in our mattresses?"

"Amy, try to calm down. I need to tell you something."

"Calm? You want me to be calm? The only home I've ever known is about to be taken from me and you ask me to be calm?"

"But Amy, if you would just listen, your dad and I have talked and I'd like to tell you if you would just simmer down."

"Silas, you never answered my question. Is Dad okay? Oh, never mind. I'll check on him myself."

Silas caught her at the door. "Amy, come back to the table and let me talk to you. I didn't realize you were so upset."

"You didn't realize I was upset?" she nearly shouted at him as he led her back into the room. "Well, what did you think I'd be with all that's happen . . ."

Amy's words were abruptly cut off as Silas snatched her into his arms and covered her mouth firmly with his own.

The kiss was not short, and Silas felt Amy go limp in his arms as his lips tenderly held hers. Amy gasped when Silas broke the kiss, and her eyes rivaled the moon for size.

While still holding her, Silas' soft, deep voice broke into the now-quiet kitchen. "If you will just sit down and stay quiet for a moment, I'll tell you about my conversation with your dad."

On Amy's nod, Silas released her and sat at the table. Silas took a chair near hers. "Your dad and I have talked, and I offered him what I have in my savings. It's not the full amount of the loan, but close enough that I think Evan will take it. We've still got a few days, so your dad wants to think and pray on it some."

Amy was moved nearly to tears and still in shock over what had just transpired, but she managed to say, "Thank you, Silas," in a small voice.

They sat in silence then. Silas studied his hands, his face expressionless. He looked up to find Amy concentrating on his mouth, and he spoke without thinking. "Did Thomas ever kiss you?"

Amy jerked as though struck and turned red. "Yes, t-twice after w-we w-were engaged." Amy realized she was stuttering and stopped in painful embarrassment. But Silas still looked at her, and she wished she knew what he was thinking.

A terrible thought coming to her, Amy asked in a harsh whisper, "Silas, are you disgusted with me? Do you think I'm cheap for kissing Thomas?"

Pain slashed across Silas' features at her words, and his voice was rough with emotion. "Never, Amy, would I think you cheap. It's only natural that you kiss the man you expect to marry."

Amy was so relieved that she nearly wept. She could not have stood it if Silas was repulsed by her.

The silence between them lengthened and grew uncomfortable. Finally Amy asked, "Would you like some coffee or anything?"

"No thanks. I think I'll go check the herd and then turn in." He spoke the words softly and for the first time did not attempt to hide what was in his heart.

Amy's own heart thumped furiously at what she read in his eyes. For just an instant their eyes held, and then Silas pushed away from the table and strode toward the door.

Grant listened in alarm as Amy's raised voice came from the other room. Silas said something in return, but Grant couldn't make out the words.

Grant froze as Amy's voice nearly raised to a shout before all went completely quiet. He continued to listen, and after a while heard the front door open and close.

Grant relaxed back against the pillows, a smile on his face. If he were a betting man, he'd place money on the fact that Amy had just been kissed.

He wondered how rough the road ahead would be. It was only a matter of time until Amy stopped mothering him and saw that the man she needed most was sitting beneath her nose. And Silas was probably sure he had just been sent by God to work in the fields, figuring Amy would never return his love.

Well, Grant knew he could not interfere. God would lead the way. "But please, Lord," he prayed, "let me be on my feet to walk her down the aisle."

You're a fool, Silas Cameron. The biggest fool to ever live. Silas had been saying this and worse for the past two hours. He had every line and splinter on the ceiling memorized as he lay in bed.

He should not have been trying to think at all for he was exhausted physically as well as emotionally. Weeks of working in the fields were taking their toll. Silas was beginning to think the life of a horse breeder was a life of ease. He was sure Luke would argue that point since he was carrying all the weight and had been for many weeks.

It was time to go home. The planting was done, and as soon as they worked out the money details there would be no reason to stay.

The savings would be missed. Silas had been praying about building his own home this summer, but Grant and Amy needed the money more. And since he didn't have a wife and kids, he had no real need for a home of his own.

No home or family of his own—that was the real reason he had to go. He had all but told Amy of his feelings. There was no way she would be comfortable around him now. At least before they had shared a friendship, but now he was even unsure of that.

Amy had made her feelings quite clear about marriage and her home here. She was more than a little attached to this farm—perhaps too much so, but he wouldn't want to take her away if she didn't want to go.

Silas lay awake for a long time thinking and praying. It was clear to him he had been used of God in the lives of these people, and for this he was thankful. But he was human, with human emotions, and was saddened at knowing his heart belonged to a woman who could not give hers in return.

It was a long time before Silas fell asleep.

Her hand going to her mouth continually, Amy could still feel Silas' kiss. Thomas had kissed her—twice, once passionately. But nothing had ever prepared her for being in the arms of Silas Cameron. Amy felt herself blushing with the remembrance.

Burying her face in the pillow, she could still see his eyes. "He's in love with me." The words were muffled and indistinct. "But he can't love me," she tried to reason with herself. "I'm like a little sister to him. Somewhere along the line, those feelings must have changed.

"And what about my feelings? His kiss made me feel like I was melting. But we're just friends. Can good friends fall in love? I don't know.

"Well it doesn't matter," she reasoned suddenly. "I have to stay here and take care of my dad. If I was in love with Silas, he would want to take me to Baxter and my dad needs me here."

"Do not build your life around me." Unbidden, her father's selfless words came to mind, but Amy pushed them away. He was just saying that! This was her home and he needed her here!

Amy snuggled deep into the covers with a contented sigh. It was going to be hard to have Silas' feelings stronger than her own, but this was where she was supposed to be, she was sure.

Amy fell asleep without remembering to open her Bible. In fact, in all her logic Amy didn't check with God at all.

27

Amy was seeing Doc Schaefer out, so Silas took the opportunity to speak with Grant alone. Silas was beginning to think Grant was a mind reader when he stepped into the bedroom and Grant said, "Shut the door, Silas. I want to talk with you."

When Silas was seated in the rocking chair near the bed, Grant seemed at a loss for words. He cleared his throat twice, and still he hesitated. Silas knew he was about to be thanked, and so he stepped in, hoping to put it off.

"I'd like to come back, Grant."

"Come back?"

"Yes. I have every confidence that you'll be back on your feet, but I'd still like to come back and give you a hand."

"You don't have to do that, Silas." Grant was very pleased with the offer, but this young man had already done so much.

"Actually, Grant, I'd be returning for selfish reasons. This is the first planting I've done on my own, and I'd like to see the fruits of my labors."

The older man's hand came out and they shook. "Thanks, Silas. I'll count on you. You come when you can."

"I'll wait until my brother-in-law Mac starts his harvesting, and then I'll write that I'm coming." Silas stood to go. "Oh, ah, one more thing, Grant. Please don't say anything to Amy about my coming back. I'd like to do that myself."

"Sure, Silas. I understand." The men nodded to one another in understanding, and Silas exited the room.

— ⊹ —

Silas sat despondently at the supper table and watched Amy look at everything but him. Even if he put a question to her directly, she answered his chin, never once looking him in the eye.

Grant didn't miss the byplay between Silas and his daughter, and he struggled to hold his tongue. He knew that whatever was between them they would have to work out. Nevertheless he would not stand for Amy being rude to Silas or making him feel unwelcome in their home.

When Silas refused both a second helping of supper and dessert and excused himself from the table, Grant determined to talk with Amy. But once they were alone, Amy gave up all pretense of eating and sat looking at the door Silas had just walked through. Just the pain written on his daughter's face was enough to stay any comment Grant had been ready to make.

Amy was miserable. She knew Silas was hurting and the relationship they'd known was changed, possibly forever. Also, Silas was leaving tomorrow, and guilt lay heavy on Amy's heart for the relief she felt. What was the matter with her? How could she be so cruel? If only Silas' feelings hadn't changed and they could have stayed just friends.

Amy would probably have sat at the table toying with her food all evening, but Silas appeared in the doorway.

"I'm not positive, but I believe Bev Randall is coming this way." Amy rushed to the window, and Grant craned his neck to try and see.

Amy turned back to the room. "It *is* Aunt Bev." She paused and then added, "I'm not sure I want to know why she's here."

"Well," Grant spoke briskly to cover his own feeling of trepidation, "that won't change the fact that she is. If someone will help me into the living room, we'll find out what's going on." Silas moved to assist him. For all Grant's businesslike words, Silas thought he looked worried.

Clearly in a state of high agitation, Bev Randall would not take a seat. She paced back and forth as Grant sat watching her in bewilderment.

"I was just furious when he told me. I stood up to Evan for the first time." Here she stopped in front of Grant and faced him squarely. "I told him to reinstate your loan or I'd be on the next train out of town."

"Oh Bev, you didn't!" Grant was truly horrified. As harsh as Evan's actions had been, nothing was worth Bev and Evan's marriage.

"Yes I did, and I'm not sorry. Evan never tells me anything until the act is complete, or we could have avoided all of this."

Bev had resumed her pacing, but again she stopped and put a trembling hand to her throat. "I never dreamed he would do such a thing. That you should suffer for . . ."

A short silence hung in the room. "Well," Bev visibly composed herself. Once again the elegant banker's wife was firmly back in place. "You're going to think me a fishwife, screeching and stomping about. Now, Amy, I do believe I could do with a cup of coffee."

"Oh, of course, Aunt Bev." Amy jumped up to do her bidding, still in a state of shock over all that had transpired.

Bev stayed a long time and told them of the situation in town. "The townspeople this week have been out of their heads, storming the bank, sure that Evan was taking their money. There were stories of 40 robberies, if you can imagine. Their panic was so great, yet no one had a single fact. They were shouting at the sheriff for justice and, believe it or not, he came to the bank's rescue. He's a good man, you know.

"Well, he told the bank patrons he had a full-scale investigation going on and that things were under control. He had already collected some valuable evidence, and none of it pointed to anyone at the bank. He was also putting extra men on the job in an attempt to curtail the thefts."

Bev left soon after her report, and Amy cleared away the cups before joining Silas and Grant in the living room. They sat and talked some, but each was emotionally drained and it wasn't long before they were all seeking their beds and thanking God for a miracle in the form of Bev Randall.

28

Silas would have given much to go to the train station alone, but that would have left a horse in town for Amy to pick up and he did not want that.

Arriving at the station, Silas assured Amy she need not stay, but she insisted. Now they stood on the station platform in painful silence, Silas towering over her, each one with so much and yet nothing to say.

The train rumbled in the distance and Silas knew he had to tell Amy of his plans to return. "Amy, I need to tell you something." Amy stiffened, mistaking his intention, and would not raise her eyes to his.

"Amy, please look at me." She did slowly, afraid of what she would see, but to her surprise Silas, the big brother, stared down at her.

"I'm coming back in the fall to help with the harvest. I think your dad will be up and around, but I want to give him a hand."

Amy was obviously surprised. "You're always so thoughtful, Silas. Thank you very much."

The train was coming into the station, and Silas raised his voice slightly to be heard. "Well, thank you for everything. I'll see you in the fall." Giving her a quick hug, he was saddened at how stiff she was in his arms.

He broke the hug, but couldn't bring himself to stop touching her. His hands lightly held her shoulders and he looked down at her tenderly.

"I'm still your friend, Amy." Silas couldn't hold back the words. "And should you ever need me, I'll come."

Amy could only stare at him, and Silas felt her relax beneath his hands. Moving slowly and giving her plenty of time to move away, Silas bent his head and brushed her lips with his own.

When he broke the kiss, he was still so close Amy could feel his breath on her cheek. "Good-bye sweetheart." His voice was a strained, husky whisper.

Amy stood on the platform and watched until the train was out of sight. Relieved that Silas was gone, she was also glad he was returning. When he came back she was sure their old relationship would be restored, and even now she looked forward to the time. He was hurt now, but they would be friends again—of this Amy was determined.

Of course, he might meet a nice girl this summer and get married before he returned. Amy refused to ask herself why this idea was not really very appealing.

29

Baxter, Wisconsin

Grandma Em silently watched Silas across her kitchen table and wondered again what had really gone on in Neillsville. It had taken her a few minutes when he had arrived the night before to get used to him without a beard. After studying him a few moments, she decided she liked it very much.

But more than just Silas' physical appearance had changed. They had talked, sharing all the latest news, but something was not quite right. Amid the family news confirming Sue's pregnancy, Luke's hard work, and how much the nieces and nephews had missed him, Silas was strangely preoccupied.

Silas had shared briefly of his stay in Neillsville and, in so doing, made Grandma Em even more sure that something was not right. He talked of the Nolans, the crops, the size of the church, the robberies and the bank run, and even someone named Thomas who was now married to Debra.

Grandma Em's mind kept returning to those two, wondering if they were somehow a key as to why Silas seemed upset. Silas evidently thought she knew who they were. But she didn't and wondered what they had to do with Silas' stay at the Nolans. She hoped in time he would talk to her of what he was really feeling or, to be specific, the real reason the sparkle had gone out of his eyes.

"Gram, is there more coffee?"

"Yes, I could use some myself. I'll get it for you." After she poured the coffee she remarked, "I haven't read my Bible yet. Would you like to join me?"

Silas smiled. "You know I would."

She read from Psalm 1:1-3.

Blessed is the man that walketh not in the counsel of the ungodly, nor standeth in the way of sinners, nor sitteth in the seat of the scornful. But his delight is in the law of the Lord; and in his law doth he meditate day and night. And he shall be like a tree planted by the rivers of water, that bringeth forth his fruit in his season; his leaf also shall not wither; and whatsoever he doeth shall prosper.

They prayed together and then shared another cup of coffee.

"How are you planning to get home?" Grandma Em asked.

"Well now, I've been thinking on that. I might just walk."

Grandma Em looked surprised. "Silas, I know very well the hard work involved in getting a crop in. You can't really be needing more exercise."

"No," he laughed, "I just thought it might be nice. It is a pretty day."

Grandma Em wasn't fooled and could no longer keep her silence. "What's her name, Silas?"

"Am I that transparent?"

Grandma Em didn't answer, not having been sure until that moment if she was on the right track.

"Her name is Amy Nolan."

"I take it you found she was no longer 14."

"No, she is definitely not 14. I almost wish she were."

"Does she know how you feel?"

"Yes, I'm afraid I gave myself away just before I left. It was the last thing I wanted. We're such good friends, and now she is no longer even comfortable around me. I don't want her hurt."

"But you're hurting yourself, Silas." Grandma Em's voice was filled with compassion.

"You're right—I do hurt. I hurt in a way I didn't know was possible. I love her, Gram. I want her for my wife, but to her I'm just a big brother and she is sure Grant would never get along without her. Her plan is to live at home the rest of her life."

The two fell again into silence and then Silas said, "I'm going back. I told Grant I would come and help get his crops in. And when I go, I'll try to repair our friendship. I'll try to put things right."

"Maybe being separated for the summer will help."

"Maybe," Silas sounded unconvinced even to himself. He missed Amy already.

"Well, I better start home."

"Yes, you better. Christine will be delighted to see you. She said it's been painfully obvious that Josh's favorite toy is missing."

Smiling, Silas felt his heart lighten some. Even the ache in his heart did not diminish the joy of knowing he was almost home.

30

The walk home worked like a tonic on Silas. He was glad that most of the way was beyond the houses of town because he couldn't wipe the smile from his face. Anyone watching would have thought him dim-witted.

Silas felt not at all fatigued as he neared the ranch. In fact, when the house came into view, he began to run. Just as he hit the porch, the front door opened and Christine ran out. Silas grabbed her in a great hug, and Christine laughed with sheer joy.

"Your beard!" Christine cried. She was staring at him, her mouth wide open. "I can't believe you shaved your beard off! You look wonderful!"

"Well, I'm glad you approve. For a minute there I wondered if you might not."

"It's just that you look so different. My goodness, you're almost as good-looking as Luke."

Silas laughed. "Now that's high praise coming from a woman in love. By the way, where is the man in question?"

"He's right here," a deep voice sounded behind them, "trying to figure out who the strange, beardless man hugging my woman is." Luke came up the steps, and the two brothers embraced.

"You know," Luke commented, "I'd forgotten what you look like under all that fur. You're not half bad-looking."

"Thanks," Silas said dryly, but he was grinning.

"Where's Josh?" Silas asked of Christine.

"He's inside. Come on. Did you walk from the train station?"

"No, I walked from Grandma Em's. I got in last night."

"Josh, look who's here."

Joshua Cameron was sitting on the kitchen floor contentedly chewing on a hard biscuit. Christine scooped him up, washed the crumbs from his face and hands, and landed him in the arms of his Uncle Silas.

Silas held this treasured little boy and said nothing. He actually expected Joshua to reach for Christine, but for the moment Josh just sat looking solemnly up at the man holding him.

Silas returned Josh's solemn appraisal, looking deep into the inherited brilliance of the Cameron blue eyes.

"Hi, Josh." Still no change in expression. But Silas didn't

care—it just felt so good to hold him. Josh's little hand reached up and tentatively touched Silas' mustache. Silas held still as the tiny fingers explored his upper lip and the hair above it. Suddenly Josh giggled.

The adults laughed, too, and Silas hugged the little boy fiercely to himself. His heart nearly burst with happiness. These people were his home.

Dear Frank,

I realize I have taken a long time getting back to you and I appreciate your patience. The job you offered me sounds wonderful, and I am greatly complimented you believe me capable, but I must turn the offer down.

I do not answer you lightly. I have prayed long and hard over this, and for this reason I'm certain I should stay where I am.

I hope we will continue to do business and remain well-acquainted in the years to come. Luke and I both greatly respect your knowledge and wisdom in our trade.

Again, my thanks and hopes you will soon find a man to take on the position.

> Sincerely,
> Silas Cameron

Silas felt instant peace settle over him upon completion of the letter. Sitting at the desk in his room, he bowed his head.

"Heavenly Father, thank You for giving me wisdom in this job offer. I could not gain perfect peace about it, and so I believe Your answer is no. Thank You, God, for this home and my work here. Please help me to know if I should build this year. I need to know what's right. And please, God, help me to accept Amy as just a friend. I don't want to hurt her, so please heal my heart and give me acceptance of her friendship and nothing more. Amen."

Silas had dreamed about Amy coming to him—dreamed that after he left she missed him so much that she jumped on the next train for Baxter. But it was just a dream, and Silas was going to have to accept the fact that she did not return his love.

True, he was going back in the fall, but he could not go expecting Amy to run into his arms. He had Amy's friendship, he hoped, and was going to work at keeping it. Every day he prayed for strength in this and knew God was already working. God had not deserted him, and Silas was determined to go on with his life.

Settled back into his work routine and doing well in his determination to move ahead, a few days later Silas saddled a horse in the late afternoon and went for a ride. He ended up down by the creek in the spot Julia had written about in her letter.

As Silas sat in this peaceful spot, he began to miss Julia so much he turned his mount toward the MacDonald farm. As he did so, he realized it would need to be a short visit as Christine would soon be getting supper on.

Silas was nearly on top of the farmhouse when he realized something was wrong. Julia and the boys were huddled together in the yard watching the house with fear-filled eyes. Spotting instantly the cause of their fear, Silas saw smoke coming from one of the kitchen windows.

"Mac's in there," Julia cried as Silas jumped from his mount. "He pushed us out when a pan on the stove caught fire."

Silas ran for the house, his heart pounding in fear, but Mac had things well under control. Silas began to throw the remaining windows open while Mac pulled singed curtains off a window near the stove.

Mac was not three steps out into the yard when Julia launched herself into his arms. Her body crashed against his with enough force to topple a smaller man.

Julia was nearly hysterical in her sobbing, and the boys clinging to their parents' legs were not much better off. Silas knelt down and hauled them into his arms. They accepted the comfort gladly and held on to his neck as the tears flowed freely.

While Julia was gaining some control, Mac released her to gather his boys into his arms. Silas looked on as they shared a family hug. His look then swung to the house. It would need to be aired out and that would take a few days.

There was little discussion as everyone seemed to be in a state of shock, but soon the wagon was hitched and Mac had his family loaded and on their way to Luke and Christine's. Silas had assured Julia that whatever needed to be done could wait until tomorrow.

Julia and the boys sat in the wagon, each with a bundle of clothes. Silas had ridden ahead, and Luke and Christine were in the yard as Mac drove the wagon in.

They saw instantly that Julia was white with strain. "Come on, Julia." Luke's voice was tender as he lifted her down.

As she looked up at her older brother, Julia's eyes filled with tears. "I thought Mac was going to burn."

"It's okay now," he said as he hugged her, his eyes meeting those of Mac who had been watching his wife with concern. "He's fine. You come inside. We'll take care of everything."

The four MacDonalds were swept inside and made comfortable. Julia seemed to be coming around, finally realizing Mac was really okay. Her eyes watched him as he went down the hall to clean up and change.

Over supper, Mac told briefly what had happened. The stove had been very hot and a greasy pan flared up without warning. Mac had grabbed the pan and moved it directly beneath the curtains. It all happened very fast and was enough to scare everyone and fill the downstairs with acrid smoke. The house would need a complete airing out and some minor surface work done in the kitchen.

Christine bustled about at bedtime making everyone comfortable. Silas was putting his two oldest nephews to bed, and Christine was checking on Julia. She was only in the bedroom a few minutes when the door reopened and Christine walked back down the hall and to the kitchen where Luke and Mac were talking.

"Excuse me a minute, Mac." Christine bent over her husband and whispered almost urgently for his ears alone, "Where are my nightgowns?"

Luke's eyes met Christine's and, though he tried to look innocent, she could see he was thoroughly enjoying this. Christine tried to look stern, but failed miserably. As they shared a long, loving look, both husband and wife were instantly back to a moment in one of the early weeks of their marriage.

Christine had just finished taking a bath in their bedroom near the stove, when she heard Luke coming down the hall. She searched quickly for a covering and grabbed the first garment she found—one of Luke's shirts.

Luke had entered and swept her with a look but said nothing. Christine had wondered about that look, but then put it out of her mind until the following night.

Luke was already snuggled beneath the covers when Christine came in to get ready for bed. She reached into her drawer for a fresh nightgown, but surprisingly only found a stack of Luke's shirts. She took one out and stood a moment in confusion. Understanding was not long in coming, and she turned to the man in the bed.

"Where are they?"

"Put away."

"Where?"

"You don't need them, Christie. Wear the shirt."

Christine fumed as she put the shirt on, determined to show him how ridiculous it looked. But once Christine was in the shirt, Luke only smiled.

Christine, indignant and angry, stomped over and stood by the bed. "It's indecent."

"What's indecent about it?" Luke found this highly amusing coming from a woman who went riding astride in her husband's denim pants, but wisely kept from commenting.

"My legs show." Christine looked down at the aforementioned members as though they themselves were the ones offended. The shirt stopped just above the knees.

"I know your legs show, but I'm the only one who will see them, so what's the problem?"

"LUKE!" Christine wailed in pure frustration, but it was no use. He was not about to tell.

Christine waited until the following day for Luke to leave the house. When he did, she tore the place apart. Every nook and cranny was searched. Nothing. She hadn't come up with a clue to where he had hidden her nightgowns.

Now husband and wife stood smiling warmly at each other. Julia needed a gown, and the story was too special to share. Luke arose, kissed his wife's cheek, and went to fetch a nightgown. Christine didn't follow him to the hiding place—she really didn't want to know.

31

Everyone spent the next few days working on Mac and Julia's house. They stayed nights at Luke and Christine's, but every minute of daylight was spent airing and cleaning. It was amazing how fast the smell of the smoke had infiltrated everything.

The first night Mac and Julia were back in their own home and the children put to bed, Mac turned his full attention to his wife for really the first time since the fire. He had sensed all along something was wrong but, with taking care of the house and the running of the farm, he'd had no time to talk with her.

"How are you doing?" They were sitting in the kitchen, each with a cup of coffee, and Mac was studying his wife's face with deep concentration.

"I'm fine." Julia answered with a small smile. The truth was that her head and back ached. But this, she was convinced, was due to the last few days.

"You don't seem fine."

"I don't?" Julia looked truly puzzled.

"No, you don't." Mac's voice was kind but firm.

"Well Mac, I feel a little achy and tired, but that's understandable after all that's gone on lately." Julia's voice told him she felt all of this was hardly worth mentioning.

Mac looked doubtful, and Julia reached for his hand. "I'm fine, honestly." Mac continued to look at her in unbelief, but he let the matter drop.

Over the next few days Mac kept a close watch on the woman he loved. She looked pale to him, but when he tried to talk with her about it, she burst into tears and said she was still a little upset from the fire. Anxiously he watched her, but he felt helpless since she seemed to think nothing was out of the ordinary. Mac prayed and tried to leave the matter in God's hands, hoping he would know if and when to step in.

The time to step in came ten days after they returned to the house. Mac was in the barn when the boys came running from the house to tell him their mother was on the floor.

"She just fell over, Pa," Calvin said with fear as they followed their running father toward the house.

Julia was just coming to when Mac ran into the kitchen. He

went down on the floor beside her and supported her as she tried to sit up. Her face was chalk white.

Julia opened her mouth to speak, but Mac cut in, his voice sharp with fear. "If you dare tell me you're fine, Julia, I'll throttle you."

That was exactly what she had been about to say and dutifully closed her mouth. Actually, she felt a bit nauseous and was glad to be still.

"Are you okay, Mom?" Charles' voice quivered with his question.

Julia turned to see her sons kneeling beside her, tears in their eyes. She started to reassure them, but Mac stepped in.

"Just as soon as your Uncle Mark sees her, we'll know."

"Oh Mac, I don't need—"

"Not a word, Julia. Boys, get the horses out. We're going to town." The boys had never moved faster to do his bidding.

Leaving Julia on the couch, Mac and the boys hitched the horses to the wagon. He threatened her with dire consequences if he found her off the couch or even sitting up.

Mac carried Julia to the wagon and tried to get her to lay down in the back, but she adamantly refused. Mac gave in just to get her to town as soon as possible.

Mac moved restlessly about Susanne's elegant living room as she sat helplessly and watched him. Julia had been with Mark in his office for over 30 minutes, and Mac was at his wits' end.

Inside the office, Mark looked at his sister, a little surprised she did not already know what he was about to tell her.

"Julia, you're pregnant."

"I'm what?"

"You are going to have a baby." Mark enunciated the words carefully as though speaking to a slow-witted child.

"But that's impossible."

Mark's eyebrows rose nearly to his hairline on that statement, but Julia rushed on. "I mean, I just never got pregnant after Charlie, and I just assumed that I couldn't." Julia's voice trailed off rather helplessly as she tried to take it all in. She was as surprised as Mark that she and Mac had not noticed any of the signs, for they had been there, staring them right in the face.

Mac! Julia's next thoughts were of her husband. She had to tell him right away.

The door leading from the office into the living room opened slowly, and Mac's entire body tensed as he watched his wife walk out followed by her brother. His peripheral vision caught Mark leading Susanne from the room, but his eyes were locked on Julia.

She walked toward him and without forewarning said, "I'm going to have a baby."

Mac's eyes closed, and he felt as if all the air had left his body. He stood a moment trying to pull air into his lungs. "Thank You, God. Thank You, God," his heart kept repeating.

When at last he opened his eyes, he pulled Julia tenderly into his arms. Julia felt him tremble, and her heart broke. He had been so frightened.

The boys found their parents in this embrace and, even though it was not an unusual sight, approached carefully.

When they broke apart, Calvin said, "Uncle Mark says you're okay and that you have good news."

Julia broke the news to them with tears in her eyes. When Mark and Sue heard shouts and laughter from the living room, they knew it was alright to return.

What followed was a joyous chaos of laughter and tears. Mark took Julia back into his office to tell her how to take care of herself and things to watch for. She had never fainted when pregnant with the boys, and he intended to keep a careful eye upon her. He insisted Mac join them since he wanted his orders followed to the letter.

A while later Mac headed the wagon for Grandma Em's. Even with the boys fighting in the back over who would tell her the news, he thought this was probably the most beautiful day God had ever created.

32

The hour was late. Darkness had long since descended over the house. In the master bedroom Luke listened to Christine rustle and thrash about. She usually fell asleep instantly, and he wondered at her restlessness.

"Christine, what are you doing over there?" Luke asked when she shifted again and accidentally brought an elbow into his ribs.

"Oh, I'm sorry. Did I wake you?"

"No," he answered truthfully. "I haven't been to sleep yet. Why aren't you asleep?"

Silence greeted his question.

"Christine?"

"I'm worried about Si." She rolled over then and leaned over her husband. She could just make out his tanned face and dark hair against the whiteness of the pillow slip.

"Did you see the look on his face when Mac and Julia stopped to tell us about the baby? I know he's happy for them, but Luke, he wants a family of his own. I can tell. Something happened in Neillsville. I don't know what, but he's miserable and trying to hide it. We're not enough for him, nor should we be. He needs a wife and children of his own."

Luke reached up in the darkness and pulled Christine into his arms. He had noticed the changes in his brother. He could hardly miss them when they worked so closely. But Silas was a private person and Luke did not feel it was his place to question him.

With Silas, Luke, and Christine living in the same house, they had become very close. But some people did not express their feelings openly, and Silas was one of them. Especially if he was upset, he kept very much to himself. Luke could not step in unless he sensed an invitation from Silas.

Christine spoke again. "With Paul not living here, it's like he's the only one without a family of his own. Not only is everyone married, but everyone has children. And Luke," Christine paused, "I think I'm pregnant, too."

Luke's arms tightened around his wife's frame. "You think?"

"No, actually I'm sure." She didn't sound at all happy about it. Luke knew if Silas realized this, he would be angry.

They didn't talk anymore that night. Neither one had answers, and each tried to give their questions over to the One who did.

It was Saturday morning and the men had just come in for breakfast. Josh was clinging to Christine's skirt, and Luke rescued him so his mother could work.

When the four of them were seated, Silas gave thanks for the food. He ended his prayer by thanking God for never hiding His will and for His ever-abiding faithfulness.

Both Luke and Christine stared at him on the Amen and Silas announced, "I'm going to build a house."

"For whom?" Christine wanted to know.

"For me."

Christine looked at Luke and knew instantly this was no surprise to him. Silas could see a storm brewing and spoke up quickly. "I've been praying about it for some time. I really enjoyed the little bit of work we did at Mac and Julia's, and the cost and availability of building materials is very good right now. But most importantly, I feel God is telling me to build."

"Where will you build?" Christine's voice was small.

"On the far side of the big oaks."

"It's a pretty spot," Christine had to admit.

"Christine, don't look so sad. It's what I really want and besides, you'll need my room eventually when you give Josh brothers and sisters."

Christine blushed and looked down at her place. Silas' eyes flew to his brother's and Luke smiled a warm, "yes" kind of smile. Silas stared at Christine in shock.

"Silas, don't look so worried, I'm fine."

"Silas, don't look so worried, I'm fine." He imitated her voice in as high an octave as he could reach. He looked at her incredulously and spoke in his own voice.

"I can't believe you said that to me. First, Sue is sick to her stomach most of the day and losing weight, and then Julia decides to faint dead away on the kitchen floor, and now you ask me not to worry. Honestly, Christine, pregnant women scare me to death."

Luke and Christine could not hold their laughter at his chagrined tone, and he was not through.

"Sue I can handle because she's married to her doctor, but I'm still recovering from Julia. Now you go and spring this on me. I may not live through it." Silas' speech seemed to exhaust him for he slumped back in his seat and shook his head in despair. Luke and Christine only laughed all the harder.

Later that day Christine stood on the porch and watched her husband approach. He was moving entirely too slowly for her and she nearly shouted at him as she met him at the foot of the steps.

"Did you talk to him? Is he upset about something? If we've done something to make him feel unwanted, I'll never forgive myself. Why didn't he come to us and why didn't you tell me?"

"Christine, he only talked to me two days ago, and he still was not sure and didn't know when he would be. He's rather surprised to feel such a peace so quickly."

"But why didn't you tell me he was at least thinking of it?"

"Because there was nothing definite."

"Well, I don't know how that matters," Christine said and Luke only stared at her. "I am not overreacting." Luke continued to stare. "Well, I'm not." But her voice was losing its forcefulness. "I just worry about him and want him to be happy. I can't imagine him not living here."

"I know you care, but Christine I've never seen him so excited. He's like a kid with a new toy. And you know Silas would never do this on his own. If he said he prayed, he prayed."

Christine nodded and Luke hugged her. "God is taking care of Silas, Christine. Leave it in His hands."

33

God was indeed taking care of Silas. Although he could not yet think of Amy without feeling pain, he felt especially close to God at this time—as though his heavenly Father was giving him special comfort.

In no way did building a house take away the yearning for a wife, but it did serve to keep Silas' mind so occupied that the summer was slipping by and he was hardly aware of the passing of time.

The house materials had arrived and you would have thought it was Christmas as Luke and Silas inspected the goods.

Silas had fallen under the spell of a house he'd spotted in a mail-order catalog. The advertisement had described the house of his dreams with two stories and a total of four bedrooms. One of the bedrooms was on the first floor along with a front parlor, sitting room, dining room and a kitchen with a large pantry.

The dining room even had a built-in china cabinet. Silas had always admired the one built into the dining room of his grandparents' home—the house now owned by Mark and Susanne.

The second story sported three large bedrooms, all with spacious built-in closets. And at the top of the stairs was a huge linen closet.

There were special touches throughout the house, such as interior doors of soft pine in five-panel styling.

Silas' grin nearly split his face as he stood in the spot where he would build. Christine and Josh had joined him and Luke out beneath the oaks. Silas held his nephew in his arms and spoke.

"Right here, Josh. This is where I'll build my home—in the lee of these oaks." Christine felt tears sting her eyes upon hearing the hopeful excitement in his voice. "Please, God," she prayed, "make it special for Silas."

The summer of 1889 was wonderful for crops, with just the right amount of rain and plenty of sunshine. The sunshine brought long hours of backbreaking work to someone building a house. On the other hand, the rain taught patience the hard way.

Silas paced on the front porch one rainy afternoon and stared out at the downpour. He knew it would not last long, but he felt a restlessness to be busy. Oh, there were things to be done in the barn—raising horses was a full-time job, but Silas wanted to build. It occurred to him, as he paced, that God had sent the rain and it was wrong of him to bemoan the fact.

Pausing from his restless walking, he wondered whether Grant's crops were getting plenty of rain and sunshine. Silas had found himself riding toward Mac's fields nearly every week, as if he could gauge Grant's progress by keeping tabs on his brother-in-law's crops.

It didn't rain all the time, and Silas worked hard in hopes of having the house complete by harvesttime. It felt good to walk through the house—even unfinished—and to imagine seeing it with furniture and homey touches.

Silas stood in the upstairs one day and looked at the three sizable rooms. "This is a lot of space for one man. What if I never have a wife, let alone kids?" Silas' mind could not stay the question. Just yesterday Christine, Julia, and Sue were talking about their pregnancies. He wondered if he'd ever see his wife grow with his child.

"God led you to build this house," Silas told himself. "And you're standing here wallowing in your own pity. Maybe you won't have a wife and kids, but that doesn't mean you won't be used of God. Maybe He will ask you to fill these rooms with orphans." Silas smiled at the thought and went back to work.

As it was, the house was not done when Mac started to bring in his crops. Luke had known all along what Silas' plans were for the fall, and so it came as no surprise to Luke when Silas told him he'd be writing a letter and leaving for Neillsville in a week.

34

Neillsville, Wisconsin

"I am not in love with Silas Cameron." Amy said the words to herself, but they didn't stop the furious pounding that started in her heart the moment she spotted him. Amy stood quietly and watched as he disembarked and crossed the platform toward her. He was so handsome. And then he was standing before her, smiling down in his sweet, gentle way, his height and the width of his shoulders blocking the sun.

"Hi." Suddenly shy, Amy's voice was hesitant.

"Hi yourself." Silas' eyes twinkled, and Amy knew that everything would be fine. She was the first one to reach and they hugged. It seemed to set the mood for the relationship they had both hoped to resume.

The ride out to the farm was filled with warm laughter and friendship. Silas was thrilled to be told that Grant was on his feet and strong but also looking forward to Silas' arrival. Amy said he was not a moment too soon; Grant had been in the fields for over a week.

Amy listened in quiet surprise to Silas' enthusiastic description of his new house. It sounded wonderful. She caught herself just before asking him if he was building a house because he'd found a girl this summer.

In fact, the summer for Amy had not been an easy one. Silas had not been far from her thoughts throughout his absence, and Amy honestly didn't understand why. For days she had thought about the way he had kissed her good-bye, and how she had allowed him to. Most of the time she had told herself it was because she felt guilt over not returning his love, and then pushed the thought aside.

But for Amy something was missing. She had never known discontentment before, never longed for things she did not have. But something was definitely missing. As the summer aged, her frustration grew and she didn't understand why. She prayed long and hard over it, but specific answers eluded her.

Amy still believed her father needed her on the farm, and that he just didn't realize it. He had admitted how selfish it would be if he expected her to give up her own life to take care of him, but Amy didn't look at it that way.

She was positive that she was not building her life around her father. The fact was he *did* need her. Amy found herself thinking this so often that she wondered just who she was trying to convince, herself or God.

"Your Aunt April and Uncle Chad send their love," Silas' voice broke into her thoughts. "I talked with them soon after I got home and told them how you were doing. And then right before I left they had me to dinner on Sunday. Your aunt sent you a present. It's in my bag."

"She wrote and said she had an early birthday present for me."

"If I recall, your birthday is in November, same day as my brother Paul's."

"Yes it is. Aunt April wrote about the gift. She said it was fragile and hoped to send it with you. Intending it as a wedding gift for me, she explained it had been in the family for years. She also said she believes I will be married someday and still wants me to have it." Amy's voice trailed off at the end, unable to believe she had actually admitted this, especially to Silas. She looked over to see Silas watching her, his expression unreadable.

Suddenly Amy felt indignant. "I don't know why everyone thinks I have to be married. Many people live long, fulfilled lives and never take a spouse."

Surprised at her outburst, Silas was speechless. Amy remained angry, and the rest of the ride home was made in silence.

Silas stopped the wagon in front of the porch and jumped down to assist Amy, but she sat quietly on the seat. He stood looking up at her. Finally, without turning to him, her voice now subdued, she spoke.

"Silas, don't you ever sin?"

"Of course I sin." But Amy only turned and looked at him, clearly not believing his simple words.

"Just because I don't often lose my temper doesn't mean I never sin. Sins of the heart, Amy—the ones no one sees—can be the most serious of all. The sin of pride has brought me to my knees more times than I care to admit.

"I'm not perfect, Amy. Don't for a second think I am. I have my weaknesses." Something in Silas' voice on this last statement caused Amy to look at him in confusion, and Silas went on almost reluctantly. "Take Thomas Blane, for instance. I'm not sure what I would do if I ever met the man: shake his hand and thank him for stepping out of your life, or knock him to the ground for hurting you."

Amy's eyes widened in surprise at this violent talk coming from her Silas. *Her* Silas? What was she thinking?

"Silas!" The shout came from Grant who was moving toward them as fast as his still-healing leg would carry him. It effectively put an end to the conversation between the two young people.

Whatever was about to be said would have to wait. Silas reached quickly and lifted Amy to the ground before moving forward to meet Grant.

Amy breathed an unconscious sigh of relief. Once again she was spared the ordeal of dealing with her true feelings.

35

Amy stood in her bedroom holding the unopened package from her aunt. Silas had given it to her when he'd come down for supper, and even her father had looked at her strangely when she didn't immediately open it. There was no way to explain to Silas or her father, as there was no explaining even to herself about the almost desperate feeling within her to be alone to open this gift.

Amy's hands shook slightly as she peeled off the brown paper and unwrapped the gift. The package contained a beautiful glass berry dish. It was about eight inches in diameter and had an ornate A engraved on the side.

The note inside read: "I so want you to have this dish, Amy. It is a gift from my heart. The dish was given to me by my mother whose name was Agatha. She had received the gift from her mother, my grandmother, whose name was Adella. My name being April, the dish was passed to me and not to either of my sisters. With no daughter of my own, I feel it a privilege to pass this 'A' dish along to you, Amy. I hope someday I'll see it in your home on your own dining table. Love, Aunt April."

Amy took no note of the tears streaming down her face. To whom will you pass the dish, Amy? The question rolled around in her head as the tears continued down her cheeks and no answer came.

For the first time Amy was fearful of praying, fearful of facing God and what His will might be. Amy remained in her bedroom, alone and totally caught up in her pain.

"Do you think Amy's okay?" Grant and Silas were sitting on the front porch, and it bothered Silas that Amy hadn't joined them.

"I suppose she needed some time alone," Grant answered quietly.

"It's because I'm back." Silas' voice held regret.

"I imagine that does have something to do with it, Silas, but I think there's more to it. I'm afraid she didn't have an easy summer."

"Well, that's not surprising. She was pretty upset about your accident."

"You're right, she was very upset about that. But I think it's something else. My guess is, she's fighting God about something." Grant paused then and turned so he could look directly at Silas. "And I think that something is you."

Silas shifted uncomfortably in his seat, afraid of where this conversation was leading. He looked out across the yard, hoping Grant would take the hint and change the subject, but Grant wasn't through with him.

"Silas, I did break my leg, but there is nothing whatsoever the matter with my eyes. You're in love with my daughter. And when she stops looking at you like a big brother, she'll realize she loves you, too."

Silas stared at Grant in disbelief, and Grant went on. "Of course, you can't blame Amy for seeing you in that light. After all, you treat her like a sister. Maybe I'm wrong—maybe she is really nothing more than a sister to you."

"You're not wrong." Silas' voice was nearly inaudible.

"Well, then do something about it. In my day when a man fell in love with a woman, he courted her."

Silas could only gape at the man, hardly able to believe what he was hearing.

"Silas," Grant's voice was gentle now, "did you think I'd forgotten what it was like to be in love? I know it's not easy for you when you're living right here under the same roof. I suspect Amy knows of your feelings for her, but it's not at all convincing when you treat her with the same sisterly affection you always have."

Silas sat in silence for a moment before admitting in a humble voice, "I've never courted a woman before. I'm not sure I'd know where to begin."

But Grant only smiled at him. "Silas, I have every confidence you'll come up with something."

Amy never did join the men on the porch that evening and Silas, knowing in the morning he'd be headed out to the fields, went to bed early. He had no trouble falling asleep, but as he waited for slumber to claim him, each second was spent thinking about all Grant had said.

36

The door slammed as Silas exited the kitchen. Amy stood near the table trying to decide if she had imagined what had just happened or if it had been real.

Her father and Silas had been outside working and Amy had washed the kitchen curtains. Stretching on the tip of her toes, she was rehanging them when she heard steps behind her and then Silas' hands covered her own. She let her own hands drop and he easily adjusted the rod, but she was unable to move with Silas directly at her back.

She thought nothing of this until Silas finished the job and made no move to step away. With his hands still high on the wall and his chest brushing her back, he bent his head slightly to the side and waited for Amy to look up at him.

When she did, he spoke as if there was nothing at all unusual about their stance. "Did you need help with anything else?"

"No." Amy's voice was higher-pitched than usual.

Silas moved then, bringing his face down until his nose nearly touched her temple. Amy stood frozen.

"Your hair smells nice." This said, Silas straightened. "Well, I best get back to work." Amy continued to stare at him as he sent her a warm smile and walked from the room.

Now she stood in bewilderment. Silas' attitude toward her the last few days had been different somehow, and Amy was thoroughly confused.

And her father—he had her completely baffled. If she didn't know better, she would swear he was matchmaking. But she just couldn't believe it of him.

It seemed that every time she turned around he was leaving her and Silas alone together. And twice he had requested certain dishes for supper, telling her they were Silas' favorites.

"Well," Amy said to the empty room, "I've got work to do. Men are just strange creatures and you have to learn to live with them."

Amy's decision to just "live with them" was fine when Silas was not around. But the truth was he had changed toward her, and she had no idea what to do about it.

For most of the day he was in the fields with her father, but those times when they were together, his actions could no longer be considered brotherly.

When he helped her in and out of the wagon, she noticed he held her just a moment longer than necessary. And when she did fix any of his favorite meals for supper, he didn't just thank her but kissed her right on the cheek—and in front of her father, too!

The real surprise came over three weeks after Silas arrived and right after he returned from a trip into town. Amy was dusting in the living room, wearing her oldest gown and her hair covered with a raggedy, faded scarf. She knew she had never looked worse.

"Amy, can you come outside a minute?"

"Oh Silas, you're back. Did you get everything from town?"

"I got everything on the list. Could you please come outside a moment? There's some—"

"Oh Silas, do we have company? I look terrible—this dress is filthy."

Silas could see he was going to get nowhere asking her. He walked toward her, took the dirty rag from her hand, and led her outside.

Amy followed mutely and listened while he spoke. "There was something in town I thought you might like. It's here in the back of the wagon. You don't have to keep it. I can take it back if you don't want it."

Silas led her to the back of the wagon and waited for her to look in. Seated upon a burlap sack was a tiny ball of black fur. Amy stared at the puppy, her mouth opening in a silent "oh." The sight of people brought the puppy to its legs, her miniature tail moving furiously, causing her entire body to vibrate.

"She looked like she needed someone to love her, and I thought you would be just the person."

"Oh Silas," Amy breathed as she gathered the wiggling little body into her arms. "She's darling."

The puppy must have agreed with Silas that Amy was the person to love her for she settled immediately into her arms and lay contentedly while Amy stroked her soft ears and head.

To Silas' surprise, Amy's face was wreathed in a smile but her eyes were shining with tears. Silas' heart overflowed with love for her and he took a step toward her, wanting with all of his heart to kiss her and declare himself.

Amy panicked when she saw his intent. "What shall we name her?" she nearly shouted at him and took a step backward. Silas looked at her for a moment as though he had no idea who she was talking about.

"The puppy, Silas, what shall we name the puppy?" Silas jerked as though stung, realizing what he had nearly done. His face flooded with color and, moving to unload the supplies to try and hide his embarrassment, he thought, "What a fool you are, Silas. Her liking the puppy doesn't change the way she feels about you."

"I'm glad you like the dog, Amy. I better get these things unloaded." Amy stood mute, not knowing what to say as he loaded a sack onto his shoulder. Silas evidently didn't feel words were necessary. As soon as his arms were full, he walked away without a word.

"Another job? Are you sure?"
"That's what the note said."
"But we haven't heard from him all summer."
"I know, and we haven't had any money either."
"Are we doing it?"
"Yea, we'll do it. Maybe this time we'll see who he is."
"Yea, maybe. When do we go?"
"Tomorrow night."

37

Laughing, Amy watched with delight as Cocoa ran in small circles in front of her. Amy had just filled the dog's dish, but Cocoa wanted attention more than food, and Amy could not coax her into the stall she'd blocked off in the barn.

Amy decided to go into the stall and, as usual, Cocoa followed her. Amy felt almost guilty at tricking the dog, but as soon as Amy rushed out and pulled the plank back into place, the puppy headed to her dish.

Leaning lazily against a post, Amy thought back on the day before when Silas had brought the little dog home. That Silas had been about to kiss her had been more than evident and, the truth of the matter was, he had no right to such intimacies. But that didn't change the fact that she had panicked and responded badly, embarrassing them both.

Amy then remembered the stilted feelings between them just before Silas had gone home. Somehow knowing he would be returning in the fall had given Amy a sense of security. She didn't feel in a rush to right things between them, but now . . .

Being busy with the puppy the evening before had made conversation difficult, along with the fact that Silas was exhausted from the long day he'd put in.

But even considering Silas' physical state, Amy could not go to bed with things the way they were. Both men headed off to bed early, and Amy had found herself alone in the living room. With determination she marched halfway up the stairs and called to Silas through his closed door.

"Silas, can I talk to you a minute?"

The door opened after a moment and Amy headed down the stairs to wait. Silas approached almost warily, his face shuttered. Amy thought instantly of how many times she had hurt him— never intentionally, but hurt him nevertheless.

"I know you're tired, but I wanted to thank you for the puppy. She's adorable, and I already love her dearly. It was very thoughtful of you."

"You're more than welcome, Amy, and please let me apologize for doing things at times that make you uncomfortable."

Amy had not expected this and made no reply. She shifted

uneasily under the intense stare Silas directed at her, but his eyes held her own. His hand lifted then and the backs of his fingers stroked ever-so-gently down her cheek. "Good night, sweetheart." His voice as gentle as his touch, he turned and went upstairs.

Now Amy stood gazing at Cocoa, thrilled to have the puppy, but totally unsure of how to deal with Silas and his feelings.

"Hello."

Amy jumped with surprise and turned as a strange male voice called to her from the doorway of the barn. She had to walk nearly the length of the barn to reach him, her look curious but friendly.

"Hello," the stranger said again as she approached. "I hope I'm on the right farm. My name is Paul Cameron; I'm looking for my brother Silas."

The first thing Amy noticed about the man was his height. The second was his voice. It was deep and perfectly modulated. The first comparison that came to her head was "smooth as honey."

Amy must have been staring because he spoke again, this time that perfect voice was filled with amusement.

"Is this the Nolan farm?"

"Oh yes, I'm sorry." Amy felt flustered and moved within arms' reach, her hand outstretched. "I'm Amy Nolan, and Silas is in the field with my dad."

"Good. I'm glad to know I have the right place. Maybe if you could point me in the right direction—"

"Oh certainly. You can go out, but they'll be in for supper anytime now if you just want to wait here at the house."

Centering her gaze on his evidently-new shoes, Amy thought, "They'll lose that shine very quickly if he walks all the way out to Silas and back."

"I'm not really dressed to go out, am I?" The amusement was back in his voice, and Amy looked up to see him smiling at her. "My word," she thought, "he's almost as good-looking as my Silas."

He was easily as tall, although his build was slighter, and his hair was just as dark, cut close to his well-shaped head. He was clean-shaven and Amy couldn't decide what was more appealing: his blue eyes with just a touch of green in them, or that full, smiling mouth filled with perfect white teeth.

Paul Cameron was doing some admiring of his own. Grandma Em had said there was someone special, but Silas had shared little with her and, other than the fact that the situation was not ideal, Gram knew next to nothing about the woman Silas loved.

Paul's first impression was how pretty she was—about Susanne's build, but her hair even more blonde. The dress she wore was a pale pink-and-white stripe. It seemed to put color in her cheeks even as her warm, blue eyes smiled kindly at him.

When Amy spoke, it was her turn to be amused. "Would you like to wait in the house?"

Paul grinned at her, totally undaunted by the fact that he'd been caught staring.

"Yes, Amy Nolan, I believe I will wait in the house. I hope my arrival won't put you out in any way."

"No, you're more than welcome. By the way, is Silas expecting you?"

"No," Paul answered as he held open the kitchen door. "I just made a surprise trip home to Baxter. It wouldn't have been a surprise if I had written ahead to see if everyone was home. I'm headed up north and, when I found out where Silas was, I decided I'd just stop in on the way."

"Well, I'm sure he'll be thrilled." Amy took his coat and bag and saw him settled in the living room with a cup of coffee. She then went to the kitchen to finish supper and Paul forced himself not to pace as he waited for the brother he longed to see.

38

Amy put a silencing finger to her lips as her father looked from her to the stranger standing in the doorway leading from the living room. Silas' head was still bent over the basin.

Paul watched his brother reach for a towel and vigorously rub his face and neck. Silas had just rehung the towel when, out of the corner of his eye, he caught sight of a fourth presence in the room.

At the first sight of his younger brother, Silas only stared, but then a slow smile began to break across his face. An answering smile was stretching across Paul's and, within seconds, the brothers were laughing and embracing, their words falling all over each other.

"When did you get here?"

"Your beard!"

"Have you been home?"

"Why didn't you write?"

"You look great!"

"So do you."

The men stopped trying to communicate and simply looked at one another and laughed. Silas took Paul's arm and led him further into the room.

"Grant, this is my brother Paul. Paul, this is Grant Nolan. And this," Silas' voice held pride, "is Amy. Have you met Amy?"

"Oh Si, you *have* got it bad," Paul thought as he studied the look on his brother's rapt face. "And I ought to know the signs."

Paul reached across the table to shake Grant's hand. "It's good to meet you, Mr. Nolan. And yes, Silas, Amy and I have met."

The two shared a smile and Amy said, "How about some supper?" The four of them talked and shared news during the meal and everyone left the table in good spirits. Silas hung back and insisted on helping Amy with the dishes.

"But Silas, you'll want to visit with your brother. He said he's leaving tomorrow."

"You're right, I do want to visit with him, but I also want him to hear you play, so I'm going to help you with these dishes so you can come out and entertain us."

"Oh Silas," Amy said, "I'm sure your brother doesn't want to hear me play. I'm sure he's heard countless piano players and I sincerely doubt he wants to hear another."

"Alright," Silas said, "I'll make a deal with you. My brother has always enjoyed hearing me play. If he asks me to play, then you're on. If he doesn't say a word, then I won't either."

"Deal," Amy said, and by the smile on Silas' face she knew she'd been had.

Amy would have loved knowing the actual amount of seconds it took Paul to ask Silas to play. Surprisingly, Silas didn't tease her at all.

"Well, Paul, I'd be only too glad to play, but you've never heard Amy play the piano and I know you would enjoy it."

Paul was sincerely delighted with the idea, and Amy cast an almost-shy smile at Silas as she moved to the keyboard.

The men sat quietly as Amy played, each one letting the music flow over him and basking in the sound of Amy's God-given talent. Grant's head lay on the back of his chair with his eyes closed, a slight smile on his lips.

Paul studied the small hands that moved so effortlessly over the keys and produced such celestial sounds, making him think of the way music might sound in heaven.

Silas' eyes never left Amy's face. He studied her lovely arched brows and the slight flush on her high cheekbones. His love found her flawless and lovely beyond compare.

Amy was nearing the end of a beautiful old hymn when she allowed herself to look about the room. Paul had joined Grant in tipping his head back and closing his eyes, but Silas was watching her, his expression loving.

Something inside of Amy began to open and grow, like a small flower beginning to bloom in the warm spring sun. "He's so wonderful and kind, and he loves me." The real truth of this fact hit Amy for the first time. The knowledge gave her such a warm, secure feeling she felt tears sting her eyes. Silas was God's child and she was God's child and together they could have a wonderful life with His blessing and beneath His watchful care. Unbidden upon the heels of this miraculous thought surfaced the doubts. "Could it really be that wonderful? Would he really love me for the rest of his life?"

Had Amy been able to tell Silas of her feelings and her fears, he would have answered all her questions and assured her of his love. But it was not to be on this night. With her father and Paul in the room, she knew there would be no time for talk. And when the evening came to an end, she had no choice but to head to bed with everything locked inside her. By morning she knew she would have talked herself out of approaching Silas.

— ❖ —

"We haven't shared a bed for a long time—do you snore?"

"It wouldn't matter if I did, little brother. This is my bed, keep that in mind."

"I take it that means you intend to hog the covers."

The men had just climbed into bed, and Silas tugged gently on the quilt in teasing. They lay quietly for a time, shifting once in a while for comfort, but neither one was close to sleep.

"Do you definitely have to leave tomorrow?"

"Afraid so. I'm already later than I said I would be."

"How many people in your congregation?"

"About 15, but the area has such potential, Silas. I just know God's going to use me up there." Paul's voice held all the enthusiasm he felt.

"I have no doubt He will, Paul, and you know I'll be praying."

"Thank you, Si. You know how much that means to me." Silence fell again.

"Silas?"

"Yea."

"Do you want to talk about Amy?"

"How did you know?"

"Grandma Em and I talked. She didn't tell everyone, but we were discussing you and she shared what you had told her. Do you want to tell me?"

"I don't know, Paul. Amy is definitely my favorite subject, but sometimes I just can't see the point. She's just not interested in me."

"Are you sure of that, Silas? Are you sure she's not interested, or is it possible she's scared?"

"Scared of what?"

"Hasn't she been engaged before?"

"Yes, she has. The guy broke if off with her earlier this year."

"Why did he break if off?" Silas didn't answer. "Was it another girl?"

"I know what you're after, Paul, but she can't think I would do that to her."

"It doesn't appear to me that you really know what she's thinking. You haven't talked to her."

"When did you become such an expert?" Silas' voice was growing cross.

"I'm in love, too."

Silas said nothing for a long time, but questions were swarming through his head. He decided to pose his questions as Paul had done.

"Do you want to talk about her?"

Paul laughed. "I'm not sure you should get me started."

"Does she love you?"

"Yes." Paul's voice was apologetic, and Silas exploded.

"Paul! How could you think for one minute I wouldn't want your happiness?"

Following Silas' outburst, silence fell once again in the small attic room. Finally Paul said, "I'm not sorry she loves me, but it seems cruel to talk about my happiness when things are not settled between you and Amy."

"I appreciate your thoughts, Paul, but I think things are settled. I can't force her to love me, nor would I want to. I want her to come of her own accord—out of love, not pity or gratitude. Now please tell me about—"

"Corrine."

"Please tell me about Corrine—where you met, everything."

Paul's voice took on an almost dreamy quality as he spoke. "Her full name is Corrine Maria Templeton. I met her up north. She and her family are members of the church I'll be pastoring.

"We've really had very little time together, but I guess it was love at first sight. I was staying with her aunt and uncle while I was speaking up there, and we met when she came to see them.

"We would have had more time together, but she wasn't feeling very well and her dad insisted she go home. But it doesn't really matter. We had enough time to know how we feel about each other."

"So it's really serious."

"Is it ever! I want her for my wife. She loves God and is just as excited about the people and the work up there as I am. She's beautiful, too—tall like Christine, only very slim and willowy. Her hair is even lighter than your Amy's, almost a white blonde. I've never seen it down, but her aunt told me it's very long."

Paul's voice trailed off, and Silas was sure he was thinking of the woman he loved. Silas' thoughts were on the same track.

"Your Amy," Paul had said. "*Your* Amy." He liked the sound of that.

"I can't give up, God," Silas prayed in his heart. "I love her so much. If there's even the slightest chance of us having a life together, I can't give up."

The brothers talked only a little while longer, a full day catching up with them. Tomorrow would bring good-byes which, though never easy, a good night's sleep would certainly help.

39

Amy's knife was putting the finishing touches on the chocolate cake she was frosting. The first thing her father had said upon seeing her puppy was, "She's as black as the cocoa you use to make my favorite cake." Amy thought the name very fitting and wasted no time in trying to come up with something better. Now, as Amy worked over the cake, she had to agree: The frosting was rich and indeed almost black in color.

She hoped Silas would enjoy it. He had taken Paul into town after breakfast to catch the train, and Amy had an inkling he might be upset or a little down when he got back. Realizing he was a little late now, Amy hoped everything was alright. She knew the cake certainly didn't make up for Paul's absence, but Amy wanted Silas to know she cared and was thinking of him.

About an hour later, Amy had really begun to wonder what had become of him when Silas drove quickly into the yard. Amy stepped onto the front porch in time to see Silas carrying Cocoa from the yard into the barn.

He was back out within seconds and striding quickly toward her, his face grave. As soon as he reached the porch, he took her hands and held them tightly in his own. Amy began to experience fear at his foreboding expression.

"Amy, I put Cocoa in the barn. I need to take you into town. As I drove Paul to the station, I could tell something was up. All through town I heard talk about your family. As soon as Paul's train left, I went straight to your uncle's. He was just on his way to get you. Your Aunt Bev is asking for you. She's been arrested for being connected with the robberies in the area."

All the color drained out of Amy's face upon hearing Silas' words. Swaying, she would have fallen but for his strong hands gripping her own.

"There must be a mistake." Amy's voice was little more than a thready whisper.

"I hope there is. Evan said she would talk to no one. The sheriff was kind enough to spare her the humiliation of the jailhouse, so she's at home with one of the town deputies."

Silas began to let go of Amy, intending to lead her into the house, but she clung to him. "Come inside, Amy. I need to go out and tell your dad. I'm sure he'll want to go with us." But still Amy would not let go of his hands.

"Please don't leave me, Silas."

Upon hearing the fear in her voice, Silas gathered her tenderly into his arms. He felt her tremble as he rested his cheek upon the top of her head. "It's okay, sweetheart. We'll go into town and get the whole story and I'll be right beside you."

God's hand was certainly on the Nolan family this day, for Silas looked over Amy's head to see Grant coming in from the fields. "Here comes your dad. Let's go tell him." Silas' large hand held Amy's as they walked past the barn to meet Grant. Silas told him all he knew and Grant insisted that Silas and Amy leave immediately.

"I'll saddle a horse and come in as soon as I clean up. If Bev is asking for you, then you need to get right in there."

Amy was nearly in a state of shock as Silas drove the team toward town. "Amy, I don't know what you're going to find when you get to your aunt's. But if she sees you so disturbed, it's just going to make her more upset than I'm sure she already is."

Silas' words penetrated Amy's painful confusion over this disastrous affair, and she started to pray. She began by thanking God for the fact that Bev had asked for her. This in itself was encouraging. Amy had prayed for years that by her word and deed her loved ones would come to understand their need for Christ and just maybe, as tragic as all of this was, it would be an open door to that end.

Amy spoke just as they entered the main street in town. "Thank you, Silas. I'm not sure what I would have done without you. If my Aunt Bev has no objections, will you come in with me?"

"I'll stay by your side as long as I'm able."

The scene in front of the Randall mansion was as close as Amy had ever come to living a real-life nightmare. Townspeople crowded everywhere. Snatches of conversations floated to the occupants of the wagon as Silas maneuvered the horses, attempting to skirt the crowd.

"If she's guilty she should be in the jail."

"The rich don't get treated like the rest of us do."

"I think she's been framed."

"It'd be easier to believe if it was him; he's certainly a cold fish."

"That's right, she just doesn't seem the type."

"Yea, she sure doesn't need the money."

Some of the sheriff's men and Bev Randall's two gardeners tried to restrain people as they trampled the landscape. Amy recognized one of the more zealous intruders as a man who worked for the town's newspaper. Unfortunately he spotted her at the same instant and began to run toward the wagon. Amy quickly directed Silas to drive to the back of the huge house. Again Amy felt God's hand on them when she saw that the guard at the back door was a man who had known her since childhood and immediately gave them entrance.

Two maids, both with swimming eyes and crushed handkerchiefs, were in the kitchen as Silas and Amy walked through. To save time, Amy headed for the back hall and stairway. The main staircase led directly to her aunt's room, but Amy was in a rush to get to the second floor and she nearly ran through the upstairs hallway to get to the spacious landing outside the master bedroom.

She stopped short, Silas nearly colliding with her, at the sight of a man standing at the door, a shining badge pinned smartly to the pocket of his shirt. His expression not at all welcoming.

Silas stepped in with the protective instincts of a mother bear. "This is Amy Nolan, Bev Randall's niece. I understand Mrs. Randall has asked for her."

The lawman eyed Silas' size for a moment before reluctantly opening the door and speaking quietly to someone within. Evan came through the door in the next second.

"Oh Amy, I'm so glad you're here. She won't talk to me." Amy had never seen her uncle so emotional, he was completely distraught. "All she'll say is 'I want to talk with Amy.'"

Amy nodded, and Evan stepped aside to let her in. Silas hesitated, but Evan gestured so he followed Amy. Evan closed the door from the outside.

Bev Randall stood in the small windowed alcove in the corner of the room and looked at the crowd below. Without turning, she spoke. "Thank you for coming, Amy. Is Silas with you?"

"Yes, he's here."

"Good. You need him. Please believe I never intended you should suffer for my conduct and mistakes. Of this I give you my word."

"So it's true you *are* involved in the robberies?"

"Yes, it's true. I hired the men who robbed those farms."

"Oh, Aunt Bev. Why?" Amy whispered in perplexity.

She turned and faced them. Silas thought she looked years older than the last time he'd seen her.

"I love Evan with all my heart. But I'm afraid the only love Evan has ever felt for anyone has been for you, Amy, and Maureen. At Christmas and on your birthdays I was allowed to spend lavishly on you. And I could buy anything for the house because, of course, a banker has a certain reputation to uphold. But never could I spend money for myself. I was never allowed anything of Evan's—not his love, his time, or his money.

"Oh yes, I have beautiful clothes to wear. But again, it's because I'm the banker's wife and we have an image to maintain.

"You wouldn't remember your mother's mother Amy, but a more wicked woman I've yet to meet. I was never allowed to forget I was not born a Randall. My family was poor and from a small town, 'hardly more than a dot on the map,' she used to enjoy reminding me."

"But Aunt Bev, he must love you. Or else why would he have married you?"

"I've often wondered that myself. I think he had just decided it was time to marry and I was in the right place at the right time. But then maybe he did love me and I killed that love because I could never give him children."

"But Aunt Bev, I still don't understand about the robberies."

"It's simple really—I wanted the money. I was sick to death of having to beg Evan for every dime I needed. Sick of being questioned about what I was spending." She gave a short, humorless laugh and turned back to the window. "The funny thing is I really believed no one would ever know."

There was a knock on the door then and Silas answered it. Grant stood on the threshold, his hat in his hands. Evan was behind him.

"Who is it, Silas?"

"It's me—Grant, Bev. Can I come in?"

She nodded and Silas swung the door wide. Somehow Silas seemed to sense their need to be alone, and he took Amy's arm and they walked from the room.

Evan was still on the landing as the door closed behind Grant and Bev. "Uncle Evan, we need to talk." Evan nodded and the young people followed him downstairs to the library.

40

Evan Randall was a proud man. It showed in his carriage, the way he spoke, and in nearly every facet of his life. But today as he faced his niece in the small library downstairs, he looked like a beaten man.

He motioned Amy and Silas into chairs, but he remained standing. "Please tell me what she said." Amy hesitated, so Evan said, "I'm sure she's upset with me or she would have talked directly to me."

Amy didn't see that she had any choice. She looked to Silas, and he gave her a small nod. Quietly and as gently as possible, Amy relayed what her aunt had shared.

Evan dropped heavily into a chair and stared at her in disbelief. "I had no idea. You mean she actually believes I don't love her?" Amy gave a small nod and fought to keep the tears at bay, his expression so clearly showing his hurt and confusion.

"Did she really say that about the money?" Again Amy nodded. "I never intended that she feel she couldn't have money. I certainly never denied her."

"But you do question her?"

"Yes, I guess I do," he admitted with a heavy sigh. "But I honestly never meant to be stingy with her or make her think I didn't care."

Other than the sound of the townspeople out front, the house was still. There were no other words to be said in the library downstairs. And the occupants of the room sat and wondered what was being said upstairs in the master bedroom.

Bev had turned back to the window, and Grant was not sure what to say or even what had led him to come into the room this way. He had not been at all prepared for the mob out front and he was still reeling with shock over the severity of Bev's circumstances.

"I'm glad you came, Grant. I asked for Amy because I guess she feels like the daughter I never had and felt I needed to see her to say—"

Grant was afraid of what she was going to say. Her voice sounded terribly despondent, which concerned him.

"I've shamed Evan, you know. He didn't deserve this. He won't be able to show his face in this town. It would be better for him if I were dead."

"You're wrong, Bev." Grant's voice was emphatic. "No one wishes you dead, and especially not Evan. I realize he's not demonstrative, but I know he cares for you. He's proud of the position you hold in this town and the work you do."

Bev only shook her head sadly and turned from the window. "I know you mean well, Grant, but—"

"No, Bev, I'm not saying these words to ease your conscience. Your involvement in these thefts was wrong, but it doesn't mean your life is over."

"You know, don't you, Grant? I asked for Amy so I could say good-bye. Evan keeps a small-caliber pistol in the closet. I haven't talked to him and he doesn't understand, but the truth is I just couldn't face him after what I've done. He's not perfect, but at least he's not a liar and a thief. I've shamed the Randall name."

"It's true, Bev, that what you did was against the law, and you have no choice but to face the judge with your crimes. But Bev, there is an area in your life where you do have a choice. How will you face God, Bev? Will He be your Judge or your Savior?"

"Grant, how can you speak to me about facing God after what I've done?" Bev cried. "It's blasphemous! I'm dirty, Grant! Maybe at one time God would have welcomed me, but I'm sure He wants nothing to do with me now."

"You're wrong, Bev, so wrong. God sent His Son, Jesus Christ, to die for the dirty, the wrong, the sinful. If we were able to cleanse ourselves before coming to Him, we wouldn't need Him. Listen to me, Bev. I may not have taken money from anyone, but without the saving knowledge of Christ I would still be headed to hell."

The harshness of his words fell on Bev's mind like the blow from a hammer. "Yes," she thought, "what I'm going through right now is awful, but there *is* worse—there's eternity without God." Bev Randall believed in an afterlife, and she knew she was not ready to face it.

Bev sank onto the edge of the bed and Grant pulled a chair close. "Bev, the Bible says all have sinned and fall short of God's glory. It also says there is hope for man in the form of Christ Jesus. He died, Bev, for the sins that make you feel so dirty. And the Bible says you need only believe on Him to know His saving grace."

"Oh Grant, I just don't know. I haven't prayed since I was a little child at my grandmother's knee."

"Bev, come as you are to Jesus Christ who loved you enough to die for you. 'For God so loved the world, that he gave his only begotten Son, that whosoever believeth in him should not perish, but have everlasting life.' "

Bev looked at Grant and tears swam in her eyes. "Please help me." She sounded like a helpless child, and Grant knew it was time. Bev Randall was ready to put her hand in God's.

"It's so simple, Bev. Just repeat after me and take God at His word." Bev nodded, and Grant began. "Dear God in heaven, I know I have sinned and I'm not worthy of Your love. But I believe, God, that You died for my sins and I now give them to You. Please take my life in Your hands, Lord. And thank You for saving me."

Bev dutifully repeated each sentence Grant spoke, and then Grant prayed when she was through. "Dear God, thank You for Your love and the miracle You have brought today in Bev's life. Please God, stay with her as she faces the rough days ahead. Help her to remember that she is now Your child and You'll be beside her. I praise You for Your Son, Jesus Christ, and His death for us. Amen."

Grant and Bev lifted their heads simultaneously and looked at one another. The crowd could still be heard outside, and there was movement at the door as though the guard outside had shifted against it.

The sounds were only half-heard by the two people within as they concentrated on the life-changing miracle that had just occurred in Bev Randall's heart.

When Grant broke the silence, his voice was gentle and reverent.

"Bev, if you believe what you just prayed, that Christ *did* die for you, then you're now His child."

Bev clasped her hands together, trembling with excitement, her voice little more than a whisper.

"Oh Grant, it's not so scary now. I still have to face what I've done, but I don't feel so alone."

The two adults stood, and Grant gave Bev a hug. He felt a bit awkward, but Bev was smiling when they parted. Grant needed to share one last thing. "You know, Bev, Maureen loved you deeply. She prayed daily that you and Evan would come to know her Savior."

"I hope she knows now."

"I'm sure she must be singing right along with the angels."

A knock sounded and Bev called for the door to be opened. Evan came in hesitantly. "Evan," Bev's voice was more gentle than he'd heard in years, "I need to talk with you."

Grant went out the door to find Silas and Amy waiting for him. They each had a final look within before the guard firmly closed the door. Evan and Bev were seated on the bed, Evan's arm was around his wife, her head resting on his shoulder. They could hear her talking quietly, but without hesitation or fear.

Grant could see that Silas and Amy were full of questions, but now was not the time or place. They made their way through the house and, with most of the crowd gone, were soon headed for home.

41

Amy woke up feeling rested for the first time since Silas came back from town with the news of her Aunt Bev. The night they arrived home, milking and chores awaited them, but over supper each shared what they had seen and heard.

Amy wept openly upon hearing of her aunt's salvation. Grant had asked Silas to lead them in prayer for Evan, whose heart had never made that step.

Grant had gone into town again the following day and returned with a lengthy report. He had seen Bev and Evan who were both holding up well and had had a long talk about the robberies with the sheriff.

The sheriff cleared up many questions and, once back at the farm, Grant relayed the information to Silas and his daughter. The discovery of who was actually behind the crimes was brought to light within hours of the Cooper brothers being arrested for the last robbery.

The men did not hold up well under questioning and soon told of the notes left for them in an old tree outside of town. Since all the notes had been saved, the sheriff could see he'd been in error in the way he'd reassured the townspeople. Every slip of paper pointed to someone at Evan's bank being involved.

In a short time the sheriff had brought in a young bank teller and it was this person who confessed to delivering "off the record" reports to the banker's home three times a week.

With this information, along with the brothers' description of the unidentified black-cloaked rider who always made the money exchange, the sheriff had soon been on his way to arrest Evan Randall.

It was Bev who gave herself away—not that she would have allowed Evan to take the blame, in any case. When the sheriff arrived, Evan had been out and Bev had just immediately assumed she'd been discovered. The sheriff had relayed his conversation with Bev to Grant:

"I can't say as I'm glad to see you, Mitchell."
"Then you know why I'm here?" the man asked, truly saddened at his findings.

"Yes, I know why you're here. You know, I really believed I would get away with it. I kept things so simple, so few people involved. I even made the money exchanges myself."

Bev, upon seeing the lawman's stunned face, soon realized her mistake. The sheriff had no choice but to report all he knew and, late as it was, it didn't take long for all of Neillsville to hear.

Silas and Grant with their work in the fields had dealt with the news better than Amy who suddenly had time on her hands as she alternately prayed and worried over all that had ensued. And always at the back of her mind was the knowledge that the crops were nearly in and Silas would be leaving.

42

Silas' thoughts were identical to Amy's. "The crops are in. Another day and I need to go home, and this time I have no reason to come back." Silas wanted to weep just thinking about it. He found himself practically begging God to give him some time with Amy.

Certain that he knew how she felt, Silas just needed to talk with her for a spell. It might be the last time for quite a while. The time came that very morning, the day before he was scheduled to leave.

The weather was turning cold and, after spending days with canning and putting her garden up, along with the stress of Bev's pain, Amy felt a desperate need to be outdoors before winter set in and made being out miserable.

The big oaks at the top of the bluff looked inviting, and Amy bundled herself from head to toe and set out for her favorite spot. She had been sitting on a fallen log for less than half an hour when Silas joined her.

They sat in companionable silence for a time, both feeling good that talk wasn't needed. The surrounding bluffs and farms stretched out before them, almost creating a valley. From their vantage point it was hard to believe there was life beyond the houses and fields they could see. And with the world so quiet and cold on this morning, it was even harder to believe people were hurting and life was not peaceful for everyone.

Silas eventually turned his head from the view and looked at Amy's profile. Amy, feeling his look, turned and let her eyes meet his.

"I'm leaving tomorrow." Silas didn't know why he said it; she already knew.

"I'll miss you."

"Will you, Amy? Will you really?"

Her heart ached at hearing the wistfulness in his voice and she answered very gently, "Yes, I'll miss you very much."

She continued to look at him, and Silas believed he would drown in the crystal-clear blue of her eyes. As before at the train station, he moved slowly, giving her plenty of time to see his intent and draw away.

Amy's heart melted within her as his lips touched hers, and Silas felt as though his own heart was going to pound through his coat as she leaned closer and didn't pull away.

One second they were kissing and the next second Amy was gone. Silas stared up at her from his place on the log. She had leapt up and was staring at him with tortured eyes, her hands clenched so tightly together that her knuckles were white. Silas stood and reached for her as he spoke.

"Amy, please—"

"Don't touch me, Silas—just don't touch me."

Standing in front of the log and holding his place, Silas spoke. "Amy, you must know how I feel. You must know that my feelings for you are deep. And you, Amy, what about you? Please don't ask me to believe you don't feel anything for me."

"Of course I feel something for you. We're friends." The words sounded foolish and inane even to her own ears, but Amy couldn't seem to help herself.

Silas looked furious. "Is that what you were just now when you let me kiss you—a friend?"

Amy shrugged helplessly, not even knowing herself why she had allowed the kiss. Silas drug off his cap and Amy watched him rake his hand through his hair, his frustration more than evident. Suddenly Amy felt angry and frustrated, too.

Taking him completely by surprise, Amy boldly stepped forward and pushed as hard as she could on his chest. Normally he would have hardly noticed the relatively slight pressure she put on him, but he was so surprised by her action that he took a step backward, forgot the log, and fell over it and onto his back.

"What did you do that for?" he bellowed from his undignified sprawl on the ground.

"Because you've ruined everything. We were such good friends, and you've just ruined it," Amy cried in pure frustration.

Silas was off the ground in an instant, knowing his brother Paul had been right. Even as Amy had shouted at him in rage, he had seen the fear written across her face.

Amy retreated as he came toward her, and Silas stalked her until she was backed up against a tree. His expression was fierce but his voice was calm. "Take a good look at me, Amy Nolan, a very good look. I am *not* Thomas Blane. I am *not* going to declare my love for you and then marry someone else."

Silas' look grew extremely tender as they both stood still, his eyes drinking in the woman he loved. He cupped her face within his big hands before he spoke his next words. "I love you, Amy. I love you as I've never loved anyone. You would but need to crook your smallest finger in my direction and I would gladly carry you down this hill to the parsonage and make you my wife today."

Silas felt as if a giant hand had reached into his chest and was attempting to squeeze the life out of his heart, so great was his disappointment when Amy did not respond to his avowal of love.

Silas straightened and moved a few steps away from Amy, his voice, if not his face, betraying his anguish. "I'll be taking one of your horses to the train in the morning. I'll leave it with the livery nearest the depot."

Turning as though he would walk back to the house, Silas hesitated. Amy hadn't moved away from the tree, and Silas didn't look at her as he spoke.

"Long after I get home I'll love you. If by some miracle you realize you can return that love, know that I'll welcome you with open arms and an open heart."

Amy was very cold inside and out by the time she followed Silas down the bluff and back to the house. And for the first time she could ever remember, she did not feel like singing at the sight of her home.

43

Silas sat aboard a southbound train, his gaze centered out the window, seeing nothing. It was actually over, and Silas was still coming to grips with the fact. Right up to the time he left he believed Amy would come to him. There was no way she was indifferent to his love, of that he was sure. But the decision had to be hers. Even if he could force her, he wouldn't want to.

The rest of the day after they had come back off the bluff had been awkward and painful. Silas found himself wishing he'd planned to leave that day. He knew Grant had figured out the problem and had compassionately said little.

In the evening not long after supper, Silas' mind was already making plans to turn in early. Grant had other ideas and asked Amy to play. Silas wouldn't have cared what the circumstances were—he would not have missed that.

As Silas brought the evening to mind, he wondered if Grant had planned it all along.

"Amy, will you play that song you wrote for me?"

"The music is in my room," Amy answered, obviously reluctant.

"Well, we'll wait for you."

The men did wait, and Amy was only a few notes into the piece when Grant interrupted her. "Please sing it, Amy."

She looked at her father for a long moment and then finally nodded. Grant said to Silas, "Amy put a poem she'd written to music this summer and gave it to me when I was laid up. She titled it 'My Rock, Refuge and Savior'."

As soon as Grant had finished his explanation, Amy played and sang. Even aboard the train, the seat uncomfortable, the air stale, and the passengers noisy, Silas had only to close his eyes to see her and hear her voice.

"Beautiful," Silas thought as his mind's eye brought up the images of how she looked and sounded. "Please God," Silas prayed as the train moved down the track for home, "please be my Rock, Refuge, and Savior and bigger than the hurt within me because she's not at my side."

My Rock, Refuge and Savior

Words by Lori Wick

Music by Timothy Barsness

44

The chill of winter was descending on Baxter in a no-nonsense way, and Silas was thankful the roof was on his house and his stoves in the kitchen and living room were piped in and working.

He was not completely finished with the house and had yet to stay a night in it, but the remaining jobs were small and rather fun, and Silas had found that the time spent on the house was a much-needed balm upon his wounded emotions.

Luke had not worked on the house at all while Silas was absent, mostly for the sake of time since he was called upon, once again, to carry the load of both men. But Luke was wise, and also held back for the simple reason that if he were building a home, he knew he would want to do the majority of the work himself.

So the house awaited Silas. Even as he worked, he harbored in his heart a faint hope, as he had before, that Amy would miss him and come on the next train. But as the days turned into weeks, Silas was forced to accept the fact that she was not going to come.

He continued to feel God's presence and to trust in Him daily for strength, but to anyone who knew Silas well, it was obvious some of the sparkle had dimmed in his royal-blue eyes.

There was even a certain young woman at church, newly widowed, with two small children. Silas thought of offering his hand, knowing that she needed someone, and thinking in time they might even learn to love each other. But he didn't entertain the idea for long; he knew it was not what God would have him do.

Thanksgiving had just passed, and Silas had found the day nearly unbearable. The women were constantly laughing about the changes in their shapes, and Mac was so gentle with Julia that it made Silas' throat ache just to watch them.

There were days when he thought he'd made a mistake about the job offer from Frank Chambers. But as always he prayed and God would show him small, but sound reasons for staying.

The main reason for staying finally came. She arrived by train in Baxter wearing new clothing from her hat to her shoes. She knew the way to her aunt and uncle's and headed directly there. She resisted her Aunt April's attempts to persuade her to come inside and warm herself by the fire, stating simply, "Thank you, Aunt April, but I need directions to Silas' house."

April Nolan wasted no time in asking for explanations, and soon Amy could be seen in the beat-up buggy from the livery, headed out of town with the wind blowing a cold blush on her cheeks.

Silas was in one of the upstairs bedrooms when he spotted the rented buggy with its one brown horse loping over the lightly snow-covered ground. He watched for a moment and almost turned away until he realized the buggy was not headed to Luke and Christine's, but to his house.

Amy was out of the buggy and looking at the huge farmhouse which loomed above her by the time Silas arrived in the yard. He approached her with a look of wonder on his face, heedless of the small flakes of snow that fell on his shirt, his coat forgotten inside the house by the front door.

"Your house is beautiful."

"Thank you, I'm glad you like it."

Silence fell with the snow.

"How's your dad?"

"He's fine. He said to tell you hello."

"Good."

The silence was longer this time. Silas looked at the woman before him, the blue of her hat a perfect frame for her lovely face and hair. He'd forgotten how breathless he became whenever she was near.

In the same state, Amy drank in his size and the way the snow looked on his dark hair. Her breath made smoky little puffs in the air, and she thought she would cry if he didn't hold her soon. Finally he spoke.

"Amy, I think I'd better tell you, if you're not here for the reason I hope you're here, you'd best say so, because you're about two seconds away from being kissed."

"Oh Silas, please don't wait two whole seconds."

Luke had seen the buggy, too, and with innocent curiosity had just rounded the biggest oak to find his brother with a petite blonde crushed in his embrace. It was obvious neither one was aware of the snow covering them or that the woman's hat lay on the ground beside them.

Luke turned and headed back to his own house, hoping Silas would bring her over to meet them. Silas had been back for weeks, but Luke was sure he'd just now arrived home.

EPILOGUE
Neillsville, Wisconsin
Spring 1890

Amy Cameron stood beneath the big oaks, not really focused in on the beautiful view. The position of the barn blocked the house, but Amy knew it was there. Her father and her husband were down in the house, supper was over, and they were discussing the planting. Her husband. Amy felt a chill go through her each time she thought the words.

It was just a year before that she and Silas had faced each other in the barn on a very rainy night. Little did she know how her life would change with the break in her father's leg and Silas' arrival. And to think she had almost ignored God's leading and let him get away.

But she had been so afraid, so afraid of being hurt again. True, Thomas and Silas were nothing alike, but there was yet another factor. Amy had not wanted to believe her father could live without her. Even as Silas had shared about his own struggle with pride, pride had brought Amy to her knees. She had known the day he left it had been a mistake. But Amy would not listen to her heart, and over the next few weeks had become more and more miserable.

It was Grant who turned things around. Amy found her gentle, kind-spoken father furious with her.

"Look at you!" he had shouted at her. "You're pale and losing weight, and for what? To stay here and take care of me when the man you love is waiting to share his life with you?"

Amy had stared at him, her mouth opened wide. But Grant wasn't done yet.

"I've never thought your skull thick, Amy, but I'm beginning to think it's going to take an oak beam along the side of your head before you see the truth. You're fighting God in this, and what you're fighting is your very own happiness. You've hurt Silas terribly and, to be very frank, I'm ashamed of you."

Amy stood on the bluff remembering his words and how they had hurt. Her father had held her and she'd cried, knowing he was right.

Thanksgiving had come and, to the astonishment of the Nolans, they had been invited to the Randall mansion. Bev had come before the judge soon after Silas left, and many had complained about the privileges of the rich when they heard about how light her sentence was—almost nonexistent. They were somewhat mollified over the high fines she was ordered to pay. The judge had ruled that Bev pay over double what had been taken from the different farms.

Only Grant and Amy had understood Aunt Bev's joy in this order when on Thanksgiving she had told them the news with tears in her eyes.

Amy now reflected on that time. The day had been a good one, but Silas was most definitely missing. Now, however, they were husband and wife, and at the moment Amy could come up with only one cloud on the horizon.

Even as she thought of it, tears stung her eyes. Silas picked that moment to join his wife on the bluff. Amy didn't turn, and Silas' arms came around her from behind, his chin resting atop her soft, blonde hair.

Silas heard Amy sniff. "Talk to me, Amy."

"I'm not pregnant."

Silas began to wish he'd never shared with Amy his great desire to fill their house with children. She was bound and determined to give him a child in their first year of marriage. And though many families started this way, it certainly wasn't written anywhere that this and this only was the correct procedure.

"Amy, we'll have children. I promise you."

"Silas, how can you possibly make such a promise?"

"Well," he thought a minute, "if we don't have children of our own, we'll take in a bunch of orphans."

"Do you really feel that way?" Amy turned in his arms so she could see his face. "Would it really not bother you if I couldn't give you children?"

"It really wouldn't bother me. God gave me you, and that's what's most important to me."

Amy smiled up at him in relief and he pressed a kiss to her forehead. "We need to go back to the house and spend more time with your dad. This visit has gone by too fast; we're headed home tomorrow."

Amy nodded, not at all upset with the idea of leaving for Baxter. Envisioning the house where she and Silas had lived as husband and wife for over five months, she linked her arm through his for the walk down the hill and began to sing.